THE MAN WITH YELLOW HAIR

MERIEL MONGIE

T0243912

ISK NCHI
African Perspectives

Published in 2024 by Iskanchi Press
info@iskanchi.com
https://iskanchi.com/

ISBN: 978-1-957810-11-9 (Paperback)
ISBN: 978-1-957810-20-1 (Hardback)

Printed in the United States of America

THE MAN
WITH
YELLOW
HAIR

He had been like this for some time now. Cool currents rocked him, rippled along his length. It was pleasant and peaceful. Above him stretched the surface, with its shadows and shapes. He admired how the colors deepened, and, at other times, were shot through with light. He had lost all idea of time. He had come from another place; he knew that. But that was all. He didn't know anymore except that he was safe. That seemed important, that he was safe. It did feel strange, though. He knew he hadn't always been this way. He seemed to be in a new skin, like he was a frog, except that frogs come up for air and he didn't seem able to do that. In fact, he was unable to move. He seemed glued to the bottom of what he didn't know.

He began to notice that the shapes came closer, made sounds, sounds that, try as he might, were impossible to make out. It was a relief when they withdrew and he was once more able to float, to idle away the hours, to dream. He knew he'd been dreaming because he found himself trying to remember what they were about. The best he could do was grab the end of a song, allow it to tremble through him, the words in a strange language. At those times, a change came over him: the snippet of melody energized him, and he imagined himself cutting through the surface of the water like some razor-finned fish, shaking droplets off his glittering flanks as he took to the air, wiggling his tail fin, scattering bubbles that sent shards of rainbow out into the blue beyond.

Of course, this too was a dream, this thinking that he could escape. His body felt like stone, like it belonged to someone else. He seemed condemned to live out the rest of his life in this stagnant pool. He couldn't even get angry about it. In the area of feelings, he was dead as well. And yet, *was* he dead? He wasn't sure. But before he could work it out, something changed.

The shapes and sounds beyond the surface didn't go away. They stayed, pushing at the surface. He tried to move away, again fruitless. The shapes became hands that rose from the dark of the water, stretching the surface until it snapped and they were through, sending prickles of unease as skin met skin. The fingers began to dig painfully into his flesh until he was in a sitting position. Pain spread through his body until he was burning up with it. The sounds became voices that spoke a strange language. Food arrived in his mouth, and he swallowed. It became a heaviness that moved down and out of him. It was a relief when it was gone. Liquids the same, passing into him and out again. Now the hands moved over him. Again, he tried to resist but couldn't. All he could do was wait until it was over and then fall back into the cradle of the water, fall back into drifting and rocking and dreaming.

He began to welcome these times when the hands and voices broke through, so much so that when they retreated, and the water closed back over him, he felt a loss. With this fresh discovery he began straining to see and hear. He tried to think his way out of it. But what are thoughts against the weight of water?

Then they were there again, the hands and the voices. This time his thighs were gripped, as well as his shoulders, and he was out in the air, bumping noisily along on some wheeled object. The sounds, the voices, hurt his ears. He wanted to tell them to stop but couldn't. He wanted to shout, scream. Then all was quiet and a voice came up close, another voice. But he couldn't understand. Again, hands moved along his body and he was rolled onto another softer surface.

With this softness, he relaxed a little. Cool hands took a wrist, held it. These were different hands with a smell that was sharp, and he sneezed, alarmed at the sound. Something cold pressed against his tongue and he was asked to make a sound and did. This was even more distressing. He could feel his heart pound against the weight of himself, the immovability that was his physical self. But it wasn't over. A cool disc was held to his chest and moved up and down. He was rolled over and the disc touched places on his back. Something soft wrapped around an upper arm, was tightened uncomfortably. Then eased up. Something small, sharp and hard pressed against the inner joint of an arm, burning and pulling at its contents.

He had been dreaming again, this time about explosions bursting in his head. He was just recovering from one burst when another came, and another, and another. His head was melting in a fire. Its bones were crumbling. The pain was a monster that had him in its jaws, shaking him. Then he was vomiting something terrible, coughing and coughing, his throat on fire. The sourness was in his ear, his hair. Something cool wiped it away. Then the blackness descended.

CHAPTER 1

I had always been better with animals than people, but this was my best friend, and I should know what to do. Faye was going to die and all I could think of was getting away from her as fast as I could.

I was visiting her in the hospital the day she was going to tell the doctor what she had decided. Until then I had been calm, as calm as you can be when your oldest and dearest friend says, *no thank you, no chemo for me.*

We had been chatting about this and that, as you do when you can't say what is really on your mind. I had come straight from helping turn out the stables, feeding the dogs, and the innumerable chores that fall to the owner of a small farm. I stood there picking dog hairs off my sweater and wondering aloud why the doctor was late.

Faye lay against the pillows I had plumped for the umpteenth time and said, "If he doesn't discharge me tomorrow, I swear I'm going to phone for a hairstylist." There had been a problem with drainage of the wound and she'd been kept in the hospital another couple of days.

I might have offered to wash her hair but already I was looking away towards a window and thinking, *she doesn't need me.* What was I doing here? She'd made up her mind.

"You do that," I said just as the doctor walked in.

Seeing his professionally cheery face and that of the duty sister must have done it, because I was muttering, "Got to go," and squeezing past.

"*Stella…*" Faye reached for my arm but I was out the door and headed down the corridor.

As I was passing the nurses' desk, I thought I'd better leave some sort of message. A dark head checked something on a computer screen. Kind eyes peered above half-moon frames. She was stout, dependable sort of person, someone you would instinctively trust.

"I'll be back tomorrow. If you could just tell Miss Morissey…" I trailed off. *Good gracious, I was going to cry.* I never cry. Well, not in public.

"Sure, Mrs Gideon."

Fergus, Faye's black Scottie, barked once, sharply, as I got into the car. I shook my head at him, but only half seriously, and gave him a couple of pats. It was all I could allow myself. He licked my ear and settled back against the seat.

Fergus had been with me since Faye went into the hospital five days ago. She had gone in for a breast to be removed, the one with the lump she'd discovered after reading an article in a woman's magazine. You were told how to do it, she told me, in front of a mirror or in the shower, lying down or standing up. Faye ended up doing them all. She even did the clockwise and anti-clockwise sweeping of the breast and underarm tissue. It was after doing this that she phoned me. It was near midnight by then.

"The doctor says that for nine out of ten women, it's a false alarm."

"You've been to the doctor already?" I was groggy, having been woken out of a deep sleep.

I wanted to tell her that she was probably one of the nine women, but I didn't want to lull her into doing nothing. Instead, I urged her to make an appointment with the doctor the next day and to make herself a mug of hot milo, tuck Fergus in with her, and get some sleep. She got to sleep afterward. I was the one who lay awake. And here we were a fortnight later. They'd got it all, the doctor said, but even so, chemo was recommended. It should be started right away.

Breast cancer is the easiest cancer to cure, I read, if caught early. Luckily, it seems Faye has caught it early. Does Faye's reason for not wanting the chemo stem from overconfidence? This is one of the many questions I hurl at no one in particular. As for Faye, when I ask her for her reasons, she says, "Speak to the hand."

I told Faye that I would check on the house before heading out to the farm, essentials like the electricity meter (I bought a top-up on the way in) and that her recycling had been put outside the front gate. I had some fynbos and other flowers in the back of the Jeep and wanted to arrange those as well as have a deco that all was left ship-shape after the housekeeper and gardener had been.

But I sat behind the wheel not moving. I was beginning to feel bad about how I had left, so I took out my cell phone and texted: **Final orders for Aggie?** 'Aggie' was how we referred to ourselves when we were contemplating some chore or other. Between the lines was, had she changed her mind? If by some miracle this was the case, the doctor was going to keep her in hospital for the start of the treatment.

The screen lit up with, **Operation Homeward Bound under way**.

She would be coming home the next day, which meant she was going through with it, this insane disregard for the doctor's advice. Until that moment I thought she would relent. Who deliberately taunted death? The treatment was no picnic, we knew that, but it was all we had. All *she* had.

I turned the key in the ignition, rammed the gears into reverse. My hands on the wheel shook. The engine roared as I backed out.

I must have spotted something in the rearview mirror, because my foot came down hard on the brake. A 4x4 passed by within inches of my bumper.

My head was throbbing as I drove through the grounds. I didn't trust myself now, and kept checking that I was adhering to the speed limit. I could feel my cheeks burn as I smiled for the sentry at the gate. I was behaving like a child.

I pulled up in Faye's driveway. Fergus had his paws up against the passenger window, ears twitching and looking out, but he was quiet.

The house was on a corner plot, below Belvedere Road. The low-pitched roof was red tile with two sturdy chimneys serving real fireplaces – one in the lounge and one in the main bedroom. Below a Cape Dutch gable, latticed bay windows looked out, one on each side. Between them the red-polished steps of the porch fanned down onto a bricked path that circled the house. Her father, a GP, had converted the servants' quarters into a surgery. These days it accommodated guests, often an overflow from the farm.

Faye had lived there most of her life, apart from a sojourn in the north-western Cape, which was where we met.

"Ready boy?" Fergus' front paws danced on the spot.

I let us in through the back door. I put the bouquet of the flowers in the sink and filled Fergus' water bowl. Counters, floor, windowsills, everything was sparkling clean. I checked for telephone messages. Most of the calls were from people at work. In her job, she was as steady as a rock. She had worked as an accountant for the same carpeting business ever since leaving university. The get-well wishes were heartfelt but there was a thread of *don't stay away too long*.

I walked through with the vase, Fergus padding solemnly beside me. At the end of the passage lay the front door, beyond it, the porch and steps leading outside. To my left, doors opened on the dining room and lounge. To my right, the bedrooms and bathrooms. I settled on the best position for the flowers, on top of a half-moon table in front of a tall gold-framed mirror. Again, everything was clean and fresh, but I had my orders. The last doorway on the right led into Faye's bedroom, originally her parents'. Almost everything was as it had always been. Faye's mother's antique silver brushes, comb and hand mirror lay on crocheted doilies on the dressing table. Framed silver photographs of the elder Morriseys' as a bridal couple, and a coy Faye, taken in her prom dress, were arranged on the opposite side of the dressing tabletop. Faye had hated the dress and her partner, the brother of a school mate roped in for the occasion. I hadn't known Faye then. We met the first year out of school. It was hard to believe that there was a time when we hadn't known one another.

I steeled myself as I picked up the photo of Faye. I had forgotten how velvet the brown of her eyes had been, how springy those dark curls, how sweet the curve of that smile. If I didn't do something, Faye was going to look even less like the girl she had been.

Anybody who didn't know me might think I was an alarmist, or worse, a fatalist. But losing my father to a heart attack when I was seventeen and a husband to a fall resulting from a brain tumor had fine-tuned my antennae for disastrous outcomes as per illness. My mother had faded away over the better part of a year. Was that how it was going to be with Faye, a lingering farewell?

I walked through to the bathroom. When Faye's mother broke her hip, Faye had the floor levelled, as well the steps outside that lead to the kitchen door replaced with a cement ramp. Handrails had been fitted on the bathroom walls and a shower installed for easy access by a wheelchair. Would her daughter be relying on these modifications in the not-too-distant future?

I made a quick exit.

On the porch I stood looking out. For one blessed moment, my mind was blank. A light breeze lifted the hair off the back of my neck. The leaves of the trees against the far wall rustled. One was in full flower. Every year Faye cursed the darn thing. She was allergic. Against Faye's present state of health, it appeared shockingly minor.

Fergus scratched the leg of my jeans. I picked him up, went over to the waist-high wall, and sat with him on my lap, smoothing the fur between his ears, scratching his neck. He grunted his satisfaction. The glossy lawn rolled down to the front wall. The edges were trimmed to perfection, the soil beneath the shrubs were freshly turned. The flowerbeds were stocked with that season's crop. In summer it was petunias and phlox, in autumn and winter pansies, in spring impatiens. Presently it was pansies. It was a little early, the soil wasn't cold enough and the roots could be attacked by fungus. But Faye, in most things, liked to get ahead.

The third of an acre was kept as spick and span as it had been when Faye's mother was alive. Maintaining the house – paintwork, plumbing, roof, electrics, you name it – was a point of honor with Faye. She was still the good daughter. This posthumous parent-pleasing nearly drove me crazy. I had tried to get her to sell up, to move somewhere more chic– or at least to somewhere that required less upkeep, less hassle. Spend the money on yourself or take a trip, I'd badger. Returning from trips with Arno, I would recount our adventures with a touch of self-deprecation, like it was childish to get so much pleasure from hearing a robin sing in the church garden where Grey wrote his famous elegy or dole out a stack of lira for an accordion-accompanied solo along a waterway in Venice, hoping she would argue that it wasn't self-indulgent but an investment in our married happiness. I could have wrong-footed her then. She always listened, asked questions, but never said how much she would like to sample these or similar delights for herself, so I couldn't. After Arno died and I had recovered sufficiently to want to get out and enjoy myself again, I asked Faye if she would be my travel companion, which meant I would pay.

But she wouldn't budge. Until a month ago. Out of the blue she asked to see some of my brochures–the ones featuring cruises.

Now this was strange. Did she have a premonition that if she didn't go she might never get the chance? I put Fergus down and walked back inside. Reliving the cruise would help both of us. It might even help Faye change her mind. Remembering how she had enjoyed herself might make her want to do so again.

In the lounge, Fergus began rushing around, sniffing everywhere. The upper half of the cabinet housed the TV set and silverware and ornaments. What I was after would be behind one of the doors in the bottom half. I walked over and opened the door.

And there they were, Faye's albums. Most people store photographs on a computer. Not Faye. She prints the best ones on quality paper, trims and sticks them on the parchment-like pages of an album interleaved with tissue paper, as flimsy and intricately patterned as butterfly wings.

The albums are arranged – typically – in order, newest to oldest, the oldest being at the bottom. On top was the shiny new one.

I sat back with it on my lap. She hadn't wasted time. It was only four weeks since we'd been back, and here was this colorful record of our holiday. My fingertips tingled as I turned the cover.

There we are, in our deck chairs in floppy hats and those oversized sunglasses people like to put on babies. We're grinning, mojitos aloft. Faye's round cheeks are flushed. My narrow face is thoughtful. It's as though I can't believe what is happening. An overhead shot catches us in the pool slathered in suntan oil, head to head on floaties. She is the one with the curves. I, the one with the twin boys in their twenties, am all angles. Moments later someone had belly-flopped, tumbling us in.

In another we giggle in fancy dress. Marilyn Monroe lifts her skirt saucily while Scarlett O'Hara attempts a curtsy in her/my crinoline. It is hard to believe our partners – John Wayne and Abe Lincoln – are kitchen staff who moonlight as drag queens in the show, *Naughty but Nice*. In the next one, at the show itself, they have dropped in our laps wearing nothing but a few strategically placed feathers. And there we are on the stage afterwards receiving a rose each.

I flipped through faster. Us at a gaming table losing hopelessly. Meeting the cast of *Hamlet*, students from the University of Cape Town – a proud moment. And my favorite, Faye with her dream come true. During his show, a Richard Clayderman look-alike, Faye's teenage idol, draws a ticket. And guess who gets to sit next to him on the piano stool, heads together, his hands on the keys and the orchestra rounding off a soppy love song?

While I look around for somewhere strategic to place my find, I see Faye's face, the one I left behind less than half an hour ago. Her eyes glint with her particular brand of determination.

I was going to have to exercise caution. No, I won't leave it out. In her present mood Faye will shoot down anything with a whiff of motive. Seeing it, she is bound to ask questions, and before you know it the whole thing will nose-dive. So I return it to the cabinet, to its place on top. Still on my knees, I marshal the spines and edges. She'll never know I've been here.

CHAPTER 2

The farm lies between the Stellenbosch and Somerset West. The sturdy bush vines of cinsault love the steepness of the foothills that morph upwards into the rugged Helderberg.

But I wasn't thinking about vines or wine as I headed out onto the freeway. I had relished the moment of blankness earlier and I suppose I was trying to go for that. I turned on the radio, listened a moment to the scrape of violins, the saw of a cello – and turned it off again, frustrated. I tried to focus on my surroundings. It always feels like I'm pulling the mountains closer. That I have hold of the ribbon of road like it's a tug-of-war and I'm the happy loser. And today it was happening again. The feeling is something like riding. It's almost as good, the release, the triumph. Leather creaks under my butt. Rock-hard belly goes like the bellows against my knees, calves. The reins and coarse mane are loose, but secure in my hands. The wind sings in my ears, my eyes water, my heart hammers, while the rhythmic thud of hooves on hard ground pounds through me. The animal and I are a unit. We are a trained partnership of intelligence, nerve, and muscle. A speed camera flashes. *Oh, hell.*

Half an hour later I am at the first gate, the sign announcing Gideon Wine Sales, and below that, Quinn Stables. Quinn is my maiden name. The aloes Arno and I planted flank the gate. They should be flaming with winter flower but they're like Faye's pansies, struggling. We've had one too many a wet winter for their liking. I should replace them with something else.

The dogs were at the second gate, barking a welcome. A different tone greets strangers. I opened a window to punch in the code and fondle the ears of the two Rottweilers known as Harry and Sally. They and a state-of-the-art alarm system that included electric fencing had been insisted on by the twins. It was first thought that Arno had been attacked. That was before the post-mortem. It was easier to attribute the gash on his head to a blow from some blunt instrument wielded by an intruder– even though there was no evidence of this– than to having knocked his head on the edge of his desk. That he had passed out in the advanced stages of an illness was unthinkable for a man so obviously in his prime. One consolation was that he didn't suffer. Not even a headache.

Now I was on the dirt road that ran along the bottom end of the vineyard. A glance at the trails of russet between the vines reminded me that we should be getting ready to prune. It was about time, too, for another blitz against ants. It made me tired just thinking about it. We were in a holding pattern. Brand, my eldest, helped out in his free time. The reduced staff and I, doubling at this and that, muddled along.

I pass the garages, the stables, and the rondavel, stacked with broken machinery and furniture, rolls of ripped up carpeting, and the twins' pram, highchairs and cots. Besides the family vehicles, we keep a truck for deliveries, a tractor, trailer, and other farming equipment. Round the back is the winery.

I pulled up in the shade of the gum trees behind the house. They keep the house fragrantly cool in summer, but it became a damp icebox in winter, necessitating a fire be lit in the centrally situated sitting room. I could have installed a heating system but I liked to keep up the traditions of Arno's parents. They had died several years ago and were buried in the family graveyard. I adored Ada and Frank. They were everything my parents hadn't been. They were always warm and welcoming.

During the holidays, the place brimmed with visitors. My parents and especially my mother put appearances above everything. Growing up, I had impeccable manners so other mothers loved to have me. However, I had trouble keeping friends because my mother would scare them away with her insistence that we eat in the dining room with starched serviettes and keep our voices down while she slept away the afternoon.

The other reason I'd been attracted to the Gideons was because the land was everything to them. They had built up the farm from scratch, worked, lived, loved, and died on it. My father had been a bank manager. We were in a different house almost every year. As he moved up the ladder, we occupied bigger and better homes, the last equipped with a swimming pool and tennis court. But he never owned one. When my father died, my mother moved into a guest house. Years later, Arno, recognizing her need for privacy and quiet, offered to add an en suite bathroom and toilet to the rondavel. He was trying to save her money, and, more than that, have her close as she was having worrying bouts of forgetfulness. Maybe it was the proximity to the horses. She could never stand them. In any case, she hadn't answered then, or when Arno tried again.

The old homestead sprawled on one side of the property. In summer we often ate out on the deep, three-way veranda. A fence ran around the house, keeping the animals off the vegetable and flower beds. The family cemetery was also in the front of the property, but in a far corner where the land dipped towards a stream shaded by smaller trees. Higher up the same stream fed the garden, and even higher, where a pump aided the process, the vineyard. The stream, which was really a small underground river, had been the clincher when Arno's father had to decide between what was to be Gideon's and another's established farm without an independent water supply. In times of drought, he had been able to supply other farms with water.

I glanced across at the three other cars as I parked. Their owners would be having their hair done by Lyle, Brand's twin, who ran a salon from the house.

Visitors on farm-related business parked round by the winery. Their numbers had dropped; I had to admit, in direct relation to the lack of inspired leadership the business was presently receiving.

The Rottweilers jostled my legs as I walked towards the house. The ancient lab, Suzi, waddled towards us wagging her tail so hard that her whole body shook. The Dachsie, Woo, yapped excitedly. Fergus followed but kept mute.

Hearing voices through the kitchen window stopped me in my tracks. "*House.*"

The big dogs settled quickly on the back step, heads high, ears twitching. Suzi and Woo slipped back into the kitchen, but Fergus was in a quandary. I looked back as I walked towards the stables. He was sitting in the middle of the path watching me. He would be there when I returned.

The cook and housekeeper, Willy, would know to carry on with lunch. Everyone was going to have to make allowances, for today at least. The groom and general factotum, Isak, and farm laborers didn't count, as my relationship with them was all about the work. But even so, I was glad they were having lunch out in the back as I walked in through the stable entrance. Individual stalls extended on either side of the open central area. The tack and sluice rooms were on the far right. Izzy's stall was on my immediate left.

For a moment I stood, relishing the odors of horse sweat and manure, the sharpness of disinfectant, and the milder rotting hay, damp earth, and feed.

Once again, I checked myself. With animals, self-control was even more vital. I took another deep breath. These days, anger was my first response. It started when Arno died. I was afraid of collapsing in a heap, I suppose. Now it was a habit. I was like a gas-fired stove. The kind that has a pilot light that snapped into flame the minute you switch it on. It didn't take much to set me off. Mostly it was inane things – things that you couldn't do much about, like, just then, the thought of people expressing their concern. It was exhausting, being angry all the time. One good thing, though, was that I slept like a baby. *Except when best friends made lousy decisions.* I had tossed like billy-oh the night before. It wasn't the way to live. If I could just be free of that, the fury, my life would be so much better. But I was at a loss about it as usual.

Izzy lifted her head from licking traces of molasses in the manger. I stroked her nose, fed her some peppermints from my jeans pocket. I'd had love affairs with each of my horses. It nearly broke my heart whenever I had to sell one or when one died. Arno used to tease me about this.

"My biggest competition is the four-legged variety," he would tell people with a mixture of pride and exasperation. They might have been inspecting the gymkhana photographs or the contents of the trophy cabinet kept in the foyer of the winery.

Stabling horses and ponies had provided a steady income. Stabling and winemaking were complementary. Horse manure fed the rose bushes that headed the rows of vines. A horse saddle was a good vantage point for inspecting the state of the vineyard. You could lean down and sample a bunch of early ripening Chenin Blanc and the later, Cinsaut, and then in between Cape Riesling, Pinotage, and Colombar. Stabling and winemaking advertised each other. People who came for the stabling discovered our wines and vice versa. We'd run a thriving two-fold enterprise. But with Arno gone, I'd had to reduce the number of stabled horses. Presently they were four, five with Izzy. We were no longer making our own wine. All our grapes went to the co-op and contributed to someone else's vintage.

Izzy snorted with pleasure as I lifted on the saddle. Her stable companion, Sweetpea, replied with a whicker, a note or two higher. Her voice matched her build and body weight. Sweetpea was a couple of hands shorter, a pony, and also younger, another factor affecting her voice. Izzy was four years old, a palomino and fifteen hands high. For anyone who knew horse breeds, her name was so obvious it was laughable, but I didn't care. The Spaniards called such horses 'Ysabellas', after Queen Isabella, who was, I'd read, besotted with their golden color.

To emphasize this, I murmured softly, "Izzy, Iz, Bella, Belle."

I held up a length of blonde mane. "Girl, you need a shampoo." I had to find the time.

Grooming the animals was how I kept in touch. It was also a way of giving back to them. Increasingly, however, I was leaving more of the tasks to the staff.

We never took the horses out beyond the front gate unless they were in the trailer because drivers seldom slowed down enough coming off the main road. The paddock behind the stable was where the groom and I –

and Brand, Lyle, and Ellie on weekends – exercised the other horses, but Izzy would expect me to take her through circles or figures of eight.

Usually I enjoyed our paces, but today I doubted I had the patience. Izzy was sensitive to my mood. Returning a troubled horse to the stable might lead to it thrashing about or even biting another horse should it come close enough. For an unrestricted ride we used a neighbor's property. But today I needed something more, somewhere that even contemplating smacked of defiance, somewhere that if we were spotted by a passerby might fetch a complaint.

To this end we headed, via a narrow dirt road, for a vacant stretch of municipal ground, a fenced square of roughly ten acres. As it came into sight, we slipped into a canter which quickly became as gallop as I leaned forward. Soon we were soaring over the barbed wire, thumping down on hooves that seemed to skim the clumpy grass before striking up a pounding rhythm as the horse got into stride. I was only dimly aware of damp clods flying up behind, a froth of horse spit breaking away and landing on my cheek, breath sucked in and expelled violently, the banging about of hearts against ribs.

CHAPTER 3

I sat at the kitchen table waiting for my lunch to warm up. I was feeling more peaceful. Willy must have gone out to the vegetable garden to pick something for dinner. I could hear Lyle's deep tones punctuating the lighter feminine chatter – all indistinct and coming from what had formerly been the lounge. The bathroom, like all the rooms of houses built about seventy years ago, was large, and three basins had fitted easily into the space formerly occupied by one. I vetoed replacing the bath and shower with more basins in case Lyle changed his mind about working at home. Of course, there had been other changes, like mirrors everywhere and better lighting, and more electric wall plugs. Then there was the new décor, featuring a chandelier, puffy Austrian blinds, a complete wall of rose-pink suede wallpaper, and imitation Louis XIV chairs. Lyle was in his element and I, when I got over the shock, had been full of admiration.

Brand and Ellie would be home from work around six, a whole half hour sooner than when they worked in town. She had been a Girl Friday for a magazine and he was selling out of the HQ of an estate agent. They met at the launch of the magazine in a house that had been briefly on the books – a 'very special house,' he was fond of saying, which I understood was code for the nature of their meeting. Because my eldest son eschewed anything that smacked of sentimentality, I took note.

It had all happened while I was still reeling from Arno's death and the mental fog from the various colored capsules pressed on me by a well-meaning doctor. I hadn't been consulted. Or couldn't remember having been. But there they were, moving in, both the twins, one with a girlfriend in tow. It must have been around this time that Brand decided to move to a branch of the agency in Somerset West and Ellie take the receptionist position at the medi-clinic in nearby Stellenbosch.

Lyle had given notice at the salon in town and opened up shop almost immediately, occupying one of the larger spare rooms until the conversion was done. Brand and Ellie had been shocked when I suggested they move into the main bedroom. Brand had refused point blank. Ellie quickly realized that moving into the main bedroom, instead of being an affront, would be helping me. She must have spoken to Brand because the next day he said, they'd love to move into the 'royal chamber', the boys' joking reference to their parents' bedroom. No one had laughed, of course, but I felt something give way. In the barren and almost blamelessness of a small spare room, I was saved from having to deal with the vacant other half of the marriage-size bed, not to mention the smells of the absent person clinging to the bed-linen. I was still ensconced there but had added little touches like new bedding, curtains, and had the carpenter, who did the alterations for the salon, knock and fit a bookcase into one wall.

I went over to the sink and ran a glass of water, drinking greedily. I was also hungry, I realized. I found the bowl of salad in the fridge and helped myself to a generous portion. The microwave pinged and I fetched my plate. Delicious steam filled the air as I lifted off the plastic cover.

There was a moment, as I picked up my knife and fork, when I thought of Faye and whether she'd been able to eat any lunch. *Just eat*, I told myself.

I was still alone when I left for the office. Arno's assistant had also had to go, which proved a blessing. Paperwork became my refuge.

———————

When I walked in later, Ellie and Brand were about to leave. Ellie had texted earlier that she and Brand were going out, and would I mind if they skipped supper?

"Where are you guys off to?"

"A dinner for work," Brand said matter-of-factly.

His brown hair was dark from the shower, and he had on one of his better suits. All my men are over six foot and rangy. Ellie, despite stilettos, barely reached his chin. She had on a slinky black dress, with silver earrings swimming like fishes against her slender neck. She lifted her dark curtain of hair as Brand helped her don a jacket of faux fur.

They looked so grown up.

"What's the occasion?" I hadn't realized until the older of the twins – by fifteen minutes – had come home again to live, how cagey he could be about work.

"The new boss wants to meet us."

"Just the two of them," interjected Lyle, as though the comment would somehow fill in the gaps for me.

"But we'll be here," said Myrna. "For a while, at least."

My smile was tight.

Myrna was one of Lyle's regulars, a divorcee of means who seemed to be joining the family for meals more and more often. When Lyle resigned from the salon in town she had brought with her a small army of friends, I hoped Lyle wasn't getting into something he couldn't handle. Myrna must have been a good ten years older. The age difference between me and Arno had been about the same, but that was different, wasn't it? Men could be older, but not vice versa. Myrna was going to get tired of Lyle – or him of her. This was a new thing for me, worrying about my children.

"Let's eat, shall we?" I lifted the lid off a pot. Most meals were taken in the kitchen. The dining room was for special occasions.

Eat was too strong a verb for what Myrna did with the contents of her dinner plate. She was all for preserving her looks, which seemed to work well for her. She was a natural redhead with porcelain skin and bone structure to die for. Lyle had used her as one of his models for a hair styling competition. He had won hands down in the fantasy section.

I didn't eat much, but that was because I'd overdone it at lunch. Lyle, like his brother, was able to consume enormous quantities of food without putting on weight, scraped the leftovers from Myrna and my plates onto his.

"What's the movie about?" I asked.

"Mom, would you like to come?" Lyle turned his big blue eyes on me, and I felt my spine jellify. Although the twins aren't identical, they're versions of Arno. Lyle has his looks, Arian blonde, when it isn't colored. Presently it is streaked with shades of metallic brown. Brand, with hair the color of ash and matching eyes, has his father's personality. Usually I'm on my guard, but tonight I fail dismally.

"No, thanks. But tell me about it."

Myrna looked relieved.

While they told me what they knew about the thriller, a sci-fi action drama with ground-breaking special effects, I noted with relief that no one had asked about Faye beyond how she was, to which I was able to reply, OK. They knew about the mastectomy but not about Faye's refusal to have the chemo. I hoped I wasn't going to have to deliver this last part. The twins loved their godmother, and her refusal of the treatment was going to hurt and confuse them. I also wanted to protect them for as long as I could from having to face the possible loss of another person close to them.

The house was awfully quiet when everyone was gone. I didn't think I could concentrate on TV or a book. I hadn't planned very well, but then again I'd only had twenty-four hours since Faye dropped her bomb. I had checked on the horses earlier when I took the dogs for a walk. From their baskets, Suzi, Woo, and Fergus watched as I stacked the dishwasher. Harry and Sally moved about on the front step. They had kennels but didn't use them. I planned to get around to showing them how but always thought about it too late. I set the table for breakfast, a task Ellie had taken on. She felt bad if she couldn't help, but she was going to be tired after her night out, I reasoned.

To get to sleep, I was going to need more wine. We had finished a bottle of supermarket grand cru during the meal. Our glasses clinked away companionably in the dishwasher. I needed something more substantial. There might still be a bottle of red in the cabinet in the dining room. The red had been Arno's baby, his *Hart Sag*. I found a bottle at the back. The boys must have been keeping it for a special occasion. Well, one had come. I took the bottle, lifted a glass off a shelf and walked down the passage.

Someone's after-shave lingered in the air. Someone's...? *Arno's*, I realized with a jolt. The fragrance seemed to come from the main bedroom. The door was open. Mostly it was closed. And quite right. Couples – especially young couples – needed privacy. I hadn't entered the room in a while and never without a fixed purpose like distributing clean linen or toilet rolls.

A shiver ran through me as I stood there. Soon, however, this was overtaken by the familiar prickle of annoyance. *Dammit*, this was my house, my home. I walked in.

Everything was very neat, including the bed. The king-size bed. Its width struck me as indulgent – past indulgence. But it had proved its worth with two growing young bodies often slipping in with us during the night. It was a shock seeing Ellie's delicate brush-stroke design – Japanese, I thought – black and red on white, instead of the old mustard and brown mosaic that had caught my eye years earlier. A teenage Lyle had called it dog's puke. Unlike his mother, he had décor sense even then.

I laughed, a dry, ugly sound. I placed the wine and glass on the dressing table and stood, looking at my reflection. My face was flushed from the food and wine, my blue-grey eyes blood-shot. My lips, with the lipstick eaten off, pursed unattractively. I muttered aloud, *you're disgusting*. Disgustingly healthy. Even my silvery blonde hair, escaped from the ponytail and framing my face in greasy tendrils, the thinness of which was the bane of my life, spoke of an unfair advantage.

I reminded myself why I was there and walked into the bathroom. I opened the mirrored door above the hand basin and there it was – the squat, opaque bottle, an anachronism among the bottles of Tommy Hilfiger and Diesel.

I stared. Why this night? Brand hadn't used it before. Anger flared and I directed it at the bottle. I should toss it. I had it in my hand when I pictured Brand or Ellie feeling the weight in the bin as they prepared to empty it. Or Willy. Questions or worse, mute concern.

I was making too much of this.

I returned to the bedroom and placed it on the dressing table. My attention moved to the wine, and I opened the bottle and poured an inelegant full glass. I sat on the bed, drinking, hardly tasting. I was pouring a second glass when suddenly I felt woozy. There seemed nothing else to do but walk over to 'my' side of the bed and flop.

CHAPTER 4

When I woke that morning, the waft of after-shave told me that Arno was up, shaved, showered and dressed. They should have named the fragrance Christmas Pudding, I would tease. I was lucky he wore fragrance at all. If you knew farmers, you'd understand why I say that.

Arno would have gone around to the office. A visiting overseas wine farmer had promised some tips on pruning. He was calling on his way to the airport, an early flight. Cinsaut produced quality wine in direct relation to how deep but skillfully the vines are pruned. Pruning cinsaut was like shaving with a single blade as opposed to using a safety razor. Dad Gideon liked to quip, the key word being 'safety'. Many a vine had been lost through clumsy pruning. Arno was always ready to learn more.

I was in my dressing gown, drinking coffee in the kitchen, when the front gate bell rang. It rings in the stables, office and house. Arno wasn't answering, an Antipodean twang over the intercom informed me.

"There must be something wrong with the wiring," I think I said as I opened the gate with the switch on the panel in front of me. "Have you called him on his cell-phone?"

There was no reply, he said.

I pulled on work gear and trainers. To kill time, Arno must be checking his recent blend in the cellar. He could go into a trance at such times. It is common knowledge that tasting wines first thing in the morning produced the most dependable results. Before a tasting, however, it helps not to wear a fragrance, but Arno must have decided to ignore this, or simply hadn't planned on blending.

The visitor, who is called Gunner, and I met at the office entrance. Arno's ridgeback, Greta, was nowhere to be seen. Something about this alarmed me. Gunner saw my hesitation, put out an arm to restrain me.

"I'll go and check. You wait here."

I remember the lack of Arno's voice and the trail of the Old Spice, stronger and more Christmassy than ever. They marked an end for me, the silence and the sickening scent. Arno and I would have been married twenty-three years.

Gunner and I have remained friends. He visits in the winter, the quiet season for wine farmers. This winter will be the third time he will have pruned our cinsaut vines, but so far, no one has dared make red wine. The boys tease me about him, but Gunner is married.

I have fallen asleep there on the old double bed.

"*Mom*."

Brand and Ellie peer at me. I sit up too quickly and my head spins. Then the throbbing starts.

"I didn't mean to fall asleep," I say, blushing and standing up. I hold up a hand against wine breath.

Ellie says, "Stella, can I get you something. Coffee?"

"Tha-anks," I say sarcastically. We both laugh. "I'll get some water. Not to worry."

I walk out keeping a straight line with difficulty. Their silence tells me they are watching. I imagine raised eyebrows. More likely they're frowning.

I am in my bedroom on my second glass of water as the memories resume.

I followed Gunner, of course. I heard Greta's warning bark and Gunner's firm, reassuring reply. There was something muted in that bark and something even stranger in the old bitch's immediate compliance.

In Arno's office she was lying next to him. She looked up as I entered and then returned her chin to her paws.

Gunner was kneeling next to Arno and had a hold of Arno's wrist. Arno was on his back, partly rolled onto his side. Gunner gently touched the blood on the back of Arno's head.

"He's gone," he said.

For some time after that I couldn't bear to hear an Australian accent and would switch the TV off if someone like Russell Crowe, the actor, was being interviewed, or even a woman, Nicole Kidman, for instance. A whole season of the Australian *Master Chef* went by without me watching, and I love that version.

To his credit, Gunner didn't try to verbalize what he thought might have happened but instead telephoned the police, our doctor, Brand, and Lyle. I remember urging him to call an ambulance, and bless him, he was about to when I realized it was pointless and called it off. Throughout all of this I hadn't cried or said much but now I bent over Arno. He looked as though he was sleeping. Death had sloughed off the years. He looked younger than when we first met. I could have been looking at one of my boys. I must have said something, whispered maybe. I remember kissing him on the lips. Their coolness was the worst. He'd been lying there a while and I hadn't known. I might have been able to get help. He might have been alive if I'd gotten there earlier, if I'd known or guessed. But how could I have? In fact, if Gunner hadn't come along, who knows how long Arno would have lain there.

I'd had to be the strong one when my father died, and here I was falling into the role once again. I heard myself greeting the doctor, the police, reassuring the twins.

An odor had opened the Pandora's box of memory. Now I 'hear' sobbing, Lyle on his knees over Arno. A boy again.

Brand was shaking and saying in a hoarse sort of bark, "Who did this? Dad's been attacked. Someone came in and cracked him on the skull. I'll bloody kill the bugger."

He began to pace up and down, telling Willy when she arrived on the scene and anyone else not to touch anything and that it was a crime scene. When the police arrived ten minutes later, he wanted to know why they took so long. Meanwhile our family GP nodded for me to take Lyle and began checking Arno. I pulled Lyle to his feet and held him while he wept some more. When he was quieter, I went over to Brand, but he wanted to attend to the business of finding out what had happened to his father. It was only later at the funeral that he broke down.

I did my crying in private. I found it easier to cry openly over the loss of a dog. Every day after Arno was gone, Greta would be waiting at the winery for us to let her in. She would spend the day in Arno's office. I would hastily check figures on his computer when the need arose, fetch files and whatever, not looking to the right or left until I was back at my desk. She barely ate. I tried force-feeding her until Lyle said, "Mom, how would you feel…?" So I shouldn't have been surprised one evening, when I came to shoo her out, to find her lifeless form under his desk, her favorite spot.

It marked the end of the raw part of my mourning. It was like that gracious creature and I had been doing it together. Now I could spend longer in Arno's office.

Brand must have sold Arno's horse, MacIver. I never asked.

Later Brand knocked on my door, this time without Ellie. It must have been almost an hour since they came back from dinner. I had been sitting on my bed staring into space for most of that time.

"Mom, I think you should have this." He handed me the bottle of Old Spice. He wasn't a fool, my son.

I turned the bottle in my hands, unable to shake myself free of the memory. "Why tonight? Why did you use it tonight?"

"Dutch courage. I thought maybe I was in for the high jump."

"With the boss? And were you – did you er…get scolded? Sorry. I'm a bit foggy." I took another glug of water.

"You're worried about Aunt Faye."

I looked at him. I shouldn't have been amazed, but I was. "A bit."

"But they got it all. The doctor said, didn't he?"

"Even so, chemo is recommended—to be on the safe side. But Faye doesn't want it and I can't understand why. She's usually so sensible. It seems out of character."

Brand sat down next to me. With the extra weight, we collided. I had been meaning to get a new mattress. This one hadn't been intended for the prolonged use it was getting. We shifted a little to get comfortable– he with his arm around my shoulders.

"I'm sure she's going to change her mind."

I kept nodding in the hope it would convince me.

"If she doesn't, Lyle and I will get over there and scare some sense into her." He was smiling. The confidence of youth.

"Don't tell anyone else. Not Lyle. Of course, tell Ellie."

"Will do." He got up.

At the door he turned. "Maybe there's something she's not telling you. Something she's scared of. Chemo can make you really sick, can't it? People lose their hair. Their nails – I dunno, something happens to them, doesn't it? Maybe she has a secret lover." He grinned.

"If only."

"Well, just remember what I said about Lyle and me. We've only got one godmother." The door closed with a resounding click.

CHAPTER 5

The next morning, I was a woman with a mission. Faye with her stop-sign hand had silenced me. But there was still something I could do. Not try and coerce her, but something else. Not words. *Actions*.

I took two headache tablets with my coffee, flung on yesterday's clothes, and went outside to check on the animals. After that, I left instructions for the day with Isak, showered and dressed in an outfit Faye liked – dressy black jeans, a black and red striped top and a red imitation leather biker jacket. I paid special attention to my makeup. I shampooed my hair. When it was dry I bent down the way I had seen Ellie do (although her mop hardly needs the sort of first aid mine does), brushed it and sprayed it with her hairspray, finishing upright with another couple of swooshes, gold hoops in my ears and a gold chain around my neck. *This is what life looks like*, it said. *Life*. Stop this dance with death. Choose life.

"Wow," Lyle said. Brand and Ellie had already left for work. "What's up?"

I almost told him then, but imagined him putting off that morning's clients and careening down the freeway in his VW Beetle with me beside him trying to calm him down.

Not the way to go. She would hug him and thank him and be as sweet as pie, promise to think about everything he said, and carry right on with what she had decided.

"I'm taking your advice, for once." Lyle was always telling me that the animals looked better cared for than their owner.

"Ellie said I should bring you breakfast in bed." He pulled out a tray from under the grill and brandished it like a choice weapon. The bacon had begun to crimp, the cheese on the halved tomatoes melted invitingly.

"Sorry, sweetheart. I'll get something to eat with Faye."

He faked a sigh. "More for me. Maybe Myrna will join me."

"Good luck with that."

"Hugs and kisses for Faye," he called after me.

Good for Brand, I thought. He hadn't spilled the beans.

Faye was sitting on a chair beside the bed when I arrived. I kissed her cheek, hugged her ever so gently.

She smiled thinly as I stood back for her to get a look at my outfit. "You look nice." What's the occasion? The angle of her head told me that particular throw of the dice was useless.

Fergus was jumping all over the front seat of the Jeep. He hadn't barked that way in days. He quieted down immediately when Faye got in but couldn't help sniffing the side of her chest with the bandages. He sat meekly on her lap as we headed out of the hospital grounds, snatching excited little breaths.

"It's good to have you back," I said.

"Most of me."

I didn't have an answer for that.

The gardener was there to lift out Faye's suitcase and bags. He had to make two trips. I remembered how she paid for excess luggage when we flew to New York. She paid her own travel expenses. I should have known she would.

The domestic had laid a tray for tea. I warmed Willy's date and nut muffins, added curls of butter to the plate. Faye nibbled. Fergus and I were gluttons.

"So. What shall we do? I'm taking the morning off."

Another smile, watery.

"How about you call Suzi to come do your hair? I'll look around, get some ideas. Get out the Rummikub." I was hopeless at this convalescent carry-on.

I had the cruise album open on my lap when she came into the lounge.

To give her time to adjust, I said, "Does it hurt?" I touched the left side of my jacket, feeling embarrassed at my own unmutilated chest.

Faye had her cell phone in one hand, waiting for a call. I wanted to hug her again but couldn't. What I felt seemed too much for that simple gesture.

"Not much. But when I wake up…it's, well, it's a rude awakening."

"Not helped by the cold, I guess?"

She nodded. She was looking more like herself, less a waif who had taken my friend's place.

"What did the doctor say when you told him you didn't want the chemo?"

"He wants me to see a shrink."

Well, of course, he does. "And…?"

"I said I'd think about it."

I didn't want to sound too keen, so I didn't comment but gave her a little home news.

It completely escaped me at the time that Faye could have been insulted by the doctor's suggestion. That he was inferring that she didn't know her mind. Faye is remarkably without ego. I would have been cursing the man to kingdom come. All I could think about then, however, was how I was going to introduce the cruise into the conversation. I was careful not to mention my trip down memory lane, and she didn't comment on my sudden departure the previous day.

"Brand and Ellie had dinner with his new boss last evening. There's something on the go but as usual, I'm being kept in the dark. Myrna is around twenty-four seven."

"Brand and Ellie went to dinner with the boss. How did they manage that?"

"The dinner was in town. Some place I hadn't heard of in De Waterkant. It was on their way, they said."

"And Lyle? I expect he's been to see you as well?"

"Er, no. But he called this morning to say he's coming tonight with Myrna. I'll send out for some snacks. Pick 'n Pay do a nice winter platter. Lyle can warm it. I can't remember what Myrna drinks."

"Nor can I."

Myrna favored dry white wine, the drier the better, I could have said, but I was acting out my pique. The twins doted on Faye and she on them. I shouldn't be surprised that they were visiting her. What was happening to me? I couldn't remember being jealous before.

Faye's cell phone rang. Suzi was coming on her lunch break to do Faye's hair. This lift of Faye's spirits boded well for my plan. Faye even helped, leaning over and tapping the cover and saying, "You've found it. I meant to show it to you, but then this happened."

She lifted her sweater and showed me the freshly bandaged left side of her chest. I put the album down on the coffee table to get a better look. The surgeon had done a good job, although, presently, the 'new' breast looked over-sized. That would be the swelling. In the hospital three tubes, one on either side and one from the lowest point of the wound, had fed into a bag containing watery blood. The quantity was alarming. I hated myself for feeling the way I did then– sick to the stomach.

Faye had endured one of the worst things that can happen to a woman. No matter how one prepares for such a thing, and despite the advances in plastic surgery that meant one was not left lopsided, it was still inevitable that one feels *less a woman*, less of what one had been. Or, if not that, then one's femininity pronounced defective. I wanted to weep and wail for her, for all women, but all I did was stare. She eased the sweater back.

I thought, it's now or never. I took the album out of the cupboard and opened to the first page– or what I thought was the first page. I had opened on us in the cruise ship's swimming pool.

"*Oh God*," said Faye. "Don't remind me." She reached across and shoved the cover down. I rescued my hand just in time.

Her eyes brimmed. "How ridiculous is this, crying for the loss of a body part?"

I realized then that we were nowhere near what I had in mind. In that first year after Arno died, well-meaning people like Ellie's mother and friends from gymkhana days would try to fix me up with dates. I knew I should be giving Faye time to adjust. But that was just it. We didn't have that particular commodity.

My eyes must have been closed, because I felt a hand on my arm. I'm ashamed to say I tensed. I'm not demonstrative. I blame my mother who only kissed hello and goodbye and that was about it. Never a pat on the back, and God forbid a hug.

"Stel, I see what you're trying to do," Faye said, "and don't think I don't appreciate it."

I waited a couple of minutes, then picked up the album and got down on my knees to the cupboard. Did she think I was trying to cheer her up, or had she stumbled on the truth? I placed the album on the top of the pile. I felt the heat crawl up my neck. Aligning the spines gave me time to recover.

"When last was this place dusted?" I asked by way of diversion, but Faye was busy dialing on her cell phone.

"Work," she said, pointing a finger at the instrument against her ear. No doubt about it, she was changing the subject.

I fetched a cloth from the kitchen and got down to business. To do a thorough job, the albums needed to come out. The top three almost fell into my arms but the bottom one was stuck fast. After a few tries I realized that leverage was needed and went off again, returning with a knife with a broad blade. I ran it back and forth under the album, trying my best not to damage the cover.

At last, it was out, and I placed it to one side. I was about to start dusting the cupboard when my eyes were drawn to the cover. My mind was still full of the cruise and my plan around it so its title, *Bethany*, didn't immediately strike home. The large capitals were handwritten on a card yellowed with age. The curling cellotape holding it in place was sticky to the touch. I checked the printing again. There was something bold, no, *brave*, in the carefully drawn letters. Unshed tears caught in my throat.

For a moment I wondered if Faye wouldn't prefer this particular trip down memory lane. I wrenched my gaze off the old album and glanced at Faye. She was frowning with the cell phone still to her ear. Her shoulders drooped.

Couldn't they leave her alone? Couldn't they do without her for a few days? Then I remembered that it was Faye who had called work. I might have snatched the instrument out of her hand then and given whoever was the cause of her distress a piece of my mind, but I thought, work... a distraction from pain.

But I wasn't giving up on *my* form of distraction. I dusted the cupboard and returned the albums all but the oldest one. I would show it to her, note her reaction, and work from there.

CHAPTER 6

In the end I returned the *Bethany* album to the bottom of the pile. Faye didn't seem to be in the frame of mind that welcomed a walk back into the past– a past veiled in the mists of twenty-something years, when we were young, and when our breasts, particularly, were young – our original breasts. Was that how she would think? I didn't want her reacting like she had over us in our swim costumes on the cruise liner. The present still held her in its grip. To get her to look at our past selves, especially hers, felt like I was reinserting the knife, and worse– turning it.

After the incident with the cruise album, she drooped some more. I cancelled the hairdo and after hot Milo and painkillers, I settled her in bed with a hot water bottle (neither of us are fans of electric blankets). I had also done some googling and knew to raise the arm on the affected side with a thin pillow so that if there was still some draining going on, this would help. I called Lyle out of Faye's earshot and told him to ask Willy to pack something tantalizingly delicious and to bring it when he and Myrna came.

Faye had taken off a mere fortnight for recovery. I was with her every day for the next two weeks. I watched her rally as work colleagues and friends called, and slump after they left. In the afternoon while she had a nap, I'd rush back to the farm, bark orders, ride Izzy, feed and walk the dogs and cart back. I spent most nights with Faye. I would give her a sponge bath and tuck her up in bed with the ubiquitous hot water bottle, read to her if she couldn't sleep. She loved *You* magazine. She always felt better about her life after reading about "other people's messes", as she put it.

Most of the time it felt like I was walking on eggshells. This was a Faye I didn't know– this closed off, *tricky* person. Worst of all, she reminded me of my mother, whom I had never been able to reach. Faye and I had always communicated openly. At least, I thought we had. I began to doubt my value as a friend. In her direst hour I was proving useless. A nurse could do what I was doing. It was the emotional side– the inspired sort of help, where I was falling short. I remembered other times when she was in pain, other sorts of pain. When her father and then her mother died, for instance. Those times had been easier, easier because we could talk. My father was the first of our parents to die, so I had that experience to draw on. Now I was out on a limb of ignorance.

Faye was having her first check-up on Monday of the last week of leave. Again, I was hatching a plan. In low moments I had continued to fret at having left the hospital when she was going to break the news to the doctor that she didn't want the chemotherapy. I had missed an opportunity to put my oar in– maybe the only one I'd get. So when Faye asked me to be present when the stitches and staples were removed, my heart leapt. I was being given another chance. By hook or by crook I would nudge the conversation in the direction of the fated treatment.

But Fate had other ideas. Hearing that the doctor had been called out on an emergency brought my plan to a juddering halt. The general pall that spread through the waiting room as the receptionist with a minimum of detail offered her apologies spoke volumes. A patient was probably dying. How one jumped to the worst of scenarios. I looked at Faye but she was deep into *People* magazine. I asked to speak to the sister. Not to worry, the receptionist said, the sister could remove the sutures. Or we could come back another day? Then I thought, a woman for us to talk to and in turn, offer advice. This is better, way better. Although Faye was happy with him, I hadn't liked the doctor, a cold fish if there ever was one. And besides, Faye was more likely to listen to a woman, and a professional at that.

The sister's opening gambit took us both by surprise.

"Doctor said I should schedule the start of the chemo." She had the receiver in her hand with a finger ready to dial.

"Is this some kind of a trick?" Faye and the sister locked eyes.

"I don't understand," the woman looked genuinely nonplussed.

"I'm not having chemo."

The sister put down the receiver and began scrolling on the computer on the doctor's desk– for Faye's file, I guessed.

"I must have misunderstood. There's no mention of the treatment here—whether you're to have it or not. I took it you were having it. I'm so sorry."

"It's an easy mistake," I said, although it had registered as unprofessional. I wanted to get the woman on our (my) side before taking hold of my oar. "I'm sure there are not many woman – and men for that matter – who refuse the treatment?"

"Not many, no. People who have health issues, other complaints like diabetics, for example, have to weigh it all up, with the doctor's help, of course. Does Miss Morrisey – do you, ma'am, have such concerns?" She scrolled some more.

Faye shook her head.

"There's alternative medicine, as promoted in the book by that movie star. A couple of our patients have gone that route."

"And a while back, Suzanne Somers," Faye said.

My heart flipped. Was Faye holding out for other remedies?

"Can we get on with removing the stitches?" Faye threw me such a pleading look that I dropped the oar immediately.

As the staples and a couple of errant stitches were removed, I thought, I have to know. I'm her friend. She has no other family, in fact, I'm *it*. As soon as we were in the car I asked the burning question, was Faye planning to go the alternative route? A car hooted for us to vacate our parking spot and Faye's reply was lost. I looked at Faye, hope popping like an old-time flash bulb. The car hooted once more, and I reversed and drove off.

I waited a moment, and then I said, "I didn't catch what you said."

"I'm happy as things are. I believed it when the doctor said he got it all. So, no treatment, even alternative."

"I hate to remind you, sweetie," I replied. We were halted behind a taxi minibus. "But the doctor recommended chemo." Which you are totally disregarding, I could have said. "You're happy to take one of his proclamations but not the other. As the daughter of a doctor, I would think you'd follow his advice." Or know better, I almost said.

This was progress, I told myself, seconds later. At least we were talking. But it was phyrric, soulless. One heard of people drifting apart after a disagreement. Their encounters were limited to celebrations of births, marriages, death. Aunts of Arno's had a disagreement over a pound of sausages and didn't speak for nine years. *Nine years*. I couldn't comprehend nine days.

The remainder of that final week passed in much the same way. Faye had another check-up on Friday, this time with the doctor in attendance. She didn't invite me in and I didn't ask how it went apart from a general question. Was he satisfied with her progress? Oh, yes, she said, smiling. The swelling was down and she could begin a graduated program of exercises. I wanted to be happy for her.

I still had no idea what I was going to do. How I was going to get her to change her mind about the chemo. I kept waiting for some chink in this new armor of Faye's, but none came. We had planned a special meal for that Saturday night on the farm with the boys and their partners. I had hoped to get Faye to come out to the farm sooner but had to accept the crumb of one night. She was going back to work on Monday. I had to do something before that. Once her head was full of the job, I would have less chance of getting through to her.

Again, I thought of co-opting the past, a past where she had been happy, where we had both been happy, the idea being to spur her on to being happy again, to doing everything in her power to ensure a happy, long-lived life. I left the *Bethany* album out to nil response. She had either become adept at looking the other way or she was genuinely not interested. Or she felt too sick to want to look at it. Or sick at heart, which in a weird way was encouraging.

But now, a week after the doctor's OK, she had begun to regain good spirits. In fact, she was the one to suggest going out to the farm. I switched to stealth mode once again. One afternoon when she was asleep, I slipped out the *Bethany* album and stowed it in the boot of the Jeep, tucking it under a box of old magazines waiting for me to offload at the vet's. It was unfair what I planned, but I had exhausted what I could do on my own. I was going to surreptitiously enlist the help of the children.

When we planned the meal, I expected Willy to come up with Beef Wellington, *smoor aartappels* (potatoes braised with onions) and pumpkin fritters, all favorites of Faye's. But my employee of longstanding raised a gnarled index finger and said, "Miss Faye has been sick. We need sick people's food."

What transpired was a velvety chicken soup with fluffy sweet bread rolls (homemade) and smoked angelfish kedgeree and steamed new potatoes with parsley butter. For dessert there was baked custard and stewed prunes. When I raised an eyebrow at the prunes, Willy said, "When you lie in bed all day, the stomach thinks it can go on holiday as well."

I almost didn't serve wine, but Brand and Lyle had mixed a jug of *gluwein* – a perfect marriage of healthy rooibos tea, red co-op wine and apple juice, bobbing with cloves, each steaming glass to be stirred with a cinnamon stick before bringing to the lips.

We invited Willy to join us for coffee in the study, which these days served as a lounge that fortunately had a fireplace– a pre-war old black metal job. Lyle had laid the fire, which was burning brightly. She thanked us and said she had to go and dream. For as long as I had been with the Gideons, Willy had told me her dreams. They arrived like installments of a gothic novel. I had given up wondering how much was the product of a fertile waking imagination, and how much was relief from an otherwise humdrum life.

"Next week we'll catch up," I said. "Last I heard you were in that whale. What happened? Did you get out?"

"*Ag*," said Willy, "From there I rode on a dolphin."

Brand and Lyle were trying not to laugh.

"Say good night to Willy, boys."

"*We are stuff as dreams are made on, and our little life is rounded with a sleep,*" said Faye. "William Shakespeare."

Lyle and Brand were frowning.

Myrna lifted a manicured hand to a yawn.

I frowned at Myrna, but madam wouldn't look at me.

Ellie said diplomatically, "We can do with a little culture around here. Anybody read any good books lately?'

This was too easy. "I have something that might interest you—a tome of family history."

I reached for the album lying on the coffee table and sat on the couch next to Faye.

"I was wondering what that was," said Brand.

"It's how and where we met, Faye and I." I stroked the label, trying to flatten the gummy cellotape. Bethany is the name of a town. Heard of it?"

"It's in the north-east." Brand offered.

"How'd you know that, bru?"

"It is close to Molteno, which has one of the lowest recorded temperatures in the country. They've had snow there a few times. Bethany is a neighbouring town." Brand, who played golf when he found the time, was constantly watching weather reports on TV.

"Snow. Imagine," said Ellie. "Did it snow when you were there, Stella?"

"We were there in the summer."

"How come? I mean, it's out of the way, isn't it?"

"Sticksville." Lyle grinned at Myrna for approval.

"Our fathers worked there. Your grandfather, Roy, managed the bank. Faye's father was doing a locum for a doctor friend. Right, Faye?"

Faye nodded.

"When was this?"

"In the nineteen-nineties. Our first year out of school."

"Come on, open it." Lyle squeezed in next to me, Brand next to Faye. I couldn't have planned it better. I tried not to get excited.

I looked at Faye. She threw me a pleading look. I blinked at her and returned to the album. I made sure I opened on the first page this time.

A waft of mustiness hit my nostrils. I wanted to sneeze, but the moment passed.

Unfortunately, the first photo was another pool shot. Why hadn't I checked? All this fretting of mine and I hadn't thought to open that album and plan my moves.

The pool was a borehole pool, a round cement tank connected to a pump that plumbed an underground water supply.

Three young people leaned over the side of the pool. Behind them, other boys and girls cavorted. Someone had just dived in, and water spilled over the sides and lapped against the arms of the three – two girls and a boy, grinning at the camera.

Myrna was the first to speak. "Who *are* they?" It came across as a complaint.

"Geez, Myrna," said Brand. "I thought it'd be obvious. That's Faye – and on the other side, Mom."

"Who's the guy?" asked Lyle. "I think I'd know if it was Dad."

"You're right. It isn't your Dad," I said. "It's a friend. Strawks."

"Strawks? What kind of name is that?"

"It's a nickname. Everyone had nicknames around Bethany."

"Did you and Faye?"

"No. We were new there. The other kids had grown up together. They all went to boarding school as there was only a primary school in the town. Apparently, the minute you arrived at boarding school you got a nickname. It was a tradition."

"His real name was Thorkild. His parents were Norwegians. It was Thorks first. You don't pronounce the 'h'. And then it became Strawks." Faye shrugged. She was looking quite pleased with herself. "There was this dance. It was on a farm, and something happened with a bale of straw."

Four pairs of eyes stared. She was enjoying this. "*I* gave him the name."

I looked at Faye. There was someone who knew her as well as me, who had cared for her as much or even more.

Suddenly I knew what I had to do.

CHAPTER 7

'Small town' hadn't prepared Stella. The first shock was leaving the tarred national road. Driving down, the countryside had become increasingly barren. Miles of flatness was broken up with thorn bush-crested small hills. A truck choc-a-block with sheep honked by in a cloud of dust, they were bound for a sale or the abattoir. Stella didn't think she was going to like this new place.

The second shock was Bethany itself. The streets were empty except for a scrawny dog. She had the door open, but her father said, "Time for that later." Lining the street was a handful of shops, among them the bank, a small hotel, the police station, and a garage offering all kinds of repairs, including fridges and primus stoves. The main street was dust like all the streets in Bethany, I was to discover. At one end was a church with a spire, once white but now stained light ochre, and at the other end, the town hall-cum-bank (*our* bank), a sober grey stone. Gravel and a resilient-looking hedge replaced lawn and the usual pride-of-the-Women's-Auxiliary town garden. Nevertheless, her father looked pleased.

For Stella, though, leaving Jo'burg would have been a complete downer if it hadn't been for the social days arranged by mothers from the surrounding farms.

She had dreaded the move more than usual, but here she was at a party, once again the center of attention. Stupid boys. They never learned. She was as likely to go out with one of them as go on a walking tour of Timbuktu. But they helped stem the boredom.

She was always marking time until she could ride again. Her father had promised her a horse. Before every move he promised her a horse.

Again, it didn't seem to be materializing, but one of these days it would. Until then, however, she was doing nicely. The farmers were generous with their animals. She made sure she did as they asked, as she wanted to be able to come back and ride again. Mostly, they didn't want her riding too far from the farm. Usually they set a landmark for her to reach before turning back. This setting of boundaries was why she wanted her own horse. She dreamed of riding as far as she could in half a day. If she was honest, she dreamed of riding away into the sunset, away from her mother. But Stella knew her limits. One day she'd have a riding school. By that time she would be an expert rider. She'd have won all sorts of ribbons and trophies. It was just a matter of time.

This was her first year out of school and she was only seventeen. The future held tremendous promise.

"You're new here, aren't you?"

Stella started and found herself looking into two enormous brown eyes. The girl had dark shining hair that cascaded over her shoulders. She was really pretty, but none of the boys had come near her.

"I'm Faye."

"Stella."

Someone had put on another record and a boy with thick yellow-blonde hair walked towards them. He stopped in front of Stella. She ignored him and turned to the girl called Faye.

"Just look what the cat brought in." As an afterthought she said to the boy, "*Hey, you.* Ask one of your friends to come over and dance with my friend."

"OK." The boy ambled off.

Faye looked down at her hands clasped in the lap of her flowing print dress. Her nails were painted pearly pink. Stella's were bitten down.

"You shouldn't have done that," the girl named Faye said.

They watched as the blonde boy returned with a tall boy with acne who wouldn't look either of the girls in the eye.

Stella whispered in Faye's ear. "Do you like him? We can get someone else, you know."

It tickled and Faye laughed. She then looked resigned. "I like this song."

She and the tall boy wandered over to the group jiving in the dance area. They were in an old-style house with high ceilings and tall, sash windows open to the cool night air. The carpet had been rolled back, the floorboards swept clean.

Faye moved surprisingly well, but the boy couldn't get the beat. A little while later, when Stella and her partner passed them, Faye was holding the boy's arms and trying to get him to feel the beat through her. In that moment Stella decided that Faye was a far better person than she was. During the breaks, Faye and Stella chatted.

Faye's father was a doctor and she enjoyed helping out in the surgery.

"Is that why I haven't seen you around?" Faye asked.

"Oh, I've been out to a farm once or twice– playing tennis, swimming, but I didn't see you."

"I was probably riding." Stella explained about horses and her plans for the future.

"In Feb I begin at U-C-T. I'm doing a B-Com."

"I took you for a brain."

It didn't come across as a compliment, but Faye didn't mind. She liked Stella. She preferred someone who was direct, who was honest. Too many girls were friendly to your face and then criticized you behind your back.

"So." Stella said. "Anyone here you dig?"

"Over there."

"The boy with the ridiculous hair?"

"He looks nice."

"You sound like my mother. He's a total push-over, but everyone to their taste."

Stella got up and went outside. She often had to do that– get away from people. Anyway, the air in the room was full of hairspray and sweat. These farmer boys had a lot to learn about personal hygiene. She thought of horse sweat and how sweet that was. Outside was cool for midsummer. Cicadas had struck up lower in the garden by the borehole pool. A moth was whirring in the light above the steps and Stella reached up to cup it in her hands. While she was releasing it over the veranda wall, the blonde boy strolled up. He was like a Jack-in-the-box, popping up when you least expected.

"Hi." he said. His hair looked like he'd given up trying to comb it.

Stella took out a packet of Texans out of her skirt pocket and offered him one. He refused. He didn't offer to light up for her when she took out her matches. *Yob*, she thought.

"What's it like in Jo'burg?" he asked. He had traces of an accent.

"Same as here. Full of spastics."

"I bet you've done it?"

"You mean kiss? Sure." She knew what he meant.

He watched as she blew smoke rings.

"Want me to show you?"

"You don't mean blow smoke rings, do you?"

Her face was expressionless except for her eyes that glinted wickedly. She wore her skirt short, and her hair was in a ponytail. She was continually tossing that ponytail. She wasn't pretty, but there was something about her that drew you.

"Yes. *Geez*."

"Come here."

He stood in front of her, eyes closed. She blew smoke in his face.

He stood looking at her and then he said, "D'you know what I can't understand, is why God gave you such a figure– I mean, look at your legs– and you hate guys."

The boy had a lot of spunk saying that to her.

"I don't hate guys," she said. "I'm not a lesbo, if that's what you think."

"Then why?"

'You're all such *babies*.'

As they walked back inside, one of the boys said, "She's out of your league, man."

Another said, "She's into men, boyo. Stand aside."

When they weren't on a farm or at a social in town, Faye and Stella began visiting at one another's houses. Stella's mother was usually in her bedroom. Stella said her mother slept during the day and paced up and down at night. Faye's grandmother had been like that, but once she went into an old age home, she was fine. She just needed company, Faye's mother believed. Faye said company was her mother's cure for most ills. Stella didn't want to discuss her mother. Instead, they got on with listening to records and checking magazines for the latest fashions and doing one another's hair in different styles. They also shared their plans for the future. Faye had helped out in an accounting firm during the previous summer and decided that was what she wanted to do. Be in business.

"I thought if not a doctor or a nurse, you'd want to be a social worker?"

"Being the daughter of a General Practitioner has cured me of that. I want a life I can call my own, thank you very much."

The house where Faye's parents were staying was full of heavy, dark furniture with equally dark paintings and photographs of forebears of the Van Jaarsveld family that owned it. Faye's mother was from England and said it was "very dour" and that she could be somewhere in Wales or the north of Scotland. Stella explained that the look was Dutch. The Van Jaarsvelds were Afrikaans-speaking. Dutch would be their ancestry. Stella liked old things. The Morriseys and the Van Jaarsvelds had done a swap for the summer holidays, which Stella thought was cool. She'd get a job in the New Year. She wasn't the studying type like Faye was.

"Perhaps you'll meet and marry a farmer – from hereabouts?" Glad Morrisey offered.

We'll be gone before that can happen, Stella thought, but didn't say aloud.

Faye's mother was so interested, so *there*. So unlike her own mother who often looked at Stella with surprise– as though she had just remembered that she had a daughter.

"It must be difficult leaving your friends behind each time you move?" Stella imagined anxious patients calling the doctor in the dead of night and getting an earful of that softly accented English sympathy.

"That's why I usually don't bother. But I think my Mom feels it. She's given up making friends entirely."

"How sad," Glad said when Stella had gone. "Do you think I should visit Mrs. Quinn?"

"Invite her around for tea with Stella." Stella had told Faye that Constance Quinn found having visitors a strain. When the bank wanted to introduce their new manager to the town, the cocktail party had to be held at the hotel.

The house where the Morriseys were staying opened directly onto the main road. Behind the house were fruit trees and a vegetable garden and a water tank that you reached the top of by means of a ladder. Almost everyone had a tank to trap the rain. Some had boreholes. The farms had tanks, boreholes, *and* windmills. The house where the Quinns were staying was bank owned. In the back it had a tank, a tennis court, and a pool. Not a borehole, but a proper, mosaic-tiled swimming pool. Her mother hung back, so Stella knocked on the door. Their shoes were covered in dust.

"Rub them on the back of your legs," said Stella, but the door was already opening.

"This is my mother," said Stella, "Constance."

"And I'm Glad. You *walked*. We walked everywhere back home. Come *in*."

"We're only a stone's throw," said Stella's mother. Her mother didn't drive. Stella did, but wasn't allowed, as she didn't have a drivers' license.

"Quaint, isn't it?"

"Beg pardon?"

"Bethany. I always wanted to live in a one-horse town." This was said jokingly, but Constance didn't laugh. She didn't even smile. "Come. Sit down. Would you like tea– or coffee? I'm un-English in that respect. I prefer coffee."

"Tea, please."

Constance sat with her knees together while Glad poured tea.

"Most of the townsfolk are pensioners. They couldn't afford a hike in rates. That's why they voted against having the national tarred road pass through."

"The wealth is on the farms, my husband says. Some of the biggest accounts in the country are at this branch of the bank."

"Then it's worth your while being here."

"It's a stepping-stone, my husband says."

Faye was amazed. Another side of Stella emerged when she was out with her mother. She pre-empted her hostess, passing the tea and crumpets to her mother, who refused all but the tea. She answered for Constance when the questions became personal.

"I don't know what I'd do if I wasn't needed at the surgery. Good thing I'm a nurse. How do you pass your time?" Glad asked.

"Mom reads a lot. She has books sent from a book shop in Sandton City."

"You should try the library-on-wheels. The selection is excellent. Most came from the deceased estate of a local farmer. Stops outside the hotel. One can order tea and go out and poke around. Lovely musty old books."

"I should."

"Do you play bridge? We need a fourth. We meet here Wednesday mornings."

"Mom always wanted to learn. How about us learning together– the four of us?" Stella threw Faye a screwy look, a cross between horror and panic.

"I should."

Stella's mother was exquisitely turned out. She wore a tailored linen dress, pearls, stockings, and expensive-looking court shoes, whereas Faye's mother wore a simple cotton shift and sandals. Mr. Quinn took Wednesday afternoons off, Stella had told Faye, to drive his wife into a neighboring town to have her hair and nails done. But in spite of this, she looked unhappy. Stella also told Faye that Constance spent the entire day after their visit on her bed.

The highlight of the social calendar was a dance on one of the biggest farms. The parents were included this time and were asked to bring salads, rolls, or dessert and drinks they chose from a list the boys and girls took home after one of the socials. The main course was lamb on the spit, which Stella promised herself she would avoid within an inch of her life. The dance part of the evening would kick off with barn dancing.

Constance looked a little flushed later as they waited for the band to strike up. She sometimes did that– drank too much because she was feeling uncomfortable. The Morriseys had been there to begin with but had been called away to deliver a baby (one of the laborer's wives on another farm). Stella had counted on Glad to break the ice for her mother with the other parents. Roy couldn't be relied upon to entertain his wife, as he was using the opportunity to promote the bank and was soon to be seen at the bar chatting to the men as they fetched drinks for their wives.

The adults sat on one side, while across the dance floor of rough cement, the girls and boys stood around a long table helping themselves to bowls of non-alcoholic punch and snacks. Balloons hung from the wooden beams of the high ceiling. Stella was reminded of an airplane hangar she had visited once at an air show with Roy. Bales of straw, one on top of the other, hid the shearing and baling equipment from view but also had the effect of giving the space a more cozy feel.

The girls had been given dance cards. Stella's was already full. She had tried not to worry that Faye's card had only a couple of names: *Plank*, the tall one with acne, and another boy called *Prop*, a two-twenty pound rugby player whom she had overheard boast of a plan to have his way with all the girls before the end of the holiday. Except he'd used an unrepeatable word. She had warned Faye, but Faye said she could handle him. Stella had told him to get lost when he tried to get hold of her dance card.

"I bet your friend won't say no," he said, smirking with opportunism.

Faye had wanted them to sit with their parents. Now Stella wondered if it mightn't have been a good idea, even without the Morriseys. She could have taken her mother's G&T when she wasn't looking, tipped some, and added tonic. Stella was amazed at how Faye enjoyed being with her parents. Stella loved her parents, but spending time with them when there was another option was unthinkable.

The square dancing was a hoot. Stella enjoyed passing Faye every so often and giggling. It was much more fun than straight jiving, so when the band struck up with the first pop song of the night, Stella went outside for a smoke. She passed Plank heading in Faye's direction. The blonde boy, who was called Thorks, followed her outside. They had bumped into one another at the stables of one of the farms soon after the social where Stella and Faye met and discovered a common interest. His parents were immigrants and poor compared to the rest of the farmers. The Johansens bred pigs and didn't own a horse, so, like Stella, he was angling for a ride. It was fun having a riding mate, especially one who'd had more practice and was only too happy to give her tips.

"D'you still want me to show you how, you know, to kiss?" She took a puff and winked.

"Geez. Yes." It had become a game between them.

"A favor, though…?"

"Ja. Anything." He stepped closer.

She put a hand to his chest forcing him to step back. "Don't you ever learn?"

"What d'you want me to do?" He had stepped forward again, cheeky sod.

"Fill Faye's dance card. But something else."

"OK…" He looked puzzled.

"She likes you, mutt. I'm not supposed to tell you. Don't ever tell her I told you. Listen– " Stella lowered her voice. "I want you to cross out Prop's name on her card. You've heard what he plans to do to all the girls before the end of the summer?"

"He's got no chance with us other guys around." He struck his hand with a fist.

"Faye's a honey, but she's clueless. I'm scared he'll spring one on her."

Thorks looked stricken. "To tell you the truth, I like Faye, but I feel I'm back in kindergarten when I'm with her."

"You've just got to get to know her. After all those dances, you sure will."

"What if she tells me to take a hike? She might guess you've had something to do with it."

"Trust me, she'll be thrilled. Tell you what. I'll go back inside. Wait a couple of minutes, and then you come in. But don't be too long. We don't want that thug getting his paws on her."

Unfortunately, Prop already had Faye in his arms. It was a slow dance. Someone had switched the overhead lights off. The only light came from lamps against the walls. Stella was sure one of the parents was going to shove the lights back on, but until then, who knew what Prop was going to get up to with Faye. One time she lost sight of Faye and Prop. Her heart thumped in her chest until she spotted them coming out of a dark corner.

"How about this," whispered Thorks when he was back inside. "Let's dance and when we pass Faye and Prop, I can cut in."

Stella's eyes widened but she said, "Good idea."

Thorks was a tad overconfident but she wasn't about to stop him, the desire to see what happened being too great.

And sure enough, when they were near Faye and Prop, Thorks tapped Prop on the shoulder and said, "I'll take this from here."

The other boy took a moment to register, then he pushed Thorks so hard he lost his footing.

Stella helped him up. "Well, that was a blast."

When Faye returned after the dance her eyes glinted, and not with joy.

"What possessed you?" she demanded of Thorks with an eye on Stella.

"I dunno," said Stella. It was no use pretending ignorance. "I thought you needed some help."

"Prop was behaving like a real gentleman."

"I'm sorry," said Thorks. "And I really do want to dance with you. Can I write in your card?" The next number was throbbing into the airwaves.

As Faye handed the card over, she looked at Stella, who pretended to be interested in the couples walking onto the dance floor.

Thorks swore under his breath. The heavy figure of his adversary was sauntering over, chuckling.

"It's uncanny," said Thorks as Faye walked away. Prop had a meaty arm around her waist. "It's like he knew and got in first."

"Now what?" said Stella. She had known all along that Faye's dance card was full.

"We'll just have to keep an eye on them. On *him*."

This was going to prove difficult for Stella. Glancing across to the row of parents, she saw that her mother had fallen asleep. More worrying was that she was leaning dangerously forward. Stella looked around for Roy. He was on the far side of the room, deep in conversation with one of the farmers. He had some target about getting new clients. It was always the way. The next step upwards depended on his success with the present one.

"Don't let them out of your sight," she threw over her shoulder.

Lucky for Stella, next up was *The Loco-Motion* and people who didn't usually dance were joining in. Even so, she smiled and tried to look as though she had nothing on her mind, but all out enjoyment as she threaded her way between boys and girls heading for the dance floor.

She was just in time.

"Hi, darling." Her mother, once again upright, spoke loud enough to prick the interest of a couple of other women seated nearby.

Stella put a finger to her lips. "S-sh."

Constance giggled.

"I'm going to get you coffee and call Dad."

"How sweet of you, darling." Constance smiled sweetly but her eyes were once again closing.

"*Mo-om.* You've got to try and stay awake," Stella muttered between clenched teeth.

On the way to the coffee urn, she passed Thorks. "I don't know where they are," he said, staring at the weaving line of dancers.

"*What...?* That's just what I didn't want to happen. Go and look for them. Earlier on they were in that corner." She pointed. "I have to get my Mom coffee. *Go, go.*"

Stella glanced back to where Constance was again asleep. At least she was upright. But it was only a matter of time. Stella decided to skip getting coffee and fetch her father.

When she was a few feet away she signaled Roy, who walked towards her, far too slowly for her liking.

"Mom's a little tipsy," she said, nodding in the direction of her other parent.

"*Good Lord.*" Constance was again leaning forward. He went across to the man he had been speaking to and offered his apologies. Father and daughter walked back together, Stella half-running to keep up.

"She knows not to drink with a valium. Silly woman."

When they reached Constance, he stood looking down at her. She seemed to sense this.

"Hi, darling." The words were less distinct now and she gagged at the end of the attempt.

"We'll have to get her home. Pronto."

"Geez, Dad. Can you take her on your own? She'll be alright. She can sleep on the back seat. I can get a lift back to town."

"Certainly not. Your mother might be ill on the way. Can you grab something, some sort of container while I walk her to the car? Say goodbye to your friends if you must, but *be quick.*"

At the table Stella looked around for a jug but there were only the bowls of punch. She could have tossed the contents but because of their size she risked drawing attention. She had just spotted a stack of polystyrene cups when someone shouted above the music, followed by a thump and a girlish shriek. The sounds seemed to come from a far corner.

Some of the dancers in the line that, by that time was threading behind the refreshment table, also seemed to have heard. In fact, the band stopped playing and the line broke up. Whatever had happened was causing a lot of excitement. People were hurrying in that direction. Just then the overhead lights went back on.

Stella grabbed the stack of cups and stood looking back towards where her father was helping her mother to her feet… her mother was protesting… and back towards the far corner where a crowd had gathered.

Plank approached, looking agitated. "Faye says I must come and get you."

"What's going on?" she asked as they walked towards the commotion.

"I don't know how it happened, but Prop is under a bale of straw. The other guys are trying to lift it off him."

By the time they arrived, the bale was off Prop and he was sitting beside it, frowning and rubbing his head. Straw clung to his hair and clothes. Faye was bending over him with her hands to her face. She saw Stella and Plank, murmured something to Prop, and walked towards them. Stella was pale except for a bright spot of color in each cheek.

"What happened?" asked Stella.

"We were there…you know…" She threw Stella a guilty look. "And someone shouted my name and, *to get back*. I looked up and there was this huge bale beginning to tip. Then it was coming right at us. *Gosh*." Her eyes were huge. "I didn't know what I was doing but I must have stepped out of its way. Prop hadn't seen it though. It landed on him."

"But you're OK?"

Faye nodded, tears pooling.

Just then, Thorks strolled up. He seemed to come from another side of the room. Straw clung to his hair and clothes.

CHAPTER 8

The events of those half a dozen weeks had rolled off our tongues like scenes from a favorite movie. One of us would carry on where the other left off. We had our favorite parts, each our version of how a particular person had looked, spoken, acted, what they had said, what they had done. We hadn't spoken of the events in years, yet they seemed as fresh as if they had taken place yesterday.

After that we just sat.

I was the first to speak. "Only a few of us knew it was Strawks who pushed that bale onto Prop. Most people thought it was an accident. I remember how we all kept quiet when the farmer came over and apologized to Prop. And if Prop guessed, or someone had seen Strawks push the bale and told Prop, he would have been too embarrassed to take it up with Strawks. Because, of course, he had been pushing his tongue down your throat and you had been trying to push him off, right?"

Faye nodded. She was staring into the fire and stroking Fergus in her lap.

We were alone. Ellie and Brand had gone to bed and Lyle was sleeping at Myrna's. The fire was burning down. If we weren't going to bed, I needed to add a few logs. Lyle had brought in vine trimmings to add fragrance to the common-or-garden pine. I wanted more of the fragrance, so I got up to add both.

As I knelt to the fire, I looked back. Faye held Fergus with one hand while she leaned forward and reached for her brandy.

"When last did you see him?" I asked.

"When last did you?"

I met her steady gaze. So that's how it was going to be.

Seated again I swirled the contents of my balloon glass. I wasn't thinking of the golden liquid, which I usually marveled at, but how best to describe the meeting. I mustn't allow blame to creep in, but I must also be honest.

"You and Strawks had broken up. He was working on the Perlheim estate in sales but wanted a job where he was more involved in the farming side of things. He asked if Arno knew of such a job. Arno didn't, but asked if Strawks would like to help with the harvest. He would have learnt a trick or two at Perlheim, which Arno was keen to get a hand on. He would dearly have loved to hire Strawks, but Gideon's couldn't support more than one heavyweight, he said. And, at any rate, Strawks would be wasted in our piddling outfit. We put away two bottles of that unlabeled plonk of ours. That was before Arno got into serious winemaking. He had enough just keeping it all going at that stage. Strawks slept over. The next morning he was gone before either Arno or I was up. We never heard from him again. He left no forwarding address. His parents had gone back to Norway. He had an older sister, though. She also stayed behind. I imagined he'd doss at her place until he got sorted." I tipped my glass, welcoming the fiery liquid as it hit my throat. I had always regretted letting Strawks go so easily, not keeping in touch.

I glanced at Faye. Her head was back, her eyes closed. It was impossible to tell how she was feeling. I wondered how much I had told her at the time because she had completely severed ties with Strawks and didn't want to hear another word about him, positive or negative.

"It's easier that way," she had said.

Strawks had been upbeat. But he had lost weight. If I'd allowed myself to think further, I would have described him as looking lost. Dealing with depressed people had never been my strong suit. Also, I felt loyal to Faye, and if Strawks and I had begun talking about the whys and wherefores of the break-up, somewhere along the line I was going to let something slip that I oughtn't.

It was all exceedingly fraught. They were both hurting. And so Strawks and I didn't get into the heavy stuff. Instead, we continued with the banter that had begun in Bethany. We were good chums, as Glad Morrisey would have said. He was the brother I never had, a *younger* brother. Funny, how I always thought of him that way. Even though we are the same age.

"His sister was called Anika."

"You speak as though she's dead. She isn't dead, is she?"

"Well, I don't know, do I?" Faye looked annoyed. She had stopped stroking Fergus, and his head was up and he was looking around.

Good, I thought. *Sign of life.*

I reached for the album and turned to the last photo. I wanted another look and I could tell Faye did, too. Myrna had been getting restless, and to keep the peace, I had flipped through the last few pages at speed.

The photo had been taken at the last social of that summer. It also happened to be Anika's twenty-first birthday. It was a group shot. Several boys and girls squeezed in around Anika, who was about to blow the candles out on a fancy iced cake. Faye and Strawks' faces were in poor focus. I wasn't in the shot, as I had already left for Cape Town. But it was a good shot of Anika. She had the same thick, yellow-blonde hair as her brother, but worn long, and china-blue eyes, also similar to his. I hadn't had much contact with her, but Faye and Anika had become friends in those last couple of weeks.

Roy, my father, had collapsed at work with a heart attack. He was dead by the time Faye's father arrived fifteen minutes later. He had been at a farm clinic. My mother fainted when she heard, rallied a few minutes later, and told me to phone her sister, Beverley, in Cape Town. Aunt Bev said, "Come and stay with me until you decide what to do." So that was what we did.

"Anika and I kept in touch until a few years ago. Strawks was getting married…" Faye's eyes, almost black under the shaded lamplight, brimmed. She's like that, Faye. She slips from one emotion into the next, whereas I would be smoldering for days, unable to move on. "There seemed no point after that." Was that a sob?

I put an arm around her shoulders– *carefully*– and squeezed her arm. "How many years?"

"Twenty-something." I released her arm. For someone whose livelihood involves dealing with dizzying volumes of numbers this could only mean one thing. "Twenty-something?" I angled an eyebrow.

She ignored this. "Let's see... Anika was working for some people on a farm outside Piketberg. That's near Darling."

"I know where Piketberg is."

"OK. And we had this discussion about how we intended celebrating. Her brother's wedding was to be her celebration. Anika, the couple– who got married the day before– and some friends had booked a special flight to Jo'burg. You know the one?"

"So it was the Millenium...?"

She nodded. Most people had heard about it. "That one that did a lot of circling over the cities where fireworks would be going off. I can't remember all the details, but it was to be the party to end all parties."

"Why have you never said?" I knew why. It was too painful. "Do you know who to?"

"Don't know. Never wanted to. Still don't."

That name would be etched, nay *carved*, into her memory. I let it go for now. But I couldn't resist, "I wonder if he has any kids. You could be an auntie. Of sorts."

Faye tipped the remains of her brandy into my glass and stood up. Fergus squeaked but landed on his feet. I couldn't remember when I had seen her this angry.

Again, I had shot myself– and her by association– in the foot.

But I couldn't let it go. I had stumbled on what I imagined would save my friend. To that end I had become almost ruthless. I had no idea then that it was my own needs that were driving me– the pain of loss, the aloneness that crouched under a coat of anger, a suit of camouflage donned as easily by a coward as a hero.

I had to get hold of Strawks. He was the one person could talk to Faye, married or not. Talk sense into her.

I drove Faye back to town on Sunday evening. She wasn't allowed to drive for another four weeks. Luckily, work had a driver. On the way back I sang, *"Come on, come on, do the locomotion."*

I couldn't wait to get to my computer.

In my bedroom I closed the door and sat at my desk. I typed Thorks full name–**Thorkild Johansen**. It is odd how details pop into your head. I remember him telling me that the 'sen' part of the surname meant 'son of'. This soupçon of memory brought him into sharp focus. If I could liken him in looks and personality it would be to the comic character *Tintin*, once featured in an animated movie, the tuft of stand-up hair above his forehead being the trademark. He was determined and resourceful, a little eccentric in his methods. Strawks was proud of his roots but embraced the new country wholeheartedly. If he had changed his mind later and decided to follow the senior Johansens, my task would be even more difficult.

My task was becoming Herculean. *Where the hell are you?* I muttered to myself. I was doing a lot of that lately.

Up came: **Thorkild Lukas Johansen** via membership at **Cape Wine Academy, Toastmasters, and Mowbray Golf Club**. All must have lapsed, but were luckily still on file so that the following details were available. **Born in Lorvik** (Gravlax was the cured salmon Norwegians consumed in quantities), **Norway, emigrated 1990-10-05, matriculated at Queens College, Queenstown 2-01-1994, graduated from Elsenburg School of Agriculture, Stellenbosch 31-12-1998**. The wine academy, Toastmasters, and the golf club would have an address. Full marks would go to the most recent.

The next morning, I began calling. My cell phone is about as basic as you can get, T-Rex to the boys, not only because of its age, but because it often gobbles up messages. For Toastmasters I had to consult the yellow pages. I had contacts in the wine industry which helped with the agricultural college and the wine academy. All addresses left by Strawks pre-dated the wedding.

Over morning coffee, I consulted Willy. First, however, I had to listen to her dream of the previous night.

"It was *lekker* (beautifully) misty, and the rescue people were out. They took me with them on their boat. We were going up and down on the waves. There was this strong light, and you saw people's hands up among the waves. They were calling for help, but none of them was my Daddy."

She was still at sea, literally. Her father had been a fisherman off Saldanha on the west coast and she had grown up fearful of his safety.

"You'll have to go back in your next dream and find him." I had done some reading on the subject of dreams. Solutions in dreams could lead to solutions in waking life.

"Yes, Miss Stella."

Willy's dream was about a search. This encouraged me to share about Strawks.

"Do you remember Faye's boyfriend? What did you used to call him?" 'Strawks' had proved too much of a mouthful.

"Mister Johan."

"That's it. I'm trying to find him. I think it would be good for her to have an old friend to talk to since she's been sick. But Willy, I don't want her to know in case I don't find him. So, *ssh*. OK?" I put a finger to my lips.

The housekeeper nodded gravely. She isn't much more than fifty. Her eyes are like two bright black buttons. She knows very little about the breakup but she would have witnessed Faye and Strawks' all too apparent happiness when they were together.

"I wondered, Willy, if you ever heard Mister Johan mentioned, perhaps that he was working somewhere?" The farming community is like an extended family. One was continually bumping into people connected with winemaking at tastings, shows, launches, and auctions. Staff loved to gossip. "He had dinner here once long ago." I tried to remember if Willy had cooked the meal, but that side of things was hazy. Willy, too, registered blank. On her days off she often visited friends in town or on surrounding farms.

"I can't say, Miss, but I can ask around."

"Willy that's a great idea. But please don't mention Faye."

"I'll say Miss Stella is drawing up her Christmas card list."

"Isn't it a bit early for that?"

"It's never too early for Christmas, Miss. Even August-month people buy presents."

I googled **Anika Johansen** next. I tried all the spellings, **Anni, Annica, Annicka, and Annicke**. I also played around with Johansen in case she spelled the surname differently. All with a nil result. She could also be married.

She had– or still did– live in Piketberg. On a farm, I corrected myself. She had worked for people on a farm. I remembered what a big part the police played in small towns. The police had come to fetch my mother and me and take us to the bank the day my father died.

"Piketberg charge office. Constable Makela. Good day."

"Constable, I wonder if you can help me. I'm trying to locate a friend who worked on a farm in the Piketberg area. Her name is or was Anika Johansen. Have you heard of someone with that name?"

"Ma'am, I'm new here. I'll call the sergeant."

"Sergeant Myburgh. Can I help you?"

I repeated what I had said to the constable.

"And your name is?"

I obliged.

"As it happens, ma'am, I do know of such a person. Do you mind telling me your purpose in locating Miss Johansen." Ah, Anika wasn't married.

My pulse quickened. What could I say? "For personal reasons."

Heavy breathing on the other side. "Could you supply a little more detail, please, Mrs. Gideon."

I could be an axe murderer, couldn't I? "A friend of mine has been sick. I'm trying to rally friends to her bedside." No sense in beating around the bush. "Do you need some ID?"

"Where do you live, ma'am?"

"On a farm, Gideon's Wine Sales, between Stellenbosch and Strand. I'm the owner."

"Tell you what, Mrs. Gideon. I happen to know that Miss Johansen has a stall at a craft market at Milnerton. She's there every Saturday. It's on the seafront."

CHAPTER 9

"I forgot to ask what she sells," I tell Faye, who is happy to have an outing planned for Saturday. She sits hunched in her anorak and pale, looking out at kites bobbing high above a patch of open green along the Liesbeeck River. She'll be regretting having gone back to work so soon but won't admit it. Notably absent is Fergus, which means we can't stay long at the market. She'll make it up to him when she gets home, she says. She tells me her whole body feels like it has bumped down a mountainside.

"What are they selling…? It has to be homemade," Faye says. "Anika was good like that. She made her own clothes, baked bread and cakes. Then there were the farm chores. She made butter and cheese, cured ham and bacon. The Johansens believed in educating sons but not daughters. She studied correspondence beyond primary school and got as far as grade ten, which I thought was admirable. Her parents needed her on the farm. She tried nursing after they left. I remember that she didn't sit for the exam. She lost her nerve and left after that. Her English was never as good as her brother's. So sad."

"Sad, indeed," I say as we wait at the set of lights before heading out towards the Black River Parkway. The mountains are clear of cloud. Veins of rainwater glint in the crevices. "They were simple farming folk, weren't they, her parents? So both Anika and Strawks did well, if you think about it." I was out on a limb. I knew very little about the Johansens.

"They did."

I had told Faye about googling Anika and also about phoning the police in Piketberg. She seemed taken aback at first, but agreed that contacting her friend was overdue.

We are both appreciating a task that takes us out of our homes and that focuses on someone and something else. We are not, as we thought, heading out on an hour drive into wheat, fruit and dairy farming– which would have been more uplifting– but across town, which is just as well with Faye feeling poorly. After leaving the freeway, we drive through industrial Paarden Eiland, blocks of structural ugliness devoted to building, motor, and related trades. Our destination, the narrow strip of land where the craft market unfurls its wares to the public, is across Marine Drive that overlooks the Atlantic seaboard and Table Bay. To the west, the coastline curves up past an array of suburbs. Some, like Table View and Parklands, are small towns.

We have chosen a sunny day for our excursion and wear our sunglasses against the low but bright sun. Seagoing craft like tankers and container ships with business in Cape Town harbor queue along the watery horizon. The sky is a basin of hard blue holding clouds like freshly laundered pillows.

I park the Jeep among twenty or so cars to one side of the row of stalls. Some of the stalls have canopies. Others take their chances against the rain, which today is replaced by a salty breeze. We zip our windbreakers all the way up. Faye pulls on purple gloves that match her beanie. I shove my hands deeper into my pockets. One would have to be keen or desperate to pursue this mode of business which necessitates exposure to all weathers. Then I remember that I am a farmer. Why do we do it? Love, I concede. And a dollop of crazy.

Nearest us is a caravan with half a dozen people gathered around an open hatch. The sign advertises hotdogs, hamburgers, tea, coffee, and sodas. I wonder if Anika could be back in there, but correct myself. A caravan isn't a stall. Nevertheless, I lead towards it. Coffee sounds like a good idea. While we wait we can peek inside and also take a look back down the row of stalls.

Anika isn't the dark-haired woman flipping hamburger patties or shaking fries out of the chip basket into polystyrene containers.

Faye sips her coffee nervously. I suggest we get started and we toss out our dregs. We stroll past machine-knitted Fair Isle sweaters, pottery, dried fruit and nuts, handmade greetings cards and jewelry, bric-a-brac, and second-hand books. I see Anika before Faye does. She is walking away from the portable toilets towards us, holding the hand of a pretty girl with long, shining, fair hair.

"Hi, Anika," we say.

It takes a minute for realization to spread across Anika's face. Her skin is weathered and her still thick hair is fading into grey, which makes her look older than she is.

"*Faye.*" They hug one another. Faye grimaces and says, pulling away ever so slightly, "I had something done to my chest. It's not completely healed."

"Oh, I'm so sorry." Anika's frown is quickly banished when she sees that Faye has brightened.

"Sorry. Stella, is it…?" Anika's accent is more pronounced as she asks this. I suspect this is because she is less comfortable with me.

"That's right. And who is this?" I smile at the girl.

"This is Valdine, my daughter. Faye and I are friends from way back, honey. From when we were girls. Not much older than you," she adds when she sees a frown appear on the girl's face. It is a beautiful face. I stop myself from staring.

"Pleased to meet you, Valdine."

Faye and I shake hands with the girl. Like her mother, she wears a sweater and jeans. But here the similarity ends. Anika, a head shorter, has loose, wide hips, whereas her daughter is slim and statuesque. Her face is fine-boned, whereas her mother's brow is heavy, her nose broad. I am reminded conversely of the teenage girls of my riding school and stabling experience. With them I have to overcome self-importance, rudeness, and sometimes open defiance. The look the girl gives us is touchingly guileless.

"We came to check out your wares," I say as we follow Anika towards a stall further along. She still grips the girl's hand.

"Wares?" the girl asks, testing the word like it is an unpleasant sweet.

"Our jams, sweetheart." Anika pats her daughter's arm, but the girl looks even more confused. Anika turns back to Stella and Faye. I have a feeling that she often has to do this– ignore her daughter in the pursuit of business. "Pity you didn't come earlier in the year. My stocks are low. I am famous for my apricot jam." She smiles coyly. "That's all gone. Ah, sorree…my partner in crime…" She beams at the woman behind the stall.

The woman, also grey-haired, stretches a hand across the table laden with jams and pickles. Faye and I shake it.

"Aletta Myburgh."

"Not the cop's wife?"

"You've met Dop?"

"In a manner of speaking."

"This is all rather mysterious," says Anika.

People have gathered and are inspecting the wares. Anika and Valdine join Aletta behind the table. We admire the display. Woven cream fabric flows over the rows of graduated height, ending just over the edge of the table. Virginia creeper, with its glowing autumn palette, winds between jars of balsamic figs and rosemary, hot tomato chili and curried bean pickle, *moskonfyt* (grape must boil until thick), gooseberry and three-berries jam, an orange twirl marmalade and something called seed compote.

I choose three jars of each. We have our own stocks of homemade produce at home. Willy will complain until she hears the reason for my purchases. Faye has bought in three figures.

"For Christmas presents," she whispers, her eyes too bright. I'm cruel, I think, subjecting her to the memories the meeting is bound to evoke.

Anika packs our purchases into cardboard boxes. She refuses payment. We try arguing, to no avail. Anika has placed a business card in each of our boxes. I can't wait to check for a telephone number, but I will have to wait until I have delivered Faye home. I wonder how I am going to be able to hide my triumph from her.

Aletta Myburgh gently shoves Anika. "Go chat with your friends." She shoves again, this time less gentle. "*Go.*"

Anika, holding her daughter's hand, comes out from behind the table. Aletta carries over fold-up stools and returns to her station. I leave Faye talking to Anika and the girl. I say I'm going to have another look around. I end up at the caravan. I order five coffees from the dark-haired woman. The trade in hotdogs and hamburgers is at a standstill. The man is over near the seafront, smoking.

I glance in his direction as I say to the woman, "I used to smoke. My husband said he wasn't going out with me if I smoked."

The woman hands me a cup of coffee and begins fitting lids to the other cups in the cardboard tray. "And you never smoked again."

I take a scalding sip.

"That mug wouldn't care if I smoked out of my bum as long as I delivered the goods." She throws an acid look in the direction of the figure leaning over the cement wall.

The pain in my tongue has subsided. "But you're needed. You'll be surprised how motivating that is. My husband died almost three years ago and I miss someone needing me, depending on me. I have to force myself to do things, the daily round. When someone close to you dies you expect grief, not boredom, not lethargy. There's no point doing anything new, either. I spend my life frustrated and angry. Wondering why in hell I'm still here, I suppose."

In the lull, the woman poured herself a cup of coffee and stands sipping.

"D'you know what I'm doing at the moment?" I don't wait for the woman to answer, nor does she look like she might. "I'm trying to fix up a friend with an old boyfriend. She's been ill and needs some advice." I grin wryly. "She's over there." I point to where Faye sits with Anika and the girl. "She's meeting up with the boyfriend's sister. They haven't seen one another since before two-thousand. She doesn't realize what I've got planned. A reunion. I'm hoping the sister will lead us to him."

"So you *are* doing something. Something new."

"Meddling." I shrug.

"They're grown-ups– this friend, the boyfriend. They don't have to fall in with your plans."

"I might be stirring up a hornet's nest— going where angels fear to tread."

"My advice?"

I nod.

"Examine your motives. If you're sure you're doing it for what you think is the best– and not, say, out of the boredom you speak of, then go ahead."

CHAPTER 10

On the way back to Faye's, we discuss the morning's activity. Or, rather, I gently probe.

"That was worthwhile, wasn't it? I tried to slip a couple of buffalos into Aletta's hand, but she wasn't having it." Hundred-rand bank notes have a buffalo on the reverse.

Faye is paler than ever and she speaks from the depths of her anorak collar. "It took me back. Seeing us like that, unexpectedly, was quite a shock for Anika, but she hid it well. Isn't her daughter beautiful?"

"Stunning. How different, mother and daughter."

"She's adopted. But there's something odd about it. Something out of sync. It's very 'in' now, single moms adopting, but the adoptees are usually black AIDS orphans."

"Maybe there are white AIDS orphans?"

"Hmm. Anika is homeschooling Valdine. They live a very quiet life on a farm. She runs a bed and breakfast business for the owner. She says we must visit. Now would be great, she says, as they're going into the quiet season."

I feel Faye's eyes on me as I drive. It is eerie, having her look at me. It is usually the other way round. Has she smelled a rat?

I brace myself as she continues, "You're up to something, aren't you, Star?" Faye only calls me that in the direst moments. Her first word when she came round from the anesthetic was, "Star?" Then she retched into the kidney bowl.

I need to keep my eyes on the road, my heart banging away. We are merging into traffic on the parkway. The plunging sun casts confusing shadows in our path.

"You knew about that poor girl, didn't you?"

"I didn't."

"Little white lies, huh? And I know why."

"Why?" When Faye is like this, it's no use arguing.

"You want me to focus on someone less fortunate." She sighs. "It can't be easy. Besides trying to educate her, she'll be terrified some guy will fall in love with her and want to whisk her away. She'll have to keep the girl in her sights at all times. Keeping her on the farm is the best solution."

"You've thought of all that in the space of what, an hour?"

There had been a time when Faye had seriously contemplated adopting, but the responsibility of rearing another human being on one's own had been too daunting. She had satisfied the mothering urge by having the twins over at every opportunity. She took leave when Arno and I took our first overseas trip.

"And it worked. I may be feeling crook physically, but I've stopped drowning in self-pity."

"Good to hear."

Her eyes bore into me again. She sighs. I wonder if now, today, and in this connection, Strawks' name will come up, for he is surely on her mind as he is on mine.

Relief runs through me, but I dare not give a sign. For now, I am out of the hot seat. The fact that Anika has a daughter is a bonus. I can't believe my, our luck. Faye has another person to think about, concern herself with.

———————————

Sunday afternoon Brand and I exercise the two older horses in the paddock. Both animals are retired– one from racing and the other from police work. After we have rubbed them down, Ellie joins us to ride the remaining three. I am on Izzy. Ellie and Sweetpea are a perfect match.

Brand's mount is also a pony– larger than Sweetpea. The ponies belong to two teenage girls. Despite my having spelled out what owning such animals will require in time and effort, we still find ourselves carrying out the routines which should have been the duty, or indeed, the pleasure of the two girls. I blame the parents, the mothers to be precise, who remain in their cars the entire time the girls are with the ponies. Just getting one of these women to open a car window takes determination on my part, let alone having a discussion about responsibility to one's ride. In the past I might have chivvied myself into doing it but so far, I have shelved the task.

In the saddle, however, I am as alive as I'll ever be. Our mounts know what is coming and we have to keep a firm hold as we trot down the road that leads to the neighbor's property. It was previously owned by a horse trainer who stripped the land of vines, erected stables, and laid out a small oval course. The new owner built a holiday house, and presently is unoccupied. Arno and I had an arrangement with the owner who lives in Gauteng. We exercise our horses on the property in exchange for a couple of cases of *Hart Sag*. I've been trading on the man's good nature since supplies of the vintage ran out. As Brand unlocks the gate, I realize that I'm going to have to deal with the matter soon. That is, when the family comes down for the next major school break in November/December. I have been regular in sending staff across to scoop the poop, so he can't complain about that.

After we have had our little race and are walking back to the gate, both humans and animals breathing heavily but with great satisfaction, I bring Brand and Ellie up to speed on the arrangement with the Gauteng businessman.

"Give him a call," says my son, an advocate of the direct approach. "You could offer his kids rides on the horses instead of the wine." Come the holidays there are usually a bunch of kids running wild. "Throw in a few riding lessons if you think he needs persuading."

"Good idea," I say.

I decide to follow his example about something that has been on my mind. "Did anything come of the dinner date with the new boss? You thought you might have been in some kind of trouble. *In for the high jump*, you said."

"Did I? He's happy with my performance."

"*Very* happy," says Ellie.

I lean forward to get a good look at Brand's face. It is deadpan.

"So?"

"So what?"

"So what is this all about?"

At the gate, Brand allows his weight to shift back in the saddle. He hardly needs to rein in for the pony to slow down. I might have admired this had I not been waiting for a response.

"The new boss comes down from Jo'burg and takes you and your partner out to dinner. That's not nothing."

He leans down to slip the chain off the pole. "He just wanted to make sure I understood his plan for the firm," he says as we walk the animals through. "Some of us have to go for training. It costs the company a wack. He doesn't want some half-ass involvement. He was drumming for support, too, I guess."

"And having your partner along... Why do you suppose he wanted Ellie there?"

"For her pretty face. Geez, Mom, you're like a dog with a bone."

I glance across at Ellie. She is frowning at Brand, but that is the extent of her support for me. Her loyalties will be with her man. I could get her alone, encourage her to talk, but then I think Brand and I should be open with one another.

When we are rubbing down, I find myself missing Lyle.

I assume he is with Myrna, but I ask anyway. "Anyone know where Lyle is?"

Brand brightens up and exclaims, "Mom, you must see what he's done."

Ellie can't contain her enthusiasm. "He's put in this water feature. Cemented it all in. She bought this kit of three beautiful pottery bowls and a pump. You switch it on from the lounge. It's going to be great on a hot night, hearing the water trickling."

I throw Brand an inquiring look. "Where is this?"

"At Myrna's new place. She wants him to do the inside as well. Like he did the salon. But different."

"He's so talented, Stella."

I didn't know Myrna had another house. "Is it a spec house?"

"I don't think it's about making money. She intends on living in the new house," imparts Ellie. "She's sold the old one. You must get Lyle to take you to have a look. Or you can see everything when they have the housewarming. Rather wait for that. It's going to be amazing." A housewarming? *They* have a housewarming? Is there something I'm not being told?

Later I unpack the pickles and jams onto the pantry shelves. I check Anika's card. There is a phone number. I hesitate. It will be better coming from Faye. I want discovering Strawks' whereabouts to happen as the natural course of events. If it doesn't, then later I can come out and ask Anika. I don't even know if Faye has told her about the mastectomy.

I call Faye instead. She is well rested, she tells me. She will go to work the next day. No surprise there.

"Have you thought about taking up Anika's offer?" The words are out before I can stop myself.

"We're booked to go next week. Friday is a public holiday. I'll spend that day in bed. Saturday she has the market. Then Sunday she wants us to come to the farm. For lunch. The whole tootie."

I take a minute.

"She would have had us stay for the weekend if we wanted to, but she's booked up. I asked if she wouldn't rather have us come another time, but she is dead keen. She says would we babysit Valdine when she is called away? People start leaving after lunch usually, and they want to settle up and she needs to check inventories in the cottages. I jumped at it. The girl liked us. She doesn't just take to anybody, apparently. She's been talking about us non-stop. She calls us 'the aunties.' Isn't that sweet?"

Surely we weren't there long enough for this special bond to be formed? But I say, wonderful, and that I'm looking forward to next Sunday.

She ends the call happier than I've heard her since finding the wretched lump. "Stel, this is such a great thing to have happened. I feel like I've found long lost family."

CHAPTER 11

Finding long lost family was how Stella should have experienced going to stay with Aunt Bev and Uncle Clive in Cape Town. No sooner were they there, though, than the Two ugly sisters of Boredom and Loneliness took hold. Gone were the farms and horses, the socials, and gone was Faye. Stella and her parents had visited the family in the past, but usually it was for a night or two before going on to a resort. Now it was open-ended.

Constance seemed unable to decide on anything, where they should live, what Stella should do. The adults were constantly going out to make arrangements or do business– everything to do with the death– leaving Stella to mind her two young boy cousins. It was a drag, but it filled the time because again, Stella knew no one, at least no one her own age. She kept reminding herself that soon Faye would be in Cape Town, but those weeks before her friend was to arrive seemed more like months– even years- to housebound Stella.

The saving grace was getting letters from Arnold Gideon. Stella took a risk writing to him. She hardly knew him. He probably wouldn't reply. If he didn't, though, no one would know and she'd be saved the embarrassment. Even Faye in far off Bethany didn't know.

But he did reply. It was strange, thinking of him reading her letters in their old home. Maybe he was even sleeping in her bed, reading her letters there.

He had flown down from Durban the day Roy died, hired a car in East London, and driven through the night. Stella heard the car engine and handbrake wrench up and she roused her mother. Dawn was breaking and Constance directed Stella to knock up the housekeeper, who came in and made him breakfast. She and her mother sat there watching this strange young man at their dining table, eating eggs, bacon, and mounds of toast. That morning, he went to the bank and was gone until evening. He had left his suitcase at the Quinns, and when he came to collect it before checking in at the hotel, her mother persuaded him to stay. The house was going to be his to occupy, anyway, until the new manager arrived, she said. Stella was shocked at this until she realized that Constance was frightened at night without Roy. The night before, she had done the unthinkable and invited Stella into the bed. Even as a toddler, Stella hadn't been allowed.

They had one week to pack up, one week before she and her mother were to leave for Cape Town. The major part of their belongings was to be packed by a removals firm chosen by the bank and would arrive some days later and go into storage until Constance decided where they would live. Stella was going to drive them down, and her mother asked Arno to help her daughter brush up on her driving, even more shocking for Stella. The lawyer in Bethany did the testing. Strawks said everyone in Bethany passed their driver's test. Even though she had driven trucks and tractors on the farms and was quite confident, she wanted those lessons.

She didn't tell anybody about the lessons, even Faye. Stella wanted to spend time on her own with Arno. The lessons took place after the bank closed. In the cool of the evening, she drove down the dusty main street with Arno beside her, stopping and starting and turning and indicating and parking every which way. There were no hills, so Arno took her up a ramp at the garage in town so she could practice stopping and starting on an incline.

After the lesson they sat in the car in the driveway and Stella would ask him all about his life until then. Arno was thirty and he had done his two-year national service in the army. He had tried a number of different jobs before settling on banking. He was an only child and one day he was going to return to the family farm in the Cape and run it. His parents never wanted to burden him and had encouraged him to try different careers. But more than anything, he wanted to run the farm and was waiting for the right time to do so.

Stella could tell that he regarded her as not much more than a child. In other circumstances this would have annoyed her, but any rancor was outweighed by the need for someone to be taking notice of her. To tell the truth, she couldn't quite comprehend that Roy had died and would no longer be coming home in the evenings, pouring himself a Scotch, stinking the place out with cigarette smoke and before settling to the paper, asking how her day was. Even though she had seen him lying there motionless on the office floor, she had knelt down and felt the coldness of his cheek with her fingertips, which Faye said was very brave. But Faye hadn't been with her the times a dog or a hamster, mice, and even rats had died or been found dead. So in a way, it wasn't an entirely new experience. You also didn't realize, until it happened to you, how important it was for what had happened to sink in. Her mother was struggling, and so Stella needed to have her feet firmly on the ground.

It was in Arno's letters that Stella learnt about the farm– what it looked like, its history, and how much he loved it. It was also in Arno's letters that Stella learnt that there were horses on the farm. A plan grew like a shoot pushing up through the earth after rain. It was a mixture of wanting Arno and wanting the farm and wanting a horse. Most of all, it was wanting a horse. Without her father she wasn't going to be able to own a horse. Her mother was talking about moving into a guest house. They had the opportunity to have a real house, their own house, and her mother didn't want one.

They could have stayed in that house and not have to move ever again.

But Stella hadn't given up immediately. She had heard of houses in areas like Constantia that opened onto shared stables and a paddock. She had discussed with her Uncle Clive how it could be managed and run. Stella would handle everything to do with the horse, her mother, and the house. But houses like the ones in Constantia (and houses everywhere) required cleaning and keeping nice (very important to Constance) and if you didn't want to do the work yourself, it required giving staff orders and seeing they were fed and went to the doctor when they were ill and were paid on time and took leave, all the things Constance couldn't bear having to think about. Roy had been the one to see to all of that. Why couldn't she learn, Stella fumed albeit silently. Her mother had been a secretary, had passed matric first class. She wasn't like the Scarecrow from *The Wizard of Oz* who didn't have a brain.

They were writing three or four letters each week. The letters continued even during the weeks when Arno was back in Durban. She received seven letters in two weeks. The letters were very much an avuncular type of letter, but they were coming from him, this man that had given her some of his precious time in her hour of need. It was all the encouragement she needed. Faye was arriving in Cape Town at the beginning of the next week, but Stella couldn't wait another minute. Her aunt and uncle had given her some money and she drew amounts from her post office savings account and her banking account, making up enough to buy a plane ticket to Durban as well as bus fare and loose change for phone calls. She told her mother that she was visiting Faye the next day and not to get up, which Constance wasn't in the habit of doing in any event.

Stella got up around five, having slept very little during the night. She had packed a backpack and asked her uncle to take her to the bus stop. He did wonder why she was going so early and she said, swallowing the fear of being found out, that she had missed her friend a stack and couldn't wait to see her. He wanted to take her all the way to a fictitious Bellville address, but she replied that she was going to enjoy the rare experience of a bus ride.

Just before boarding the flight for Durban, she rang Faye from a callbox and told her where she was and what she was about to do. Faye squealed down the line and said, "*You're joking*. How exciting." And in the next breath that she was worried for her friend's safety. What if some man got hold of her? At which Stella said that she had it all planned. She would make sure that wherever she was, there were other people present. A kick in the nuts would take care of any funny business. Faye also didn't like deceiving Stella's Mom, and Stella said, not to worry, she would be telling her mother where she was later, and that her mother thought very highly of Arno so everything was going to be just fine.

Balmy air greeted her as she walked off the plane at Louis Botha airport. She had to catch two buses to get to the Berea where Arno lived and worked, with some waiting in-between. She was too late for the bank and went straight to Arno's flat, thumbing a lift when it was growing dark, which was the first really dangerous thing she had done all day. But the driver, an old *toppie*, drove her right up to the gate to Arno's apartment block. Before he took off, he waited for her to go through, up the stairs and wave before she disappeared through Arno's door.

He stared, first at her and then at the backpack.

"*Good God, Stella*. What are you doing here?" His blue eyes were wide and his blonde hair stood up from lying on the couch and watching TV, which made him look even more shocked. "How did you get here?" He was in a T-shirt and shorts and barefoot.

"How did you think? Lift, bus, plane, bus, taxi." She was definitely not going to tell him about the lift to the gate.

He stepped towards her, grabbed her, almost like he wanted to shake her. His thumbs bored into the soft flesh of her forearms. In other circumstances she would have shaken herself free, or at worst cried out.

"Does your mother know?" He was almost shouting. He looked into her eyes for long minutes. She willed herself to stare back. Then he released her. With the shock of it, she nearly lost her balance.

"No, don't tell me." He was shaking his head and had turned away, like he couldn't bear to look at her.

"I'm going to phone her now. May I?" She made to lift the receiver off the handset in the hallway.

He marched into the kitchen. She heard him switch on the kettle.

Then he was bursting out again. She heard his footsteps and then he was silent. He had seen that she was crying.

"*Come here*." He said softly.

He held her while she cried it out. He said with his chin on her head, "Of course you would come here. We'll phone your Mom and explain." He found her a tissue and waited while she blew her nose, waited some more until she was looking at him. "I know what it is." His voice was gentle. "I'm your replacement Dad."

Constance *was* shocked. She had no idea. Stella almost felt sorry for her mother. "Mom, can I stay here a few days? I'm going to help Arno in the bank."

He shook his head. He was grinning from ear to ear. Then he was shaking his head some more.

"Help me in the bank?" He was laughing.

"And why not?" She had her hand over the mouthpiece.

"Security reasons, silly. This is not Bethany where anything goes. This is the big city."

When she had said goodbye to her mother he said, "You are such a child."

She sulked after that and wouldn't eat the omelet he made for her and began crying again.

"Geez, Stella. I never knew you were such a handful."

"I'm a handful with you. With everyone else I'm fine."

"That's probably because you have everyone else wrapped around your little finger. Here, I'm the boss. If you're going to stay with me, we're going to have some rules."

She had taken out her packet of Texans and a box of matches.

"Starting with this." He snatched the cigarettes and matches out of her hands. "As long as you're with me there'll be no ciggies." He dropped the box of matches into a drawer and thrust the packet of cigarettes at her. "Go chuck it in the bin."

When Stella flew to Durban that first time, she had no plans beyond putting some distance between herself and her mother, driven by the looming reality that she wasn't going to be able to own a horse. Staying with Arno, even though he was treating her like a younger sister that needed keeping in line, was pure heaven. She had a future. She had her whole life ahead of her. In the morning she would lie in bed until Arno had gone to work, get up and wash the dishes, tidy the flat, and the rest of the day was hers. She couldn't go back to staying with her mother. Even having her new and best friend in Cape Town, who was jumping up and down to show her the sights, shop, and go to the movies, wasn't enough to shift Stella from this conviction.

She began making inquiries about business colleges in the area. She needed to get a job as soon as possible. Being independent of her mother drove her forward. She still felt guilty, though. To counter this, she began thinking ahead. Flying down to see her mother on long weekends and when she had leave should satisfy both her mother's and her own sense of responsibility. Constance was going to be OK, Stella told herself, because she had her sister, Aunt Bev, and family. And if she wanted friends, there would be the other residents at the guest house. There was also Glad Morrisey, who had promised before they left Bethany to collect Constance and take her to tea or for a meal, or to shop– in fact, anything at all that Stella's mother would like to do. At the end of a week Stella was enrolled in Miss O'Donnell's Secretarial College for a six-month basic course of typewriting, bookkeeping, and office routine, subject to payment of a deposit. She called Constance, who sounded relieved, but wanted to speak to Arno when he came home from work. Constance asked Arno to arrange for a transfer into Stella's bank account.

Stella used some of the money to buy herself work clothes– slim skirts, blouses, jackets, and high-heels. Lunchtime the next day, she dressed in one of the new outfits, snapped on pearl earrings, and twisted her hair into a French roll to complete the look of someone who knew exactly where she was heading, and arrived at the bank and invited Arno out to a meal at the nearest Wimpy.

"What's this about?" She could tell he was trying not to grin, but didn't argue when the waitress handed him a menu.

"Constance is paying, so have a steak if you want," Stella said.

After they ordered– toasted cheese and tomato sarmies and cokes– she said, "Mom has agreed for me to do a business course. Six months. But I can't continue staying with you. It wouldn't be right, she says."

"Fair enough." The sandwiches had arrived, and Arno bit into his.

"You're not offended?"

"No, I'm not offended. I want you to spread your wings, meet people-"

"Go on say it– people my own age."

"Let's not turn this into an argument."

The owner of the college, Phyllis O'Donnell, although a martinet where work on the course was concerned, had a soft heart for recently bereaved daughters, Stella discovered. Phyllis arranged accommodation with one of the teachers, which included a lift to and from college. There'd been a necessary fudging of the truth. Stella was staying with a friend of the family, who had encouraged her to come to Durban to try her luck in the business world there. His flat was a 'bachelor' and therefore awfully cramped. Constance said Stella could have Roy's car when she passed the course.

Was Stella going to come back to Cape Town, find a job there, and stay at the guest house? Stella said she didn't know, but secretly determined to land a job in Durban.

Arno collected her every Sunday for a pub lunch. He drank beer but refused to allow her even a beer shandy. Stella, meanwhile, was going to parties sometimes on Fridays and Saturdays– *and* drinking alcohol. She wondered what Arno was doing at these times and other times when he wasn't at the bank and wasn't with her. Did he have a girlfriend, she wondered, someone that matched him in looks and was as mature and experienced and worldly-wise as he was? It did occur to Stella to spy on Arno, but that would have meant it mattered.

There was to be a cocktail party to celebrate the graduation of their class and having no close family in Durban, Stella invited Arno. They were encouraged to apply for jobs. Miss O'Donnell's was known for turning out proficient workers and had the edge on graduates from equivalent institutions thanks to subjects like deportment and etiquette. Employment agencies and firms were constantly asking Miss O'Donnell to recommend girls for a variety of jobs. Stella had responded to a number of adverts, but as it turned out, the college receptionist was leaving to have a baby and Stella was asked to fill the position. She grabbed it, even though the salary was bottom of the scale as it meant having four holidays a year.

Stella's landlady told her that what had clinched the job for Miss O'Donnell was that Stella 'kept to herself'. In a job where she was surrounded by women it was important that the person chosen didn't gossip.

So for her it was a double celebration as she clinked glasses of champagne with Arno and Miss O'Donnell after the diplomas were handed out. Miss O'Donnell liked to do things in style and Stella had received– as did the other graduates– a corsage of miniature carnations set on feathery maidenhair fern, now pinned to the shoulder of her black taffeta sheath dress. Which should have made her feel more grown-up, but as usual, in Arno's presence she was feeling anything but.

What helped ease the discomfort was the envious looks of some of the girls. He wore a sports jacket, open-necked shirt and slacks– all in creams and camel which suited his blond tanned looks. She had just begun to introduce him to her principal and now boss when the latter interrupted with, "We know each other, don't we, Arno?" The older woman was dimpling. Stella glanced from one to the other. Phyllis O'Donnell was probably only half a dozen years older than Arno– at most, ten. Joan Collins, Liz Taylor, and Tina Turner had made the older woman eminently desirable.

"That we do." A waiter topped Arno up.

Stella placed her empty glass on the tray.

"Your mother must be looking forward to having you home?"

Stella balked at the word *home*. "She is, Miss O'Donnell." Although what Constance thought was anyone's guess.

"I'd love to stay and chat, but I must be away to do my duty. Stella, see that your guest does justice to the smorgasbord and yourself as well.

There's a cash bar for when the champers are finished, which I hope won't be until much later. Excuse me."

Arno and Stella watched as the older woman moved to the next group of girls and guests, her ample but corseted hips swaying delicately, her voice and manner the perfect advert for her business.

Stella shot Arno a questioning look.

"The bank," he said. "The college is a client. I thought you knew." And then, because she wasn't saying anything, "You must drive your Mom out to the farm. I'll be down for Christmas. We'll always be having parties, braais. We farmers are always looking for opportunities to drink our wine. Bring your friends, Faye and what's his name, Strawks?"

Will we be allowed to drink wine, she wanted to ask, but it would have looked even more childish. But she couldn't stop herself saying, "Faye has parties and stuff to do *this* long." She demonstrated with an outstretched arm.

"Bring the party to us. The more the merrier."

Arno drove her back to the teacher's house. At the door he kissed her on the cheek.

After the holidays Stella would have her father's car and wouldn't need Arno to drive her places. She would also have her own pad– a furnished bachelor flat, the lease of which Arno had signed using the power of attorney arranged with her mother through the bank. She couldn't wait until she was twenty-one and had legal authority. She also planned to tell him that he needn't take her out to lunch on Sundays. She was a member of a group of young people that went to the beach and that partied at one another's houses. He didn't need to know that half the time she was alone. But soon she wouldn't be. She had taken the first step towards having a horse. She had joined a riding school. When she came back after the holidays she would have her first lesson. Eventually she would have her own horse but for that she needed to work on her mother. She was sure that by the end of the holiday, Constance would have agreed, as she had agreed to almost everything that made up Stella's new life in Durban.

CHAPTER 12

The Jeep isn't ideal on the freeway. We perch on hard seats. But as soon as we are on the narrower roads, winding up between the mountains beyond Piketberg, we are going to be grateful for its sturdiness. The ploughed wheatlands with their secret seeds slide by on either side. Their nakedness and hope of success to come touches me and tears prick. Nature is so trusting. I look across at Fergus with his head on Faye's arm and modify the thought. His eyes are watchful.

Following my gaze, Faye says, "It's like he knows this is a new route for us."

There was a sense of excitement as we started out, but the couple of hours on the often straight highway lulled us. The newness of the terrain of low hills with farms nestling in treed valleys invites something to talk about other than our daily routines. Like Moses striking the rock, the Bethany album has opened a flow of the past into the present. Now I am eager to fill the gaps with the times Faye and I were apart. When I share this, I need explain very little. It is obvious she has her own nostalgic inner feed running.

"When I arrived from Durban that first July holiday, you and Strawks were an item. You were always together, off somewhere, chatting, arguing."

"I only took him on the one. He nearly got himself killed. What a dunderhead. Life in small-town Norway had been so insular. He saw his first black man in Cape Town. He kept on about how great a country South Africa was. *Ok for you whites* was yelled at him. He didn't realize what he was dealing with."

I had sensed a connection between Faye and Strawks at the barn dance, but Roy's death soon afterwards had blurred events. "I was never sure when you guys got together. Was it in Bethany or when he was at the agricultural college?"

"At first, we were just friends. Anika suggested I call him at Elsenburg to find out how he was doing. She had to stay with her folks, work on the farm. She wouldn't have had the money to visit him. Pig farming wasn't the money-spinner they thought it would be. He didn't know anyone in the Cape apart from a couple of guys from home who were also studying at the college. When he called back, I hardly recognized him. He was no longer the cheeky kid we knew. He was homesick. Big time. My Mom only needed to hear that once and he was invited over for the weekend–weekends into infinity, if he wanted."

"And he wanted."

I glance across. My God, she is blushing.

"Remember out first sleep-over at Gideons?" she says. "You were in a huff most of the time, but we had such fun. Well, Strawks and I did. I couldn't understand you. Arno was the perfect gentleman, but you were a right little bitch. And his folks were so great. Those meals that overlapped. The swimming and riding gave us those roaring appetites. Remember how we collapsed into bed at night? We were asleep before our heads touched the pillow."

"Not me. I'd lie in bed wondering when Arno was going to make a move. Of course, he had Mariekie hanging around. Mostly, though, I would be thinking about a horse and how I was going to get one."

"The girl he thought his parents wanted him to marry, whereas they didn't. Now Strawks' parents had a Norwegian girl earmarked for him."

"And that's what was holding him back from declaring love to you?"

"I thought he was being a perfect gentleman."

"So we both had *perfect gentlemen*." The last two words are in unison, an oft repeated rounding up of the story. Our comedy of errors. We look at each other and laugh.

Faye's laughter is like a monkey's wedding, raindrops colliding with sunbeams. Our eyes meet, hers are moist and my heart leaps. Everything is going to be fine. I just have to keep telling myself that.

The Jeep had been grinding away up the last slope. Now we are at the top of a small mountain, one of several in this landscape of surprises. Soon civilization emerges in the form of workers' cottages, fenced orchards, clumps of non-indigenous trees, like pines, wattles, and oaks, and rooftops– even a railway line opening up ahead. We wind around the staggered foothills, losing height all the while, passing signs but not the one we are looking for. At last it appears, needing a freshening of unimaginative white paint on wood, *Akkerstroom*. I stop the Jeep, get out, and open the gate whose metal frame is dented, I imagine, from much hanging onto and swinging from by local children. Here there is no intercom and no guard dogs. I drive in, stop, and slip the rudimentary loop of wire back over the gate pole.

I remember Anika saying that people liked the simplicity of the farm. There is no electricity in the cottages, but there is gas, if I remember rightly. Anika has to have electricity and a telephone line for internet bookings and to be in touch with the police and medical services.

We drive through orchards of clementines, olives, almonds, and smaller groupings of stone summer fruits. It is all organic, which means no insecticides or pesticides are used. A homeopath is called when the fruit trees become diseased. Water from tanks situated at the highest point on the property irrigates trees, flowers, and vegetables. Like Gideon's, they also have an underground stream from which they pump water, powering it from a small generator. The pines, wattles, and *oaks* (the derivation of the farm's name) have to go, Anika said, because they are too thirsty. But they keep putting off the task.

The grounds clear as though a giant hand has pushed back the trees, exposing the first of a row of some ten cottages. Each has a chimney and a small, roofed patio with a cemented stone grill with a funnel to direct smoke away from the front door. There are cars parked beside some of the cottages which lend a more populated feel to what would otherwise have a deserted look, a look it wears during the week, I imagine, or outside of holiday times. Our directions were to continue on until we came upon a separate cottage with a low wall, which we do, at last. It has a pretty garden and a bigger roofed patio. Its door is bright yellow and opens as we draw up. Anika appears, holding Valdine's hand, and motions for us to park on the far side.

Fergus growls a little, but more for show. Faye gets out and lets him walk and sniff about while she comes around to receive her hostess and daughter's hugs. I am similarly greeted. I notice that this time Faye is careful not to flinch.

"You've arrived all in one piece."

Anika's looks and manner strike me as being eminently compatible with her surroundings. Her skin and hair are coarse and dry, much like the vegetation, whereas Valdine seems to have been shaped by hands not of this world. There are gold flecks in her eyes and her skin is like silk. Even as I chide myself for an imagination gone crazy, I gawp.

"Come in. Come in."

In the cottage, the girl releases her mother's hand. I almost sigh with relief. How restricting for both women, I think. The girl presses a button on a CD player and the sound of a tinkling piano fills the room. I am encouraged by her execution of this simple task. Fergus trots up to her, wagging his tail.

"You can pick him up, Valdine. His name is Fergus."

She tries valiantly to pronounce the name but gives up when Anika says, "That's OK, sweetheart." She glances from Faye to Stella. "Let's have a pre-lunch drink, shall we? What would you like?"

"What do you have?"

"I have *Glögg* ready to heat."

"Now that takes us back. We'll have that," Faye beams.

The weekend has been successful, Anika tells us, as we sip the welcome warmth of the beverage. Her first advert on radio has aired. A number of that weekend's guests are a direct result.

"Henk is pleased," Anika says. Henk is the farmer. "He'll join us later. He's giving us a chance to catch up."

The girl is humming along with the piano melody and watching Fergus, who is still trotting about and sniffing.

"We have mice," explains Anika, glancing at the dog. "One can't stop them coming in from the fields. Valdine loves to catch and pet them. Don't you, sweetheart?"

"Come here, Fergus," scolds Faye, "On second thought, I'll put him in the car." She stands up.

"That's not necessary," says Anika. "Sit." Faye obliges. "Henk has a dog, and so we're used to it. Valdine knows what to do." She looks directly at me as she says, "In the country, animals have to learn to get along together."

I smile reassuringly.

The girl lifts Fergus onto her lap. "Better. Wolraad."

"Wolraad is Henk's German shepherd. He has grown too big for Valdine to lift onto her lap. She is saying that because she can lift Fergus onto her lap, she prefers him."

"You spoiled thing," Faye says to Fergus, whose eyelids are lowering in ecstasy.

I look around myself as Faye and Anika move into the tiny kitchen to get lunch. All surfaces are as far as possible left in their natural state, from the lime-washed Malay plaster to the ceiling ribbed with poles unrelieved of nodes and bark. Small windows feed my musings about a giant who, in this case, has thumbed them out of the eighteen-inch thick walls. The Johansen parents and forebears stare grimly from heavy frames. Against these the sheepskin rugs seem ready to be swept off the unpolished stone floor by a breath from the giant of my imagining, only to be enticed back by the heat from the logs of wattle that snap and crackle and shoot sparks out of the maw of the hearth.

Anika signals for us to join her at the table.

The *Glogg* that Anika served earlier, because it is similar to Gluwein, hadn't rung any bells, but now as Anika offers a loaf of grainy bread, an aromatic reveille resounds. The culprits are cardamom seeds that pop out as we tear off pieces.

That Christmas in Bethany, Strawks' parents had us around for a typically Norwegian array of dishes unattractively hot for the southern hemisphere. I remember the bread is called *Julekake*. Faye and I had giggled when we heard it, *kak* being the Afrikaans word for human feces.

And here we are, eating it again together with *gravlaks* with piquant mustard sauce and *fiskeboller* (fish cakes) and local, Cape Malay *rostes* wrapped around curried chicken.

The girl eats with the abandon of a child. She helps herself to more *fiskeboller*, unwraps the *roste*, eats it, and leaves the filling. She picks cardamom seeds out of her piece of *julekake*, lines them up around her plate, only to discover she is too full to eat the bread itself.

We persuade Anika to check on her guests while we clear away. Anika takes Faye aside and says that on no account should we leave the cottage, even if Valdine begs. But no sooner have we washed, dried and tidied everything away, than our young charge does just that, going to the front door and doing a good job of acting out her desire.

"We'll hold her hand all the time. Like Anika does," I say. "It'll do us good to get out. Perhaps there is some little animal or bird in a nest that Anika hasn't had time to take her to check on." I am thinking how it would have been for me had I grown up in such a place. I change tack. "You want to foster the relationship, don't you?" Indeed, the girl has been sitting next to Faye ever since our chores were done.

Valdine pulls us along a track that leads up a hill. Fergus follows, excited by movement in the course grass, but the girl continues relentlessly and the little dog is forced to scamper after us. Faye is pale and out of breath by the time we reach the top. We sit on the ledge of one of the tanks, lean hot and sweaty backs against the cool metal and admire the view. Among the trees below are visible the roofs of a house and a series of sheds, where I imagine the business of the farm is carried out. Beyond is the panoramic spread of undulating countryside.

Mercilessly, the girl leads some more, down another hill and into the cool darkness of scented pines where a narrow path opens onto a sunny clearing. There is a bench in front of six simple graves with handmade cement headstones. Faye is about to sit on the bench, but the girl pulls us towards one of the graves.

She bends down, lifts a shriveled bunch of carnations out of a vase, and tosses it onto the grass. She grumbles and throws us angry looks. We should have brought fresh flowers, she seems to be saying.

Faye leans in to read the roughly carved cement. I seize on the worst scenario. *Strawks is buried here.* I shudder, too afraid to look. I look at Faye instead. She is absorbed in the task, displays no sign of distress. Fergus sits, panting.

"Estelle. Beloved wife and mother," Faye announces. She throws Valdine a questioning look.

"Ma," says the girl. "Want Ma."

She seems to have forgotten about the flowers and doesn't look particularly sad, which is puzzling. I understand from the ease with which she led us to the spot, that visiting the grave happens on a regular basis. If there was sadness, it has played out.

"There are dates," I say, recovering from my delusion, although my legs still feel rather wobbly as I lean in.

Faye reads: "MCMLV – MM. Good Lord."

_____

CHAPTER 13

Miss O'Donnell had hammered Roman numerals into our girlish heads.

"1955 to 2000," I say.

The buried woman could be Valdine's mother. Maybe 'Estelle' died giving birth.

"Your mother... your *Ma*?" I touch the girl's arm.

She stares at the ground.

"Valdine?" I say. "Is anything wrong?"

She turns, and before we can reach out a hand, she steps back. We stare as she takes off up the stony track. I take off, calling back, "Faye, you take it slow. We'll wait at the top for you. Don't strain." Fergus stares after us.

The girl has picked up speed. The slope is steep and the distance between us grows instead of lessening.

"*Valdine*." I call. "*Wait*." Through frantic breaths I shout, "Why are you running away?"

At the top of the hill, she swerves away from the track and with deep strides– almost falling onto each foot, as she makes her way down among gum trees now, and the rough terrain that leads to a clearing and the house I spotted earlier. Small stones loosen and roll, and twigs snap and scatter as I follow. This must be the farmer's house, I think. Ahead, the girl runs up the front steps. She opens the door, which she flings shut behind her.

Now I am inside and hear a woman's voice. Help at last. I walk down the passage, which leads through to a kitchen at the back. I am gasping but manage to call, softer now, "Valdine, where *are* you?"

There she is, with her back to me, also panting. I move closer. My only thought is to hold her. I can't let her get away again and I come around so that I am facing her. I try to hug her, but she steps back.

"What's happened? We're friends, Faye and I. You know that, surely?"

Her eyes are wild. Her mind is somewhere else.

I become more aware of the woman, aproned, and the table, sink, and window of the kitchen. This must be the housekeeper. She takes hold of the girl's hands. Valdine's breathing is becoming more regular. So is mine. I think, it's going to be OK, but then the girl is shaking off the woman and is looking around like a trapped animal. If I can just hold her and transfer some of my calm which used to work with the twins when they were small?

But the girl is crying and thrashing about with her arms. I make a final bid and she vomits against me.

I ignore what has just happened and hold her. I feel whatever has caused this will leave her. At last, she is limp.

"It's alright, Miss Vally. You are going to be alright," is said in Afrikaans. We take the girl to a chair. At first she won't sit, holds herself ramrod stiff, and then she becomes limp once more. The woman reaches for a wet cloth hanging near the sink and begins wiping the girl's chin and T-shirt.

I take the girl's hand and instantly there is a change for the better. She is looking at me, seeing me. Her breathing quietens. She sits there, meek now and spent.

"My name is Edna. I work for Mr. Verwey."

"How d'you do. I'm Stella. A friend and I were taking Valdine for a walk. We are visiting Anika."

Edna takes the girl's hand. "The bathroom is down there." She points towards the bedroom area. I wash as best I can. There is a very masculine deodorant stick in the cupboard above the basin and I drag it across my neck.

Faye hasn't arrived.

"Would you mind coming with us to Anika's cottage? I'm hoping my friend has found her way back there." I am grateful to be with someone who knows the girl.

"Certainly. Poor thing," she says. "Miss Anika does her best. She is our wild thing. Our *bokkie*. Aren't you, Vally?" She touches the girl's cheek lightly, turns and gives me a look. She is going to say more, I suspect, but just then a man walks in.

"What's going on?" he says in Afrikaans. He is smiling until he sees Valdine.

He is tall– as tall as Brand and Lyle but bigger, wider, a craggy tower of a man. He has a mop of dark fly-away hair and equally undisciplined eyebrows above grey eyes. A beard like a bib conceals the opening of his worn cabled cardigan. His corduroys are also worn, and he wears sturdy leather boots– they are so big I imagine he has them specially made. *My giant*, I think.

"My heaven," he says, nostrils wide. "We've had a little accident have we?"

"We were exploring, then something seemed to alarm the girl."

"No need for explanations," he says. "I'm Henk Verwey. You must be a friend of Anika's. Which one are you?"

'I'm Stella. Stella Gideon." My hand is squeezed until it hurts. I want to rub it but don't.

"Edna saved the day. She was about to come with us to Anika's cottage."

"If you wait five minutes, I'll go with you."

The German Shepherd, the too-big-for-Valdine's-lap Wolraad, is about to accompany us but Henk sends the animal back with a firm, *"Bly."*

I think that now I will receive illumination on what ails the girl, but Henk wants to know how we know Anika. I tell him that Faye, Anika, and I are girlhood friends. That we met the year after school in Bethany. That Faye and Anika grew close after I left for Cape Town.

"I hadn't heard about you a week ago and now you're coming to lunch, taking Valdine for a walk. Anika almost never has visitors." He is the girl's protector, I think. Or is concern for Anika his true motivation? One wouldn't want to cross swords with him.

I realize then that I am either going to have to tell Henk the truth or not say anything at all. But he seems genuinely interested. I feel to blame for what has happened to the girl and wonder if I can ask him to put in a good word for me with Anika on Faye's behalf.

"Faye has been ill. Meeting Anika and Valdine gave her something, someone else to focus on. If you've ever been sick, you'll know that it's very easy to fall prey to self-pity."

"I'm sorry to hear that your friend has been sick. My late wife was ill for a long time, so I know what you're talking about."

"Is– was– her name Estelle?"

"I guessed that was where you had been, that is, where Valdine dragged you." He says this with a smile, albeit sardonic.

"Isn't that cruel, allowing her to believe Estelle was her mother?"

"*Gats*, I don't know what she believes. One never knows what is going on in that pretty head." He looks down at the girl. "You're full of surprises, aren't you, *Bokkie*?" He turns to me, "She goes there to bury dead animals." And to the girl, "Isn't that so, Vally?"

"S-s-s." The girl is trying to get her tongue around the word, 'surprises', maybe?

"It was my idea to go on the walk. I wonder if you'll explain that to Anika. When we're gone, that is."

"I'm sure there's no need. Just remember, we are all learning how to handle this kid." He whispers this against my ear. It tickles and I giggle, releasing some of the tension. He gives me a searching look.

Faye is outside the cottage waiting for us when we arrive. She is pale with worry and I feel doubly bad about what happened. I also notice that Anika is displeased, but hiding it.

"Let me get you something to change into," she says brusquely, and I follow her and Valdine into the only bedroom. She opens a drawer in the dressing table and pulls out a T-shirt and hands it to me. She leaves me to change. In the bathroom she speaks softly to the girl, but the words are endearments, nothing that sheds light on why the girl behaved the way she did. While I change I look around. There are more family photos but none recent. I am tempted to open drawers (the wardrobe door, for instance) but desist.

Over coffee and *blotkake,* Henk replies to questions about the farm. We learn that he supplies Prince Charles with fruit. Henk had been negotiating with the Prince's agent to supply the royal with Anika's jams made only from organically grown fruit, which is a stipulation. Various samples are being tested in a laboratory in Cape Town. Conversation quickly turns to the B+B business. His plans are to start up a colony of artists and writers as has happened in other country areas like the towns of Arniston and Stanford.

"We have to try a bit harder because we aren't at the beach or near it," says Anika. She no longer seems angry. Or has she tamped it down? Being a fellow sufferer, I am super aware.

"How do you propose to do that?" asks Faye, who seems oblivious of undercurrents where her friend is concerned.

"There are a number of free magazines. We advertise in some of those, but the best way is if someone writes an article about us."

There is a knock on the door. A car engine is running. Another guest is taking his leave. Anika and Henk leave to attend to business. Valdine hands Faye a book to read to her, lying back on the couch, pale, but her beautiful self once more. Faye begins with Fergus on her lap.

On the mantle above the fire, among the drabness of the other mail, the colors of a postcard catch my eye. I stroll over and examine it, lingering over the moss-covered ramparts of what looks like a castle. Underneath in small print I read, *St Bernard's Abbey, 1480 AD.* A tourist destination. Someone has been travelling. I flip it over and notice the stamp bearing the profile of Queen Elizabeth II. *Dear Sis,* it begins. *We're done harvesting. Now it's prayer and more prayer.* My eye flips to the signature, *Bro. Thorkild,* but not before I have checked that Anika and Henk are still outside with their guest, Faye absorbed in her reading. I check for an address at the top, but there is none. However, there is a date. The card was written roughly a year ago. Henk's bulky presence fills the doorway. I return the card to the mantel as unobtrusively as possible.

Leaving the girl asleep on the couch, Anika walks with us to the Jeep. Anika tells us, "Valdine overdid it at lunch. She was nauseous but couldn't tell you and so ran away."

Faye and I wonder about this as we drive out of the valley that holds *Akkerstroom* and several other farms in its fertile clasp. I feel bad that it was me that suggested we take the girl for a walk. Yet I am also oddly triumphant. If Valdine's bolt and vomit was digestive and not due to some mental disturbance, then we did some good taking her out into the fresh air. Are we reading too much into what happened at the graveside? We are clueless where the girl's speech difficulty is concerned, if that is her problem. And as to who her mother is, and indeed, who her parents are, will have to remain a mystery for now, although we can't help being curious. Anika's parting words were to come for a weekend, soon. Our, or my, misdemeanor doesn't seem to have counted against us, which is a relief.

CHAPTER 14

Home and its chores and responsibilities are waiting for me. Among the messages on my cell phone is one from Gunner. He has had to postpone his trip to South Africa by two weeks. This time he is staying longer. A month. He has booked into a hotel in the Stellenbosch. Fish and house guests go bad after ten days, he quips. Perhaps he is bringing his wife and doesn't want to impose?

I text back: **Stay with us, wife and all**.

Am I playing the good hostess or Curious Cat?

The reply comes: **Just me. Won't you get tired of my Aussie ass?**

Probably, I text. **But stay anyway. We can always get you magicking up a wine to keep you out of our hair. We kept back a few thousand liters. You might like to tinker with this while you're here. But don't stress.**

What am I thinking? I have asked an almost stranger to blend for me–us? I know he makes his own wines, so he's equal to the task, but this is like allowing him to use my toothbrush or inviting him into my bed. Luckily for me, he is married, so there won't be any awkwardness in that department.

If Gunner wants to blend a wine, I'll have to tell Brand. I have no right offering Gunner to help us blend. Up until now Gunner has been sensitive to a fault, constantly checking that this or that is alright for him to do. But so far it has been all about the pruning. *Damn.*

What I need to do is text Gunner and withdraw my offer. It occurs to me then that I have been taking advantage of Gunner. He won't take a penny for his services. My offer was an attempt to repay him, I realize. I decide there and then that, no matter what, I am going to pay him for the pruning.

Gunner, I text, **second thoughts on blending. We're not ready yet for this step. I think you'll understand!? Terribly sorry. Looking forward to yr arrival.**

The reply comes: **Stella, it wouldn't have worked anyway. The new wine, when it happens, must be the work of the owner of Gideons— someone who loves those vines. Seeing you will, as usual, be the highlight of my year.**

After we sign off, I am sad. The 'someone' who loved those vines is gone. Good 'ol Gunner, I think, always the gentleman. Another gentleman? My heart skips a beat.

It is after midnight when I google **St. Bernard's Abbey**.

Perhaps I am tired, but chanting monks grate. What the heck is Strawks playing at? The monks wear grey or white habits and either kneel at their prie-dieus, restore ancient manuscripts, hammer metal into religious objects d'art or snip a rose in an immaculate garden. Nothing I can imagine Strawks doing. I am treated to a virtual contemplation of an ornate altar ablaze with candles, exquisitely vaulted ceilings and a walk down dim corridors with marble statues of holy men holding wooden crosses, a stalk of St Joseph lilies or an infant Christ.

Next I try Wikipedia and learn that the abbey is in Wales. It was built in the eighteen hundreds. Henry VIII had an abbot, and several monks executed but despite this the order continued. Rebuilding began after a German Dornier Do-17 bomber discharged prematurely in WWII.

I try a site featuring a visit by a history group from which I learn that apple wine is made on the premises and sold countrywide. Wine, I think, I'm getting warmer, but *Bro. Thorkild*? Is he really a religious brother, or is it a joke between brother and sister?

Another website lists a Craft and Wine Shoppe with an address in Chester and a phone number and an e-mail address. I'll start with the shop, but the lateness of the hour requires that I try in the morning. I lie in my narrow bed and scenes from the now previous day run through my head. What a strange day it was. My last thought before sleep takes hold is, I hope it hasn't put Faye off. I dream of a giant carrying a screaming Valdine through a dark forest pursued by Gunner and me. I keep telling Gunner I'll pay him so that he doesn't give up the chase.

———————————

I am chewing toast liberally slathered with Anika's orange swirl marmalade when the farm phone rings.

"Good morning, Stella." It is Henk Verwey. "Fancy dinner in the Strand tonight? I have to visit our packaging crowd over on your side."

"Is it business or pleasure, Henk? I don't date."

"Six of one and half a dozen of the other."

"I don't want you to waste your time."

"What a tough cookie you are. But that's what I like about you, Stella Gideon. Six OK? I'd like to check out your place before we head for the restaurant."

I know I sound inhospitable (Ada and Frank will turn in their graves) but I can't bear someone else's scrutiny of the farm. He's bound to pick up on my lack of enthusiasm, of direction and offer advice I won't be able to take. A favorite saying of wine farmers mocks me as I think this— the worse the soil, the better the wine.

"I'll meet you there. Can you give me the name of the restaurant? Shall we say seven?"

After lunch, I phone long-distance to Chester, England. A soft-spoken gent answers. The accent flips me back to trips with Arno. No, he doesn't know of a Brother Thorkild, but I should try the abbey. Only after I ring off do I wonder if I should have mentioned that the person I am trying to get hold of is South African. I ring back and mention this. They usually see South Africans at harvest time, he says. But apples picking is over for the year. Is there someone else there that I can speak to? I ask.

A woman says, "There was someone here that could have been a Kiwi, an Oz or a South African. Forgive my ignorance."

"The person I'm looking for was originally from Norway."

"That would explain it, then. He talked funny, as my grandkids would say."

My pulse quickens, my mouth is dry. I have so many questions. I explain about the postcard and the name of the signatory.

"The person I am thinking of was here, oh, a year ago. He most definitely wasn't religious. He was in charge of the orchards back in Llangollen, that's where the abbey is and where they make our wonderful St Bernard's Nectar. He came to check out our display and offered suggestions. Would you like to order a case, we have a special on at the moment…"

"Not at the moment, thanks. This person, what did he look like? Color eyes, hair, height?"

"Are you from the police?"

I laugh. "I'm a friend. We go way back." I take a deep breath. "I have a friend here in Cape Town who is sick and I'd like him to know."

The warmth flooding the airwaves is palpable. "Medium height, thatch of yellow, cheeky blue eyes."

"That sounds like my friend. His full name is Thorkild Johansen. He had this nickname…"

Soon we are chatting. I tell her that Faye has breast cancer and refuses to undergo chemotherapy. Thorkild, or Strawks, as we call him, is my one hope of getting Faye to change her mind.

She ends off saying, "Give me your details. The minute I see or hear of him I'll get in touch."

"There's one other thing," I say. "There is no phone number on the abbey website. Do you have it, perhaps?"

"I'm sorry," she says, and she does sound genuinely contrite. "We are not allowed to give it out. The monks are a contemplative order. Big word, I know," she chuckles. "They eschew any contact from the outside world. I've known people go there in person and knock on the door and… nothing."

I sum up my progress. Strawks– I am fairly sure it was he– was at the shop a year ago. He was working for the monks of St Bernard's Abbey in Wales, running their apple harvest. It is also a year since he wrote that postcard. He could be anywhere. I have one more lead. Read Fort Knox for St Bernard's Abbey.

One of the websites I haven't tried is YouTube. I type in **St Bernard's Abbey**. Up comes an aerial view of the abbey. A lively piano thumps away as a forklift truck enters the grounds and begins an inspection and repair of the tiling and gutters of the steep grey slate roof– all in time-lapse photography. Three men in yellow hard hats and jackets over blue overalls perch on a small platform that is winched upwards via the arm with its two joints and circular mobility.

If they can get in there, I can too, I think. I would need some pretext. There must be someone in reception dealing with visitors. I read on their website that contrary to what is generally believed about the habits of monks, they do not eat only bread and water. There is fasting during Lent, for example, and leading up to the feast days of certain saints, but on the whole they eat a balanced diet and drink every kind of alcoholic beverage. I could offer them a gift of South African wine, but I have no contact numbers.

Anika would have the answer to most of my questions. Perhaps it is time to come clean. Except that Faye isn't ready for the other woman to know about the mastectomy in case it puts her off allowing Faye to help with the girl.

———————

Henk has chosen what describes itself as a *family restaurant, De Herberg, estab. 1950*. The middle-aged owner and a grey-haired woman (whom I assume is his mother) welcome us. They know Henk and I can only guess that he brought his wife here all those moons ago. Should I be honored, even a little worried?

As far as dinner-wear is concerned, he has pulled on a tweed jacket with elbow patches over a flannel shirt. The beard covers most of his tie. I am in a jacket, slacks, and polo-neck sweater– all demurely blue and grey.

Henks' *raison d'être* for the dinner, and why he agreed to my terms, is quickly revealed.

Our main courses arrive, Duck à L'orange for Henk (one of the few places that don't get it dry, he boasts), and Filet Mignon with Truffles for me (I want him to know I don't come cheap even if it isn't a date as such).

He offers me a fork load of duck and sauce. I chew as he says, "I've never brought Anika here. Not to any restaurant. She won't leave the girl."

"What about leaving her with your housekeeper? She seemed fond of the girl."

He hails for more orange sauce and pours. "You know the song, *The Farmer Wants a Wife*? Well, I've found her."

My heart thumps. "Anika?"

He nods. Relief runs through me. Now I can focus on the steak that is proving to be every bit as delicious as hoped.

"Except she won't leave the kid for five minutes. Did you go into the bedroom?"

"Yes?"

"They sleep in the same bed. I don't profess to understand what ails the girl, but it sure isn't helping her being coddled by her *ma*."

"Has Valdine always had difficulty– um– with speech? Was she born that way?"

"It seems so. There was a school that was prepared to take her, but Anika would have had to move to Cape Town. There were people prepared to have the girl as a weekly boarder. I offered transport so that Anika could keep working for me. She is like that—independent to a fault. The bottom line is, I don't think Anika believes anyone else can do as good a job as her. But it's none of my business." He checks that I am finished eating and then nods to the waiter to take our plates. "Anika and I have spoken about marriage and she's keen, but it won't be any kind of marriage the way things are. I'll come right to the point, Stella, but first, how about dessert and coffee?"

After we order, he continues. "Seeing you and your friend with Vally and how she might come out of her shell had me thinking. Especially when you said your friend finds helping someone else gets her mind off her own problems. What I had in mind was leaving the girl with you and your friend for a few hours, then a day and eventually, say, a weekend."

"You haven't wasted time."

His eyes steel up. I imagine him brooking no trouble with staff.

I say, "I'm happy with that. However, Anika would have to agree."

"What I thought is that you work from your side and I from mine."

"I can do that. Now *I* need something."

"Anything."

"It's about Faye. I'm breaking a confidence in telling you this, Henk, but after what you just shared, it could be of mutual benefit." I pause, winging a prayer for Faye to forgive my betrayal. "The oncologist has recommended Faye have chemotherapy. She refuses. And she won't say why. She says, speak to the hand." Henk *tsk-tsks* with disbelief. "*And* she doesn't want to go in for alternative remedies. I've checked with her."

"She's your friend. She's got to listen."

"I wish. She's been there for me at every turn. Now when I can do something for her, she won't let me."

"*Bliksem.*"

"But there's one person she will listen to. Might listen to."

"Oh?"

"He's Anika's brother, Strawks. Have you met him?"

Henk's expression swings from hope to eyes narrowing, nostrils flaring. "*That bugger?*"

"Strawks? What's he done?"

"I'm sworn to silence. I'm already going to get it in the neck if Anika finds out what I'm up to." The dessert and coffee have arrived and he gives the bowl of ice cream a fierce stir.

Then he pushes the bowl away, knocking the coffee over and bringing the waiter running.

"*Leave it,*" he barks.

The waiter quickly steps back, stuttering an apology.

His next words come out like he is scolding me. "You say he's the one who can talk to Faye? What's the connection?"

This is new for me, defending Strawks' corner. "They were engaged once. She broke it off. He adored her and would have done anything for her. But she was adamant. She wanted nothing more to do with him. Strawks was in a low state afterwards, as you can imagine. I'm ashamed to say I lost touch." Henk looks doubtful. I feel the need to add, "He took every kind of job after that, trying to better himself with the hope Faye might relent and take him back."

"Well, he's gone to the dogs since. That's all I'm saying." Henk put his hands flat on the table as though Strawk's fate, unpleasant in the extreme, is final.

I wait while Henk receives a fresh cup of coffee, hoping he will elaborate. When this isn't forthcoming, I empty my cup and firm up my backbone. I see again seventeen year-old Faye glance across at the boy with the yellow hair and say, *He looks nice.* Then I look Henk in the eye.

"In spite of what you've said, I have to get hold of him. He's my only hope. Do you have his details? A phone number, e-mail address, street– um– address?"

"Not a clue. You'll have to ask Anika. She hears from him from time to time. She expects so little back for what she does. She's like that with me… everyone. And he takes advantage. *Bliksem.*"

CHAPTER 15

Arno had promised Constance during that first holiday home after meeting the Quinns that he would keep an eye on her daughter when they were back in Durban. This was easier said than done. Stella had her father's car now, so offering her a lift was out, and she had made it plain that Sunday lunch was for old fogies, shades of her mother, and the residents of the Cape Town guest house. Her social life was hectic, which meant he never knew when she was home, and he felt too embarrassed to contact her at the college for fear of bumping into Miss O'Donnell or having the latter pick up the telephone. It was enough to have to field the old girl's inquiries about Stella at the bank.

"I lost my Dad around the same age," was how one of those conversations began. The woman always asked for him. It was as though she knew how he felt about Stella and enjoyed seeing him squirm.

The one chance he had of pinning the girl down was at the riding school.

He took his time about going there. He didn't want to cramp her style. Besides the fact that she loved horses and riding, he felt that it gave her an edge over her friends, Faye and Strawks, who were doing graduate courses. The school was out of town, among rolling hills of sugar cane. The wealth of the sugar farmers was legendary, but he couldn't get excited about sugar. You couldn't do much with it, not like grapes.

His Ford Cortina was small fry among the Mercs and BMWs parked along the white fence. But there was Stella's, originally Roy's, Opel Record and, unbelievably, a free space alongside. So he *had* got the day and time right, he thought as he walked between the rows of stables towards the practice arena.

He was quite unprepared for how Stella had improved. He was close to tears as he watched her canter around on the gelding, Ensign. The school had arranged the purchase of the horse, which was the one time Stella asked for his help. She had been so offhanded as he indicated where she should sign to the extent that Mona, the head clerk, had asked him who *that snooty kid* was. It's all an act, he wanted to say, but that would have revealed more than he wanted to another staff member.

Most of the arrangements with the bank had been made in Cape Town with Constance, so there wasn't much to do, and he rather regretted this. He would have liked them to have a drink together to discuss– under the pretext of how the riding school account was to be administered– how they could settle their differences.

"Can't we be friends?" he had ventured that time, to which she had retorted, "We are," and flounced out with a toss of the ponytail that poo-pooed the lies he had been telling himself.

The lies that told him his waking hours weren't spent remembering how she had looked when she woke up with her hair messed and her blue eyes sticky with sleep (when she stayed at his flat) or in the bank the day the purchase of the horse was finalized (he had thought then that she was going to kiss him and only just stopped himself from grabbing her), that told him his dreams weren't a sweaty storm of their thrashing bodies. In short, the lies that told him he wasn't in love with Stella Quinn.

Again, he was defeated. He had waited in the car while she showered and changed, emerging a good half an hour later without makeup– which he loved best– and fresh in a crisp blue cotton shirt, belted jeans, and flip-flops, with her wet hair twisted into a knot. He was already out of the car, grinning a welcome.

"What are you doing here?" She shoved on her sunglasses, climbed into the Opel, and tossed her handbag onto the passenger seat.

"I'm a member at the club down the road. Care for a sundowner?"

"What for?" Goodness me, she was impossible.

"A friendly chat. Friends *do* chat from time to time. I thought it would be something different. You wouldn't be able to go in otherwise." He liked to think he had some value in her life. That she still needed him, that he could offer her treats, luxuries. Damn, he was being an uncle again.

"You mean because I'm not twenty-one? I do have friends that are over the legal age. Or do you think you're the only one?"

Why did they always end up with the age debacle?

He leaned into the window. He could smell the shampoo in her hair. She had fine down on her upper lip. He wanted to run his tongue along it and down to her mouth. Her lips looked so soft.

He was glad she wasn't looking down to his crotch. With the shades he didn't know where she was looking. "I thought a quiet drink, watch bowls, tennis. We could put our names down for a game. They have a braai later. You cook your own meat or ask one of the waiters to do it for you. We could catch up. We hardly spoke when we went to the bank in Cape Town. Your mother was there, full of her new life. And then when you came out to the farm, there was always someone around. Ma and Pa do that. Invite the whole of the Cape when I'm home." He was watching her face. She looked sad. He tended to forget about her Dad because she hardly ever mentioned him.

Now he needed to cheer her up. "You ride like a pro. Soon they'll have you entered in gymkhanas."

"I have already entered."

"Congrats. Good show. I want to hear all about it."

She turned the key in the ignition, revved a couple of times. Then she seemed to change her mind. "I've been entered as a novice. My favorite is the flag race." She almost smiled. "You ride towards these flags, pick yours up, and ride back with it to your team."

"Let me know when. I'd like to be there. I can take pics for your Mom."

"I have to go." He couldn't see her eyes. He thought there might be tears there. "So long."

She began reversing out before he had quite pulled away from leaning, this time, on the roof of the car.

When he flew home for Christmas, he learnt that she had become a regular visitor at the farm. She and his mother were as thick as thieves. He'd come across them laughing over photos which they wouldn't let him see. He did manage to spot one before Stella snatched it away. He was carrying a puppy in the blow-up pool, buck-naked. She was different on the farm. She still ignored him, but she was happier. She loved hearing about his parents' childhoods in England and how they had come out to South Africa after the war and searched for the right spot for the farm, how a divining stick had helped his father decide, how they lived in a caravan until the house was built. How having a wine farm was a dream come true. People who called thought she was a niece, she fit in that easily.

Of course, the main attraction was the horses. Stella rode all four animals for practice, but it was Bathsheba that Stella loved with a passion. She was an old brood mare that had a habit of suddenly walking backwards, and often bit her handlers. But not Stella. She allowed Stella every sort of liberty, like checking her legs for lameness (you bent a foreleg back sharply and then had the animal stand on it), and cleaning her hoofs with a pick. Bathsheba often had some sort of ailment. If it wasn't the lameness, it was colic. She was always eating weeds, the toxic ones. But Stella seemed to like the contrariness about the old girl.

His father liked the way Stella wasn't 'afraid of elbow grease', as he put it. She would muck out the stables, measure and mix the feed for the horses. She knew their weaknesses, which one liked turnips, the special biscuits Willy made for them. Stella wasn't afraid to discipline them. Bathsheba no longer nipped people for treats as they walked past her door.

All had been going well. Then the old mare had stumbled in the paddock. At first it looked like the usual laminitis but when they called the vet, he diagnosed one of the top bones of the leg as being cracked. As soon as he heard this, his father had taken him aside and asked him to take the shotgun to her. In the meantime, Stella had begun pleading with the vet to save the horse and before they knew it, he had immobilized the leg with plaster of Paris. In his favor, the man had remarked to Stella that the horse's age was against her.

Now, a day and a half later, it was Boxing Day, and his mother was having a crowd over. He had looked in on Bathsheba earlier and she hadn't looked good. He should have telephoned Stella. But how could he tell her what his father wanted him to do? That she should come and say goodbye? So he had done nothing.

He was aware that Stella had arrived because Constance came to where he was laying the fire and said hello. There was no point in asking how Stella was because mother and daughter communicated on a very superficial level.

Now he was immersed in getting the fire ready. He checked beneath the grid. There was still some flame, and instead of shaking salt over it, he decided to wait. Because he had only the weekend and the public holidays, his time on the farm was short. At this time of the year, it was one braai or party after another. Somehow, even when he went for a ride, there were others with him, turning everything into a game and robbing him of quiet reflection.

He walked away from the fire and stood looking down into the garden, golden in the sunlight of an early summer evening. The air was clear and wind-free. He could already see the first few stars pricking the deepening blue. Only on rare occasions could one hear the sea– in the middle of the night maybe, but definitely not in holiday time with cars and motorbikes careening by at all hours. Just knowing it was there, however, was enough.

He turned back to the house, noisy with music and laughter. Faye and Strawks were around somewhere. He envied their friendship, their ease with each other. Mariekie came down the steps with a refill of beer. His father and hers were wine *maats*, in that they traded quantities of one cultivar for another for blending purposes. Arno suspected his father of trying to carry the success of this over into marriage between Arno and their daughter. The girl seemed to be at his elbow at every turn. Stella was bound to have noticed, but short of being outright rude to a guest, there was little he could do. It took a while for the *sosaties* and *boerewors* to get done. It was time he put the steaks on.

"Mariekie, will you fetch a dish for the steak, please? Willy usually leaves one here. She must have other things on her mind," he said in Afrikaans. It was he who had other things on his mind.

"*Seker*." Sure.

He watched the girl waltz away. She had brown wavy hair to her waist and a good figure. She'd be a catch for someone.

Faye and Strawks came down the steps.

"That looks good," said the Norwegian. Arno always thought of Strawks in terms of his nationality. Even before he spoke, you knew he wasn't local.

Faye was frowning. "Arno, have you seen Stella?"

Someone shrieked behind them on the veranda. Someone else turned up the volume on the record player.

"I was thinking of going to look for her." Arno began turning the steaks. "I wanted to get these done first."

"I can do those," said Strawks. "You go and see where our Durbanite has got to. Should I baste them with the marinade?"

"Please."

"This is one of the best things about being in South Africa. The *braaivleis*," Arno heard Strawks say to Faye as he walked around the side of the house towards the stables. If he walked through the house, he was bound to meet Constance, who would ask about Stella.

He could hear the horse's moans from outside. She was lying on her side on a bed of straw. Stella was directing air from an electric fan onto the horse's head and neck which were wet from a sponging down. The mare's head was on a pillow fashioned from sacking and hay. This detail affected Arno more than anything.

He knelt on the straw beside Stella. Her eyes were red from crying.

"The painkillers have worn off," she said in a croaky voice. She had switched the fan off.

"If we give her too much, she'll think she's OK and try to stand up."

She began to cry. He wanted to hold her as he had when he had been mad at her for turning up at the flat, but they were way past that.

"We have to end this, don't we?"

"It was never your decision to make." He wanted to spare her the guilt.

"But I made it mine. I asked the vet to save her. I was thinking of myself. Oh, *God*."

He took the fan and placed it on the floor behind him and took her in his arms. She lay unmoving against his chest in the awkwardness of being on their knees and twisted towards one another.

"Do it," she said against his shirt. The warmth of her breath seeped through to his skin. In his mind, she was a small bird that he had captured against him. Soon she would fly away again.

He crept back into the house through the kitchen and telephoned the vet. Constance came in and he explained what he was doing.

"You can go through to the stable," he said, thinking she might want to comfort her daughter or at least show solidarity.

Constance shuddered. "I've had enough of that for a lifetime."

His father came in then and Arno told him what he had decided. Frank nodded. "Good boy. Poor girl has suffered enough."

"Who?" Constance looked confused. She began prattling about some old dear in the guest house who'd had a stroke and was in hospital. She was like that, Arno noticed, apt to change the subject at the drop of a hat, sometimes mid-sentence. He put it down to the shock of her husband's death.

They each laid a hand on the horse as the vet administered the barbiturate overdose. It seemed an eternity. His father stood by with the vet. His mother stuck her head in but went away again to their guests.

Faye and Strawks seemed to have been standing there for some time. Faye came forward and the girls embraced.

"Bloody shame," said Strawks.

Stella was quiet for the rest of the holiday. She was at the farm much of the time, his mother told him, riding, mostly. She had cleaned out Bathsheba's stable. That was the last time she was going to cry, she had told Ada. He could hear the smile in his mother's voice. She had grown fond of the girl.

"That's what you think. But once you fall in love, there's no getting away from it – the joy and the pain."

But Stella had changed. It was like she had heard what his mother said and taken it to heart. The first time he noticed was after the gymkhana when she came to where he was sitting in the stand and asked– as open as a summer day, "How did I do?"

"You have the proof, don't you?"

She was holding a small silver cup, and a much-coveted blue rosette was pinned to a lapel. Her figure contoured the jacket and stretched the jodhpurs. The masculinity of the shirt, tie, and boots only served to emphasize the woman in her.

The cap swung from a finger. "I would have won that other cup, but my chinstrap wasn't fastened properly."

"Congrats." He was determined not to say more or offer treats.

"Are you still a member of that club…?"

He stared at her for a moment.

"If you wait for me, I'll come with you. Some of the others are going with their folks." His heart flipped and then sank. *Folks.* He was in the parent category.

CHAPTER 16

It is past seven and still it is dark as I go through for breakfast. The vacuum cleaner is humming as I pass the salon. Willy likes to get in there before Lyle arrives. It has been only a couple of weeks since he has been sleeping at Myrna's. I will worry less as time goes by, I tell myself.

"Morning." I kiss Brand and Ellie on the cheek.

I stand at the door. It has stopped raining. Suzi and Woo have already been outside and return smelly and damp and ready for their morning cuddle. Harry and Sally wait for me to step outside and reward their patience. They're wasted here, I think. As I scratch their ears, I promise myself that sometime soon I am going to find someone who really needs them.

Ellie says, dark eyes sparkling over the rim of her glass of orange juice, "And where were you last night?"

Despite the almost platonic nature of the previous night's encounter, I blush. I don't have to explain, but I do anyway.

"Doing a deal with a farmer."

Brand perks up at this. I guessed he would. He has been quiet over the past couple of days, and I want to engage him.

"A deal of a personal nature. Faye and I are planning to help Anika with Valdine. Henk Verwey, who owns the farm where Anika works, wants the same thing. He wants to marry Anika but as things stand, he gets very little time with her." Brand and Ellie know about our outing to Akkerstroom and about Valdine, but in broad terms. I told them, for instance, that Valdine struggles to communicate, but not that she ran away and vomited on me.

"What's your part of the deal, Mom?"

"Reassuring Henk that Faye and I are serious about spending time with Valdine. I can't wait for you guys to meet her. She's a special kid." I help myself to fruit salad. We have fruit salad all year round, another of Ada's practices I have kept up. "I plan to have them over."

He returns to last night's paper.

"Looking for a job?" I ask.

Now it's his turn to blush. Ellie puts a hand on his arm.

"Of course not," he says, without looking up from the paper.

Ellie comes to his aid. "He's been made assistant manager at the Durbanville office."

"It's a bigger branch. Fifty-million more on the books."

"Then why so glum?"

Brand pouts, "I'm not."

He is seldom childish, which alerts me. His cell phone rings and he takes it outside.

Ellie says, "It's a sideways move."

I remember the excitement in the air when they left for dinner. "But the boss took the two of you to dinner."

Ellie's frown suggests there is more to this. Brand is suddenly back, saying they have to go.

I am still puzzling over this when Lyle walks in. He loads a plate from a serving dish in the warming drawer, pops two slices of bread in the toaster, and sits down. I pour him a glass of orange juice, ladle fruit salad into a bowl. I watch him devour food and drink, relishing having my son to myself. I sure as hell am not going to ask after Myrna.

Lyle anticipates this and says, "The tilers are coming today. I've left strict instructions. Myrna's given me a free hand seeing as I'm going to be living with her."

"You're what?"

"Yeah. Permanently. I'll be running my salon from there."

I feel the shock of this run through me, but try to maintain outward calm. "Have you thought this through? Aren't you going to feel obligated?"

"Mom, I thought you'd be pleased. We're pretty cramped here. When Gunner comes, I won't have to sleep in the junk room."

He is exaggerating, but I don't say. Instead I tell him that our Aussie visitor is coming two weeks later than usual.

"Is that OK for the vines?"

Since when is Lyle worried about the vines? I have a mind to go around to Myrna's while Lyle is busy and tell her to quit cradle-snatching.

I need something else to think about, so I call Anika.

I jump in with both feet. "Henk and I had dinner last night. Did he tell you?"

"He did say something to that effect," she says in her mild manner. I sigh with relief. Dealing with the green-eyed monster is a complication I can do without.

"Did he tell you what he was going to talk to me about?"

"He did. That man lives in a dream world."

"How's that?"

"He knows marrying him is impossible."

"Not so impossible with Faye and me around."

I want to err on the side of caution. If Faye doesn't get the chemo and her health takes a nosedive, helping out will depend on me, and I don't know if my commitment will stand up without Faye at my side. Her welfare is, after all, my chief motivation, the reason I am making this call at all. For this reason, I decide that disappointing Anika and Henk is a risk I must take.

"We've been talking about helping with Valdine on a permanent basis." I offer Henk's suggestion of gradual involvement.

"Faye's life is in flux. You could say she is at the crossroads," I add. I check that Anika knows about the mastectomy. Faye told her at the cottage, before Henk and I returned with Valdine. But the fact that Faye has put the kibosh on chemotherapy is news. As I expected, she wants an explanation, which I am unable to give her.

"Which brings me to my second reason for calling," I continue, "one which will go a long way to ensuring, I hope, Faye's continued help with your daughter– and my help, naturally."

I marvel at how conniving I have become. It's all for a good cause, I remind myself.

I bring up the matter of alternative therapies and how Faye has shut the door on this avenue. "She has no family that I can appeal to. She is godmother to my sons. I'm hoping to settle this without involving them. Meeting you again brought back how close Faye and your brother once were. And I thought... I just feel if anyone will be able to convince her to have the chemo, he will."

I hear the humming and guitar chords. Neither is tuneful.

"I don't know..."

"He loved her desperately. They understood one another."

"She *did* cancel the wedding." Anika pauses. She must have found it hard to forgive Faye's apparent cruelty.

I have to try another tack. She doesn't know I have seen the postcard from overseas.

"So, what's he been up to lately?"

"Farming apples and making what they call scrumpy. That's English for apple cider." She mentions the abbey.

"You must miss him."

"And Valdine. He's over there earning pounds to help with her." The pause is so long I begin to wonder if we have become disconnected. "You see, she is his daughter."

Now *I* am silent.

"I haven't adopted her. She is Thorks and Crystal's daughter. They are divorced. He has full custody. I tell Vally she is adopted. It is less hurtful. She has only dim memories of a mother. There's no shortage of money on that side, Crystal's. There's an allowance piling up in the bank, but Thorks is too proud to use it. He couldn't get a job here in South Africa. He tried and tried."

While she lists positions Strawks failed to land, I grapple with these revelations.

"What about Henk? Wouldn't he appreciate another pair of hands?"

"They don't get on. Did he go on about Thorks…?"

"Somewhat."

I hope for an explanation, but none is forthcoming. She goes on, "Finding a job here is even worse if you're a white immigrant. Then he trawled the internet, found this job, managing an apple farm in the UK. We had apples in Norway, you know. We fed the rotten ones to the pigs. So that's where he is, I think. I haven't heard from him for some time. I've been telling myself it is summer over there, so he'll be busy in the orchards. Vally wouldn't understand."

I don't want to worry Anika, but I suspected that by this stage of the summer, the picking would be done.

"Doesn't the farm have a phone?" These days communication is the least of one's worries. "Does Strawks have a cell phone?"

"Abhors the things."

I am glad Anika can't see my face. As the father of a teenage daughter, separated from her by an ocean, how can he afford to shun this most readily available means of contact? I am beginning to wonder if I am seeking help from a crazy person, certainly an irresponsible one. But I press on. "Do you have a number?"

"Can you hold? I'll get my notebook."

I hear Anika, away from the phone, say none too sweetly, "Play in the bedroom, will you…?" A twang and a thump follow. A tantrum? The very basic picture I get of the girl cheers me.

"Here it is."

I am bowled over that Anika has given me access to her brother. At one point in the conversation, though, I thought I might be cast out into utter darkness. *She did cancel the wedding.* Anika is a strange cat. I shelve this thought as I replay what she told me. Strawks is divorced. The man is free. Free for Faye and him to get together. To reconcile. To marry. Girlish romanticism bubbles. So long have I wanted this for my friend that now that there is even a hint of hope, my imagination runs amok. I see him on bended knee, and in quick succession, standing before an altar while he slips on a ring. As she turns to him, a radiance not seen for years transforms her face, a face, last seen as she waved me off after our trip to Akkerstroom. A face that looked like it hurt to smile.

And all the while there has been this beautiful girl, Valdine, there for the taking. Someone who has close connections to the love of Faye's life, who is the very fruit of his loins. Could the connection be any closer to the man she still loves but won't admit it?

I am on a high and no use to fish or fowl. I saddle up Izzy and head for the municipal ground. The earth is firmer under the pounding hooves. Now, instead of damp clods, sand and small stones fly up behind us. Soon we are both sweating. I dismount and walk her home.

I want to share the news with Faye. But this is not the sort of news I can blurt over lunch. Not only will Faye be under pressure to get back to her desk, which I find irritating at the best of times, but it's likely that in my haste I'll bungle it, leaving her to knuckle down afterwards with the tumult of thoughts short-circuiting any success she might have had with those figures of hers.

It's also the sort of news that can't wait. Before I rub Izzy down, I take out my cell phone.

"How do you fancy takeaway Chinese in front of the fire?"

"Sorry, I have to do an all-nighter. Playing catch-up."

This is another moment to thank God for Izzy. Otherwise I might have screamed over the phone. Instead, I say, borderline acid, "You just don't get it. You are still in the convalescent stage. You shouldn't be at work at all, let alone doing twenty-four hours at a stretch."

We've thrashed out the subject of temps. It always ends with her saying that she is the only one that can do certain things, be it the quarterly report, income returns, or year-end accounts. Any help would be cancelled out by her having to explain this and that. She will need to catch up on sleep, I reason, so it would be better if we leave it until the weekend. Once she hears my news, she will wonder why I didn't bash down the door of her office and bawl it via a megaphone. But I give in, as always.

Back from the stables, I see that Anika has left a message for me to call her.

"Have you called the abbey yet?"

"No, I haven't. I must confess I've gone a bit crazy since I heard who Valdine's father is. Crazy happy, that is."

"Have you told Faye?" Of course, she realizes I will tell Faye. Again, I have to say no.

"Good. I was so pleased that you wanted to contact my brother that I left out something important."

I sit down. "What is it, Anika?" I am at the kitchen table and Suzi gets up stiffly and comes over to sit with her grey snout in my lap. Woo, in her basket, arches a pretty eyebrow.

"You need to know what you're up against. You see, he may not want to come back. Still, you may succeed where I have failed. Maybe just hearing about Faye's condition will do it."

"You don't sound terribly sure, Anika."

Willy comes in, points at the kettle, and I wave her back to the laundry and the ironing.

"Before I tell you what he's done, I must explain something." Again she pauses. "Thorkild has been depressed." *Not again*, I think. "He feels he's messed up his life. First, by letting go of Faye too easily and then by being seduced by that…that woman. His ex, Crystal. He regards Valdine's handicap as his punishment."

"Surely not." I want to say how Old Testament, how medieval, but the approach might stem from their Norwegian upbringing, and I don't want to be offensive. "If anyone should be punished, it's the mother."

Anika doesn't answer.

I say, "My father used to say everyone is allowed one major mistake in their lives. We all need something to learn from."

"He was wise."

"Yes, he was, although I didn't appreciate it at the time. I'm sorry it didn't work out for your parents in South Africa. Do you miss them?"

"I do. They are both alive, you know. They're well into their eighties."

"Mine are both dead. My mother had Alzheimer's."

"I'm sorry."

"Thank you."

I wait a bit. "So what has ol' Strawks done? Robbed a bank?" I am determined to be optimistic, although his being in prison would explain much— his unavailability, for one.

"I told you a white lie. That I wasn't sure where he is. It's embarrassing. You see…" She is taking her time. "He is at the abbey. He's decided to throw his all in with the monks of St Bernard's."

"Work there permanently? That would mean promotion, wouldn't it? Good news, surely?"

"He is entering the novitiate."

All I could think of then was that it explained why he wasn't using a cell phone.

CHAPTER 17

It was the year they were turning twenty-one. It was also the year Stella learnt about women's liberation. Faye was coming to the end of her studies and had reported some lively debates on the subject. She had read Germaine Greer and Gloria Steinem and passed on quotes in the letters that lopped between Cape Town and Durban. Stella admired this but found it heavy-going.

Princess Di had seemed such a wonderful role model standing up to Prince Charles, only to die tragically the year before. You wanted your role models alive, like Calista Flockhart in *Ally McBeal,* and Madonna wearing lingerie on top of her outerwear, and Cher in an almost naked but divine dress on the red carpet. But outshining all of these women was Gonda Butters in a framed photograph on a wall of the foyer of the riding school.

In 1955, on her horse Gunga Din, she broke a South African record with a jump of 6 ft 8 in. It wasn't that she was only twelve or that she went on to win other championships all over the world, notably representing South Africa in the summer Olympics of 1992 that mattered most to Stella. What impressed Stella was that it was on Gonda's own horse that she won the under 18 Provincial show jumping competition at age 8. Unfortunately, though, it was not flaunted on the walls of the school.

Everything was going so well. She was still with Miss O'Donnell, who was 'Phyllis' in private and 'Miss O'Donnell' everywhere else. Stella might have looked for a job, say, as a legal secretary– the top of the secretarial pile– but she needed every extra ounce of energy for riding. She was a teacher now at the riding school and had trophies and ribbons to take home. Home was a misnomer. 'Home' was her flat in Durban, she supposed, but she was hardly ever there and had done nothing to improve it. It had the same curtains and furniture Arno had helped her pick out. She seldom brought anyone home. Her life was work, parties, and riding, riding, riding. The beach was for exercising the horses.

She stayed at the farm or at Faye's when she wasn't visiting Bellevue House, where Constance languished until she died soon after Stella turned twenty. The second holiday of that year, her mother kept calling her Maudie, the name of her personal maid at the guest house. The next holiday, she hadn't recognized Stella at all. Then Aunt Beryl called long distance. Her mother had gone missing from the guest house a couple of times– once overnight. She had been found sleeping on a bench in a nearby park. They were advised by Constance's doctor to book her into somewhere where you needed a code to get in and out, where there was round-the-clock supervision. Constance wouldn't even know where she was, her aunt remarked with a sob.

Constance had used up the greater part of what Roy had left them, but Stella had enough for a small house, but not enough for stables as well. She felt lonely just thinking about living in a house on her own, but a riding school with a rented flat nearby, now that sounded fab. She had her eye on a riding school up in the Westville hills, just outside Durban. It needed some fixing up, but that could be done gradually as money came in from fees.

She had no worries about drawing custom. She was gaining a name for herself in riding circles. Arno could help her with a business plan. She knew he was dying to do something. She didn't want to appear a total brat. But she couldn't help the feeling of glee at the thought of signing the purchase agreement or deed of transfer or whatever documents you needed for ownership without having to rely on his and her mother's pesky power of attorney.

Of course, Faye wanted her to move to the Cape. Her selling point was that Stella no longer needed to put a thousand miles between herself and her mother.

Lately, Faye couldn't seem to make a point without backing it with numbers. Being near Faye and Strawks and the Gideons was something to consider, yet being independent had become a habit. She wore it like a badge of honor. *This is me, and I don't need anyone.*

She only saw Arno in Durban at the bank or at gymkhanas. She couldn't believe that she had once panted after him. He was never going to make a move, and now she was pleased. She was free to live her life as she wanted. At the farm, they behaved like buddies. They teased one another. They weren't afraid to tell one another off when they thought the other one needed it. He understood why she held out for Durban. Mariekie must have become fed up with waiting for him to propose because she had married another wine farmer's son. They had a baby and their farm was in the Overberg, which meant that these days they seldom saw her. Arno dated other girls, Ada told her, but Stella had yet to meet one. Perhaps that was what he told his mother to keep her off his back. Either way, Stella didn't mind.

"You are the daughter I never had," Ada said recently. Stella didn't think Ada would have said that while Constance was alive. She was touched. Arno was born when Ada was forty-five. Stella had difficulty imagining that tiny frame pregnant with lanky Arno. They thought they were going to be childless, Ada told her. "Now we have two children." Her face had lit up. She was well into her seventies, but you wouldn't have guessed.

She took Stella to her bedroom and opened her jewelry box. "I want you to have these when I'm gone," she said.

Frank, too, had his ways of expressing affection. The day after Bathsheba was put down and when all of their guests had gone home, he asked Stella to come into his study. He quietly closed the door and took her in his arms. It was one of those long hugs that you half enjoy, and half want to get away because it was too tight.

"I never realized how much the old mare meant to you," he said, holding her away from him and looking deep into her eyes. "You are one of those people who feel animals are our equals, don't you? That they feel everything we do, understand everything, but just can't speak. I had a sister like that. Long gone. You're just like her. She was always at loggerheads with my father when he had to put animals down, about expensive treatments at the vet she considered necessary and over who he sold animals to. The way some of the animals were transported– to the abattoir, for instance, distressed her."

Faye and Stella had some fun times. The best was after Constance died and while Strawks was away in Bethany helping his parents pack up for Norway. Faye tended to cling to her folks, but Stella, now with money to spend, talked her friend into a weekend in Knysna. It was a day away by car. Any further, and Faye wouldn't have agreed. But it was far enough to give them that feeling of release, of freedom from responsibility.

They got quite drunk the first night, abandoning Faye's Mini at the restaurant and walking back to their chalet along the edge of the lagoon in the moonlight. They spoke deep into the night. Faye and Strawks were getting engaged on Christmas Eve, just days before his parents flew back to Lorvik. There was the party to talk about, who was coming and what they were going to wear. Inevitably, the subject of sex came up. Faye and Strawks had had sex a few times in his digs in Stellenbosch, Faye said, but had decided to hold off until they were married, which would be as soon as they had jobs. They had each gone for interviews, some of which looked promising.

Stella wanted to know why they had stopped having sex. She wouldn't have dared ask, but the wine (they had opened another bottle when they got in) had made her daring. She felt like an ignoramus where sex was concerned but would never have let on.

"For the sex to be good, you need to be together all the time. You don't know one another properly until you live together. Plus, the walls at res are paper thin and you share a bathroom with several others."

"How was it?"

"The first time was an utter disaster. Strawks was lasting a little longer before we decided to stop. I found this old book, *Sex Manners for Men,* and I gave it to him to read."

"You didn't." Stella kicked her legs in the air. They were lying against pillows on one of the beds, and wine slopped onto her pajama top. She drained what was left in her glass, remembering how Strawks wanted *her* to instruct *him*, and now here was *Faye,* handling it like a pro.

"And you? Any luck in that department?"

Stella shook her head, suddenly sober.

Faye reached across to the bedside table for the wine and filled their glasses. "I don't know how you do it– holding off all those guys pounding on your door."

"I'm known as the Ice Maiden, don't you know." She took a glug of wine. "Guys have always found me a challenge."

"What's that supposed to mean?"

"Oh heck, I don't know." Stella leaned back against the pillows. "Perhaps I'm going to be one of those horsey spinsters. They get it from riding."

"What, from rubbing up and down on the saddle?"

"*And* bouncing up and down."

Giggling ended that one, but a couple of days later, a Sunday, lingering over lunch in the Wilderness on the way back, the two women had turned off the national road and found this little place nestling on a slope among trees. Craft, furniture, and art shops peeked out between the thick trunks. You had to step over tree roots and read directions off quaint little signboards.

The restaurant was wood-framed and surrounded by big glass windows, kept warm by an old-fashioned anthracite stove at its center. The smoke was what had attracted them, funneling out of a chimney in the pointed roof and filtering through the branches of some special trees with plates with the botanical and English names screwed into them.

Faye didn't want to be away more than two nights. Stella would have loved to spend longer.

Why, she thought, have I chosen a friend who is still attached by the umbilical cord? Opposites attract, seemed the answer. She admired Faye's loyalty, something seemingly lacking in herself. Faye was going to be a wonderful wife, but they would need to live near Faye's parents, Stella decided. She couldn't see her friend ever immigrating.

"Has Strawks said he'd ever want to go back to Norway?" Stella asked.

"He's never going back, he says. They're in the dark ages over there. You've heard him say that?" Stella nodded. "He'd never seen a deodorant, let alone used one, until he came to South Africa. Also, everyone is the same. Boring, he says. He loves the diversity here. The opportunities. The politics don't faze him. Above all, he loves the sun."

"He hasn't suffered under it, though, the politics. He hasn't had to do national service, for instance."

"You mean do the two years, like Arno? He was in the army, wasn't he? Did border service. That must have been rough. Ada said how worried she was when he was in Angola. Does Arno moan about that– about people who for one reason or another get out of it? Some people hate immigrants. They say they live on the fat of the land but don't contribute."

"Arno doesn't like to talk about the army. He certainly hasn't moaned about Strawks. He does say, though, that *it knocks the shit out of you.*" Stella attempted a deeper tone, a tone Arno sometimes adopted when he thought his young friends needed to be put right. They giggled until their eyes watered.

"As long as he doesn't say it would do us women good to do the time."

"He'd never say that. Not to me, anyway. He's very careful what he says to me. Oh, we joke, but keep away from anything too serious. I learn a lot from him about business. And horses, of course. But he never tells me what to do."

They thought about that for a while. The waitress asked if they wanted anything more. They ordered coffee and watched as she hurried off to the kitchen.

"She's dying to knock off," Faye said. They were the only ones left in the restaurant. She turned to Stella. Her big brown eyes glistened. Stella was always a little scared when Faye was like this– super serious. "What have you done to make him so wary of you? I thought by now you would have made up. You never forgave him for putting Bathsheba down."

"I didn't need to forgive him. The vet did it. I needed to forgive myself for making her linger." That had been a turning point. She had been very green, very open and vulnerable. She felt more grown-up now. More his equal. "We're friends."

"On your terms."

"What do you mean?"

"You don't let him in. He adores you, you know. Just one word and he'll be in like a shot."

"Oh, stop it." Stella was blushing.

Winding down Sir Lowry's Pass, which signaled their proximity to Strand and the farm where Faye was going to drop her off, they began finalizing the party arrangements.

"Have you decided what you want to do for *your* big two-one?" Faye asked.

Faye's birthday had been in the spring and the Morriseys had booked a private dining room at the Mount Nelson Hotel below Table Mountain. The menu was specially chosen and there were wines for every course. Faye's birthday gift had been the Mini, pink and sparkling new.

Stella's birthday was on January 2nd – *tweede Nuwe Jaar* (second New Year) as it was referred to by locals. It was the day the city center was roped off for the colorful and lively Coon Carnival in which bands, whose members were essentially of Cape Malay descent, competed for top honors.

"We'll all be at the Parade during the day, won't we?"

Faye nodded in response.

"You'll be wearing your diamond. I can't wait to see it."

"Neither can I. I've told him to get bottom of the range. We'll need our money for furniture and so on."

They were nearing the end of the descent and Faye was slowing down as the turn-off came into view.

"Come on." Faye flicked a glance at Stella. "It's your birthday, mutt. What can we expect?"

"Oh, gee. Ada wants to have a braai. Willy whispered that a band has been booked. Frank has bought firecrackers. But let's just focus on you and Strawks' great day, shall we?"

Stella couldn't help feeling excited. She had bought a new dress and was going to have her hair done for once. Really though, it was what the birthday represented that was giving her a buzz.

She recited the famous lines from the poem by William Ernest Henley:

"Beyond this place of wrath and tears
Looms but the Horror of the shade,
And yet the menace of the years
Finds, and shall find me unafraid.

It matters not how strait the gate,
How charged with punishments the scroll,
I am the master of my fate,
I am the captain of my soul."

"Too masculine, you think? Ms. Steinem and Greer wouldn't be too happy."

"I like masculine," murmured Faye, looking starry-eyed.

———————————

They drove to the engagement party in separate cars. Ada and Frank weren't going to stay until the end. Ada wanted to do some prep for the Christmas lunch before she went to bed. Willy always left to join her family in Upington on the morning of Christmas Eve returning a week after New Year. Stella said she'd help when she got in.

"I've got a better idea. Why don't you and Arno sleep over and drive back in the morning? You don't want to find you've missed some of the fun. Arno can have an extra beer or two and not worry about safety issues."

"The Morriseys have a full house."

"Oh gosh, I'd forgotten. They have four extra. Mr. and Mrs. Johansens, Strawks and their daughter. What's her name?"

"Anika."

The Morriseys' place was more Christmassy than usual. They had ordered lights for the outside– unusual in South Africa, and inside, bunches of balloons added to the usual streamers as well as tinsel, holly and mistletoe. The fireplace in the lounge was lined with fresh pine branches and moss on which was arranged a hand-carved nativity scene, a gift from the Johansens, Faye told her. Her friend looked excited, even feverish– Strawks equally so, as he pulled Faye's arm through his.

"How are you feeling?" she asked them, utterly unaware of what was to follow.

They looked into each other's eyes. It began as a question, deepening until their eyes locked. Stella was stunned. Until then they had hidden it, she realized. Out of politeness or out of diffidence, she wasn't sure. She felt shut out. They had forgotten she was there, or anyone else for that matter.

A wave of embarrassment hit her. She felt stupid standing there– juvenile, a babe in arms.

How had she missed what had been growing under her nose? The intensity, the intimacy that burrowed into the very heart of the other, this knowledge of one another that was alien, foreign because it was entirely outside her experience.

Why hadn't someone warned her? Anger flared. She wanted to bash their smug faces together.

"Come," Arno said at her elbow, leading her out onto the front porch. He handed her a tumbler of pale gold liquid.

She sipped. "What's this?" she said, grimacing. "Whiskey?"

"You looked like you needed it."

Only family and close friends had been invited, which made the atmosphere more intimate.

When the time came for the announcement, Strawks asked Faye to climb up a ladder (wound around with brightly colored crinkle paper) in order to retrieve the small box in the grasp of the angel on top of the tree. They had a good view of Faye's curvy legs in her peacock blue silk party frock. Laughter rang out as Strawks called out instructions for the untying of the bow holding the precious package in place. It was obvious Faye had been completely taken by surprise, because when she was down again, and had turned to face her audience, she was blushing right down to her décolletage.

The record player clicked into action as Strawks slipped the ring on Faye's finger. *You are my Special Angel* by Bobby Vinton, she learnt later, flooded the room. All sickeningly old-fashioned, was all Stella could think. Later Arno told her Glad had helped Strawks with the choice of song. The thought of how this must have proved to Strawks that he was accepted by the Morriseys should have crossed her mind, but she was too lost in her own misery.

Now the mistletoe, hanging from a central light, justified its positional worth. She squeezed her eyes shut.

She hadn't ever felt this wretched, even after her Dad died. Frank and Ada left soon after the cake and 5th Avenue Cold Duck. They wanted to get back before it was dark. Frank's eyesight wasn't as good these days and Ada had never learnt to drive. Stella felt their absence keenly. They had a wonderful stabilizing effect on any gathering, or was it just on her? Perhaps if the other oldies had taken themselves off and the young ones were left to roll back the carpet, dust off an LP like *The Springbok Hit Parade* and rock the night away, she might have loosened up and begun enjoying herself.

But around eleven, Mr. and Mrs. Johansen announced timidly that they needed to get ready for midnight mass. Miss Goody-Two-Shoes Faye took up the clarion call. Strawks, Anika, Glad, and Bert Morrisey followed suit, effectively breaking up the party.

Stella and Arno were the last to leave, bar Faye and Strawks in Faye's Mini. Stella and Faye called to one another through the car windows: "Happy Christmas. See you soon."

Faye, "Roll on the big two-one."

"You bet."

Arno tried making conversation as they whizzed along in his pride-and-joy BMW he'd driven down from Durban. He'd been saving for it since *klaar*-ing out of the army. Behind, the sky glowed purple, and ahead, it was slate black. She should be happy for Faye and Strawks, but resentment boiled like larva ready to spill over the banks of her carefully laid plans. Because that was what was at the root of her new mood, a realization that her life as she saw it panning out lacked that essential ingredient, what her friends had in spades. Everything paled beside this commitment of theirs, and she has been blind to the extent of their happiness. Against it, the prospect of her birthday palled. That cynical expression came to mind. *It's just a number.*

Arno was saying, "It's tough for them starting out with Strawks' folks in far off Norway. Will they come back for the wedding, do you think?"

"I doubt they can afford it," Stella said crossly.

She felt him looking at her, but she refused to look his way.

If only she could have shared what was troubling her. But what could she have said? *I had a glimpse of love and it shocked me.* What could he say to that? What was there left to say after that? So they drove on in silence.

CHAPTER 18

I am in the Jeep heading for town along the N2 highway. Another storm is on the way. A strong north-wester pummels the driver's side, sending stray plastic bags and other litter across my path. It is eerily dark at five in the afternoon, which makes one almost long for the heavy downpour that is predicted. The first big drops smear the screen for fearful seconds until it clears, revealing the mounting traffic. The pelting on the roof begins, and I switch off the radio.

I am feeling happier than I have for a while. I have this wonderful news to impart. Faye had sounded vague, even fretful when I checked at lunchtime that she had remembered that I was spending the night with her.

"Since when do I forget something like that?" she grumbled.

This is to be expected, I tell myself. You don't get over a brush with death in five minutes, the thought of which adds to my determination to fill her in about Strawks and Anika's strike out of left field. That part– that he is training to be a monk– can wait. I am still grappling with it. And as for contacting him, I have no clue how I am going to proceed, especially with all efforts on that score rendered *verboten*.

"Unless it is a matter of life and death, he is not to be contacted for nine months." I could hear the despair begging for dominance. How awful for Anika to have her parents return to the old country, and then her brother leave her stranded *and* with his kid, whom I know she loves like her own, but *still*.

Learning about the conditions of the novitiate was like being flung back in time. Monks scratching away with quills on parchment came to mind. Strawks will spend much of that time on his own. This is to ensure that he comes to the right decision. He has nine months to decide if the lifestyle is for him. Then he does another two years, the novitiate proper, which can be extended to as much as seven years, before he takes the final step. These days what the men give up in the way of personal freedom, possessions, and sexual activity is referred to as a donation. So instead of making a vow, he will be giving a donation.

The kitchen is in darkness as I arrive, *Chinese meal for 2* and a couple of bottles of cab sav in hand. I have my key, turn it, and am inside. I switch on the light. Fergus comes pattering towards me, tail down. I pick him up, give his beard a little tug to cheer him up and we head for the bedroom.

Fergus hops onto the bed by way of a footstool and fills the space next to Faye. He whimpers, and then rests his head on his paws.

"Faye, wakey wakey." I kiss her on the cheek.

"Star." Her breath is foul.

I have only switched on the bedside light, but she shades her eyes.

"It has an infection." She points to the recidivist boob.

My heart pounds. "And…?"

"We're trying an antibiotic. I may have a stitch or something left in there. It's the body's way of pushing out something it doesn't want. If it goes on too long, he'll do a local. Snip it out."

"How long have you been on the antibiotic?"

"A week."

"And it's no better?" *And you hadn't thought to inform me?*

She nods. "Can you get me some water? I'll take a couple of painkillers."

Afterwards I make tea for her and pour red wine for myself. We lean back against the pillows, and I stroke the top of her head. I can't bear it that my friend is once more suffering. That she has been in touch with the doctor, I am grateful for, and a Plan B is in the offing, should the discomfort continue. That's for now. For her *future* health, as far as that can be reckoned, I have my secret plan.

I can't hold it in much longer. There should be a drum roll. Faye doesn't look ready for any sort of news– good or bad. Perhaps I should wait until the painkiller has worked and we have eaten?

Then I think, *darn it.*

"Faye, I know who Valdine's father is." No reaction. "And her mother as well." The 'mother' part is a downer, but that can't be helped. The 'father' part will overshadow it.

A reply muffled by the duvet, "Who?"

"Strawks."

"Strawks," she says dully. This is not what I expected at all. She thinks for a moment. "Well, where is he?"

"That's what Henk said."

"Henk? Henk told you?"

"Anika told me. Henk just thinks badly of Strawks because he has gone off to work in England to make money for himself and Valdine. Henk wants to marry Anika but it's pointless as long as she has the girl around her neck. We know that. There is plenty of money, but Strawks is too proud to use it and couldn't get a job here so he found one in England."

"Totally confusing. Who is the mother?"

"Strawks' ex, Crystal. She's given Strawks full custody. She has arranged for money to go into Strawks' account every month but he's too proud to use it. Oh, I said that didn't I?"

When Faye puts her hands over her ears, I realize I've made a complete dog's breakfast.

She has barely moved except for closing her eyes. After a while she says, "I went to the shrink, you know."

This time I wait. No more charging in.

"He says my not wanting chemo is a cry for help. A cry for help, I ask you. I have all the help I need. There's you, the doctor, people at work. If I'm not there they phone, come around. Take a look in the fridge. It's full of food. Sorry. You've brought something. I should have told you I have all this lasagna, breyani ..." She sighs and again closes her eyes.

She doesn't want dinner. She also doesn't want mashed avocado pear on toast. That used to be a favorite. What about a small bowl of Rice Krispies, or banana 'pennies' and custard? Nursery food, but what the heck. But no, she doesn't want anything. I warm the chicken chop suey and pick desultorily. Fergus is beside me and I fill his bowl. The boy is hungry. I clean and fill his water bowl. The leftovers in their polystyrene boxes would add to an already congested fridge so I stow them in the freezer compartment. In the lounge I pull the TV set on its wheeled stand away from the wall, unplug it and push it down the passage. Why hasn't Faye ever invested in a second set, I wonder. Does she feel it will desecrate her parents' memory or is it just more of her lack of self-indulgence. The set fits at the end of the bed like it was meant to. I track down an extension cord and connect up. Lying beside Faye I scroll from *Animal Cops Philadelphia* to *World's Greatest Motorbike Rides* to a replay of *Downton Abbey*.

A rasping breath wakes me. For a moment it's Arno snoring and I am ready with an elbow. But it's Faye. Fear replaces disappointment. I place my hand on her forehead. Roy used to say I was 'in tiger country' when I ran a fever. Well, Faye is in there now, the jungle of ill-health. I fetch a bowl of lukewarm water liberally squirted with Dettol. I pull back the duvet, carefully slip a couple of clean bath sheets underneath her.

"Huh...?" she says.

"Nursie here," I sing.

I remove everything except her underwear. She lies mutely while I squeeze excess water from the sponge and begin my pogrom against bacterial invasion. Her face and neck shine with moisture that will catch the cooling air. Then I turn my attention to her shoulders and arms. I work around the injured breast. The flesh is bright red on either side, the micropore plaster covering the troubled area at the base.

I wipe around her other breast, remembering how the doctor asked if she didn't want both breasts removed. He said that some women didn't like the idea of being lopsided. Also, he said, many women want both breasts removed to obviate the chance of a lump appearing in the other breast. It didn't necessarily follow, he had said, but having both removed is recommended. Not surprising, Faye stuck with the first option. Does she hate herself? Is this what is motivating her?

She had asked how not being lopsided was achieved. In the case of the single mastectomy, he'd said, a particular type of implant is used allowing for an adjustment of size down the line, the first to be carried out after the swelling has subsided.

Well, the swelling is back. I drag the wet sponge down her tummy, along each leg and the tops of her feet. I lift up an arm and she is giggling even before my sponge makes contact, resulting in fresh agony. I continue grimly, rolling her onto the side with the healthy breast, wiping down the exposed surfaces of her back, arms, legs, feet. Again she giggles, but this time ends with a spasm of shivering, signaling success.

I *have* to get in touch with the doctor. I will discuss this with Faye in the morning. For now, I slip on a fresh pair of pajamas, ever so carefully, and hey presto, she drinks a glass of milk. Soon she is sleeping peacefully.

I am wide awake, however, and cloaked in a blanket from the linen cupboard. I walk out onto the porch. Fergus hasn't followed me, which is telling. The storm has worn itself out. The first fingers of light creep up behind the line of rooftops softened by the lace of trees. The faint rumble of traffic and cold air tainted with exhaust fumes alerts me to the working day. I rest my denim-clad buttocks on the wall to wait for the sun.

How much will Faye remember of our earlier conversation, I wonder. I am not so naïve as to believe that there won't be some unfinished business to be worked through before she is able to welcome Strawks back into her life, even as indirectly as through contact with his teenage daughter.

And as to getting hold of him and persuading him to come back to her, I believe I am on the right track. What the psychologist said confirms my reading of Faye's decision to forego chemotherapy. It is not a reasoned decision. It is a reaction to her life, to where she is in her life. No one can know what is truly in someone else's heart but my reading of her is that she is stuck. *Join the club*, I think. I am also in a stagnant phase. We are put on this earth with others of similar leanings, coupled with others from whom and with whom we can learn similar or complimentary lessons. My quest for Strawks is just as much her quest. We are journeying together.

I don't know how, but I will find a way to bring Strawks to her. I have to. Not only for her sake but mine.

CHAPTER 19

Faye hadn't known that she needed anyone until she met Strawks. Life with Mum and Dad had been absorbing, if demanding– although Faye wouldn't have thought of it in that way then. She was too full of love and concern for her father and her mother indirectly. Few people knew that Bert was a diabetic and had been injecting himself since the age of sixteen– what had sown the seeds for his leaning towards medicine. He had read up on diabetes and it had grown from there. A thirst for knowledge, followed by concern for others who suffered similarly, culminating in, and most important of all, how there was help at hand. Glad, twelve years older, had been a theatre nurse at one of his first tonsillectomies and had been instantly attracted. There was something about the young doctor you simultaneously admired and wanted to protect.

Glad and Bert had emigrated with five-year-old Faye after a receptionist in Bert's practice in a village in the West Country had told everyone that the reason their doctor had been out of action was because he was a diabetic. He was young then, and hadn't learnt to balance his jabs with food and rest and work. He teetered on the edge of a coma for ten days. His patients, fearing that his disability would interfere with their health needs, left in droves. Another country (there were other advantages) and a big city like Cape Town was less likely to hold the same dangers. Friends who had emigrated reported back on the famous South African hospitality, a general lack of small-mindedness, and a touching trust of the medical profession.

It had become second nature to help make sure her father had his egg or fish for breakfast, that he rested in addition to eating when he came home at lunchtime, that he was shielded from patients who might harass or drain him, but above all, that his secret remained hidden. Mother and daughter had become so adept at concealing the secret that Stella hadn't known about it until after his death.

Faye had friends before, but they never lasted because sooner or later they became curious. Stella hadn't asked questions. She seemed to accept everything at face value. She had her own parent issues which occupied her when she wasn't thinking about or enjoying her horses and riding. When Stella slept over, it wasn't a cause for concern because Bert medicated himself at his surgery. Besides, he was such a warm, cheerful person– playing golf and generally looking so good, that you would have had to be a Sherlock Holmes to guess.

Faye and Glad had been a little worried when he took on the locum to help a friend, a fellow student from medical school. By its size, Bethany reminded Glad of the village they had left behind and the likelihood of gossip. It had to be admitted, Bethanites and farmers were curious, but it had more to do with who would be foolish enough to come to their off-the-track dusty backwoods. Bert, it turned out, was a fresh breeze after their dour regular man, and they began popping into the surgery at the merest sniff or ache to get a look at him (if they hadn't met him before) or quiz him on life in the big city. Also, six weeks wasn't long enough, Glad and Bert opined, for skeletons to come sneaking out of the cupboard, and they were right.

Strawks wouldn't have stood a chance against the Morrisey laager if he hadn't, firstly, won Faye over when he pushed the bale of hay onto Prop, and secondly, persisted with an offensive, albeit clumsy, charm. Stubbornness was his strength. It was also his undoing, as she discovered much later. Back in Bethany, in the weeks before Stella's Dad died, he, Stella, and Faye did everything together. Then after Stella left, Anika made a third as they swam, played tennis, and danced. Then, he had been simply a friend– a bumptious clown given to practical jokes, like putting a moth down the front of her blouse to hear her scream, mounting an untrained horse so she could see him get bucked and laugh, and then, arriving to pick her up for a fancy dress party as a Goth, in this instance, to hear her gasp.

Besides being in black from head to toe, he had combed black shoe polish through his hair, used a black khoki pen on his lips and eyebrows, and hung some old bicycle chains around his neck. His methods were always over the top, which meant you just couldn't take him seriously.

Then he was in Cape Town. He called from the farm to ask her to meet him at the station and her mother cooked a special meal and Bert drove them to Stellenbosch. They even trooped up to inspect his room. Glad and Bert bade their farewells, leaving the young ones to say theirs.

Ever since she saw him waiting with his suitcase outside Cape Town station, she had felt differently about him. Their third wheel was missing, leaving them to face one another and their feelings. She wasn't ready. She had only just turned eighteen, and then there was her concern for Bert. She had been part of his support system for so long that it was difficult to imagine any other sort of existence. If she had ever imagined meeting someone and getting serious, which was seldom, she would have been well into her twenties, studies completed and well-established in her profession. And the person, too, this supposed man of her dreams, would be tall, dark and handsome and also a professional, an architect or university lecturer– someone whose intellect she would fall in love with before anything else. And here was this gawky boy of middling height, with the ridiculous hair and not particularly good-looking– someone who cleaned out pigsties, broke in horses, and checked bunches of grapes for powdery mildew.

"Can we go steady?" he asked.

"Go steady. Isn't that for school kids?"

"Just say yes."

"OK. Yes. But it doesn't mean open season with me."

"No. OK. I'll phone you. If I don't, it's because I've run out of cash, not because I don't care."

They had gone downstairs after that, and he had waved them off. He hadn't kissed her, she realized, on the way home. *Well, you weren't exactly encouraging*, she told herself.

The first month he called sporadically. He sounded glum. Then her mother said Faye should invite him for the weekend. He took a train and a bus. When he arrived, he looked different. He had lost weight and some of his bonhomie. He said he was missing home.

"But you emigrated and went to boarding school. You should be used to these sorts of changes," she said.

Then the truth came out.

"I hate studying," he said. "Books and I don't go well together. I didn't know there was going to be so much theory. We're going to be farmers, chrissakes."

"Next time, bring your books," Glad Morrisey said. "Faye is good at studying. She'll help you. Come every weekend."

"That's very kind," he said, but he didn't look confident.

Later he told Faye that he didn't have money for the train and bus fare. When her father heard about this he said, "The boy needs a job," and arranged for Strawks to caddie a professional golfer at the club, quickly proving Bert's confidence in him.

And so they settled into a routine. Strawks caddied on Saturdays and studied with Faye on Sundays. He returned to the farm in the longer breaks, but at Easter and Michaelmas he and Faye went on jaunts in Glad's runabout. He was used to being regarded as foreign and therefore different, so things that might have bothered someone who had grown up in Cape Town didn't bother him. He went on political rallies, to begin with, but he kept praising the Nationalist government who had smoothed the way for his family to emigrate when he should have been shouting it down. She was afraid he might get beaten up by the stick-swinging lot– the ones who smashed cars and shop windows– and talked him out of it after that. He gave in so easily that she realized he had only been participating to please her.

He sat with her at Sandy Bay. She had always wanted to go topless, and Stella thought it stupid and wouldn't go with her.

"I'm blushing," Faye said.

"You're sunburnt, is all," he had countered.

He glanced at her breasts like they were apples on the farm in Norvik. She might have been disappointed, had she not been squirming with embarrassment.

Then he spotted a crop of marijuana growing in the next-door garden, climbed over the fence and came back with a handful, roots and all. To her they looked like any old weed. He was going to replant them in the Morrisey's garden, but she stopped him. He would have been expelled if he had been discovered with them at the hostel, so he hung them in the garage to dry. If her father noticed, he didn't say anything. Faye thought Strawks had forgotten about them. Then, one evening when her parents were at a social function, he brought the dried-up things in, crushed them between greaseproof papers, took a packet of Rislas out of his haversack, and rolled them each a *zol*. They took a blanket out onto the lawn and a bottle of wine. She'd had the most wonderful time, singing and dancing in her bare feet on the grass while he became more and more morose, saying he should be helping his folks on the farm and not sinking their money into varsity fees. (It was true that his parents weren't doing well on the pig farm, but usually he was quite pragmatic about it, listing alternatives for them like selling up and trying another sort of business or getting jobs.) To cheer him up, she tried to kiss him. That was when he swung away and vomited into a flowerbed. Then he had to run into the house. He had diarrhea.

"Never again," he said, and that was that.

Another time they had visited a sex shop. He bought a dildo for her and some cream for himself that promised *twenty-four hour pleasure*. Of course, she was wondering when they were going to use the gadgets.

He knew what she was thinking and said, "My roommate is going away for the long weekend. We could try them out then."

Not the most romantic offer, but he surprised her with the gift of a rose when she walked in, a table set for two with plastic knives and forks, a bottle of wine and a three-course dinner cooked on an electric hot plate.

Stella had warned her about varsity students and smelly socks (Stella had once raided a men's res in Durban with girlfriends). The room smelled strongly of air-freshener, but otherwise looked clean and neat. After the meal of cheese rolled in slices of ham, tinned spaghetti, and shop-bought pots of chocolate mousse, they washed the saucepan and two plates and cutlery in a hand-basin down the passage in the bathroom.

They lay side by side on his single bed. His fingertips touching hers sent shocks up her arms. Her dildo was till in her handbag and his cream was nowhere in sight. There was only the light from the candle flickering on the table.

He turned to her, hitching himself on an elbow.

"Faye Morrisey, will you be my forever love?" His accent seemed more pronounced. Its foreignness always gave her a thrill. He smoothed her hair to one side and kissed her gently. She realized with a gasp that she already was his forever love.

"I don't have a ring, but I just wanted you to know— before we do it— that I'm never going to leave you. If there's ever going to be any chasing away, you'll have to do it."

"So I'm stuck with you?"

In answer he closed her mouth with his.

———————————

Soon they were talking about marriage. The finals loomed. Then, unbelievably, graduation, and finally, their engagement the Christmas Ma and Pops Johansen were heading back to Norway. (Their return was being subsidized by an aging uncle, who needed help running his pig farm).

She was taking instruction as a Catholic, although Strawks only seemed to go to mass when his parents were around. This was also why they weren't sleeping together, which she hadn't told Stella because she didn't think Stella would understand. Stella, as well as Glad and Bert, wasn't a churchgoer, but Faye loved the ritual with the changes each season brought. The altar and priest's vestment went from the everyday green to purple in Lent, a season of fasting and penitence, for instance, to white for the heady celebration of Christmas with extra candles and brass bowls of poinsettias everywhere. Then there were the hundreds of years of tradition. You felt safe against the ravages of time, like her father's energy levels which were waning. Because of this, he had taken on a young partner to share the load of the practice and was playing less golf. When he did play, he complained about other players holding him up or about the poor state of the greens. Even about the inroads of Egyptian geese that hissed when a player came near a nest. Glad and Faye shared a look but didn't dare sigh or show any sign of what they were thinking. Worried thoughts were what they were thinking— thoughts about Bert retiring and having quality of life before it was too late. Oftentimes, Faye heard her parents' raised voices when she was in bed at night.

Of course, this didn't help her relationship with Strawks, because as with Stella, Faye hadn't told him about the diabetes. She knew she would have to eventually, but she kept putting it off. The years of restraint held in place by fear of the consequences were just too difficult to surmount.

How it affected their relationship was that, without consciously admitting it, she was allowing the arrangements for the wedding and the busyness of their new working lives to crowd out the possibility of coming clean.

She had curtains to make for the flat which was to be their new home. Hilliard Carpets, her employer, was fitting carpets at a hefty discount. Strawks slept on the new double bed in a sleeping bag but the rest of the time he was at the Morriseys, when he wasn't at the Cape Wine Academy working towards Cape Wine Master or Toastmasters to give him a better command of English. He didn't complain about his daily commute to the Simonsberg district of Stellenbosch. Driving along in the work van, he experimented with different sales pitches, he told Faye. Having the use of the van had tipped the scales over jobs with more hands-on farming. But there was plenty of time for that and he had his spade in to a certain extent with Perlheim Estate because although he was in sales, he could work in the vineyard out of business hours. He wasn't getting paid, but the experience was invaluable. His course at Elsenburg had been general because at that stage he hadn't known what sort of farming he wanted to do. Spending time with Arno and his father helped him make up his mind, but by then it was too late to change courses. On advice and sponsorship from Bert, he had joined the golf club, something else that ate into his and Faye's time together.

"It's the best and most enjoyable way to do business," his future father-in-law said. "Invite customers to play a round or two."

Strawks hadn't the heart to tell her father that customers would expect him to pay for them. But that would happen as he moved up the ladder at Perlheim, he assured Faye.

Her target was to get the books up to date at Hilliard's before the wedding, so she could go away on honeymoon, a week in Mauritius, with peace of mind. They took her on after being without a bookkeeper for several months. That she was her own boss outweighed the extra hours she was putting in. The auditors had promised help, but already Mr. Hilliard Sr. was complaining about their fees. Pride kicked in. She would fill in the missing pieces herself. All the while she was tracking down invoices, bank statements, and stock sheets, she was getting to know suppliers, bank staff, their own staff, and customers.

Glad and Bert loved Strawks. He would have stood no chance if they hadn't. This was another thing that she kept to herself but did wonder about in the middle of the night. It was the case of the chicken and the egg. Did she love him because her parents loved him? Would she still love him if her parents didn't? Which led to– if her parents' opinion was so important, then did she love her parents more than him? And what sort of a question was that, anyway? You loved your parents and your fiancé in different ways, didn't you? But the torture continued. Did she love him enough for the lifelong commitment they were contemplating? She was more certain of *his* love for *her* than *her* love for *him*. Not the best way to be preparing for marriage. But it had worked out well so far. Everyone was happy, weren't they?

Then her father collapsed on the golf course. She was at the flat where they hadn't yet installed a phone. Strawks arrived back from Perlheim to an empty house. A note beside the phone read, *Dad in Vincent Pallotti*

Hosp with cardiac arrest, Mom. That was when he remembered Faye saying she would be sewing curtains at the flat. He had careened around there, banged on the door and blurted it out. He hadn't realized how devastating the news was.

When she was calmer she said, "I knew something like this was going to happen."

They dashed to Casualty, but it was too late. All that Faye could think, as she gazed at the still form on the gurney, the silver chain and medic-alert disc visible above the neck of the blue cotton gown, was that now everyone would know the truth. When the sister told Glad to take Bert's ring, watch and neck chain, Faye took Strawk's arm and turned away. Old habits die hard. He probably thought she was giving her mother a private moment, which Faye supposed later, she was.

Strawks called his parents long distance, and then Stella. Arno came and went. Through a wash of tears Faye was dimly aware. Stella said she would be on the next flight.

It was evening before they were alone. Her father's young partner, Nico, had prescribed a sleeping tablet for both Glad and Faye. Her mother had taken two and gone to bed. Until then she had been a dynamo, handling the undertakers and making the first tentative funeral arrangements, but now she was exhausted.

Strawks had brought them mugs of hot chocolate, although it was a hot February night.

"Aren't you going to take your sleeping tablet?"

"I want to be alert in case Mom needs me."

"I think you should forget about her." He was quite cross and Faye, although wrung out and dull, was startled. "You should think about yourself. You're always thinking of them– sorry, he's no more."

This was the nub of the few disagreements they had in the past. Usually he backed down.

She looked at the drink.

"Want whiskey in that?"

She nodded. She wept again while he shifted bottles in the liquor cabinet. He came back and poured a capful into her mug.

She said, wiping her eyes with the sleeve of her cardigan, "What about you?"

"Don't need it." He sat quietly while she sipped. Then he leaned forward. "What did you mean when you said I knew something like this would happen?"

"He– Dad– had been getting tired lately. You remember how he was on the golf course? It was a warning, and we didn't heed it."

"*He* didn't heed it. Honey, your Dad is– was– a doctor, he would surely have seen and felt the signs. Wouldn't he have had pains across the chest or something beforehand?"

"There's more to it than that."

"What do you mean?"

She realized then that it was over. The need for guarding the secret. Her father's career was over, and with it, the need for keeping knowledge of the diabetes from his patients. There would be no more patients demanding, needing him. No patients to be kept from knowing the truth. No more danger. The danger and the secret had gone with her father. And in the next breath, she realized, she didn't need to tell Strawks.

She said, "It's just that he was such a proud man. You've heard the expression, *physician heal thyself*. The last person a doctor thinks about is himself."

"That's why you and your Mom fuss over him so much. I know." He thumped his forehead with his knuckles. "Why you and your Mom *fussed* over him. I'll never get used to this."

He looked at Faye, aware of a new calm in her. Something had happened that he didn't understand. But Faye looked happy. In the midst of tragedy, his darling was happy.

"Can I kiss you?"

She kissed *him*. "Oh, honey. You're so good to me. Always looking out for me."

CHAPTER 20

Stella knocked on the door in the early hours, overnight bag in hand. They stared at one another, then she stepped forward. The hug she gave Faye was stiff and awkward. But Faye had felt the warmth. In that moment she knew Stella loved her. It was just difficult for her to express that love. Now, Faye grabbed Stella, and they held one another and Faye sobbed and sobbed.

Then Strawks was there with his arms around the two of them. It was the longest hug in history and it ended in giggles. He looked satisfied now that they were smiling and went off to make more hot chocolate, afterwards handing the whiskey bottle around for top ups. They didn't speak about Bert. Stella told them about people on flights in the middle of the night. One old guy said he was expecting his homing pigeons to have arrived when he got home. Strawks said how his folks wanted to fly over for the funeral, but they could only afford one trip, so he had put them off until the wedding. Faye said how strange and empty she felt. Was she callous, she wondered aloud. The friends were adamant. She was in shock.

Stella's eyes were wide with trying to stay awake and not cry. They unanimously agreed to get some sleep. Stella went off to the spare room, where Strawks usually slept, while he took a rug and lay under it on the couch in the lounge.

The next day he cooked eggs and bacon and made a pot of fragrant, *real* coffee. Stella played doorman to the priest, undertaker, lawyer, Bert's young partner, and a stream of friends. Arno was coming for supper and would take her back to the farm. He arrived with messages of comfort from Ada and Frank, although they had already spoken to Glad on the phone. Whenever Faye was offered the receiver she shook her head, fresh tears sliding down her cheeks. Arno also brought a big tin of homemade biscuits.

"For visitors," he said to Glad. "Not you."

He eyed Strawks, who was famous for his sweet tooth. Faye knew Stella wouldn't relax completely until she had said hello to the horses. Because it was term time, and she would be flying back to Durban after the funeral.

She was back at Faye's the night before the funeral. When they were alone, Faye said her mother was running around like a mad thing, whereas she, Faye, sat around most of the time weeping or locked in some kind of a stupor.

"Your Mom is so *strong*." Stella said. "Total opposite of how mine was."

Faye hated it when Stella maligned Constance, even posthumously. As regards, Glad, her mother was on some sort of a high, arranging the funeral and playing hostess tirelessly. Had Nico given her an 'upper,' Faye wondered, but not aloud. The night before the funeral, Glad took another two sleeping tablets and went to bed. Strawks, after making another round of laced hot chocolate, realized the friends needed to talk and said he'd doss in the spare room until they were done.

"I don't feel anything," said Faye, wringing her hands in her lap.

"At Dad's and even Mom's funeral I went around comforting everyone else, if you remember," Stella said.

Faye nodded. If she didn't feel anything, why tears? Were they for herself bereft of a father? For her mother? Glad was going to be alone when Faye and Strawks were married. The flat was just up the road, but it wouldn't be the same as having someone close at hand. If her mother cried out in her sleep, as she had done almost every night since Bert died, Faye wouldn't be there to whisper comfort, to slip in beside her mother and hold her close until she was asleep again.

"You won't feel anything for a while. When the animals were sick, I cried over them. I realized only recently that crying for them was me crying over Mom. I was so used to holding everything in."

"Did you cry over your Dad?"

"All over Arno, I'm afraid. He was the handy shoulder when I arrived unbidden at his flat in Durbs."

"Like me with Strawks."

It seemed indecent at that stage to talk about the wedding, although Faye was sure Stella must be dying to– herself, she wasn't sure. Any thought beyond the immediate future refused to take shape. Instead, they spoke about what they were going to wear for the funeral and who would be there. Neither Glad, Stella, nor Faye wanted to wear black. Something dark, it was decided, was a good compromise. Already bowls of flowers, homemade casseroles and lasagna, cakes and chocolates were arriving at the door as well as letters and telegrams of condolence.

At the funeral, Stella and Faye walked either side Glad, arm in arm. Also in the front row were Strawks and Anika, and Arno with his parents and Bert's partner (now former), the young doctor, Nico, who was running things superbly at the surgery, according to Strawks, who had been around running errands. The church was packed. The priest who was giving her instruction and who would be marrying them had offered to have the funeral at the parish church. Faye gazed up at the altar with its tall candles and waxy St Joseph lilies and down to the marble altar rails and statues in alcoves. Through the stained glass windows the morning sun was throwing a rainbow of color across people's heads. She loved the service, the hymns Fr. Rob had helped her choose. She felt proud. All of it was proof that she was grown-up, that she was able to make decisions. That she was her own person and not simply an extension of her parents' lives, now her one parent's life. In a matter of weeks the church would be decked out in frothy white and the hymns ringing out would be a jubilant blessing for a long and fruitful life of togetherness, instead of this solemn and lonely goodbye.

Glad had ordered a lavish send-off for Bert at the golf club. You knew Bert must have touched many lives, but seeing so many of them gathered in one place was a shock, a happy shock. Nico hosted proceedings. A couple of Bert's old friends spoke glowingly of times together, one of them quite the joker. Strawks and Stella stood either side as she began reading from two hand-written pages, *"The Readers Digest* used to have a regular slot entitled, *My Most Memorable Character*. My most memorable character was my father, Albert Churchill Morrisey."* If she hadn't had those pages to check on afterwards, she wouldn't have known what she said. Those moments up there were a blank.

At the airport Faye and Stella reminded one another that they would be together again in a few weeks. Stella was flying down a few days ahead for the firming up of arrangements and the fitting of Anika's and her bridesmaid dresses. Arno and Nico were best man and groomsman, and their ties were being made from the same blue satin as that of the bridesmaid dresses. Faye felt coy about the bride's dress. She was keeping it a secret from all but her mother. Here, again, Stella didn't pester her for details, although she had expressed her curiosity. It was what made the friendship work, this respecting of one another's privacy, this allowing of one another to follow each their lights.

That night Faye was woken up by the sound of something crashing. Strawks met her in the passage.

"What was that?" She shook her head. "I'll check the front."

"No. Let's go together," he said.

She thought they might have had a break-in. They walked through to the front door. It was still securely locked. The lounge and dining room seemed undisturbed. None of the windows had been tampered with. They checked the main bedroom. The double bed was empty.

Faye was running by that time, towards the kitchen, the only other room they hadn't checked. They heard the groan before they got there. She didn't see her mother at first because she was on the floor behind the table. She must have grabbed the tablecloth before she went down because broken crockery and cutlery were scattered everywhere. Faye pulled the cloth out of Glad's clutches, bunched and tossed it in a corner.

Glad was moaning and clutching a place high up on her buttock. At the same time her eyes were closing like she wanted to go back to sleep, right there on the floor.

Her mother, drugged from the sleeping tablets, must have missed her footing and fallen. When they tried to get her to sit up Glad roared an objection, a sound Faye remembered from a farm in Bethany. A young bull was being castrated. This was so unlike her mother, always ladylike.

"Make your Mom comfortable while I phone Doc Nico," Strawks said.

"What?" The stupor that had been bothering her since her father died was there again.

"Get a pillow and some blankets. We can't move your mother in this state. She needs to be checked out first."

"Looks like her hip," the young doctor said when he arrived in minutes that seemed like days. "I'll give her an injection now and organize for her to be admitted first thing tomorrow."

"She's broken her hip?" Faye whispered, alertness having returned, thank God.

He nodded, grave. She wondered if she imagined it. He had looked a little guilty before professionalism took over and he began dialing the hospital.

Between them they carried Glad to bed. She gasped and moaned all the way. Faye could tell her mother was more aware this time of their presence and, with extreme control, was tempering her outbursts. She was still groggy from the sleeping tablets, though. Just think, Faye said to herself, if she hadn't taken them and felt the full extent of the injury? Or perhaps she fell due to the drug. This seemed worse than seeing Bert on the gurney. Her father was out of it by then, his suffering over. Her mother, however, was aware of every stab of discomfort and all without her beloved Bert at her side.

Faye lay down beside Glad who dozed and groaned. With her thoughts churning, it was impossible to sleep. She thought again about the young doctor's behavior. He hadn't seemed surprised by her mother's fall. Was that because he expected a reaction of some sort after the shock of her father's death, all that rushing about that her mother had done? Or was there something else, something he wasn't telling Faye? Or was this Faye again fanning concern into angst? Strawks would agree, wouldn't he? He had to work the next day and had gone back to bed, otherwise they could have discussed it.

It was still dark when Nico arrived. Strawks had made coffee before he left. Faye had called Mr. Hilliard and he said, take as long as you need. He was big on family, another reason she had taken the job. Faye made sure both she and her mother were dressed when the ambulance arrived. Again, her mother's gasps sent agony echoing through Faye, each one freshly tortuous. She didn't know how she was going to endure more of it, but she knew there was going to be more, and so she had to be strong.

Glad needed a hip replacement. Decalcification was so advanced the doctor was surprised she could walk at all. After a decent interval– enough for healing of the first operation to take place– she would have to have the other hip done. Nico had known about her corroding hips but Glad had kept putting off treatment. She had been on a cocktail of cortisone, painkillers, and what-have-you. She was waiting, the young doctor said, until Bert retired. And her mother hadn't thought to tell her? Nor her father, who must have known? And now who was bearing the brunt of it? She felt bad thinking this. All she really wanted to do was curl up and die. She had to get a grip.

Two weekends later they had the house to themselves. It had been a tough week, with Glad in pain after the operation. Saturday had been a little better, Faye thought, Sunday they should have a talk– she and Strawks.

"What about?" He sounded defensive.

She hadn't answered.

She was calm now; she had made a decision. She was getting used to making decisions, which wasn't a bad thing, seeing as she was going to have to make many more along the way, she and her mother.

Stella told her later that he had called her from a payphone that morning before breakfast. Faye remembers him calling out while she was in the bath, something about getting milk and the Sunday papers.

He needed advice, he told Stella, although why he should call her, she didn't know. She was crap at that sort of thing. *And* he seemed to have it all under control. He was expecting to have Faye tell him that they must postpone the wedding. Which wasn't a train smash, Stella assured him. If Glad was going to welcome her guests with any sort of dignity, she needs time, months and for each hip.

"Hang in there, mate," she said.

Flights could be cancelled (his parents). There would be some losses, like the air tickets, unless they received a discount for bereavement, and the deposit at the Mount Nelson where the reception would have been (he was already thinking past tense). The flowers had been paid for, suit hired, and so on. Faye would jolly well have to make sure she didn't put on weight in the interim or her dress wouldn't fit. These were bum fluff compared to Glad Morrisey being comfortable. Because he knew Faye's concern for her mother was at the heart of what she wanted to talk about.

When Faye emerged steaming and perfumed, he was already home. He had made hot chocolate again, laced from a bottle of whiskey that he had bought. He hated living off her family, he said, when he had produced it days earlier.

She was in her pink dressing gown sitting on the couch in the lounge when he came in with the steaming mugs. Her face was rosy and shining, her hair still twisted up out of the way with a rubber band. She patted the space next to her and he had obliged, placing the mugs on a side table. When she turned to him, she was dry-eyed. Again, Strawks had the feeling he was missing something because lately Faye cried for everything, it seemed. She might be talking about hiring or buying a Zimmer frame or whether they should buy take-away fish and chips for supper.

"You know what I'm going to say, don't you?"

"That you want to postpone the wedding?"

His face was so full of hope that she had to shut her eyes. "No."

"*What?*"

"Strawks, you know I love you?"

He looked at her with a mixture of hope and dread.

"And I always will."

THE MAN WITH YELLOW HAIR | 161

Now he stared at her, puzzled. His eyes moved from her eyes to her lips and back to her eyes. He looked like he might silence her again with a kiss and she shifted towards her side.

"But not enough. I've been thinking about it for some time. It's not enough for a life together forever." The last three words were whispered.

He was staring again. She almost hated the blue of those eyes then. True blue, she thought. It's a bit late to be thinking that now, she told herself. The full import of what she was about to do didn't seem real. But only for a second. Then the reality of her situation returned. There was no other way. She had to do this now. The longer she left it, the harder it would become.

"I can't marry you," she said. "My mother needs me."

She had been holding the ring in a fist. Now she held it out. He was shaking his head, uncomprehending. Gently, she placed it on the couch between them.

"You must have known this was coming. I thought you must have guessed how I would be thinking."

He continued to stare at her. Then he opened his mouth, ready with an argument, or was it a proposal?

She had a hand to her nose, as if to stop herself crying. Her other hand was up as if she was in class and wanted to ask a question. Then he realized it was to stop him saying anything.

"No," she swallowed. "It's no use. There is nothing you can say that will change my mind. But before you go, there is something I must tell you."

"*Before you go?*" He repeated the words dumbly. He leaned forward with his elbows on his knees. His hands were covering his mouth, as if this was the only way he could prevent himself saying more.

"Dad had diabetes." And she told him the whole story. How Bert had lost patients in England because of it when she was little. How they had emigrated on the advice of friends. How they had kept it a secret for fear of the same thing happening.

At the end, she said, "I was never free. I'm sorry I led you on. I led myself on."

He must have said something, asked questions, but like the eulogy, it was gone.

CHAPTER 21

I called Faye's doctor on Saturday morning. He prescribed another antibiotic and put her off work for the next week. Maybe a day or two will do some good, but a week off work will probably have an adverse effect, I think. I leave her early Monday with the advice that when she does go in, to at least come home early if she didn't feel well during the course of the day.

"Sit out on the porch," I said, "with a glass of wine."

Who am I kidding.

The sky is an icy blue and flocked with scurrying clouds. Along the vineyard fence I slow down, gravel crunching, Harry and Sally alongside. I cast an eye upwards. Did I imagine someone among the cinsaut? I look again. But, no, there is no one. I immediately wonder about that new date of Gunner's. It can't be too long now before he arrives. The date will be on my mobile. I'll check when I get in– that and the many other tasks waiting for me. I groan aloud. Being with Faye was a holiday of sorts, but now it is over.

Something makes me stop, but I leave the engine idling. I look up again. There are no signs of life yet on the wizened branches. Vines, during the dormant season, generally remind me of old men. Why not old women, I ask myself. Women are, after all, the bearers of new life.

I turn off the engine. Nearer the fence, the chenin blanc hang for dear life onto the trellises. Like Christ on the Cross, Arno once said, awaiting their sacrifice. Today they display a heartening rash of baby green. The dead leaves and weed growth have been ploughed in, I note, pleased. After the pruning, we'll fertilize. The number of cold fronts lately will have helped Gunner's postponement. I return to the aesthetics. The rows of vines heading up the slope are pale brown lace on a dark gown. The outline of the mountain above is the scalloped neckline against the deep blue of what? Never mind. It's the thought that counts. How often do I take a moment to enjoy what I have, what has been given to me. The money left to me by Roy and Constance paid for additional stables, the riding school, and general setting up of the business. It isn't their fault my enthusiasm has dwindled. Neither is it Ada and Frank's fault Arno died and with him that elixir of life, a lusty red wine. Here I am, finding fault with Faye yet continuing down the same road. I am expecting her to take a few days off work, and here I am, reluctant to spend a few moments admiring my kingdom. Yes, it is my kingdom, and I it's queen. I laugh out loud. It's a good sound.

I walk into the kitchen feeling recharged. I kneel to Woo. Suzi takes a while pulling herself up and out of her basket.

"Come on old girl," I say. The prescription I give her for arthritis is no longer effective. Cortisone is next.

"Tea, Miss Stella?"

"Egg and bacon?"

"*Dis klaar.* I can make toast."

"Lovely. And let's try another of those new jams."

I sit down with my cell phone.

"Has Miss seen the pruning man?"

I grin. So that's why there is no hot breakfast.

"Have you seen Gunner?" Lyle walks in, grabbing my slice of toast and *moskonfyt*. He bites, swallows, licks syrup off his fingers. Today his hair is red and cut into a cap-like oval on top of his head. He has a line of matching moustache that meets under his jaw.

"That must have been him among the vines."

I check with the calendar on my phone. Gunner has come on the first date he gave me. I wonder what has happened to bring him sooner.

"This time I don't have to abscond to the laundry," Lyle says, looking pleased with himself.

I'm not sure how I feel about it. "Are you still planning on moving the salon to Myrna's?"

"That's on hold."

She's bored with you? I want to say. *So soon?* I badly want to smile.

"You'll see what I've done tonight. You *are* coming?"

"Of course." I butter toast to hide my embarrassment.

Lyle returns to the salon. Girlish giggles tell me he has cracked another joke.

My spirits take another leap upwards. This is what I need– a fresh face about the place. I check with Willy that the bed in Lyle's room has been made up with fresh linen and that we are having fish for lunch– kabeljou, in particular. Luckily, we have some in the freezer. I remember from past years that this is Gunner's favorite meal.

"I'm dreaming about butterflies now," she says.

"Doesn't that have something to do with death? A butterfly lasts for only twenty-four hours, symbolizing the fleeting nature of life." Then I remember her offer to ask after Strawks. "Did you find out anything about Mister Johan?"

"No one saw him around town. But Josie's baas used to talk about Mister Johan working on a boat."

" A cruiseliner? A fishing boat?"

"Those oil boats."

"Oil boats?"

"Those bi-ig boats out to sea. They get oil out of the sea. I saw it on television. They send long pipes down."

"Oh, an oil rig. Mister Johan worked on one of those?"

Her eyes disappear behind wrinkles as she smiles. I'm not sure how this will help except to explain why I never bumped into Strawks in Stellenbosch.

"Thanks, Willy. Keep asking, though, will you? You never know what comes up."

I check on the horses and walk round to the winery. A silver Lexus, Gunner's hired car, I assume, is parked beside the two-ton farm truck and the battered Mazda owned by the groomsman. Once I counted twenty cars. It had been summer, mind you. Winter is always quiet, but not this quiet.

Before I settle to the pile of mail and handwritten messages left by Brand and the staff, I walk into the cellar. Part of this is avoidance. It is the end of the month again. But part is the need to crank up the part of me that, like the vines, has lain idle. The de-stemmer, roto tank, racking and filtration equipment are in adjacent rooms, as well as the bottling plant and packing tables. I feel the pressure their presence inflicts. Too often they sit idle. I pass through the low-ceilinged shelved area. The depleted stock is another downer. Through the arched doorway the ceiling rises into the domed, cooler, maturation section. Only in midsummer do we need to switch on the air-conditioner. There is enough moisture for us not to need a humidifier. Even so, I check the gauges. Oak barrels of varying size fill one side, stainless steel tanks the other. The wine I told Gunner we kept back was in the 250 liter oak barrels for six months before being fed into the stainless steel tanks where it has remained ever since. I can't say why I kept it back. I've never envisaged myself as a wine maker. But I do know that resting in this way can only do good. A young wine needs to stabilize for its flavors to become more complex.

Arno is in my head thinking these thoughts. In fact, the odors of earth, wine-must, and wood bring him so close that it is difficult not to expect him to come walking in and ask, what I am doing? To which I might answer, sweetheart, I've no idea.

But I do need to do something. Or rather, something does need to be done for the farm, firstly, to become a more viable proposition, and secondly, to bring honor to his memory, never mind Ada and Frank. Somehow I don't think Brand's heart is in making wine. Even so, we need to sit down and talk. Gunner, by his presence, is bringing these thoughts to mind, and not a day too soon. When I have to juggle payment of another pile of accounts, drag myself to the bank and argue for an extension of the overdraft, I will discover my resolve, I'm sure. It is only a matter of time.

The aroma of buttery garlic greets me as I turn the corner towards the house. Gunner gets up from the grass verge where he has been changing muddy boots for shoes. He picks up the boots and slings his bag of tools over a shoulder. Then he sees me.

"Stella." He drops both and comes towards me, arms outstretched. I all but disappear in the bear hug.

He is a big, muscled man. I know I shouldn't, but I can't help comparing him to Arno. He is Arno's opposite in every way. He is medium height, and he has thick salt and pepper, dark brown hair, neatly clipped, strong features, a craggy brow, and navy-blue eyes. I once shone a torch at his eyes in an argument with Lyle about their color and won. Gunner roared with laughter at the time. His name hails from his Royal Navy days and suits him. His given name, Doug, pales beside it. Perhaps this is the clue to his personality, disciplined, no-nonsense.

He retrieves the boots and bag. The dogs make a fuss of both of us, all four.

Willy is radiant with Gunner's compliments regarding the cooking smells. He succeeds in getting her to sit down to a meal with us– something she will normally not do. I want to know why Gunner postponed, then came on the original date. Also, why he is able to stay a whole month? But I don't want to interrupt the easy banter. He and Lyle are planning to catch snoek out beyond Table Bay and tie up ends in this regard. Myrna, eating very little but apologizing to Willy, interrupts to say she will see us all later. She is assuming I will be at the housewarming. I look at Gunner and he senses my hesitation.

"You don't need us old fogies there," he jokes.

"You're not old, Gunner. Old is my Gran. No, Lyle wants all his family there. Mine are a grouchy lot. We need some balance. No, you *must* come." Although she hasn't addressed me directly, this is the first positive thing I have heard Myrna say in a while.

Gunner drives Brand, Ellie, and me to the party. The prices of cars are so good, he tells us, that he decided to buy a car instead of hire one. He'll find a buyer easily when he needs to, he reckons. We drop Willy off at a friend's house. Lyle invited her to the party, but in this instance, Gunner isn't able to persuade her out of her idea of what she perceives is socially acceptable. The men are in shirts, slacks, and loafers. Gunner's shirt is soft and white, Brand's stiff and patterned. I am in my standby, a black dress, but Ellie has draped a shimmering pink and lilac scarf across my shoulders and fastened a pair of her earrings in my ears that mirror these colors. She wears a dress of crushed strawberry that fits her like a bandage, leaving us in no doubt of her womanly curves and further stunned by her shapely arms and legs.

I am the only one wearing a jacket but discard it as soon as I get out of the car. The wind has dropped and the air is surprisingly warm. A thumping beat calls to us as we walk up the front path bordered with solar-energized lights, colored ones wreath the entrance. Judging from the raised voices, celebration is well underway.

"You have to see the water feature," says Ellie and leads us to one side of the garden.

Lyle has fashioned a grotto sheltering pottery bowls, statuettes of water birds, reptiles and insects that look quite at home among the beautiful plants, a mix of textures, intricate leaf patterning, and simple clean lines. Water trickles from bowl to bowl. Light seems to come from nowhere. Butterflies hang suspended, also by some cleverly concealed means. They remind me of Willy's dream, and I promise myself I will bring her over at the first opportunity.

What I can see of the décor makes me wonder why I haven't made more use of Lyle's talent. Of course, it could be Myrna's taste, but I think not. There are no carpets, but gleaming wooden floors and minimalist leather, glass and metal furniture. Embossed wallpaper in biscuit and tangerine, large mirrors, abstract paintings and sculptures relieve the severity. It doesn't feel homely. I know if I say this I'll be shouted down, so I take a mid-path and admire with restraint.

Myrna's Gran instructs Lyle to bring chairs for us to sit on the veranda.

No sooner are we seated than she asks, "You can't be happy about your son and Myrn?"

She doesn't wait for a reply. Not that I have one.

"Cradle snatching, that's what it is. She had a perfectly good husband but wanted more. Something better. Of course, she only wants your son for what he can give her."

"As long as they're happy." I feel like a fraud saying this. Well, it's half right.

"It was the same with her ex. Took him to the cleaners. They have a sports equipment business together. It almost folded— she milked it so dry. He's stopped her getting an extension to her bond, you know, for the hairdresser shop. Wouldn't sign the papers. She wanted to have it joined on the side of the house. There." She points to the side away from the driveway.

Gunner pops his head out and I throw him a pleading look. He brings another chair across and a bowl of chips and says, offering the bowl around, "Lovely to see a brick house. On the way over I called in on some New Zealand friends. They're turning more and more to wood. Even in Auckland, which is not in the fault zone."

"You're from Australia. You don't sound like it."

"From England originally, hence your puzzlement over my accent."

"Puzzlement. That's a good word. Puts in a nutshell why my granddaughter has to build a big house like this when she doesn't want children."

"So she can throw parties like this," Gunner adds. Lyle pointed out earlier how the dining room had fold-back doors providing an area for entertaining the size of a small tennis court.

An elegant grey-haired woman appears. She is wearing an apron over a tailored dress.

"Mom, I hope you're not telling tales?" She turns to Gunner and me. "Petra Leibrandt, Myrna's Mom."

We introduce ourselves.

"This gentleman is from Australia. The lady is the boy's mother," the grandmother adds.

"So you're Lyle's Mom. He tells me you have a riding school. I have a niece who needs lessons."

"Had, I'm afraid. I closed the school after my husband died."

"That's a pity. There's a great need for it in this area. Lots of small-holdings that have stables and horses."

"These people will pay anything. Spoiled kids, but who doesn't love a horse at that age. I wasn't allowed to ride." Petra frowns at the reply from her mother.

"It's never too late to learn," I counter. "All you need is a love for the animal and a willingness to learn. The rest comes naturally. Man has always ridden horses. Will always, despite the invention of the motor car."

Gunner says as we walk back inside, "That was a wonderful sales pitch. You should have taken the woman's number."

"I might have to reopen the school," I say.

"But you'll love that, won't you? It's your passion."

"If I do reopen, I want it to be because I want to, not *have* to."

Gunner looks thoughtful as we walk in. *You're Beautiful* is playing. I settle into the song that I previously labelled corny. Gunner's after-shave is lemony musk. I enjoy that I don't have to look so far up for our eyes to meet. I used to get a crick in my neck with Arno– a symbol for our relationship, I muse. I was always trying to beat him at something, from the success of our businesses, to who could ride best. With Gunner there is no need. I'm not sure why. Maybe it's the difference in their personalities. Arno was more uptight. Gunner is far more forthcoming, easy-going. I haven't caught up on the sleep I missed when I was with Faye. I think about resting my head on his shoulder, but I might fall asleep.

"How come you postponed your arrival, then came on the original date?"

He takes the hand that is on his shoulder and leads me out into the garden. The grandmother waves. The rocks around the grotto are helpfully smooth and we sit each on one.

"You aren't cold?" he asks.

"I'll need my jacket if we stay too long," I say.

"What I have to say won't take long. I postponed my trip to please my wife. It was another of my attempts to save the marriage. When I realized that it wasn't working– again– I decided to come when I originally planned. I'm also staying longer because I want to look around with the idea of investing in property here. I'd like a house here so I can come over in summer. Brand is going to show me some."

This is more than Gunner has ever said about his wife and marriage. "So far you've only experienced our winter."

"If your summers are as good, I might stay longer."

"You're welcome to stay with us whenever you come, winter or summer. And for however long. You know that, surely?"

We return to the dance floor. I have things to tell him as well, about Faye, principally. He might even have suggestions. But it can wait. For now, I am enjoying having a dance partner– someone I know and who isn't going to grope me. Gunner steers me skillfully as the dance floor fills up, but once or twice we collide. It is almost deliberate, and I don't mind. I am ready for this innocent touching. It is uncomplicated.

Who would have thought this day would end with me dancing with a man, I think as I glide passed other dancers, my children, and their partners. Life is full of surprises.

CHAPTER 22

Stella caught another midnight flight. Talking to Faye over the telephone hadn't helped. Her friend had retreated behind grief, a soggy curtain that Stella was powerless against. It made her shudder. She was glad Faye couldn't see her. And Strawks had been no help, insisting that it was all a mistake and that Faye would come round.

"I hope you're right," Stella said.

She was missing Glad, who would have come on the telephone and told Stella to be patient with Faye and that everything was going to be alright. But Glad was out of action. Very much out of action. Stella hadn't known Glad to suffer from anything more than flu. She had been the dependable one in Faye's life, in Stella's, in everyone's. Glad had told patients that they were going to be as right as rain, and mostly they were. She had comforted Stella when her dad died and again when her mother died. No wonder Faye was in a state.

"I've told her I'm not leaving, not going away." Strawks kept saying, like a stuck record. She wanted to tell him not to be a ninny. He should be bearing it in silence like Arno would have, or charging in, caveman style, hoisting Faye over a shoulder and carting her of. Anything rather than this martyr stunt.

On their way from the airport, Arno said of Faye, "It's a lot for anyone to handle. Losing her Dad, and then her Mom ill and in pain. But it is radical, turning away the one person who can give her strength. Not to say you aren't a great help, Stel. But you know what I mean."

"Do I?" Even Arno thought she was useless at this personal stuff.

At three in the morning, there was Strawks, sitting in his work van just inside the gate, looking utterly miserable. They hadn't said much, he, Stella, and Arno as Stella wanted to get to Faye and try to sort out the mess.

Arno waited in the car. Hearing about Bert's diabetes helped, but it still didn't convince Stella that Faye was doing the right thing. Still, all those years– most of her life– keeping that secret and them wham, the need for it gone. It would throw the strongest of persons off balance. Stella remembered how Faye stood up in front of everyone at her father's wake and spoke. Stella had left that sort of thing to others, to her Aunt Bev and Uncle Clive. Faye would triumph in the end, would see sense, realize she was overreacting.

Apart from explaining about Bert's diabetes, she wouldn't say more, but wept quietly.

Stella told herself it would be better to talk the next day when they were fresh, when she'd had time to think about what Faye told her. She kept telling herself that as they drove to the farm, that Faye would regain her equilibrium, but she felt wretched nevertheless. She should be sleeping over with her friend, but she didn't feel she had anything to offer. To be honest, the sight of her friend red-eyed, her hair grown long for the wedding and as yet unstyled and hanging in greasy rats' tails, braless in a washed-out shirt, disgusted Stella.

Constance, in her last days, had still been asking for her powder compact and lipstick.

Strawks was there, she also told herself. He'd go in, wouldn't he, and check on Faye? She wouldn't do anything stupid, would she, like taking sleeping pills? Stella's heart began to pound. She didn't think so, but she still felt worried as the farm gates came into view. She couldn't wait to see and touch the animals. They would restore her so that she could come back and be the kind of friend Faye needed, the kind of friend that would offer comfort, and help steady her so that she could think straight, so that she could get over this crazy need to destroy all she had built with Strawks.

But the next day was worse. He was there again in the van waiting inside the gate. He hadn't gone to work. He intended staying there, he said, until Faye took him back.

"If I park outside the gates, the police will tell me to move on," he said.

He hadn't shaved, looked gaunt. He probably hadn't eaten either. Arno dropped her off and went back to persuade Strawks to have a beer and a pub lunch. Arno had succeeded but came back with Strawks to collect Stella, looking glum himself.

"I told him to give Faye some breathing space. That Faye just needed time to process everything that had happened. That she would come round. That they had so much going for them. But tonight, he says, he's going to sleep on the front porch. Oh, geez."

Talking to Faye again didn't help. She was almost monosyllabic in her replies to concern from Stella. Stella, who was no cook, had done her best mashing avocado pear and spreading it thickly on toast with blobs of mayonnaise and salt and ground pepper the way Faye usually liked it. But Faye ate nothing. Stella offered to make hot chocolate and Faye screamed, "*No, not that.*" Very strange. After that, she sat red-eyed or weeping and saying she didn't love Strawks enough, not enough for marriage. That Strawks loved her more.

Twaddle, Stella wanted to say. You can't measure love. This one loves more, that one less. But what did she know?

Arno drove Stella and Faye to the hospital. Stella had persuaded Faye into the shower and helped her find and put on clean underwear, a blouse, and a skirt. She helped Faye with her hair, drying it and brushing it until it shone. She had to smooth salve into Faye's dried and cracked lips before applying lipstick. Faye looked a hundred percent better, although she wouldn't look in the mirror.

Glad was surprisingly chipper.

"It's the drugs," Faye hissed behind her hand. "Could do with some of that myself. Nico has prescribed something, but I'm afraid I'll get hooked although he says I won't. I need to remain alert for Mom's sake."

This spirited outburst should have encouraged Stella, but Faye's reasoning squashed that. Everything, all her efforts, were directed at remaining free and strong for Glad's sake with no mention of her intended. But at least Faye wasn't suicidal.

Out on the freeway again, Stella and Arno were quiet. Stella wondered at that stage if coming to the Cape was serving any purpose at all. Except for one thing. Faye had asked her to do all the cancellations and to collect their dresses and the men's ties. She realized that she couldn't ask Strawks. For him it would be admitting defeat whereas Stella would have something to do while she waited and hoped. They could always undo the cancellations or find a new and better venue and so on. The wedding gear would still be there in a week or so's time.

She made Arno promise to be with her when she tackled the list Faye had given her.

"Don't you think you should wait?" Arno asked her. "Faye could still change her mind."

"I'll wait a few days. Then we must get on with it. I have to work, don't forget. I'll be getting the sack if I take off any more time." Then out of nowhere, it hit her. That Faye and Strawks might never get back together. "They were so right together," she said. The world had gone dark. "They loved each other so much."

Talking about love to Arno felt strange. She watched his face as he said, "They still do. Once you love, it's for keeps."

"You really believe that?"

Coming from Arno it didn't sound ninny-ish. She didn't know what to say. They drove on in silence.

Ada wanted to hear all about it. Frank listened in the background.

"I had a friend," Ada said, "whose fiancé was reported missing during the war. She turned away other suitors believing that someday he would return to her. Years went by. My friend never married. Then he returned. He had married an Italian woman. It was an act of heroism, of unselfishness inspired by extreme fear and need. That's what war can do. But listen to this. The woman, the wife, had died after a struggle with cancer. He asked my friend to marry him, and she did."

That was fine *then*, Stella wanted to say. But for our generation it is different. We have Women's Lib. Women's Lib thinking is that you don't need a man to be whole, to function in the world. A man was there for your pleasure. You used him. In the light of this, Stella wondered why she was even bothering with Faye and Strawks and their engagement. If you approached the problem as a Women's Libber, Faye was doing the right thing. She was putting her own and her mother's needs first. She was being realistic when she said she didn't love Strawks enough. Faye is a pragmatist. But why did the thought leave Stella feeling hollow?

"What would you do if you were me, Ada? Should I work at trying to get my friends back together? Or should I leave them be?"

"You've had your say. You've tried. Now it's up to them."

Frank said, "But that young man at the gate, sleeping in the car. He needs to get on with his life. Bending another's will to one's own is not the way to go."

"I'll tell him what you said, Frank."

"Hell no, Stella. But do get him thinking about working on his career. Focusing on being the best he can be so that if and when the young lady wants him back, he'll have more to offer."

Armed with this advice, Arno and Stella went to work on Strawks and he responded beautifully. He was going to speed up his studies on achieving Cape Wine Master, and at Toastmasters, 'knocking 'em dead,' as he put it. He spoke to Faye about the flat he and Faye were to have shared, the subject of which he had been avoiding since the break-up. And for once she listened, culminating in them deciding he should sublet and split the rent income with her. He knew of cheaper digs closer to Perlheim and was going to use any free time to work in the vineyard. He would be gaining more experience as a wine farmer. It was only a pity he wasn't being paid for it.

"I'll see if I can get them to pay me. Then we'll be able to have an even better honeymoon," he said, and Stella felt tears catch her throat and she swallowed hard. Poor Strawks. He was definitely not giving up.

She then asked if he was going to cancel their week in Mauritius? He had nodded, tears pooling. It was the pits seeing a man cry. She remembered, then, that Anika was working on a farm and she asked if he had been in touch. 'Big Sis' would be spending a weekend with him as soon as he was settled, he said. Stella felt a little better after that.

The biggest deposit was with the hotel. Stella related how the bride's father had suddenly died and how she had been going ahead with the wedding, then the mother fell, and hip replacement was the prognoses. Stella cringed as she added that the family needed the money for the medical bills which wasn't strictly true. The deposit was refunded in full.

"You're good at this," Arno said. "You don't need me."

But the farm did, a refrain down the years, and understood by Stella, well trained by her diligent bread-winner father, Roy. So Stella was left to handle the rest. The tale of woe didn't work with the florist, the suit hire firm, and the band, although they weren't unfeeling and all promised to render their services should the wedding be re-scheduled. She wished.

Fr. Rob, the Catholic priest, was on the list. He hadn't been paid and thus no refund was possible, but Stella visited him anyway. Maybe he could get Faye to change her mind, a last desperate bid. It wasn't too late. They could re-book everything. Stella would personally take care of it all. She was like that, ding-donging between acceptance and hope.

"Marriage is a serious business," he said. "If a couple aren't sure, it's best to wait. We do an excellent marriage preparation course. But I will try. I wonder if you know Faye was coming to me for instruction?"

All the more reason to call on Faye, Stella thought, and no, Faye hadn't told her. Something else not confided. Stella wondered if there was anything else she wasn't being told.

She had collected the bridesmaid dresses and the men's matching ties. She planned to give Anika's dress to Strawks for him to give to her. She wondered where the bride's dress was.

Faye hadn't said. When she next visited the hospital, she would ask Glad– out of earshot of Faye, naturally. Stella wondered what Glad thought about Faye having cancelled the wedding. Up until then, Glad had been too sick for the subject to be raised. Conversation had been about the success of the op and how the doctors and nurses were treating her and so on. And when Glad satisfied them regarding these, she asked after Ada and Frank and was Faye eating properly? There had not been one word about the wedding, whether it was on or not, especially now that Glad was up and about and sounding more like herself by the day.

The more Stella thought about it, the more certain she became that Glad didn't know about the cancellation. She was also sure Glad wouldn't want Faye refusing to marry Strawks on her account. That was the kind of person Glad was. She would want the very best for her daughter. *And* Strawks. She had taken him in like he was her own. His parents had stayed with the Morriseys until they left for Norway. She might even feel responsible to the Johansens for their son's happiness– married happiness, that is. As well as her daughter, she would want Strawks to be happy. She would be concerned for him as well.

Maybe Stella could pay Glad a visit without Faye, without anyone else, for that matter. She had a sneaking suspicion Arno wouldn't want to be part of what she proposed doing, although this time a white lie wasn't needed. She had the perfectly innocent means of introducing the subject.

Next to Ada, Glad was Stella's favorite mother figure. Although Phyllis O'Donnell had been caring in a multitude of ways, she and motherhood were like unmatched socks. Stella wanted Glad to be happy again. Glad had been looking forward to the wedding. The wedding would be a sign of hope in the face of a second op looming. Stella, not given to metaphors, found herself thinking the wedding was the one bright star in the awful dark night of her beloved Bert's passing. And she, Stella, was the angel come to restore this source of great joy, she thought, as she peeped around the door of Glad's private ward with its mass of greeting cards and bowls of flowers and gift baskets of fruit and chocolates and biscuits, the outpouring of concerned former patients of Bert's, and a lifetime of friends.

"Stella. This is a nice surprise. What brings you here?" Glad was no fool. Stella without Faye was unusual.

She decided to get right to it. Glad was in a chair, rosy-cheeked and smiley, with a hand resting on the trusty Zimmer frame.

"I've collected the bridesmaid dresses and was wondering where Faye's dress is?"

Glad frowned. "Have you and Anika had your fitting?"

"Not necessary, seeing as Anika and I won't be needing them."

Glad's brown eyes searched Stella's. For long moments she waited while Glad trawled recent memory– the days since she fell on the kitchen floor and underwent major surgery, all the times her daughter had sat there talking and trying not to weep.

"So that's it. I wondered. You all looked so shocked. More than this silly body of mine warranted. So that's what my girl has been keeping from me." Glad's eyes glittered with unshed tears and righteous anger. She had a right to be angry, Stella decided. A decision had been made that affected her as well as the protagonists, and she was being kept in the dark.

Glad sat there trying to digest what she imagined had happened. At last she said, "She's given the ring back? Told the priest, the hotel…"

Stella nodded. "I've been round to tell the florist, the suit hire people and so on. When I collected our bridesmaid dresses I wondered about Faye's dress. I thought you would know where it was– and then I started wondering if you knew the wedding is off."

"Has she told people? The guests?"

"I don't know. I haven't seen her writing letters or even phoning anybody. She's in a state of shock, I think, at what she's done."

"I have to speak to her."

"Glad, you can't– mustn't say I told you. Ple-ease. Faye will never forgive me."

But Glad didn't seem to hear. "Stella, help me to my bedside phone. I have to stop this." She hesitated. "What about Strawks? Is he going along with this?"

"No. Certainly not. He's out of his mind. He parked for days inside your gate refusing to budge until she took him back. Until Arno and I persuaded him back to work." Stella thought it better not to pull punches.

"I'll get Faye to come here. And then I'll get the two of them. There's no need for this. It's madness."

"Remember not to say I told you. Tell her you guessed. That mothers know these things." Again, Glad seemed not to hear. Or was she choosing not to, Stella couldn't be sure.

Then Glad said. "It's in my wardrobe. Her dress." Her eyes softened. "It's a beauty– all guipure lace and satin with a sweetheart neckline, a puffy skirt. I can't wait to see her walking up that aisle. She has to, for Bert's sake."

"Tell her that, you know, that Bert would want this."

Stella got up. When she was at the door Glad said, "Faye's going to thank you for this. I don't know what she was thinking. Well, I do know, can imagine, but it has to stop. It isn't necessary."

Stella thought she'd give it a night or two for everything to settle, but on the third day, when she still hadn't heard from Faye, she decided to call. She had been promising Phyllis to return but hadn't booked a flight. She had bargained with God. I'll give up the job and, after she'd thought some more, Ensign, if you'll grant me this. Bring my friends back together again. Make the wedding happen. (Another voice whispered, you can find another job, but…. And then a sneaky thought, *no one will want to buy Ensign.*)

"Can I come round?"

"Yes. Come." Faye didn't sound weepy. She sounded awfully serious– sort of quiet and deliberate, but Stella wasn't going to dwell on that, although her heart did begin thumping heavily. She thought of calling Strawks, but it seemed wrong. And they didn't need him, not yet. Faye had been her friend first. It had been them, and then Faye and Strawks. Their friendship had to mean something, had to be able to endure anything. They had to be able to help one another, otherwise what were friends for?

But she continued feeling uncertain, uncertain of her reception, and wondered if she should ask Arno to come with her to town. But that sounded cowardly. Again, she reminded herself that Faye, in importance in her life, came before Arno.

All the way to Cape Town she continued the inner proclamation of their friendship. How they had met. The recognition of a twin soul no matter how different in personality. The tests, like being apart and choosing divergent careers. How they had been there for one another through the deaths of Roy and Constance and Bert. This was just another hurdle to mount, to stagger under the strain of, but to continue steadily onwards and upwards.

She half wished Strawks' van was in the driveway. While he was there, there had been hope. The house was quiet.

She knocked and let herself in the back with her key.

She almost jumped with fright. Faye was sitting at the kitchen table. There was something on the table, something in a see-through plastic cover, something floaty and white.

Stella couldn't help the smile sliding across her face. Warmth spreading up from her heart.

"*Is that it?*" It was the dress.

"That's it." Faye was smiling too, but it had a stiff look about it.

"Are you going to try it on? You've probably lost weight and it'll need taking in. Back to the dressmaker…"

Faye sighed and looked at Stella. Her lips were pursed like she had tasted something nasty. "No. I'm not going to try it on." She continued looking at Stella who had remained standing with the car keys in a limp hand and her handbag dangling from a shoulder. "I want you to take it, sell it, give it to someone, do what you like with it. Only, *get it out of my sight.*" All this was spoken slowly and enunciated in a clear monotone, the last few words raspy and in her throat.

Then Faye lifted the poofy, white plastic-wrapped contents and threw it at Stella in one smooth movement. It fell to the floor and Stella bent down and fumbled about until she had it safely in her arms. My, but it's *big*, was all she could think as she stood up.

"What happened? Did your Mom tell you I told her?" Stella knew now that she was for the high jump. There was no point in mucking about. "Your Mom called you from the hospital and you went round?"

"I had an awful job convincing Mom that not marrying Strawks is for the best," said Faye.

"But you love him, and he loves you. Your Mom doesn't want your break-up blamed on her. Don't give her this terrible burden of your unhappiness to carry about." She was shouting and leaning forward. She wanted to grab Faye by the shoulders but couldn't seem to let go of the dress.

"It's not because of her. Yes, the hip fracture prompted me, but I would have come to the same decision over time. It has saved a protracted on-and-off stop-start affair. I've thrashed it out with Mom. She gets it now."

Faye looked at Stella in a way that was new. Stella wanted to shudder again, but for a different reason. She would be shuddering because she wanted to weep. She couldn't remember Faye ever seeing her weep. Not when her father died, or her mother. Oh, yes. She was remembering when Bathsheba died. But crying for animals was different. It was simple and pure, free of guilt and blame. Animals never held anything against you. They were always only ever grateful and loved you back whatever you did and didn't do. She was feeling suddenly lonely and cold. She shivered. A deep chasm had opened up between her and Faye that she knew words wouldn't help her cross it.

Faye continued in the same dull voice with crisp consonants. "But the way you did it makes me wonder about you. Then I came to this conclusion. You really are the Ice Maiden. Where your heart is, is a block of ice. I wanted to argue with you when you told me people called you that. I thought I knew the real Stella. But I don't. I see that now."

In all this time Faye had hardly moved. Now she licked her sore-looking lips. "I was going to tell Mom in my own time. Now, thanks to you, she needs more of her sleeping pills to get a night's sleep."

"Faye, I'm so sorry. I just wanted to help. "

"Go now. I'm still your friend. But I don't want to see you for a while." Faye's mouth must have been dry as well because she swallowed. "And I don't know when I'm going to want to."

CHAPTER 23

It is Monday morning, Gunner has left for the vineyard, and I have dialed the number for St Bernard's Abbey. A male voice with a broad Yorkshire accent tells me the monks are at prayer. I call again only to discover there is no message service. I call at different intervals throughout the next day, and the day and evening after that. No one picks up.

I try the Catholic Church in Mowbray and ask to speak to Fr. Rob Green. He retired several years ago to a 'village' for that purpose in Vredehoek, Cape Town, I am told. I jot down his telephone number.

The Irish lilt is unchanged in twenty-something years, and he remembers I was to have been Faye Morrisey's bridesmaid. One of two bridesmaids, I want to add, but I am stunned into silence.

I tell him a little about myself. He could have retired 'back home' but with a bequest from a generous parishioner has settled beneath 'your wonderful mountain'. I want to argue that Table Mountain is just as much his as mine but hear a gong being struck in the background and decide to get on with the business in hand.

"How is Faye these days?"

"Well, that's why I am calling," I say. "She has breast cancer, has had a single mastectomy but against the advice of her doctor refuses to have chemotherapy."

"I'll visit her. They've got me doing hospital rounds. Keeps me in pocket money."

"It's several weeks since the surgery and she's back at work. It's kind of you to offer, but that's not why I'm calling."

"You want me to try and persuade her into having the treatment?"

For a moment I am thrown back to my conversation with him all those years ago. I never knew whether he did try to persuade Faye into making up with Strawks. Whether she continued with the Catholic faith for a time, I have no idea. She has no involvement presently. Glad's memorial service was conducted by a local dominee in a chapel near the farm. None of this matters now, but something about what I am doing strikes me as an egregious déjà vu.

"Nothing as direct." Pull yourself together, I tell myself. "I am hoping someone else will do that. Her jilted lover of many moons ago, Strawks."

"I never forget a name, but that one is in neon." He quotes the derivation, from Thorkild to Thorks to Strawks. He knows that Faye gave Strawks the name, and even about the bale of straw incident.

"That's, well, It's amazing that you know such details."

"It's in the job description. I take it Faye hasn't married."

I murmur, yes.

"And himself?"

"Married and divorced. He has a thirteen-year-old daughter."

We reflect on that for a moment.

"See what you make of this. Anika, his sister, told me that he is at St. Bernard's Abbey in Wales with the view to becoming a monk. That was weeks ago and no word since. To begin with, or should I say, before that, he worked for them, managing their apple orchards."

"St. Bernard's in Wales. I know of them, and that's about it. I can inquire, if you like?"

"I've had no luck phoning."

"Don't you be worrying. We have our ways."

I mention having contacted the Craft and Wine Shoppe in Chester and I give the address and phone number, as well as the address and phone number of the abbey.

Three days later Fr. Rob calls. Someone he had been in the seminary with in County Cork, now a bishop in Dublin, made some inquiries. Thorkild Johansen was rejected as a suitable candidate for the cloistered life.

"The reasons are confidential, that is to say, they will probably die with the abbot and the candidate." Father Rob chuckles. "As a church, we're big on secrets, what hasn't helped the predicament we have found ourselves in recent times."

Ah, the reports of sexual abuse of minors by priests. He relays Strawks' forwarding address – Akkerstroom Farm, P.O. Piketberg, Western Cape, RSA. Well, he sure isn't there, I want to say, but don't, remembering Henk's opinion of Strawks.

No sooner have Anika and I greeted than Henk comes on the line. Speak of the devil. He invites Faye, me, and my family to Sunday lunch. I have a guest from Australia, I say, so it would make better sense for him, Anika, and the girl to lunch with us at Gideons.

"I'll be in touch," I say.

Anika asks after Faye.

"She's had an infection. That's why you haven't heard from her. But she's on the mend." I wonder if Henk is hovering. "Can you speak freely?"

"You'd like more jams?" she says. She gets it.

"I'll call you around ten. Will the coast be clear then?"

"Sure. Three of the *moskonfyt*. Is that all? I'll have them ready. Bye."

"Give her a dozen of each," I hear Henk rumble in the background.

"Tell me about this *kêrel* of yours." Henk has the receiver again. *Kêrel* equals boyfriend. Oh, dear.

At ten that evening I call Anika. I repeat what Fr. Rob told me.

"At least," I say, "your brother wasn't the one bailing out."

"He's never the one. Crystal was the one who wanted out from the marriage."

"So you have no clue where he could be?"

"None."

"Might he have gone somewhere for consolation? He must have been feeling hellishly frustrated. Even this most noble and courageous step has been thwarted." He can't seem to get anything right, I think, but don't say. "Where was he happiest?"

"Bethany." Anika has stayed in touch with folks there, in particular with two spinster sisters, and offers to make inquiries.

"I was checking my passport the other day with the idea of flying over to Wales and pounding on that big wooden door."

"What a good friend you are to Faye."

"Maybe. I nearly lost her years ago when I interfered." This time she might say she *never ever* wants to see me again.

The next morning at breakfast Gunner tells me I look stressed. I don't offer an explanation, but we arrange to take Izzy and Sweetpea to the neighbor's racetrack after lunch. It looks like it will rain but Gunner is game. We gallop the horses in a gale that whips our cheeks red and waters our eyes.

While we walk back to the road I tell him about Faye. I tell him how we met and how Strawks was there from the beginning in Bethany, how they fell into friendship and then love. How her father died and that I hadn't known about his diabetes. How she couldn't break free of responsibility to her parents, and especially her mother when she fractured her hip which led to her cancelling the wedding. How I am only now discovering that

Strawks was married and subsequently divorced– someone we haven't met– and has a daughter of thirteen. How he tried being a monk in Wales. And now Faye has cancer and has had a breast removed and won't go for the chemotherapy and how I have to find Strawks because he is the only person that has a chance of getting through to her. I tell him that Strawks has been turned down as a monk and has given the farm, Akkerstroom, where his sister lives, as his postal address. That Anika and I think that he might have gone back to Bethany.

"We think he might have gone there for consolation."

"But you really don't know where he is?"

I am feeling foolish with my talk of consolation. Men, like Gunner– and Arno for that matter– don't, *didn't* have much time for the intangibles.

We continue in silence. Gunner is like that. He knows when to speak and when not. It reminds me of a line from Proverbs about keeping one's counsel.

"We have to assume he's on South African soil." He says. "Where is Bethany?"

"North-eastern Cape. A day's drive away."

"Isn't there somewhere closer he might go, like nearer Akkerdaal? That's our clue, isn't it?"

"Well, he was fairly happy at Elsenburg School of Agriculture, and then Perlheim, a wine farm, where he worked before Faye broke up with him. Both are nearby."

The next morning, I call Elsenburg. The secretary asks, would my friend be giving lectures or a tutorial or supervising in one of the labs? She can e-mail a list of the departments, she adds. When I say I'm not sure, I am put through to someone in HR who says they don't have anyone of that name on the staff and have I tried the Visitors Centre? Back to the main switchboard and on to someone in PR. The voice, still in sales mode, wants to know what my friend's intention is in visiting the college. Describing Strawks' motivation as nostalgia leads to me writing down a private telephone number– the secretary of the alumni. I haven't tracked down Strawks, but I have found someone who remembers him. Her son stayed at the same B+B as Strawks. He was in his first year and in awe of Strawks, who was in his final year. Out of politeness I hear how the son's career in wine farming has gone from strength to strength.

"How has Strawks done?"

I tell her about Strawks' attempts at farming, but all too soon Faye is in the picture and my need to find him. We end with her wishing me luck and offering an invitation to visit her son's farm to taste their wines and enjoy a meal with them while there, I only have to call.

"How did your inquiries go?" asks Gunner when we are left alone after lunch.

"I have the address of a house in Stellenbosch where he used to board, but no landlady or landlord's name and no telephone number."

"I'll be finishing the pruning by the end of tomorrow. We can take a look after that, if you like. And Perlheim?"

"I'm calling this afternoon."

I can never think of Perlheim Estate without feeling embarrassed. I tell myself that the petty jealousy– to put it bluntly– that Arno allowed to fester and boil towards Perl Javinski must be allowed to die with him. But I don't know if I can do that.

For as long as Arno made red wine from the cinsaut grape, the top honors had gone to Perl, the owner and winemaker of the estate. Every time we went to check out the bottles on the long tables at the Stellenbosch Young Wine Show, Arno would spot his *Hart Sag* with a tag like 'much improved young wine' or 'shows promise' and I would know he'd be churning up inside. (He made other wines, but how they fared didn't seem to bother him.) Every year, he and Perl went head-to-head in the cinsaut category. They were like siblings from different mothers but the same father– jealous of Daddy's affections, Daddy being *mein* host, the Stellenbosch Farmers' Winery. If the winemaker had been a man, there would have been no problem. Arno would never admit this. For my part, I kept up the charade of smiles and friendliness. Hence, I have never known how I really felt about Perl, even to myself. Now I will be finding out.

Entries at the wine show came well after Strawks had left Perl's employ. I have always wondered if he was asked to leave, especially when he told us that sales of Perlheim's wines, for which he was responsible, had plummeted. The fact that he was probably a square peg in a round hole doesn't ease my discomfort as Gunner and I make our way along the Strand Road, elbowed on our right by mountains with the university town of Stellenbosch ahead and the cream of South Africa's wine farms, wine estates, and co-operatives.

"Perl doesn't know why we're coming?"

"It was hard to get a word in." Perl's loquacity, though normally irritating, in this instance meant I wasn't under pressure to explain why I am paying her a visit out of the blue. I can't remember when I last saw her. Probably at Arno's funeral. I certainly haven't been out to the estate. "Before I knew it, she was inviting us for lunch at the restaurant, singing its praises and the whole enterprise. She's dying to catch up, she says. She's curious about you, knows you prune for us."

Gunner is at the wheel of his Lexus. I admire his big, strong-looking hands. He is quite hairy, which I discover I don't mind. There is something very masculine about it. He is one of those men that could shave twice a day, that have to decide how far down their necks to shear.

"How would she know that I prune for you?"

"It may cover a large area, but it's a small world as far as winemaking is concerned. We all meet once a year at the shows, to catch up and gossip. Or I used to."

"Do you miss it?"

"It was Arno's thing. He was very jealous of Perl winning every year." Gunner knows about Arno's wines, but not about the Perl saga. "He went through hell every year."

"Fool. His wines were– are– superb. He didn't need anyone telling him that."

"He was human. Aren't we all?"

We are idling at a set of lights on the outskirts of Stellenbosch. He looks at me. "How's it going?"

So much is unsaid, so much implied by the question that a sob catches in my throat and before I can stop it, tears spill down my cheeks. I hunt for a tissue in my handbag and blow noisily. When I am done Gunner covers my hand with his big one.

We drive along for a while not saying anything.

"So. I should beware of Perl– Javinski, is it?" His hand is back on the steering wheel.

I giggle and sniff. "Something like that."

CHAPTER 24

Faye pitched them straight into one another's arms, Stella and Arno would maintain later, privately, of course. But the afternoon Stella returned from the row with Faye, they were still just friends.

Stella went to the stable immediately after she arrived at the farm. She saddled up placid old Washington and took him out to the field and kept him lumbering round and round. The thud of hooves drowned her sobs.

Afterwards she washed her face at the tap outside the field and sat on the ground against a fence pole, allowing Washington to cool down and crop grass, and waiting for the hiccups to stop and her eyes to look less red.

She was flying back to Durban the next day. She booked immediately after she left Faye. Being mid-week, she was able to secure an early morning flight. She was longing to be on her own in the flat. The thought of those empty rooms was like a drink of water in the blistering desert of the proximity of Arno's parents. She hadn't told them where she was going, so maybe they wouldn't guess. If they did ask, she could tell them she had run more errands for Faye. Or she could simply say she went to say goodbye. If they picked up that she was behaving or looking different, it could be attributed to the fact that she was going to miss Faye, or was worried that she was leaving Faye at a time when she needed help and support with Glad. There was also the dark cloud of regret about the break-up with Strawks, which Stella would be expected to feel more deeply than anyone else apart from Strawks himself. They knew the wedding was off, and it was still off. For Ada and Frank and Arno, nothing was changed. There was really no need to talk about it. And Stella was usually good at this sort of thing– keeping quiet about issues, especially troubling ones.

Nevertheless, the prospect of getting through the next few hours rose like Mount Everest in her path. The tears kept rising in her throat and she had to talk and swallow and smile through it. Everything made her want to cry. The dinner, for instance. Willy and Ada had gone all out. There were candles on the table and snow-white table napkins, flowers. Roast chicken and bread-and-butter pudding were on the menu, her favorites, but she anticipated a struggle getting them down.

Arno opened a bottle of wine he and Frank had made together. Arno was going to make his own next season. In Durban a few months earlier, he had surprised Stella by inviting her to his farewell party at the bank. Frank was retiring 'while he still had *vuma* (power) in him,' Arno explained. It seemed a good time, as he and Ada wanted to visit their relatives in England for which they needed an extended period. Frank called it 'a final round-up.' Stella didn't allow herself to think about how it would be at the farm when Ada and Frank were away. This time she wouldn't be able to stay with Faye. The thought made her want to cry some more. The fact that Aunt Bev and Uncle Clive were always ready to have her stay with them didn't help, either. Whenever she was with them, memories of Constance, a mixture of regret and self-blame would envelope her like a damp, prickly blanket.

She went to bed early saying she had some final packing to do. This was accomplished in ten minutes, after which she sat on the side of the bed wondering what Faye was doing. Was she regretting chasing Stella away, or did she feel free now, free to live her life the way she wanted, pouring all her love into caring for Glad, the love she had previously had to share with Stella, and, yes, Strawks. If only Stella had kept her big mouth shut. If only she could have let things be. The Beatles song floated through her mind, and she began to hum the tune, rocking backwards and forwards with her arms folded across her middle. She remembered how the song came out just as Paul McCartney was leaving the band.

When I find myself in times of trouble
*   Mother Mary comes to me*
Speaking words of wisdom, let it be
*   And in my hour of darkness*
She is standing right in front of me
Speaking words of wisdom, let it be, let it be.

Ada insisted Stella have breakfast. This time she had to refuse all but coffee. She didn't know if she could keep any food down. Arno was outside giving orders, she supposed, while Ada was showing Willy how to use the new coffeemaker. Her thoughts turned to arriving in Durban. This would be the first time Arno wouldn't be at the airport to collect her. It reminded her of the first time she flew up. Roy had just died, and although she was sad then, terribly sad, life had looked hopeful. She had been on her way to Arno. *Oh God. She mustn't think that way.* Think of Ensign and the riding school and her next gymkhana. Think work and Miss O'Donnell. Think of the flat where she would find quiet and peace. She could do the flat up. Invite people from work and the riding school so it would feel more like a home. Throw a dinner party.

But it was all hollow. The heart of it was gone. She thought about telling Arno she had changed her mind about going back. Miss O'Donnell would understand. She was always willing to accommodate Stella. But what about *me, my* independence, *my* badge of honor, Stella wondered. Where was the battle cry she had been so keen to belt out? The prospect of owning and running a riding school seemed bleak now, lonely, the impetus gone. What about those plans? What was different now? Faye had never been part of it. Granted, the wedding had been a distraction, but she couldn't blame Faye that her plans seemed to have come to a standstill. What was stopping her? She was her own person. *I am the master of my fate, the captain of my soul.* With or without Faye.

"When is your next holiday, Stella? We may be in England then," Ada said as they walked towards Arno's truck, loaded up with her suitcase and the box of veggies and a case of wine that was going to collect a penalty at check-in.

Ada would have included a pocket of potatoes, a couple of scratchers and a leg of mutton if Stella had allowed it. As it is, she was going to have to distribute the spoils at Miss O'Donnell's. In Durban, she lived on bowls of cereal and Aeros and the occasional take-away fries which Ada had no way of knowing and Stella would never tell her for fear of hurting her feelings.

Stella frowned. "My next holiday? End of June, middle of July. I can check if you like." She began scrambling in her tote.

"Don't worry." Ada's hand was warm on her arm. She gave Stella such a knowing smile that Stella had to swallow a couple of times. "Nothing is definite yet. We'll keep you posted. And in any event, when we are away, Willy will be here, and you can have Faye over. Faye and her Mom. So you'll hardly miss us. Dear sweet Glad. How is she?"

Frank said, "Arno can fit a ramp to the back door. There's always someone around to lift the wheelchair if Glad is still in that, or help her up and down the stairs."

Now her eyes did fill. *No.* She couldn't let Ada see the effect of those words and she scrambled some more, this time for a tissue, and blew her nose fiercely. She thought she had succeeded when Ada said, "Wherever we wander, remember we'll always be coming back."

They hardly said a word to one another on the drive over. Arno kept on looking at her, opening his mouth to say something and then changing his mind. Finally, they settled on discussing her entries in the coming-up gymkhana and his plans for extending the vineyard.

What is it about airports that tug at one's heart strings? Every other couple or family they passed was hugging or kissing, shouting exuberant hellos or murmuring tearful goodbyes.

When they were at departure security, she said, "You don't have to wait until the plane has taken off. I know you have plenty to do at the farm."

She wouldn't look at him and felt her body stiffen as he moved to hug her. "Please don't," she said.

He gave her a probing look. Silently she repeated, *I am the master of my fate, the captain of my soul.* He dropped his arms to his sides. Again, he was about to say something and again, changed his mind.

She was sobbing again on the walk to the aircraft. It didn't matter now. It didn't matter who saw or heard her. Now she could sob as much as she liked.

——————————

Arno didn't follow Stella's suggestion. Instead, he made his way back to the wide look-out windows. What he saw mobilized him. For hours, days, months, dammit, *years*, he had been doing what she wanted. Well, this time he wasn't going to. He went straight to the airline desk and booked on the next flight to Durban.

He also rang Ada and Frank from a callbox. He had never discussed his feelings for Stella with his mother. Always inhibiting had been the cradle-snatching aspect. That he was going to ruin Stella's young life. Her nursing his crippled old man self was a particularly mesmerizing and off-putting scenario. The other one was his John Thomas folding on him. Although Frank was still going at it with his mother. Arno had surprised them recently when a fire had broken out one night in the vineyard and he couldn't find the key to the shed where the spare water hoses were kept and knocked on their door.

"Ma," he'd said now, dropping a few more coins through the slot. "I'm going after Stella."

"What?" Ada must have been nodding off in a chair.

"I'm flying to Durban this morning. I'll call you when I've arrived." The line was quiet. "You there, Ma?"

"You're flying to Durban. To see Stella? But you've just seen her."

"Ma, didn't you notice how unhappy she looked? Something has happened, and I've got to get to the bottom of it."

"Well, she did get teary when we said goodbye. She's usually so reserved. And here's another thing. Dad found a bride's dress on the seat of the Jeep. Looks like it could be Faye's. I've hung it in the wardrobe in Stella's room. Will you tell her?"

Of all the things to be telling him then. *Women.*

He telephoned Ada again on arrival to say he'd arrived safely. Next he tried Stella's flat. She had probably nipped out for fresh supplies. Then he realized she would go directly to work. She'd remarked once or twice lately that if she took any more time off she was going to lose her job. But Stella wasn't at work.

Phyllis answered. "I'm a little worried. Stella said she would be in mid-morning and there's been no word. It's so unlike her."

He should have known it. She would be with her horse.

"Are you back at the bank?" Phyllis had been at his farewell.

He had to think of something. He took a wild leap. What did it matter, he was already acting crazy. "Her horse is sick. Hasn't she told you? That is why I'm here. The vet gives advice, but the owner is the one that has to make the decision. I'm here to help if the news is bad."

And then came the inevitable, "What's wrong with the horse?"

"We're not sure. It could be equine flu. Or strangles."

"Oh dear. Then you better hurry out to the stables."

Stella would have some explaining to do, but he wasn't going to think about that yet.

It was after lunch, but the roads were still busy. He took a route across Berea and down past the Windermere golf course, turning left at Umgeni Road and along Athlone Bridge through to Durban North, heading via Redhill for the inland road to Verulam. The coastline and its heat haze disappeared over to the right, giving way to the now familiar rolling green of canelands. He had passed another high white wall and imposing gates when the fence and buildings of the club appeared where he and Stella had had drinks after a gymkhana. His membership ended when he left the bank. He wondered if they would realize that if he rocked up now, but this thought was quickly overcome by anticipation of seeing Stella again. And not without some anxiety. Too often he had been given the cold shoulder. He needed to amend that to the *frozen* shoulder. Frank had suffered from the ailment once and said it was extremely painful. Arno thought that maybe emotional pain was the most overlooked form of human suffering. He'd had an easy ride himself. But now Stella… Poor darling must have had some hellish thing happen for her to bawl that way.

The riding school was busy with afternoon lessons. Several young people in riding gear, mostly girls, hung around the front entrance. They gave him a cursory glance as he parked, then went back to chatting. He had spotted Stella's Opel, but it was hemmed in on either side by other cars. He remembered how he had parked beside it that first time at the school. He wondered, briefly, if it was an omen. For the first time since he had made the decision to follow Stella and hop on a plane, it occurred to him that he might be on a hiding to nothing, that he had misjudged the situation, that Stella would be back to her standoffish behavior, and he would find himself once again shut out.

For a moment he watched the behavior of the girls nearest to the few boys. The toss of a swathe of hair, a hip thrust forward, a trill of girlish laughter got a boy's attention. He'd watched a program once on body language. The man that could read the signs best in a girl, got the girl. But Stella didn't do any of those things– or did she? She was about the most undemonstrative woman he knew. He reminded himself what had brought him there. The picture of Stella clutching her tote to her chest, shoulders shaking with sobs as she walked across the tarmac below flashed rivetingly. The fact that she had concealed so thoroughly the reality of how she was feeling made it all the more shocking.

He felt fired up again. This time he wasn't taking the brush off. This time she'd have to fight him off.

Armed thus mentally, he entered the school foyer. The receptionist had seen Stella rushing by the desk on her way to the stables. But it was odd, the girl said, because Stella's name wasn't in the appointment book for that day. Although she did sometimes appear unscheduled, she added. She offered directions to Ensign's stable. Arno said, thank you, but that he'd been there before.

Arno stood looking at the empty stable, the food trough. Any extra saddles, bridles, and other tackle were kept locked up in the tackle room, so he didn't have the give-away of missing gear. He looked for clues on the walls. Stella had cello-taped pictures of other horses and scenery to the wooden partitioning. She was always looking for ways to make the horse happier and often played music while she rubbed him down. Music players too would have to be locked away or they would get stolen. Which explained why it looked so bare, but not deserted. Deserted, perhaps, was symptomatic of his state of mind. He had to remedy that immediately.

He just avoided colliding with the groomsman. To Arno's inquiry the man said, "I'm surprised you didn't see them when you drove in, sir." 'Them' being Stella and Ensign, he explained.

"Do you know where they were headed?"

"One of the farm roads?" He shrugged.

"Is there anyone else that might know?" There were easily a dozen farms in the area, he knew from dealing with them at the bank.

"Boss Lady, maybe. But she's not here today."

Arno spent the best part of an hour driving down each of the roads fanning out from the central hexagon. All of them but one led to locked gates which offered intercoms that either gave no answer to his inquiry or replied that they had no knowledge of the girl and horse he described. The last road, a rutted dirt road, led past the green shimmer of cane. He had driven down it a couple of miles and was about to turn back when he spotted movement behind a gum tree. It looked like a horse's tail. He couldn't be sure it was Ensign, and there was no sign of Stella, but he stopped anyway.

And it *was* Ensign, tail swishing and chestnut rump glistening in the low sun. He was enjoying the grass, fully saddled up and waiting for his mistress, who sat on the ground leaning against the tree.

The horse looked up first.

"Hi, Stella."

She turned. It occurred to him that if he hadn't spoken, she wouldn't have moved. It was like she had come to a dead halt, literally and metaphorically. There was no sign of the tears of earlier. Mind you, it was almost a whole day later. The sun was fast disappearing over his shoulder behind the lush countryside.

"Arno." She must have thought she was dreaming. He would have expected her to ask what he was doing there– employing some of her usual cheek, spunk– but he could tell from the shadows beneath her eyes, her blanched cheeks and trembling lips that ordinary considerations were beyond her.

She didn't attempt to get up and he was forced to go on his haunches. He had donned a suit that morning, and he loosened the tie. It was only then that he remembered he'd had an appointment that morning with an advertising agent in Cape Town.

Ensign had taken a step closer and was sniffing the back pocket of his trousers, where he had saved a couple of mints from the plane meal.

"Not now, boy."

Ensign tossed his head and trotted back to the grass.

Arno looked at Stella until she was gazing fully at him. "I watched you walk to the plane."

It took a minute for that to sink in. They continued to stare at one another. He watched the tears wash over blue, becoming a sea that rolled down her cheeks.

"Faye doesn't want to see me again," she said between sobs. It tore him up to watch and listen, but he knew she must get out what was bothering her.

He dug into his jacket pocket and came out with a clean handkerchief. He shook it open and handed to her.

"What happened?"

"It's warm," she said of the handkerchief. She blew her nose, and he waited while she recovered some way. "I told her Mom she had cancelled the wedding. Her Mom didn't know. I thought her Mom would get her to change her mind. It was a last ditch on my part."

"And?"

"It didn't help. The wedding is still off." She began to cry again. "I interfered, Arno. Faye is furious. She was going to tell her Mom but when she was more recovered. Her Mom is everything to her. She doesn't want me or Strawks or anyone else. She just wants to be left alone to care for her Mom." She blew her nose again. It was a raw red. "She is still my friend, she says, but doesn't want to see me for now, for I don't know how long."

She might have wept again but then something occurred to her. "I left it on the seat of the Jeep. *Oh, hell.*"

"Faye's bridal gown? I know. Mom told me. It's in your cupboard at home." His legs were beginning to cramp up.

"You said home." She was smiling a crooked smile. Her eyes were a warm blue, but her face was blotchy, her eyes puffy and bloodshot, her lips swollen where she had bitten them. To Arno, however, she had never looked more beautiful.

"Come home, Stella." His legs gave way and he fell backwards.

She got up and crawled on all fours until she was over him. "You OK?"

But he was laughing. She watched him for a full minute then she was laughing too, so much so, that she collapsed onto him.

CHAPTER 25
_____

The sun has played Hide and Seek all the way into the Simonsberg. Out of the warm car, Gunner helps me into a jacket.

It is a Friday, and busy. The restaurant proper at Perlheim has spilled over into the cellar and tasting room where Perl Javinski leads. In one corner a jazz band is playing, *In the Mood*.

"May I call you Gunner?" Perl asks. She dimples. "I don't know your real name."

Perl is looking smart. Her stylish bob has the dull look of colored hair. The shade is a close match to the chocolate brown of her jacket. The cream ruffles of her blouse cover her neck where, perhaps, her age might show? But she is still an attractive woman. She has been a widow forever, running the estate until her sons were ready to come in with her. I should be learning from her example, although changing the name to incorporate her own– I can't see myself going that far. Little is known about her husband, and the estate made little mark on the industry while he was alive.

"It's not worth the paper it's written on," Gunner says. He isn't going to tell Perl, which I admire him for.

The tasting room has a closed-in feel being without windows, which is customary in cellar construction. It has more to do with Perl's personality, I realize, which is the kind that leaves no stone unturned. We have placed our starter and main course orders. Here, she makes suggestions which feel more like orders, which we follow out of courtesy and she has ordered the wine she deems best for the dishes we have chosen. Now she wants to know where Gunner learnt to prune and what his secret is.

"Self-taught," he says, "and off the seat of my pants."

"Can I have your card? I have a proposition."

He pats various pockets in his shirt and trousers with nil result. He laughs his great bull laugh. He has led us on.

"When I'm on holiday, I'm on holiday," he says.

"But you prune for Stella."

"That's *in memoriam*."

I experience a mixture of pity for Perl, gratitude to Gunner for his continued kindness, and an ache of longing for Arno. While I take a couple of deep breaths I sneak a glance at Gunner. His head is to one side as he listens to the band. He has an almost childlike ability to enjoy himself. I wonder about his marriage. He and his wife must have loved one another once. Does he miss that? Does he want to try and find love again, or has it put him off for good?

Our wine has arrived. The sommelier, a young black man with a crisp English accent, wears white gloves. He offers the bottle to Perl, who indicates Gunner will play host. Who reads the label and asks about vintage and origin and whether and for how long it was in the cask. The cap is unscrewed, the mouth of the bottle wiped with a clean white cloth, and a third of a glass of the light straw savignon blanc, *Arresté,* is poured for Gunner to nose and roll around his mouth. Satisfied, he nods, and the glistening liquid rises to the correct two-thirds level in firstly, mine and Gunner's glasses, and then Perl's. All through, Gunner seems to be humoring our host. Our starters arrive as we take a second sip.

"Arnold and Stella. That was a match made in heaven," Perl says, taking over where Gunner left off. "But, my girl, you've stuck yourself away far too long. Glad to see you're venturing out at last."

I have no idea how to reply to this.

"You've been widowed for how long, Perl?" Gunner asks.

She almost drops the blob of snoek pâté off the end of her knife.

"I forget," she says blushing and spreading a slice of bread. "Twenty-five, thirty years. Why do you ask?"

"And how long before you were ready to date again?"

Now Perl looks miffed. I admire that she answers. She must realize she doesn't have to.

"Never did. I had a family to support. Make the farm profitable. My husband left me with a pile of debt."

Just then, our mains arrive and we never get to hear more about the late Mr. Javinski.

"So who is going to be making wine at Gideon's?" Perl looks at me.

"I've been meaning to talk about that to Brand, although Lyle is the creative one." I want to mention Lyle's interior decorating skills but the link with Myrna puts me off.

"What's wrong with you giving it a try?"

Is she teasing? But there is no give-away twinkle. I decide 'twinkle' and Perl are unlikely bedfellows.

Gunner is nodding and smiling as the band returns from a break. He whispers in my ear, "What's your favorite?"

I shake my head. My mind is a blank. He writes something on his paper napkin and hands it to our waiter who takes it across to the band leader seated at a keyboard.

The tune is new to me. Perl has been called away by one of her staff.

Gunner is grinning and nodding appreciation to the band leader. "I wasn't sure they would know the tune. It's new. Written by *Shari,* a young gal from home."

"Home as in Melbourne?" I ask. "Do you know the girl?"

"I do. She served me coffee for years at a café round the corner. On Sunday nights she would play the guitar. Some of the songs were her compositions. Some friends and I convinced her to make a CD. Go on YouTube. She did. In a year she went global."

I wonder why Gunner is telling me this. Gunner is the sort of person that does nothing without intent. "If she never tried she wouldn't have known how successful she could be. That's all I'm saying."

Perl returns, apologizing for her absence.

"Perl, you're probably wondering why I'm here today."

"To introduce Gunner to me and the estate? Taste our wines?"

"That, yes, but I have a rather pressing need and I'm hoping you're able to help." The staff member is back, and I decide I must hurry or lose the opportunity. "I was wondering if you have had any contact with Strawks Johansen recently – Thorks Johansen?"

She deals briefly with a query and returns her attention to me. I see that I have surprised her.

"How recent?" she asks, leaning back in her chair.

She gives me a sobering look and I feel as gauche as a schoolgirl as I say, "Within the past few months, weeks preferably. I was hoping he might have come looking for a job."

The employee is at her shoulder. It is the young man whose request resulted in her leaving us earlier.

Still facing us she says, "Makes you wonder what they teach them at hotel school, doesn't it?" She says something to the young man who turns on his heel. I admire his composure.

She leans forward. "I had to let him go. He was hopeless as a salesman. He would end up having the most interesting conversation with the target person and get back to the van and only then remember what he was supposed to do. But he showed promise in the vineyard. He had a feel for the vines. Something like you, Gunner. But I couldn't have paid him the salary he wanted." She signals for the waiter to take our plates. "But that was years ago. Why do you want him now?"

So when Strawks came looking for a job from Arno he had already been 'let go'. Or was that later? After the harsh but only too real vignette of Strawks, the hopeless salesman, confidence for my task plummets, accompanied by irritation at her patronizing of Gunner, not to mention dismay at her treatment of the hotel school intern.

Outside sunlight breaks through the trees and I take heart. "A friend is ill. He'll never forgive me if anything happens to her and he didn't know."

"I see. Sorry I haven't been much help. Dessert?" She waves the menu, but we decline.

When we say goodbye outside, she says, "Think about making your own wine, Stella. Gunner here, can give you a few tips." She kisses me on both cheeks. "I need another sparring partner. It keeps me on my toes."

Gunner says before he turns the key in the ignition. "Pity we didn't get to hear about her old man. He must have been a scoundrel to have put her off men for life."

"But she said she had a family to support. That's why she didn't date."

"Don't you believe it. All that coquetry is a front."

I sigh. I can still get the personal angle wrong. But on the positive side, all the embarrassment about Perl has evaporated. In fact, something new has replaced it, something I haven't felt for some time. Hope? A challenge? How difficult can it be? A little bit of this, and a little bit of that. Taste and taste again. You'd need to measure and record the volumes, vintage and a whole lot besides. But I need time to think. I need to speak to Brand and Lyle.

Driving through Stellenbosch with its wide streets and ancient spreading trees, its Cape Dutch university buildings and hostels, I imagine a younger Strawks on foot or riding a bike. Gunner pulls up beside the pavement in an older part of the town. The iron roof has a weathervane that creaks in the breeze and dormer windows. Its deep verandas sport white *broekie* lace trim overhead and waist-high fancy railing.

A sign above the gate reads: *Bella's Bed and Breakfast,* and below: *Daily and Monthly rates. French and German spoken.*

Into the intercom I say, "Hi! My friend and I–"

Before I can say any more there's a buzz and the gate swings open. We side-step giant pink crocus flowers on the brick path that leads to the front steps.

A stout gent in a worn cardigan and slippers reclines in a wicker chair. He lowers the newspaper, peers over readers and asks, "Looking for a room?"

Gunner says, "Any vacancies?" winking at me.

"No idea. But the nosh is good. Dinner is at seven."

I frown at Gunner.

"This way we can come at it by-the-way," he says as he pulls a lever over an antique-looking bell arrangement at the door, unnecessary as we have already been buzzed in.

"I'm Cilla," says the reed-thin person at the door. "Missus is at the market. Maybe I can help?"

Gunner introduces us and says, "We're looking for a room. Could we see one? We've done the rounds and some of the places we've seen are not up to scratch."

"Tell me about it," the woman says. "They're going to have to bury me from here."

She has a loose bun of iron-gray hair and a pair of reading glasses with a dangling chain sits on the end of her aquiline nose. She reaches for a key behind her on a board with several hooks.

"Are you going through with this?" I whisper to Gunner. I want to match his seriousness, but I feel a smile break through.

"You'll be surprised what comes out glancing across a double bed. And you never know, you might want to get away sometime." His reply is without undertone, but I feel a frisson up my spine.

We follow Cilla along the passage past a small lounge where half a dozen elderly folk are playing cards.

"How much longer…?" a ginger-haired woman asks, drumming her fingers on the table.

The door is opened on flowered wallpaper, curtains, and covers on a brass four-poster bed. The carpet is soft underfoot. The air is full of lavender and all-purpose cleaner. The afternoon sun streams through a window that overlooks the pretty back garden and swimming pool. I think Gunner has a point. I could spend a happy couple of days here. I also realize my bedroom at home has reached its sell-by date.

"How long has the pool been there?" I am wondering if Strawks, the student, took study-break dips. "I have a friend who boarded here in the late nineties."

"We're also wondering if the friend, Thorks Johansen, stayed here recently?" Gunner adds.

Our guide drops the spectacles onto her washboard chest and looks thoughtful. "I've really no idea. But Mrs. Wood will be home soon. She might know. Or– there are the guest books, they go way back. Would you like to look through them?"

"That's very kind," I say.

"And the room? Will you be taking it?"

I look at Gunner, who looks at me.

"Shall we?" he says, and I laugh.

Our guide looks at us, grins, and ushers us out.

In a nook off the main lounge, our informal guide hands us the books. A waitress in a frilly white apron and mop cap brings us tea and biscuits. We decide to start with the present and work back. I hold the one in current use that begins with February two years previously. Gunner has the one that precedes it. Because Bella's has a large percentage of permanents the pages fill up slowly, except for the warmer months, September to April, where home addresses crisscross the globe. Running a finger down the names on the far left of each page, the process is quicker than I imagined it would be. To amuse ourselves we read aloud an occasional entry in the comments section on the far right. *A scene from Miss Marple*, Gunner reads. *Ghosties lurk in the cupboards*, I read, *but otherwise A-OK*. I almost miss the scrawled *TSJohansen*. The date he booked in is May last year– fifteen months ago. The date he booked out was a week later.

Mrs. Wood has arrived. Her youth surprises me. She is thirty-ish, pretty with a tumble of brown curls, and a young child on a hip.

She notes my surprise, "Bella was my grandmother. I'm running the business for the family trust."

Cilla who had been hovering explains our quest.

"Thorks Johansen? I do remember. Suzie was born two months later." She pats her stomach, and I smile at the child who is set down to totter down the passage, Cilla solicitously following.

"Shame," our host exclaims. "He had a job on one of the wine farms. He paid the deposit– a fortnight's rent. A week later it was off. We have a policy of no returns. I felt bad. But he said money wasn't a problem, although, to be honest, he looked shattered. Turns out it was the way it was done. No why or wherefore. It was a family business. A mother and sons, I think he said."

I look at Gunner. Is he thinking what I am thinking?

"Did he mention the name of the farm?"

"Sorry. I did ask but he wouldn't say. Before he left us he tried some other farms and businesses in the area but with no luck."

Back in the car I say, "Perl. It's got to have been Perl. She didn't give us the whole story."

So Perlheim was one of Strawks' fruitless attempts to find a job before chancing his luck overseas.

"All the more reason to get that wine out."

On the drive back Faye texts: **Call me after work. At home.**

We'll be back at the farm by then. The terseness of the message worries me. Even if it is something frivolous I prefer to find out in the privacy of my bedroom. I don't want Gunner or the children to see how I tense up when anything to do with Faye enters my orbit.

We are on the last few miles before our turn-off.

"It's up to Anika now," I say to Gunner. "She was going to contact people in Bethany. Let's hope she's come up with something. Imagine if he went back to work on one of the sheep farms."

"How would you feel going back after, what is it, twenty-something years?"

I count in my head, forty-six minus eighteen. "Twenty-eight. The thing is, I left under the cloud of my Dad's then, recent, death. I'd be returning under another cloud. Which is a shame as most of the time there– all but the last week after my Dad died– I was happy. They were some of the happiest days of my life. We were so full of hope. We had plans."

"If you don't mind me asking, what plans did you have?"

"I don't mind. I was a simple creature. All I wanted was my own horse, to begin with, and then a riding school."

"And you got both. No plans to find a man and get married?"

"None. The man just happened. I had no idea what I was missing until he came along." I look across at Gunner. "Here I am, spouting about me when it's you I want to know about. You never talk about yourself."

"Boring," he says. I keep looking at him until he says, "What do you want to know?"

"Everything. Where you were born, went to school. Did you go to university? Did you have brothers and sisters? When you joined the navy, and where. Where and when you got married?"

Gunner has a daughter and a son. I know that. In fact, I know more about them than about him. His daughter is training as a dentist in Melbourne and shares a house with other girls that she went backpacking with in her gap year. His son is also in the navy and is four years older. He is married with two children. Gunner is proud of them and likes to talk about them.

"I went to the University of Liverpool. I have a brother and a sister. They're both in England. They have two kids each who are roughly my age. I was a change-of-life baby. My mother was forty-eight when she had me. My brother and sister left home when I was small, so I hardly know them, and their children even less. Moving to Aussie didn't help. I went to the Royal Naval Academy in Dartmouth, Devon. Transferred to Aussie immediately. I was commissioned. Met my wife on shore leave in Sydney. Marriage to a naval officer is tough. You hardly see one another. When I retired to farm ten years ago I thought it would save us, our marriage. But it seems it was too late."

"Arno was also a *laat lammetjie*. A late lamb. A child born well after the other children. Except in Arno's case, there were no other children." We are off the main road, have slowed right down, with the gates in sight. I don't want the conversation– and I have to admit– the day to end. "Your wife didn't take to farming?"

"You guessed right. About winemaking, she says, 'What's all the fuss. It's just fermenting grape juice.' She prefers the supermarket plonk to my wine."

"Next time you come you must bring some of your wine. I don't know why you haven't brought any before." I shoot a look at Gunner as he takes the turn-off.

"Coals to Newcastle?"

"Gunner, you're too modest for your own good. I bet it's delicious."

I shut my bedroom door and sit on the bed. For a moment I close my eyes, allowing the events of the day to wash over me. I had a good time today. Did I tell him? I can't remember, because I walked into an argument between the groomsman and one of the laborers who failed to help turn out the stables and worked in the vineyard instead. It is not the man's fault, but a failure on my and Brand's part to clarify who should be doing what, where, and when.

I dial Faye's cell phone number.

"Hi." She sounds groggy.

"Have you been asleep?" I ask. That's good, I think. "You'll never guess where Gunner and I went today?" I'm spinning out our conversation, putting off the moment until I hear why she has called. "We had lunch at Perlheim."

"With the Wicked Witch from the West?"

I chuckle. "Yes, with Perl."

"Is she still sweeping the tables at the young wine shows?"

"I don't know." I pause, waiting to drop my bomb. "She wants me to make wine so she can have a sparring partner."

"Sorry to burst your bubble, sweetie, but that's so she can enjoy the triumph of winning again. Trumping another Gideon."

"Hang on. How d'you know *I'm* not going to sweep them tables?"

"Since when did you want to make wine?"

"Since today." I say, serious now, "I have to do something. We're not breaking square."

"I've told you. Let me have a look at your books. There's bound to be a number of ways you can cut costs."

It's tempting. She has turned the carpet business around more than once, so her talent and skill are without question. I could certainly do with the help, but I know it may, no, will lead to arguments. Our friendship would suffer, and I can't let that happen. I am sorry now that I mentioned Gideon's finances. The success of the day with Gunner has given me a false sense of what is possible.

"So what did you want to tell me?"

"I have another lump. It's the size of a pea, mind you…"

CHAPTER 26

Faye couldn't help but be happy when she received the invitation to Stella and Arno's wedding. Happy for them, but oh-so-sorry for herself. She should be the Maid of Honor, but not just that. Her friends had got together without her knowing. All the delicious details were closed off from her, and, through her own hastiness, her own fault, something she had been reminded of every time her mother wanted to know how Stella was and what she was doing which was every couple of days, then weeks, then months, and Faye had to make up something. Then Glad had stopped asking.

Faye had filled in the RSVP with its attached postage stamp. It was a case of holding her breath as she dropped it into the mailbox. She didn't know how she was going to bridge the gap, what she was going to say. All she knew was that suddenly she knew she wanted to see her friend again.

It was almost two years since she or her Mom had seen Stella, and they were both full of questions but not saying much as Faye drove into the country. The ceremony was in a chapel just outside Stellenbosch and the reception afterwards at the Gideon farm. She had warned Glad that if the vibes weren't good they weren't going to the reception. Stella was perfectly in her right to be guarded when they were faced with one another again. She wouldn't know if she was forgiven, and Faye wasn't sure about that herself. She had spent many a night sobbing about how Stella had been prepared to jeopardize Glad's health, that she hadn't understood how Faye's mother's health and welfare came before everything else in Faye's life, and worst of all, how Stella had gone behind Faye's back and told Glad that the wedding had been cancelled. But the occasion was just too tempting. Curiosity killed the cat.

Trailing was the thought, a surprising source of joy, that Arno was landing the woman he had loved for so long.

The map that came with the invitation was easy to follow, and they arrived with a dozen cars already parked in the treed grounds. Faye dropped Glad off near the door with her stick. Glad had had her second hip replaced and had made good progress according to the doctor but was still in a lot of pain when she walked. For the occasion, though, she had taken a hefty dose of painkillers, and had more in her handbag.

It had rained along the way and the pines were still dripping as Faye made her way over the rough ground to the miniature stone church. Inside, she was assailed by a sensory rush of perfume and after-shave, underpinned with the damp thatch of the roof and woodiness of the oak beams and pews, the peppery red polish of the floor and the melting beeswax of the candles. Overriding all was the heady scent of the deep orange Stargazer lilies on the altar. The brilliant color of people's outfits, especially the women's, and more flowers in convenient nooks, completed the scene of heady pleasure.

Faye stood looking towards the front row and in that moment, Glad was forgotten. Arno's head stood out above the others in that row. For eerie seconds her eyes locked onto the male head beside him. But it was a dark head. Not yellow-blond. She swayed sickeningly before shifting her gaze to the opposite side. A strange woman sat closest to the aisle wearing a picture hat of blowsy pink roses, next to her was Stella's Aunt Bev in a turquoise toque. The woman in the big hat should have been her. Faye thought she might break down then, but her mother was beside her, nudging her into the back row on that side.

They kept on having to shove up as more people arrived. Eventually it was only standing room inside and a small crowd swelling outside. Ada and Frank arrived with what appeared to be relatives. Their English accents floated back as they walked up the aisle. The priest arrived in a white lace-trimmed surplice over a black cassock with a white and gold stole. A woman in a grey felt hat with a feather sat at the small organ wheezing through a medley of hymns, playing ever so softly when the priest spoke.

He welcomed everyone and then ten minutes later appealed for patience–and then again more nerve-tugging minutes later.

Faye wiped her hands as unobtrusively as possible down the skirt of her blue silk dress. She was about to do it again when Glad took the hand nearest her in her lace-gloved one and held it firmly in her lap.

The familiar chords of *Here Comes the Bride* pumped out and the congregation stood. Faye looked over her shoulder. Framed in the arched doorway stood Stella, flushed but radiant with upswept hair crowned with creamy orchids. She was wearing a pale yellow satin dress that strained against an enormous stomach bulge. One hand gripped her Uncle Clive's arm, the other a large bouquet.

But after seeing the bulge and what it meant, the other details retreated like vision after a flashbulb had popped. She must have been staring as her mind struggled to accept what was there before her eyes. Stella wasn't only getting married, but she was going to be a mother. The shock of this, the naked indecency of it, what it implied, that Stella and Arno had had sex, and that good, well-brought up girls didn't have sex before marriage, and especially, that *Stella* had had sex, and all without Faye being aware of, without being part of, blotted out for a moment the fact that Stella was staring back.

Her eyes were enormous. Faye knew that look. She had seen it at Roy's funeral when Stella entered the church with Constance and again at the latter's funeral. But Arno had been at her side then. Now he was way up the front of the church.

Faye turned some more. "*Star,*" she hissed. "You look fab." And then, and she didn't know why, she said, "God Bless the bride."

"Faye." Stella didn't need to say anything else, but she did, "*You came.*"

———————————

"We were waiting for Ada and Frank to come back from England before getting pregnant. But then it happened. When they heard the news they jumped on the first plane."

Faye was looking at Stella's stomach again.

"It's twins." Stella grinned. "If they're girls I'm calling them Faye and Stella."

"When is it– *they*– are due?" They had so much catching up to do.

"Twins come early, so anytime." At Faye's concerned look she said, "We've passed thirty-two weeks, so they'll be alright."

"So have you two of everything?" Faye didn't know what else to say. She was desperately trying to think of anything she could say with regard to pregnancy and childbirth, but she couldn't think of anything.

"Sorry, I had to give your place to Phyllis. I thought of having no one but she has done so much for me. It was a way of saying thank you." Stella waved to Miss O'Donnell at the main table chatting with Ada. Her ex-boss beamed broadly, including Faye.

"So glad you're here," Arno had whispered in Faye's ear outside the church. "She's half herself without you," which, with Stella's present size, was the joke to beat all jokes.

Now he smiled a big warm smile that included Faye and Glad as he held out a hand to Stella for the first dance. Then as she moved into his arms the smile transformed into something quite different. Faye turned away, moved, and, yes, embarrassed. It was like she had walked in on them naked in bed.

The carpet had been removed and the floor polished for the occasion. A three-piece band played *Can't Help Falling in Love*.

They were about to start dancing when Stella, still in Arno's arms, leaned across and said, "Hey, Faye?" Faye turned round. "We don't have a special song. We're just letting the band do their thing."

"This is our song, then, hon," she heard Arno say as they danced away.

"That's *so* Stella." Faye said to Glad.

Just then Ada came over. "Won't the two of you join us? I want you to meet our UK family." She added, as they walked across to the main table, "It has all worked out so well. Now Arno will have company when we go caravanning. We're retired. The gallivanting has begun."

Faye tried to enter into the conversation with the Gideons and their relatives, but her attention kept being drawn back to the couple on the dance floor to feast her eyes on their beauty, their happiness. It was strange but so right, seeing the two of them together in this way. This was a different Stella– a full-blooming, womanly Stella. A Stella exuding the warmth and brilliance of new love. Faye couldn't stop the tears rolling down her cheeks. Tears of joy for the couple, for their friendship healed and restored. Her mother looked across and smiled. For now Faye felt part of this wonderful celebration and was grateful, so very grateful that she had decided to come. Later she might weep about her own celebration of love that never was but might have been, although she knew that if she had it over she would probably do exactly the same thing. She looked at Glad in lively conversation with Ada, Phyllis O'Donnell, and the English families, and she was happy. That was the bottom line. That was her reward, her mother, happy and well.

It would only be a matter of months, and they would all –well, the main players– be gathered in the tiny church again. Then Faye would be upfront cradling a twin in each arm in her role as godmother. Stella and Arno had broken with tradition in that there was to be no godfather, which was a way of saying that she, Faye, was enough.

CHAPTER 27

It's been another tense wait at the hospital. The doctor emerges gowned and with his mask still around his neck to inform me that Faye has come through with flying colors. Flying colors? Poor thing stands to be cut away body part by body part until only her skeleton remains, and even then she might have to endure being chiseled away or sawn into before this horror story is over. I want to hammer fists on his falsely proud chest for failing to persuade Faye to have both breasts removed. And then there's my part in all this. Why hadn't I tried to persuade her? Without hesitation I could turn those fists on my own chest, two blithely unscathed and unconcerned breasts.

And here it comes. Is he going to ask if Faye has changed her mind about having chemo. No, he doesn't. Then, I think he's probably thinking she'll be convinced now, with two boobs gone west.

But I must be grateful for small mercies. She is over another hurdle. I will remain at the hospital until she has surfaced a tad more, and we can exchange a few coherent words, both of us. I take the elevator to the coffee shop on the ground floor where I will make calls to Brand and Lyle, to Gunner and to Anika. People from work have already called. I reply with less vigor than the doctor, but positive nonetheless. I will go home later and then return to spend the night at her bedside. To maintain sanity I have to have my ride on Izzy. If I didn't need to, I could go back to Faye's and have a kip. Gunner has insisted that I allow him to drive me back in and share the vigil. There's another mercy.

To begin with, the drive back into Cape Town is soothing. Gunner doesn't need to fill the silence, and I appreciate that. However, to ward off worry about Faye that buzzes in my head like a trapped bee, I ask Gunner about the houses he has viewed so far. He says most of them need too much upkeep to leave empty during the months he would be away, which, in any case, Brand and other agents have advised him against. The laws governing renting agents in South Africa aren't stringent enough from a property owners' perspective, which I'm aware of and agree. It is also not unheard of for squatters to move in or tenants to refuse to vacate. It can take a year or more to have these undesirables legally removed.

"We're talking gloom and doom," I say, and by unspoken agreement we continue in silence with me making lists in my head for chores to be done the next day as a way to shut out the angst.

When we arrive, Faye is awake and after a brief exchange, Gunner leaves to get coffees.

"It's better this time," she says. "Remember how I vomited when I was coming around last time?"

I nod.

"I told the anesthetist and he gave me something different. The woman in the other bed," Faye nods towards the other bed from whose pillows loud snores erupt, "has had a complete hysterectomy. Also cancer. Her breasts were first to go. All of this *with* chemo. She's heard that there's some medicine that prevents the cancer spreading from the breasts to the rest of the body, but the government won't allow it to be imported because it's too expensive. I'd love to get my hands on *that*."

I want to say that each course of chemo will have extended the woman's life. Who knows, she might have been dead by now. But Faye is no fool. She will be aware of this. It occurs to me that hankering after a medication that is out of reach is another form of avoidance, of ignoring what is possible for her, available to her here and now.

"Hon, just get over this," I say, and she doesn't argue.

When Gunner returns she is sleeping, but fitfully. He fetches the other chair in the ward so he can sit beside me. He hands me a cappuccino and we sip in silence. He nods off but I remain awake. I study his face in the half dark. He looks younger and vulnerable. I want to touch his hands so neatly clasped in his lap, but don't.

Gradually Faye's murmurs and sighs become less until finally she is in a deep sleep. I wake up to the sister whispering that she has checked on Faye, which includes the watery bleed into the bag that hangs down the other side of the bed, Faye's pulse, blood pressure, and so on, all done while we dozed. Gunner opens his eyes as the woman is giving a thumbs up. We should go home, she says. She is sure Faye will be fine from now onwards. I glance at Gunner with a raised eyebrow, and he nods. I kiss Faye on the cheek and we creep out. At the nurse's enclosure I give the sister my telephone number and she promises to call if she feels my presence would help or if Faye asks for me. Otherwise she will call with a report before the end of the shift.

The next morning the sister calls. Faye had a peaceful night and wants to talk to me.

"Hi," she says in a thick voice. "Deserted me, did you?"

"You were sleeping like a baby, so we made a turn at a nightclub."

I shared the good news with Gunner when he appeared for breakfast. He is going to oversee the overdue spraying of insecticides. He and Brand have done a deal. In exchange for board and lodging, Gunner has a checklist of vineyard tasks. I like that Gunner treats Brand as he would have Arno, as an equal. After my share of farm and office tasks I catch up with Anika.

When I reported back to her the results of Gunner's and my day of inquiries she told me that she didn't think Strawks would be at Perlheim *or* at Elsenburg. Why tell me? She must have guessed that I would go anyway. I didn't tell her about his recent approach of Perl Javinski, or that she employed him for a week then fired him without giving him a reason. It would only have added to the indigestible knob of discouragement she struggles with on his behalf. To mention that he had stayed at Bella's B+B, also recently, will serve no purpose, so I leave it out completely.

"And what about Bethany? Don't you think he is there either?"

"I really don't know, Stella."

"Have you any contacts there?"

"I'll make some calls, but don't get your hopes up."

"You're not worried? You don't think he's done something stupid, do you?"

"You mean harm himself?" Anika had paused, leaving me to gasp at my crassness. "I don't think so. No, definitely not. He loves Vally too much. He knows she needs him. She talks about him every day."

What could I say? Our promise to help with Valdine has so far come to nothing. I also have to shelve my plan to have the Akkerstroom three to lunch, Anika, Valdine and Henk. I had hoped to include Gunner, but he flies home in a week. I was looking forward to the two men meeting. It would have been an opportunity for Henk, that old bigot, to give me some feed-back on Gunner. Is he for real? Can someone, a man, fit so spoon-like into a person's life without there being some snag? I could Google him as I did Strawks, but I would have no way of checking the between the lines stuff. I am a horsey girl after all, wanting to check the horse's mouth.

I call Anika again with the news of Faye's good start to the day and her delight is shared with Valdine, listening in the background. She and Valdine will say a prayer of thanks after the call. If we never find Strawks, and a quiver of disquiet shoots through me at this thought, I will have made a new friend, and in the case of Faye, renewed contact with an old friend.

A day later I wake with a throat that feels like it has been sand-papered. My pajamas are wringing wet. I know if I don't stay in bed, the interval before it is safe to visit Faye without the chance of infecting her will be prolonged.

Gunner knocks on the door with a tray of orange juice, coffee, and a bowl of fruit salad. There is also a glass of water and two Disprin. He pulls up a chair and watches as I down the water with the dissolved tablets. I am unable to do this without screwing up most of my face.

"Willy's doing?" I whisper hoarsely. I glance at the meal, knowing I am going to disappoint her.

"You look like something that washed up after a storm," he says.

"Does everything have to be about the sea? You don't look too frisky yourself."

"Are we agreed then, to take the day off?"

I nod. "I'll text Faye."

"Let me do that." He takes the cell phone.

Faye is happy to have a morning to herself, he says. Then his cell-phone rings and he apologizes as he leaves, shutting the door behind him. His voice is raised as he responds but the words are indistinct.

By the next day the phlegm I cough up reminds me of frogs and tadpoles.

"You must stop smoking." This is our doctor's standard comment whenever he sounds my chest. A sick joke if ever there was one.

I call Anika and hallelujah, she agrees to stay in Faye's house with Valdine so that she can visit Faye with greater ease while the latter is in hospital. She has also offered to stay on and help Faye if I am still laid up when Faye comes home. And there I was champing inwardly at Anika's tardiness in things Faye-related.

Later that evening Brand brings me a hot toddy. Does he have my permission to continue taking Gunner house-hunting?

"You know you don't have to ask me that."

"I dunno, you have him pretty sewn up here. And what's this about you making wine?"

"Perl Javinski issued a challenge."

"So I heard."

"You don't mind? We can each have a go. The more shots at Perl the better."

Brand gives me his best grown-up look. "Winemaking is not for me, Mom. I'm thinking of doing an MBA."

"You did well with the estate agent exams."

"The courses are worlds apart. I may go part-time at work to make sure I pass. It takes two years. Ellie will be the main breadwinner, although we have savings from the sale of houses."

"You've thought of everything."

Brand looks as happy as when he sold his first house. I will find out eventually what was bothering him.

Lyle is next. The boys are taking advantage of my ensured presence. Have I been that unavailable?

"Mom, is it OK if I come home when Gunner has gone? Myrna and I need a cooling-off period."

My sore head throbs with joy. "Of course."

"I can't tell whether it is her I like or the opportunities she's given me to decorate. She is also majorly encouraging." And I wasn't? I have been preoccupied, I realize.

I call Faye.

"Has Anika been to see you?" I enunciate carefully hoping this will compensate for a voice-box squeezed out of existence by an unseen hand.

"And Valdine. She would make a good nurse. She's so gentle. She has a wet face cloth pressed to my forehead."

"Wonderful."

"We've been talking about her Dad and how she misses him. I've told her how he and I were friends. That he was my best friend but that we lost touch. She said that when he comes home he and I must 'find touch'– her words, isn't that cute? Sounds like rugby."

"And what did you say?" I cough into the duvet against my mouth.

"I said that it sounds like a good idea."

Already I am losing concentration. This is better. Sleep, the refuge. I feel my eyelids pressing down.

But I can't abandon my quest, even when the rest of me is screaming, *stop*.

Any chance this second butchering has made you change your mind? The words start as a tickle in my windpipe, crawl up my raw throat and dance around seductively on my chapped lips. But instead of the magic words, I am in the grips of a spasm of coughing. I have to end the call with a whisper, "Good night. Take care." After which I realize it is still afternoon.

I wake later with the dance of my cell phone on the bedside table.

"You're sick, Stella. Why didn't you tell me?" No, softly murmured, 'Star'. Faye has been in touch with the boys.

CHAPTER 28

They say you can't fill the gap left by one person with another. The arrival of the twins put paid to that theory. Perhaps it worked because there were two.

From the moment Faye stood at the window of the hospital nursery, she was hooked.

"They're not identical. See, the little guy on the left has dark hair and the other one fair." Faye looked into Arno's eyes, intense with pride, and back at the tiny red faces peeping out of the blankets. Later she would notice that the dark-haired baby had a long, thin face and often frowned. Stella called him 'old man.' Whereas the fair one had a round, contented looking face. He was 'Mister Sunshine.'

"Thank goodness they're not identical," Arno continued unabashed. "I was dreading getting them confused."

"They're ugly," was Stella's pronouncement when Faye returned to the bedside.

Faye wanted to argue that they were beautiful but shockingly small. She had to make allowances for Stella. Arno had warned Faye over the phone that it had been a natural birth but difficult. The twins had gone almost full term and were chubby. As a result, there was extensive internal and external suturing. He also told Faye that Stella had had a tubal ligation.

This seemed harsh, but perhaps that was what had enabled Stella to lavish her attention on her babies, Faye reasoned. This was her friend's one chance at motherhood. She was firm, though. Arno said he was often the one that had to be stopped picking up one of the babies when they cried. Whereas Stella would count off on one hand that they were fed, burped, had on clean diapers, were warm, and no fastenings were too tight. It was time to sleep and that was what they had to do. She would switch on their musical mobiles, close the door, and retreat. She left them to cry a little too long, Faye thought, but Stella was their mother and was going to do things her way no matter what. When they cried like that Faye retreated to the garden and kept walking until she couldn't hear them.

That Stella was willing to share her babies never failed to amaze Faye. She was sure she couldn't have done the same. Once the twins had passed the milestone of six weeks, Faye was allowed to take her turn. Stella would bring one of them, then the two, for a few hours. Saturday afternoons saw the lounge, the kitchen, and her bedroom a fall-out of Pampers and the whole range of Johnson's baby care, a thermometer, just in case, the baby chairs, blankets, bibs, rattles, soft toys and mobiles, formula, fruit juice and bottled water, later rusks and wands of biltong and jars of Purity. Eventually Faye would get on top of the situation, but to begin with she was in a flap, and Stella, wisely, left her to it.

In fine weather Faye took them for a walk in the neighborhood with the 'double-cab,' as Stella called the twins stroller. What a delight having people pop a head under the canopy and ask their sex and age and pay the most flattering of compliments. Faye began by correcting people when they assumed she was the mother but then later she thought, what harm could it do? She wasn't actually lying. An outing, say, to Kirstenbosch Botanic Gardens, was akin to preparing for a climb up Mount Everest. The supplies that had to go on board. She planned in detail before they left, but even then something unlikely would happen, like a strap in the stroller that came loose, causing little Lyle to fall forward when a boy carted into Faye from behind. Lyle had been holding a lollipop at the time and luckily it hadn't been rammed down his throat. But he did have a grazed lip. Luckily it didn't bleed for long and the little chap smiled through it all.

Then came the first sleep-over, first with Willy, then solo. She dreaded them waking up together. Brand was bellowing, so she fed him first. Lyle emitted little squeaks to let her know he was there. In general, you had to remind yourself to do things for him because he hardly ever complained.

You also had to keep track of who had what when. Faye had devised a chart that she thought was natty. She offered it to Stella, but Stella preferred to wing everything. She was a natural, which Faye put down to Stella's affinity with animals.

Her mother was the stabilizing force with her nursing experience and having had Faye. She wasn't able to help other than hold one of the infants on her lap at bath time or mealtimes. They stopped crying immediately. It was like they sensed this person knew her oats. Stella said Glad reminded them of Ada, whom they adored and who played a similar non-intrusive supportive role.

All too soon the twins were at nursery, then preschool, and then primary. Faye tried to get to all their events, be it sport or school concerts, prize-giving and excursions to a sweet factory, for example, or the aquarium. Brand did well in schoolwork and sports. Lyle was in the percussion band and won prizes for art. Faye loved best the longer spells with them, that is, when Stella and Arno took their holidays overseas. For those weeks they became hers and they grew really close and confided in Faye. Lyle told her about a teacher who had made Lyle his pet, which antagonized the other children, who then picked on him behind the teacher's back. Encouraged by his brother's openness, Brand told her how another player down in the rugby scrums regularly twisted his testicles and he had to hide the pain and couldn't report on the other boy for fear of being called a *moffie*. When she told Glad, Glad was quite firm about the boys telling Stella or Arno, so that they could take action. Which Faye did and which had the desired effect. Afterwards she felt robbed. They would probably never confide as freely again.

The best of times was when they stayed with her in town. For those days, she had them to herself, whereas at the farm they were gone all day, ate lunch with the laborers in the vineyard, returning exhausted. Persuading them to bath was a struggle. They gobbled enormous plates of food, after which they flopped into bed, offering her a sunburnt cheek to kiss, and in seconds were asleep. Ada and Frank provided much needed adult company. In later years, she became more aware of her being alone at the farm, maybe because it was a family home with married parents whose absence was conspicuous. But in town, the three of them went to the movies or ice-skating or took boat rides to see the seals around Hout Bay or in the harbor inspected ships open to the public or rode the cable car up Table Mountain. Because of the pain these sorts of movement would have caused, Glad elected to stay home. But she accompanied them to kid-friendly restaurants like the Wimpy and the Spur steak ranches. They stayed up late to watch television, not allowed at home. Over mugs of bedtime Milo, they had lively debates about the heroes and baddies in the movies and TV shows. They loved to hear tales of Auntie Glad's childhood in England. They went to the office with Faye, where they made books from wastepaper and stapled them together, which Brand filled with figures and Lyle covered with drawings.

Then the owner of Hilliard Carpets died and the son, who had inherited the business, already had a car sales business of his own, so he put her in charge. Although running a business was a dream come true, it came at a bad time as Glad, after years of procrastination, had decided to have the first hip redone. Walking had again become painful, and life lived almost exclusively out of a wheelchair loomed. It wasn't an easy decision because she had developed high blood pressure, diabetes (in sympathy with Bert, Faye wondered), and arthritis. She had to lose weight before the op. Holding her mother to the diet and using every means at hand to keep her spirits up, like taking her to restaurants that served the pretty but scant servings of nouvelle cuisine, and back and forth to the farm (she and Ada were bosom buddies), used up any energy Faye might have had after work which meant that she didn't have the twins around as much.

Glad never came round from the anesthetic. She was in a coma for two days then slipped away not having uttered one word.

Faye couldn't face arranging the funeral at the church where Bert's funeral had taken place. This would be a smaller affair, and if patients and people who remembered her mother from her days in the surgery felt the need to attend, they could take a drive out to the stone chapel in the country. The dominee who had married Stella and Arno took the simple service. Stella saw to the flowers, choice of hymn, had the order of service cards printed. Without Glad to trigger a guilt trip Faye felt eerily lightheaded. It seemed so easy.

Attending was another thing entirely. At her father's funeral her preoccupation had been concern for Glad. Now the focus was on herself. She felt exposed, like a Siamese twin brutally severed from its sibling. She made herself greet people at the door sustained by a 'cocktail' from Doc Nico. As it was winter, almost everyone was in a coat. The twins, in their school uniforms, pink-kneed from the cold, sat between Faye and Stella. Faye might have kept them away from the funeral had she been their mother. Being sons of a farmer they were acquainted with death, she realized, oh so grateful for their fidgeting and questions about cremation and what 'the hereafter' meant, so that she had little time to think. Ada and Frank, looking frail and diminished– they were to die the following year– sat on the other side of Brand, but when their eyes met Faye's, the warmth they conveyed filled her with renewed strength. Arno, on the other side of Stella, stretched his arm across the back of the pew and gave Faye's shoulder a firm squeeze.

People were invited back to the farm. As always, there was loads of wine and food. If the twins hadn't been present she might have got drunk. Instead, she soldiered on mildly tipsy through a fog of sympathy and snatched moments, sitting on the front steps and watching them play with the dogs or lying on her stomach on one of their beds, chin on hand, listening to Lyle strum his guitar while she and Brand tried to remember the words to a song. She spent that night at the farm but the next morning she kissed their sleeping selves, each on a cheek, gathered her wobbly self, and headed for work. There, she would hopefully be able to forget her sorrow. Stella was going to sleep over when she next got the chance. Faye clung to the thought like a lifebelt.

And yet when Stella did come, Faye felt worse. Without her mother she was like a boat without a rudder. Everything from then onwards– her job, people, even Stella, came at her like the waves of a high sea. Although on the surface she must have looked and sounded the same because people responded to her as they always did, or seemed to. She was in no shape to judge because she was going through the motions, doing everything from habit. She heard herself speaking, acting, checking her mail, making entries in spread sheets, directing staff and replying to Stella, who had begun to sound and look worried. But it was Stella who had a family, the farm, her animals, so that every word of concern and consolation, and Stella being Stella, these were blessedly few, clanged like a buoy on those choppy seas, distant, belonging to a former life, one that had no bearing on the present.

Weeks passed, and months. Gradually she began to feel less shattered, less broken. A thought began to stir from somewhere deep, like the shoot of a winter bulb. Maybe now she could have a life of her own. Do the things she might have if she hadn't had her mother in her life. Bless her mother, bless Glad. Faye wouldn't want her life to have been any different. But now there was an opportunity for something else. For dreams she hadn't dared dream. For that shoot to grow, develop. A dream of having her own children. She would be thirty next birthday. It wasn't too late. She would always want the twins in her life. Always be grateful for their bouncing affectionate selves, but having her own, now that would be nothing short of a miracle, a glorious and unexpected miracle.

She hadn't dared think about Strawks in that way, as the father of her children, as her husband until then.

Over the years, Faye had kept in touch with Anika, who gave her news of Strawks. He was a job forager, it appeared, working in the wine industry and then veering off into maintenance and HR at a hospital or management of the gardens of a chain of hotels or joining the technical team on an oil rig, only to return after a spell to what best held his interest. He worked in a cooperage, for a wine-rack producer, a wine center offering tasting and videos on winemaking. Although Anika assured her that Strawks was happy and doing well, that he liked ringing the changes as regards work, she couldn't help thinking that if they had married she would have kept him steady, helped him clarify what it was he was after. She knew that he wanted to own a wine farm. They could have saved together for one.

Anika was careful to avoid mentioning any women friends, and even when he was getting married, Faye might not have heard about it had toasting the new millennium not come up. Faye received the news like a blow to the chest.

It was then that the dreams began. She was always getting ready to marry but never actually marrying. Sometimes they got as far as the altar and then a bale of straw might fall through the ceiling and flatten the priest. Or her father would arrive on a gurney, and she would try to get him to stand up so he could give her away, with disastrous results– he died, or he went off to attend to a patient, or some other crazy intervention. Or she was in some unsuitable item of clothing like pajamas and she would run back down the aisle to change only to find her wedding dress was missing. Once she was pregnant and her labor started just as the priest opened the book with the marriage service. Another time the church was on fire, and they had to run to safety.

Then she bumped into him at Jo'burg airport.

She had flown up to sort out a stock problem with a supplier and was in the business class lounge when she felt a hand on her shoulder.

Then he was bending over and kissing her.

"You're on the way back to Cape Town, too?" Her heart was thumping, her hands shaking so much that she had to clasp them in her lap.

He was nodding, all smiles. He seemed taller and broader. There was a sheen about him. He had a smarter, gelled haircut and wore an expensive suit. She remembered the Goth outfit and how he liked to dress up and wondered if he was playing a part, the part of the successful businessman. But there were lines around his eyes, and she felt bad thinking that. His lips had been dry on hers. She took a stick of Lip Ice out of her handbag and handed it to him.

"Always looking after me." He was chuckling. "Remember how you made me study?"

"Made you? If I remember correctly, you begged for help. You would have failed without me."

His eyes darkened. "Sorry about your Mom." He touched her hand. "Wonderful lady."

But his eyes were twinkling as he stroked the wand across first her top lip, then her bottom lip. She'd forgotten how mercurial his moods.

"All the more reason to kiss you again." He leaned in but she pushed him away gently and took the Lip Ice from him.

"You're married."

"Mind if I sit down?" He looked suddenly all in.

She patted the seat beside her. "We can still be friends."

It was an almost macabre déjà vu of how she had patted the seat that last time they spoke. Except this time, she was sending him away because of something in *his* life.

His shoulders in the beautiful suit sagged. He seemed to search for words. "...big mistake."

He threw her a stunned look. "You're the first person I've said that to."

"Our friendship?"

"No, my marriage."

"We keep in touch, Anika and I."

"So you know I'm married. It works both ways, you know. That's how I heard Stella and Arno got married. Stella had boy twins, Brand and Lyle. I did pop in at the farm once. I embarrassed Arno when I asked for a job. Decided I wouldn't put us through that again. Then I went undercover at Sports Day. To check out the *lighties'* running races. If anyone asked I would have said I'm an uncle, come to see my nephews. No one did."

He hadn't come over. He'd been at the twins' school and he hadn't come over.

"I knew when I saw your Mom, especially walking with a stick, I'd get the brush-off. There's only so much a guy can take. That made me decide enough was enough."

"So you got married. I'm giving myself too much importance aren't I?"

"Hey, let's enjoy this. This hand of fate." He smiled. With Strawks, a smile was never far away. "You're lookin' good, Faye Morrisey."

She swallowed hard. "And you, Thorkild Johansen. Er, Strawks." She was grinning in spite of herself.

"It's stuck. The name. That's how I introduce myself."

"You *don't*."

He looked sad again. "You've left your mark on me."

"Hey. Cheer up." It was her turn to lighten the mood. "The hand of fate?"

They sat looking at one another, the familiar pleasure in one another's presence moving through nerves, muscle and blood. She wriggled in her chair. Her panties were slippery wet.

The call came to board. They walked across the tarmac arm in arm. Fifteen minutes in the air he was asking the woman next to Faye if she wouldn't mind changing seats with him.

"She's my drug mule," he said. "I have to protect my investment."

The woman threw him a nervous look before scurrying off. She never returned. She must have found another seat.

Faye was still giggling when he told her the trip was to check on the kind of farming in Gauteng.

"For a job interview," he said, like an afterthought. "You're still with Hilliards?"

She nodded.

"If you ever want to make a change…" He took a business card out of his top pocket. "These people are ace. I owe my illustrious career path to them." He was writing something on the back as he said, "Ask for Merrilees."

She took the card. On the back he had written a phone number, his private number?

"Will you take it, do you think?" And when he looked puzzled, "The job in Jo'burg?"

"My wife's dead keen. She loves the social life. More of that in Joeys. But the farming is grain and cattle, market gardens. I love my vines. I've become a real Capie. Can't see myself making the move. So in a way, I'm kidding myself about the job. I could commute, like every fortnight or so, but that would eat into my salary. So I'm stuck."

"Can I visit you?" He asked out of the blue.

She shook her head.

"You said we could be friends."

She looked at him and sighed. She knew what would happen. They'd fall into bed and would soon be having an affair. She thought too highly of him and herself, for that matter, to allow them to sink to that level. She wanted so much more for them. It was that, or nothing.

He wanted to know about her, how it was with Glad, and afterwards without her. About the job, Stella and Arno, the twins. What he was really asking was– did she miss him, did she regret anything? But those details would have made it all the harder to remain firm.

The trays came with their meals. Remembering his sweet tooth, she gave him her dessert.

"What the heck," he said, digging his spoon into the second tub of chocolate mousse. "The wife has me on a diet."

He shrugged, but he gave her his cheese and biscuits. They were like an old married couple, anticipating one another's needs. It would be so easy to be his mistress. No one would know. His visits would be clandestine. He could still be a husband, a father.

When the trays were gone he tried again. "I will need to visit my sister. That's if we move to Joeys. And if we're still in the Cape… I'm often out nights visiting clients. No one need know. Not even Stella. We can meet at a hotel on the other side of town if you're worried about the neighbors. Some place no one you know frequents."

She knew she couldn't do it. But every time she flew up to Jo'burg– which was once or twice a year– she would find herself hoping she might bump into him again. But it never happened. She wondered if he had taken the job in Jo'burg. But by then she had stopped contacting Anika, who had never been in the habit of contacting her, so she never knew.

CHAPTER 29

To begin with, I get worse. Even after a course of a second, more potent antibiotic, the phlegm keeps bubbling up, ever so slowly changing from swamp slime to sun-bleached slime to the transparent effluvium of the tormented air passages of my lungs. The doctor remarks on the 'looseness' of my chest. One winter I had the 'tight' kind, and a physio came twice a week to pound my back as I hung over the edge of the bed.

I consume little for the first ten days, causing Willy to fret so much that I almost wish *she* would get sick herself and leave me alone. If you haven't suffered a bronchial infection you won't know about the taste it leaves in your mouth. Obviously Willy hasn't or is too darn dogged in her nursing. But I do drink an enormous amount of water. For weeks I can't stand tea or coffee. Later I progress to diluted fruit juice, and then Willy's homemade ginger beer, also diluted– to her disgust.

For a while, the world is dark. My lungs are leaden, toxic clouds that pin me down, determined to bury me alive. My nights are full of dreams that tear through my consciousness, and I wake up gasping for air. I grope for the bedside light to dispel the threatening image of a doctor with a Medieval-type instrument, a cross between an eggbeater and a drill that he uses to dig around in my chest.

In amongst the horror I hear Gunner speak. Is he on the phone or is he speaking to me?

His face is close as he waits for me to focus.

"Anything I can do?"

Turn off my mind, I might have said. I try to sit up, but he gently presses me back down.

"You're wet through," he scolds as I imagine he might have an unfortunate midshipman.

He switches on the bedside lamp, looks around the room. It is his first time there. I might have cringed had I the strength.

"Where d'you keep your pajamas?" He opens a door of the built-in cupboard. Before I can reply, he has a pair.

He helps me to a chair. "Put these on while I change the sheets."

"Also in there." I point to the other side of the cupboard.

"You sure live neatly. You'd do well in a sub."

Yellow Submarine. Something about this makes me want to laugh but I daren't. A coughing spasm can bring me to the edge of wondering if I'll ever catch a breath again. He keeps his back to me while I change.

"Wow," I croak when I see how he has made the bed.

"Mine was the best bunk on training." He helps me back in. He picks up the damp pajamas and linen and I hear the linen basket lid in the bathroom click back after he stuffs the bundle in.

"OK. What now?"

I point to the medicines on the bedside table.

I can't remember him leaving.

———————

Two weeks have gone by before I realize Gunner hasn't left for Australia. He has often brought me a tray or changed my sheets, found me my favorite program on local radio, or read to me from the newspaper. He is making the bed one day when I find myself admiring muscles moving as he smooths and tucks.

"You're still here." I sit up, shaking my head. How selfish I am not to have noticed.

He steps forward and I bark, "I'm fine." I walk back to the bed stiffly.

When I have my breath back I ask, "What made you change your flight?"

"I haven't found a house yet." He pulls me towards him with a hand on my back. I might have caught a whiff of his aftershave, but my sense of smell has abandoned me. But I do become aware of the breadth of his chest and the prickles of his stubble through the crown of my matted hair. He is the sort of person whom you feel has a third hand somewhere invisibly doing something else because everything gets done most efficiently.

I lie back against the most perfect of bolsters. "I thought you were giving up on the houses?"

"I'm like a dog with a bone. And your son is willing."

Tears spring to my eyes. I put it down to weakness wrought by the infection. With difficulty I say, "You're welcome to stay as long as you like."

I am puzzled but don't feel up to questioning him. Then I remember that Lyle wanted the room so he could get a breather from Myrna. I am torn, but for now all I can do is hope Lyle isn't in a hurry. Gunner has to go eventually, but that is also something I can't get my mind around.

It is the first day I decide to get dressed and stand in front on the long mirror in my underwear. A scarecrow girl stares back.

Fortunately, horses don't mind how you look. I am not strong enough yet to ride but I can visit and talk, snuggle and kiss.

"How have you been, my lovely?" I ask each one.

The groom and laborers, the twins and Ellie have done a good job. I feel dizzy standing beside Izzy, whom I leave until last. I look around for Isak, the groom, and he brings me a stool. I tell him how pleased I am with the condition of the animals and the stables.

"Mister Gunner, he also rides and helps in the stables."

"Back home he has a farm and horses. He will be missing them."

"*Nee*, Miss Stella. There's nothing to miss. He sold his farm. The one in Australia?"

How many farms does Gunner have? "There's only one that I know of."

"That's it, Miss. Australia. Melmouth…Melbit…"

"Melbourne."

"*Korek*."

Gunner will tell me all about it, I am sure.

Each day I can do a little more. I am still brought my meals in bed. My visits to the stable are in secret. I slip out after lunch when Willy is taking her break, when Lyle is busy in the salon, Ellie at work, and when Brand is out showing houses to Gunner or at work. A few days later, after I have greeted the horses, I stroll down to the garden taking care to keep well away from the windows of the salon. I am getting myself fit for an inspection of the vineyard, something that weighs heavily.

Spring is everywhere. The oak trees nearest the stables spread their lacy green mantles for me as I pass. The coral tree, until recently, known as the *kaffir boom* is coming into the glorious color of its name. As littlies, Brand and Lyle shelled 'lucky beans' out of the black pods. Had they been girls they might have made necklaces, but being boys, they used them as ammunition in their homemade 'catties.'

I stand beside the vegetable patch and try out my breathing. It is almost normal. After the fallowness of the past few months, the rows of young carrots, beetroot, baby cabbages, and a variety of lettuce and rocket are a cheering sight. Climbing beans and tomatoes poke through the trellises against the wall of the shed. I rub basil and then coriander leaves between my fingers and sniff. I am almost there, smell-wise. I pick a strawberry, then another and another. Juice runs down my chin. I wipe and lick the back of my hand. Away towards the fence, the flowerbeds dazzle.

The world has moved on without me, a world from which I was absent. I inhabited another plane, a driven one. I pushed and pushed. My body, no longer able to keep up, folded on me.

I walk up the steps and flop, hoping my head isn't visible from the salon. The bones of my buttocks through their inadequate padding object. My breathing, although much improved, still snags on bubbles in my chest.

I shiver and pull the edges of the cardigan together. I hug my chest, which gets me thinking about Faye. I expect to feel resentment– or, heaven help me, jealousy – or at least defeat, that Anika is with her instead of me, but I don't. I'd like to think this is because I have gained some wisdom, a notch of maturity, but feeling anything other than self-pity or resignation requires strength and energy. I can console myself, however, that my friend has a substitute and a pretty good one. Not some stranger, but a friend. If I was able to feel strongly about anything at present it would be that my search for Strawks has juddered to a halt. But even in this respect I fail. Zeal is for the healthy.

In my room, I am about to lie down, when Willy knocks on the door.

She hands me a note in her childlike cursive that reads, *Tilly* and a number. "It is for Mister Gunner," Willy says. "The young miss said it is urgent."

Tilly is Gunner's daughter. Wherever he is, and I imagine he is looking at houses again, he has switched off his cell phone.

I decide to call her. I have never spoken to Tilly or her brother and it suddenly seems a good idea.

I am about to give up when a young voice answers.

"Hi. This is Stella. Gunner's friend."

"Hiya, Stella," she is breathing fast, as though she has been running. "Dad told me you are sick. I'm sorry to have disturbed you." She pauses, snatches another breath. "I told your housekeeper not to bother you. Soon after that I got hold of Dad on his mobile." She apologizes once more. "How *are* you?" She sounds genuinely concerned. What a lovely, bright person, I think.

"I'm very much on the mend. I thought it was time we were acquainted. Although I feel like we've already met. He talks about you a lot. He's a proud Dad."

"Silly man. I'm two a penny over here. Every Aussie girl goes walkabout and then studies something."

"But not everyone is one's daughter."

"True. Has he been behaving himself?"

"Put it this way, he only lacks the papers. In every other way, he's a tip-top male nurse." Tilly giggles and I say, "I feel bad. He is meant to be on holiday."

238 | MERIEL MONGIE

"I'm glad he is making himself useful. He is on holiday all the time or will soon be. Hopefully. That is why I called. They've brought the date forward for the auction of New Bordeaux."

New Bordeaux is Gunner's farm. Isak, the groom, must have got his tenses wrong, a common mistake for Afrikaans-speaking people. So, the farm hasn't been sold, or not yet.

Tilly wants to know more about Brand and Lyle. I tell her that Brand is thinking of doing an MBA. She is full of questions about the course, and I share what little I know. I boast unashamedly about Lyle's forays into interior decorating, mentioning Myrna and her house, by the way, but nothing about his proposed relocation of the salon. As I do with her father, I issue an open-ended invitation to come and stay, and for as long as she likes.

"I may just do that," she says. "The Cape sounds amazing."

"But you have marvelous scenery and places to visit in your country."

"But not all in one place like Cape Town. We must talk again," she says, "I have to get back to class."

Now it is my turn to apologize. "I'm so sorry. I've taken you away from your studies."

"Between you and me, he's an ol' drone, the Prof. But I need credits before I can sit for the exam. So sadly, it has to be. I've really *really* enjoyed talking to you, Stella." She pauses. "Dad's going to kill me for saying this, but he has a major crush on you. Again, bye-e."

Well. My mind is spinning. I could do with walking off what I've just heard. A stiff walk. But common sense returns and I can put Tilly's postscript down to girlish mischief. She is certainly full of fun. Brand and especially Lyle are going to love her.

I am lying back, running over the purpose of Tilly's call, namely, that the date for the auction of New Bordeaux has been brought forward, when Willy again knocks on the door. Did I telephone the 'young miss'? After I tell her I have, she stands for a moment. She has spotted my flushed cheeks and wants an explanation.

I feel well enough now to eat my meals with the family, I say, doing my best to tone down whatever has arrived by way of expression on my face, that is, I try to smile and look as normal as possible, and not like a rabbit caught in the headlights. So please, Willy, I add, lay a place for me at the table for dinner? I don't want Gunner to feel bad about flying back for the auction sale of his farm, but this I don't say.

CHAPTER 30

Two days later Gunner is leaving. Because I haven't been out of the house yet (officially) we won't, as a family, be dining out. He had it all planned, Ellie told me, and then I got ill– dinner at a five-star hotel in Cape Town. But I am in for a surprise. The night before he leaves, Gunner is cooking, and from Willy's reports, it will also be a meal to remember. Gunner invited her to join us, but she is using the opportunity to visit a friend.

A man in the kitchen. I can't resist. The minute I hear pots clattering I am at the door, asking if I can help.

"Only in an advisory capacity," he says, and I sit at the table. I am good with eggs. I make a fluffy omelet and poached eggs with Hollandaise sauce that doesn't curdle. But that's where it ends, and I think Gunner knows this, otherwise he wouldn't sound so cocky.

He is in an Old Navy T-shirt he tells me was a gift from Tilly when he left the navy. *Old* navy. One of Ada's old aprons (Willy must have given it to him) is tied around his middle. To complete the picture of preparedness he wears shorts and flip-flops. When he grins his teeth flash white against virulent stubble. He'll have a proper beard by the time he gets home, he says, rubbing his chin when he sees where my gaze has landed.

He is making crêpes, which he will fill with spinach and ricotta cheese, smothered in a tomato sauce, and bake. He stops to squeeze oranges into a tall glass, adding a splash of tequila, ice cubes, and a twist of the rind before handing it to me. We sip, looking at one another across the rims– he from a tankard of iced water bobbing with slices of lime. That cooks can drink wine and still perform miracles is TV-chef codswallop, he says.

"But it's O-K for me to drink?"

"What you have there is medicinal."

I watch as he spreads a hammered flat pork fillet with fruit, nuts, and spice before rolling and tying with string. I admire his deftness with knots. He says he can also dance the hornpipe, and promptly begins prancing around knees high, toes pointed, hands on his hips. My delight ends in a bout of coughing. But it is all bark and no glob. He apologizes profusely but is still grinning as the pork follows the rest of his stash into the fridge. He asks if I'm up to destalking green beans, and I nod.

Suzi hasn't stirred during all this, but a worried Woo asks to hop onto my lap.

When he begins the desserts, I feel my eyelids lower. I leave him with the last of our strawberries, a carton of cream and a 2-litre block of vanilla ice cream out on the table, half disappeared in a cupboard hunting for something 'to liven it up'. Back in my room I realize I forgot to ask him why he never cooked for us before, and then it occurs to me. It is typical of Gunner not to want to queer the cook's pitch. I also realize that if I hadn't got sick I would never have discovered another of this man's many talents, and I wonder as I lie back what else I might have learnt about him if he hadn't been called away. He hasn't bought a house, and I wonder if that means he won't be back. He also told me during the pruning that he gave Brand and our head laborer a crash course on his 'method'. No one should be indispensable, he said at the time, and that it wasn't he being pushy, but good management.

I wake from a nap and pad along to the dining room. The table is laid with what looks like an orange curtain, lacquered placemats I haven't seen since Ada died, silverware, and cloth napkins in the crystal glasses that are so ornate I don't think even Ada used them. The garishness is so male.

I smell smoke. Stepping through the French doors I see Gunner on the veranda. He lifts the lid off a Weber Braaimaster with a flourish. This is where the pork and sweet potatoes will roast, he tells me.

"In another half hour they'll be ready," he says of the coals.

"Where did you get that?" I cast a doubtful look at the Weber.

"My gift," he says. "I also found you a gas-fired model. It's in the shed. It's an Aussie thing. We like our barbies mobile. I'm guessing you have a lot of wind in summer?"

I glance down the garden to the bricked structure that has served the family ever since I've known them. It has a double grill with a warming shelf of the same width above, storage below for wood, charcoal and fire-lighting paraphernalia on one side, crockery, serving dishes, and utensils on the other. I have a flash of Arno slathering steaks, us later queuing with plates.

Gunner sees my lack of enthusiasm. "You still have that for your bigger events. In winter you'll be glad not to have to stand out in the cold."

"Thanks, Gunner," I manage.

What's wrong with me? I've been given something. The man has anticipated my needs. I am obsessed with the past. That's what it is. I need to let go. As I lie in the bath, I tell myself it's a small thing. There are many ways to pluck a chicken, lay a brick, fire up a barbecue/*braaivleis*. But it feels big. There's a name for it. Change. And it's strange that it should come up on Gunner's last night. It cuts through sentiment, warning that allowing someone into one's life will mean adjustment. But I may never see him again, I tell myself, so all this introspection could be pointless, and is probably the last of the illness blustering through, doing some final mischief before I am fully restored.

As I climb out, I hear voices– a laugh. That will be Lyle. I hear Brand object to something. The women's voices are like the tinkling muzak of a shopping mall, or in this case, a restaurant.

Ellie pops her head round the door as I stand at the mirror in my cupboard. "Lyle asks do you want help with your hair?"

"Please."

Minutes later he appears, brings a chair across, and I get an up-do. Ellie takes one look, goes off to her room and returns with a pair of pearl drop-earrings. She has also brought a floaty rainbow-hued scarf which she ties around my neck, shakes her head, and then swathes my waist in it, leaving me with curves that make Lyle whistle.

"When you're up-and-about, we're going shopping," Ellie declares, tying the ends at one hip. She asks me to sit down again, fetches her make-up bag and applies more blusher, hunts for a brighter lipstick, and strokes that on as well.

"I should do this for a living," she says, standing back and admiring the effect.

"So *this* is where you are."

"Come in," Ellie and Lyle chorus.

I haven't seen Myrna since I got ill. She stares at my reflection. I turn around and greet her. With my newly restored mojo I could have hugged her, but she remains determinedly near the door.

"Glad to hear you're better," she says, and I have to be satisfied with that.

We begin with sparkling wine. Gunner, with the help of Ellie, paces out our courses. Brand and Lyle keep our glasses topped up with a choice of wines. The pork is tender with deliciously crunchy crackling, the sweet potatoes toasted caramel. I try everything but my appetite lags. I refuse the ice cream bombe but enjoy the deliciously light strawberry fool.

We take our Irish coffees out onto the veranda. It is a surprisingly warm night, but even so Brand fetches the duvet off my bed and bundles me in it.

Conversation hovers around Gunner's departure the next morning. He recalls highlights like Myrna's housewarming party, fishing off Table Bay, horse rides, golf, and most important of all, house-hunting.

"We've left no house unturned," Gunner quips. "This guy has the patience of a saint." He lays a hand on Brand's shoulder. "I don't know if you are aware –" he looks around the circle of eyes in the half dark, "but the sale of my farm fell through while I was here. I'm going back for the auction." He grimaces, an expression at odds with his personality, I think. "So it's just as well I didn't sign for one."

Later, when Lyle and Myrna have gone and Brand and Ellie have said goodnight and leave to clear the kitchen, Gunner says, "My wife and I co-own the farm. There were a couple of pages of the sale agreement she didn't initial. The buyer used the opportunity to duck out. Some bungle with his funds. Better to find that sort of thing out sooner than later."

"When did you decide to auction?"

Gunner looks embarrassed. "The sale fell through when you were sick. The response to the ad has been so good (I remember his replies to his phone)– much better than the first time. In fact, so good the agent suggested we bring the date forward. Tilly was calling to confirm."

"I'm so behind with all this. Just to put me in the picture– when you postponed coming and then came on the original date, did it have something to do with the sale?" Why didn't he tell me he had sold the farm, I wonder. I remember our day at Perlheim and in Stellenbosch. He had plenty of opportunity then.

"No, but it had to do with the farm which was already sold. There were two months before the buyer took over. Greta, my wife, hired a movie crew to make an ad there– she sells silk flowers– and wanted me to waltz attendance while they were there. When I realized she was free to do it herself and was just using me, I re-booked. She hated living away from town. It got so bad she couldn't bear spending a night at the farm.

"She gave me quite the wrong impression when we discussed buying the place, though. She was going to grow real flowers. But as soon as she realized that she would have to be there and supervise, she dropped the idea. I had this romantic picture of us watching over our crops– her flowers, my grapes, while we sipped my wine, discussed watering systems, soil enhancement and insecticides. We kept a house in town, and she began spending more and more time there.

"Stella, I'm sorry I kept everything from you– the sale of the farm and when it fell through, the arranging of an auction. I wanted to hand you a fait accompli. I wanted to have a house that I could invite you to here."

"You know you're welcome."

He puts a finger to my lips. "No protests, ma'am. I have my pride. I wanted to be able to invite *you* to stay with *me*– and the rest of the family, of course. But all in good time." His eyes are black in the half light. I want to shine a torch again to make sure of their color. Confirming their color suddenly seems vital.

"None of this has turned out the way I planned. Selling my place, buying a house here– I couldn't buy a house until the sale was through."

He sucks air into that almighty ribcage. "There's something I want you to think about while I'm gone– and I'll be back, make no mistake, as soon as I can. If that's still OK with you?"

Before I can give my standard reply he says, covering the hand nearest him, the one that is clutching the duvet, with one of his, "Don't answer yet. In fact, don't answer at all now. I'm going to call you when I get home. In any case, I'll be giving you an update from time to time." Now he takes the hand, and it disappears between his two. "And if you agree to this– even to just thinking about it– and *you*'ll also have to be patient. I have my side to wind up." He looks into my eyes, then off into the impenetrable distance across the garden– green where the light reaches, purple in shadow. He looks as though he is searching. For a moment I feel sorry for him. Men are the ones who have to go on bended knee.

I take the opportunity to close my eyes. I am praying, I guess. It had seemed complicated enough, years ago, when Arno asked me to 'come home.' The 'will you marry me' had followed fast on its heels with my breathy and heart-in-throat 'yes' in reply. After the thrill had subsided I was faced with sorting out my commitments in Durban involving a job, a flat, and a horse. Surprisingly that first night of unbridled, gaspingly glorious coming together in my flat (Arno flew back to Cape Town the next day) didn't lead to me being pregnant. I wouldn't have been ready mentally anyway. Arno understood this, saying we would get engaged when I was ready. Months later, when I was ensconced at the farm we behaved like friends until Arno's parents left for their longed for and well-deserved holiday in the UK. A few weeks later I was pregnant. At twelve weeks it turned out we were expecting twins. We could have left getting married until after our babies were born, an unthinkable (but practical) alternative back then. In the end we broke the news to Ada and Frank, and they flew back in time for the wedding.

Now another tricky situation loomed with an expanse of ocean in the mix. Then the birth of our children forced a decision. Now there is no pressure– external, that is. Only our own– Gunner's and my– needs and desires.

I breathe in the tranquility the veranda offers, the cool night air, the occasional flutter down of a leaf of the bougainvillea but I am unable to draw on it that anxious am I feeling. Gunner stands. I remain sitting.

"I have a proposition, Stella. I feel bad asking you in your weakened state. I was going to wait. Then the sale of the farm fell through. Even then I had time, but as you know Tilly called with the new date of the auction." He grins boyishly. "It's so great you and she have met– in a manner of speaking. She thinks you're sweet."

A proposition? *She thinks you're sweet.* Gunner is a direct sort of person, so I am surprised at him beating around the bush like this.

"I had been thinking along these lines for some time. Then the night of the housewarming you mentioned not wanting to have to reopen the riding school. You looked so stressed the next morning, and even though you explained so beautifully about going after Strawks on Faye's behalf, I wasn't convinced. Brand confirmed that things are tight. *Money*, to use a dirty word. That the bank is balking at extending your overdraft.

"I don't want you to *have* to open the riding school and I don't even expect you to make wine– although I'm sure once you get started you are going to love it. After all you have been through, you deserve a period of consolidation, a period of finding your feet, of discovering what you want to do. I know what I want to do. I wasn't completely truthful when I said I want to invest in property. More specifically I want to invest in a business, a going concern, and most particularly in a farm. I've had plenty of opportunity to check wine farming from the South African perspective. I can help you manage, take the load off your shoulders, if Brand doesn't want to. That is between the two of you." He takes a breath.

"We get on so well. I think we would make excellent business partners. Getting along with all of the Gideons is a bonus. And if you're worrying about me coming in and changing anything, you needn't. Arno has left an excellent model. We can modernize for sure, but the essential Gideon enterprise will remain."

How strange, I thought. The first time love came into my life I was unaware, and it took the man to spring it on me. This time I'm feeling it, and the man isn't. What a risk Arno took. I might have turned him down. I had certainly shut the door on him several times before.

But I don't have that sort of courage now.

I feel heat spread up from my body and I push the duvet away. Then I realize it is the most God-awful blush that is breaking out. My cleavage is on fire, my neck, my face. If I spit on a finger and put it to an ear it will sizzle, I'm sure.

Later it came to me. What had I been thinking? At no time had he said he was getting divorced.

CHAPTER 31

I didn't go to the airport the next morning. I had the perfect excuse as I lay there against the pillows. The way I had coughed during the night would have told anyone with half an ear how I was faring. I hadn't bothered to brush my teeth, comb my hair, dab on perfume or any of the palaver, I might have indulged in had I not had my dreams squashed the night before. But I was a big girl. I'd been round the block, as the saying goes. I wasn't the ingénue of twenty-something years ago– although at the time I would have argued until I was blue in the face that I was the dead opposite, a girl who knew her mind and where she was heading.

So, when Gunner gingerly tapped on my door, I met his "Hi. How are you?" with a steady look and questioned him as to his readiness for the flight. When we had done with these niceties he bent forward and kissed me goodbye on the lips. I thought of the axiom, lip service. It was the first time we'd kissed. Hours earlier I would have been over the moon but now I wanted to pull away, but of course didn't. I wasn't even sure if he was a friend. A true friend.

I waited until the expensive whirr of the Lexus had completely faded before I got up. It was a Saturday morning and Ellie and Brand had piled in with Gunner. They were going to pick up Lyle and Myrna. Gunner had bought the car as he said he would and was leaving it for any of us to use, Ellie and Myrna included. He had sorted with the insurance company. Because I wasn't sure about any of what Gunner had proposed the night before, both his wanting to invest in *and* manage the farm, I found the arrangement with the car irksome. It was like we, the boys and *I*, were being smothered in goose down. I wanted to be done with the man and his trappings, his methods, the subtleties. The boys were going to object, but as soon as Gunner called, I was going to tell him that I didn't want the responsibility of the car. That he had to make other arrangements. When I made my decision about the business– in consultation with the boys, of course– I wanted to feel free, not having his generosity impinge, which could be manipulative or quite innocent (I was giving him the benefit of the doubt).

I sat on the side of the bed feeling wretched. This very minute my children were being brainwashed, their wills slowly bent to his. I felt like my family had been taken over by an alien, a very clever alien. Gunner had us all eating out of his hand. We were going to lose our identity if we allowed the man into the business, despite his assurances to the contrary. But I wasn't going to think about that now, though– the financial side. I wasn't in good enough shape. Besides being emotionally wound up, I was feeling nauseous. I wondered how much the rancor over the previous night's proposal was due to being below par physically and how much to a bruised ego.

Best not to think too much now. I was good at that– not thinking, even not feeling. Except the anger. Where were the blazes when I needed it? A fit of temper would act like a stoked steam engine sending me hissing through the day ahead. I tried to laugh at myself, but the sound was more a groan.

First, I needed to down some Enos. After the simple diet of the past few weeks, the big meal of the night before wasn't sitting easily in my stomach (another cause of the nausea?). After a fizzing glass of the salts I burped and instantly began to feel better. I washed my face, brushed my teeth, dressed, pulled a comb through my hair, tied it back, and applied lipstick.

Someone had made coffee– Ellie, probably. I could smell it as I walked down the passage. I poured a cup, black, with Woo at my heels. I lifted her up and cuddled her for a second, feeling the warmth beneath the fur speak to me about the love of God's creatures for us and our love for them.

I hadn't expected Suzi to get up but now I saw that she was lying quite still. Was she asleep? Or were her joints too sore to even sit up? Damn, I still hadn't called the vet about her medication. Her tail wasn't wagging either and her head lolled against the side of the basket. Her mouth hung open. Her pale tongue protruded half an inch.

I knelt at the basket, sucked my finger and held it against the old lab's nostrils. Nothing. I was surprised the children hadn't noticed. They must have been too occupied with getting ready and helping Gunner with his luggage. I felt another ugly twist in the region of my heart. The man had dazzled us all, even to ignoring our pets. I took one of Suzi's paws in my hands. It was still warm. It had just happened. Gunner was excused of this, but of the rest? Don't think, I told myself.

Woo padded over and we contemplated our friend. The Dachsie whined pitifully. I leaned my head against the box of Suzi's chest covered in velvety fur, stayed there letting the tears drip. No more beating heart in there. She had been such a lady, always with none of the cheek of Woo. It had been a good partnership. Opposites attract even in the animal world. My shoulders shook as I allowed the grief full rein. Woo began to lick my face.

"I still have you, baby. Thank God." I kissed her snout.

It was then that I saw the envelope lying on the floor face down between the basket and the skirting board. It must have been propped up against something– the kettle perhaps– and been unwittingly knocked down. How long had it been there? I picked it up and turned it over. It was addressed to Mrs. S. Gideon. I slit it open. Inside was a page of note paper, torn out of the book I leave near the telephone.

Dear Miss Stella,

My Mommy is ill. Yesterday, while visiting my friend, I got the message on my cell. My brother says it's SERIOUS. I must come straight away. I think it is mos your butterflies. So I will take a taxi and a bus and I will be in Uppington tomorrow morning.

Yours truly,
Wilemina Moses

She had been in earlier. I wondered if she had encountered the Gunner's children. She would be on her way. All I needed now was for something bad to have happened to Faye.

Anika answered.

"How are you guys?" I ask, my heart thumping.

"We're all fine. I'll give you Faye. We're having a late breakfast."

"We're having pancakes. Hi, Stella. Pancakes with strawberries." A girlish giggle tickles my ear.

"Hi Valdine."

"Hi Stel. Everything OK?" Faye has the phone now. I thought about the tone of a loved one's voice. Did love give it that timbre?

I feel the tears coming and just manage, "Someone's come to the door. I'll call you in a minute."

She is OK. For now, anyway.

I look out of the window, swallowing, sniffing. Harry and Sally.

"Hi guys! Come in, come in." The two pairs of sharp black ears point heavenwards then lower slightly. Tails wag. They can't believe their luck. They have a good sniff all over the kitchen– the bin, the floor beneath the table, Woo, looking alarmed, and finally, Suzi. They don't seem surprised at her lying there motionless. Tonight I will bring their baskets and bowls inside. Willy won't like it, but I can do with more company in the house. Perhaps I'll tell her she can have a long leave when she calls. She and I were coming up for twenty-five years, give or take a couple.

I am ready to make my call.

So, are you ready for your chemo now? But I don't dare. She knows what she has to do. If two boobs gone west don't do it, then she really is in trouble. She really was crying for help. All the more reason to resume my search.

"Who was at the door?"

"Harry and Sally. I've decided they can sleep in the kitchen from now on."

"What brought that on?"

"Suzi has died on me."

Silence at the other end, then, "*Oh, Star.*"

More silence while I fought for control. "She was struggling. I was going to call the vet. It's better this way. But how are *you* doing, sweetie?"

"Wonderfully. With my young helper."

"The children have taken Gunner to the airport."

"How was your meal? Did he do himself proud?"

I was still too upset to talk about Gunner. But I could talk about his food. I ran through the menu, mentioning the Weber braais. I had yet to check on the gas-fired model in the garden shed.

"What are you going to do about Suzi?"

I could give Isak a ring. I often had one of the laborers come in over a weekend, especially if the twins were going to be away. Staff welcomed the overtime. But I didn't know what arrangements had been made while I was sick. I had a flash of Gunner instituting a more economical system, like keeping the carcass in the freezer until the staff arrived on Monday morning. *You're being nasty*, I told myself. But I wasn't listening.

"The boys will be home soon. We can bury her together."

"Like old times," Faye said. I could hear the longing in her voice. Often she had been with us when we had one of our sad little ceremonies— Arno and I and the boys, when they were available. We had driven to Cape Town when it was her turn to say goodbye to a faithful friend.

Afterwards I walked outside. The air was startlingly warm. The sky had a milky look over towards the jagged horizon. It was a *berg* wind, a wind blowing off the mountains towards the ocean. It usually presaged a cold spell, even rain. I inhaled deeply, and to my surprise, didn't cough. The first crop of hard, green baby grapes would be feeling the unexpected warmth and draw the juice up from the roots, up along the wizened but by-no-means passed-it branches, through to the new tender stems and into their confined spaces, pushing outward against the frosted stretching skins. The leaves would unfurl some more, preparing to shelter their progeny from the sun even now capable of frazzling the buds on the later varieties. If I listened intently I might hear the sprinklers come on. But, no, it was too early for that. But it wasn't too early for a ride.

Back in the house, I took an old but clean blanket out of the linen cupboard in the passage and covered Suzi. Then I pulled on thick socks and riding boots, shrugged on my anorak, wrapped a thick woolen scarf around my neck, and zipped up the jacket. It was like stepping into a Turkish bath, but I wasn't taking any chances.

I told Woo, Harry, and Sally to 'stay', and walked purposely along the path and across the courtyard to the stables.

"Isak. What are you doing here?" I could hear Izzy whinny as I stood there, contemplating the groom. Just walking over had me breathing heavily.

"Mister Brand asked me to come in today."

He threw a doubtful look at me as he helped saddle up.

"Just the paddock today," I said. "But you ride Sweetpea."

Isak looked relieved at this. I waited while he saddled up and then together we walked the horses behind the winery.

There is nothing better than to feel the strength and equine grace beneath one, especially when these two combined in the schooled small and big circles and figures of eight. But first we had to allow our rides to expend their energy, which I often imagined was like blowing the froth off a tall glass of beer, so easy was it. And today was no different. Isak and I kept to the perimeter going in opposite directions, beginning with a trot, then a canter and finally a gallop. In this last stage, however, more concentration was required due to the limits of the area and the proximity to one another, and, more than anything, my unfitness.

But Izzy and Sweetpea knew the routine and hardly needed more than a nudge, a tweak of the reins, the pressure of a knee. Sweetpea sometimes became excited at this stage and kicked out. But she was more timid with Isak, maybe even a little afraid of him, and so today, she was behaving impeccably, which suited me in my present state. After a half an hour of this, we walked to settle them and then took our first steps in the dance, as I like to think of our paces.

Somewhere in all of this my spirits lift and I feel peace spreading from the deepest place and outwards through to fingertips and toes, to the top of my head until my whole body tingles. Then I am glad that I wasn't angry, wasn't propelled by my unnamed nemesis, the disquiet that had haunted me over the recent past. But I knew I hadn't resolved it, hadn't got to the source. That it was waiting to grab hold of me again and would do so until I had faced whatever it was that needed facing.

After the ride I asked Isak to take Suzi to the garden shed. I didn't like leaving her where she was. The children might come back from the airport while I was showering and see the covered remains. He brought along a wheelbarrow and we wrapped her in the blanket and lifted her onto it. Harry and Sally sniffed the blanket as Isak passed by. Woo, in my arms, whined softly.

I had heard the car arrive as I showered. Now I stood in the kitchen doorway. They were in the middle of an animated recalling of something that had happened at the airport. A group of visitors from another African country– Ghana, maybe, and ahead of them in the queue– had tried to bring on some fresh food, the juices of which had dripped out of the cardboard boxes during the weigh-in, giving them away. Lyle and Brand were laughing as they took the previous night's leftovers out of the fridge, wondering as they did so, if those visitors' food was anything like what Gunner had left them– a still magnificent feast.

I watched as bowls and dishes arrived on the kitchen table. Myrna was laying out clean plates, cutlery and glasses.

Brand said, "Hi, Mom!" Then, "Where's Suzi?"

"She's in the garden shed," I said, trying to sound matter-of-fact. The laughter was fading from of his eyes.

"She died?" He didn't look surprised, wise, observant Brand.

Ellie said, "When?" and before I could elucidate, she added, "I thought she was rather quiet when we left. Usually she follows us to the door.

We hadn't noticed what she was doing before that. We were desperate for coffee before leaving. After last night…"

"I can imagine," I said. I hated the way my presence had dampened the gathering, and most of all the sad news that I'd had to deliver, and on the heels of the high of the previous night and what I assumed had been a cheerful send-off of Gunner.

"She might have been dead while I made coffee!" Ellie collapsed onto a chair, hands over her eyes.

Myrna said as calmly as ever, "She wasn't enjoying life so much lately, was she?"

Lyle had a hand over his mouth. I was dreading his reaction.

"Faye rang just now," Lyle said, bending to the grocery cupboard and noisily shoving cans aside.

"The tomato ketchup is in the fridge," I said.

"She says she is definitely coming over tomorrow. She's driving, she says, and blow the doctor. She's bringing Anika and Valdine. Faye's had another op, Mom, and you didn't tell me. Why has she had another one? Didn't the chemo work?"

Brand stared at me. "You told me not to tell him, Mom. And so I didn't."

"Tell me what?"

"That Aunt Faye doesn't want chemo." The boys hadn't addressed Faye as 'aunt' since she asked them not to when they began high school. It made her feel old, she said. Brand walked over to the fridge, took out the bottle of Heinz, gave it to his brother, and closed the fridge door. Then he sat down.

"*What?*" Lyle was standing with the bottle of bright red in one hand, looking from me to Brand. "Did *you* know, Ellie?"

"So many times I wanted to tell you but– yes, I did."

"And you, Myrn?"

Myrna shook her head. Brand offered her the basket of bread rolls and she took one. She broke it apart but instead of spreading it with butter, she sat looking at it.

"Everybody but Myrna and I knew. I bet Gunner knew and Willy and Isak and the whole bang universe."

"I thought if you knew you'd dash over and try and talk her into it."

"*Well, of course!*" Lyle was shouting. "She's going to damn well die if she doesn't get the treatment. This is her second boob gone. Go figure."

We sat there in silence. No one was eating. What harm could it do now. Perhaps her– dare I think it– favorite twin would be able to do what I and the doctor – and I didn't know who else– hadn't been able to do.

"She is coming here tomorrow, right? You'll have your chance. Brand can join you. He wanted to try and persuade her, and I stopped him."

Lyle looked at me questioningly but didn't say anything. Then he began to sob. I got up and took him in my arms.

"First Suzi, now this," he muttered between sobs.

I wondered what Myrna thought. Would she be feeling inadequate? Would she want to be comforting her boyfriend in place of me, but didn't know how? Was she feeling jealous of me and wished I wasn't there? Or was she quite glad not to have her shoulder become wet?

But she did step forward and take the bottle out of Lyle's hand.

CHAPTER 32

The next morning, over an early breakfast, the boys laid out their plan. First of all, Lyle was driving to town to fetch Faye, Anika, and Valdine. He had already telephoned to arrange this. After lunch we were going to bury Suzi, setting the tone, after which they wanted their godmother to themselves. The rest of us were to get the tea ready in the kitchen while they sat with Faye on the veranda. I was bursting with advice as to how they should go about this, but my track record in this regard was scant recommendation, and so I silently entrusted them to Fate.

Lunch was a hodge-podge of the seemingly elastic (was I never to be free of the man's presence?) left-overs and a sausage braai, a trial of the gas Weber. Lyle proved best at it, being both patient and finnicky. He took over from Brand, reducing the flame to its lowest and turning the sausages frequently so that they browned evenly. He'd heard that you could get a rotisserie to fit a Weber and said I should get one for the future. Or he was jolly well going to go out and buy me one. He sounded cross as he said this. He was still angry with me for not telling him about his godmother's refusal to have chemo.

I'd had an (unexpressed) hissy fit of my own– with the matter of the Weber gas model. I'd planned to return it. The boys could use the braai version. But the next morning, when I walked out onto the veranda Brand already had it out and spread with fat coils of *boerewors* and paler strings of pork bangers. In any event, making a fuss and crying about it would raise questions I wasn't ready to answer, that I hoped I'd never have to answer. The fate of the Lexus and a pow-wow about the business could wait. Once again, my concern for Faye was taking precedence, and in the hierarchy of need, it should.

Anika had brought *agurksalat* (Norwegian cucumber salad), *karikal* (lamb and cabbage stew), and *kringla* (figure of eight, crisp cookies) and a Norwegian sour cream and raisin pie for tea. I jokingly asked if she hired out her services. I was going to need some help while Willy was away. To this, Faye, less jokingly, said she wasn't parting with Anika until she absolutely had to. This was code for until Henk began jumping up and down. She seemed happy enough, with pain kept at bay with prescribed analgesics.

To make it easy, we ate at the kitchen table which seats eight comfortably. Faye kept Fergus on her lap. We were all, in our various ways, aware of the missing lab, so much a part of past meals taken in the kitchen. Compliments regarding Anika's contribution to the meal abounded as we passed the bowls and dishes round.

"Ma is going to teach me to cook, the Norwegian way."

All eyes were on Valdine, who, like Faye, had been quiet until then. My family were as stunned as I had been by her beauty, and warmly welcoming, as I knew they would be. Ellie was particularly friendly, admiring Valdine's blouse and tights and the gold sleepers on her ears. Anika had only days earlier allowed Valdine to have her ears pierced.

"I want to be a chef one day. Faye's been helping me with my reading and writing."

"It's amazing how interest in a subject facilitates learning. Faye and Vally are using one of Faye's mother's cookbooks like a school reader." Anika looked pleased.

"I keep a picture in my mind of what the word means all the time I am saying and writing it. I'm going to a culinary school one day."

"One thing at a time," cautioned her mother.

"I thought you might want to be a nurse," I said, "seeing as how well you've cared for Faye."

"I made the cookies."

"You'll have to show me how to make them," said Ellie.

"Today?"

"Next time you come. When we have more time."

"You'll have to come for a sleepover, Valdine," I said.

"I could stay tonight." Valdine glanced at her mother and a look passed between them. "But I haven't brought my pajamas."

"You see the shape of your cookies er – *kringla*? We call this a figure of eight in riding. Next time you come you can watch how our horses pace out that shape in the paddock."

Valdine looked perplexed. I thought of the teenage girls at the riding school and their quick of-the-mark objection, "T-M-I!"

"Would you like to see the horses? They're in the stables. We can go after lunch."

Valdine smiled but checked again with her mother who nodded.

I half wondered if any attempt had been made to teach Valdine to ride, but then decided Anika wouldn't have been happy about that. I thought that one day I would like to teach the girl– one day, further along the road of our acquaintance, when trust was in full flower like the girl's womanhood.

After the meal I left the others to clear away and took Valdine by the hand. Anika walked outside with us. She whispered, out of earshot of the girl who was patting Harry and Sally, "Stella, I appreciate all you're doing. But –I don't know how to put this– you don't have to single out Valdine. She is used to sitting quietly and listening. She's used to being the child among adults."

But I wasn't to be outdone. "But she's with family, so it's different. We want her to feel important, that she has a contribution to make." I wanted to add that already I could see a difference. At that moment Valdine wasn't holding my hand and her speech and understanding of what was going down in the group had noticeably improved.

"Well, in that case, it's fine."

She turned and was about to go back into the kitchen to help clear away, when I said, "Come with us. There are plenty of hands in there."

I was hoping she could give me news of Strawks. Faye had already asked if she could lie down.

"Just a catnap," she said, with Fergus tucked under her arm.

Lyle and Brand had been listening, and I noticed a look pass between them. I wondered then if their plan was going to work, hoping for their sakes that it would, for everyone who loved Faye's sake, and especially for Faye herself. That we wouldn't need Strawks didn't occur to me.

A wind had sprung up, whirling before its clouds of dust and winter's fall of papery leaves, but it was welcome after the closeness of the kitchen and its food smells. Valdine loved feeding Izzy and Sweetpea with the slices of apple and carrot we had brought. I showed her where to stand and how to offer the treats on an open hand. She was a farm girl, but I was making sure. We fed the other two horses the leftovers and patted and spoke to them as well. I explained that Sweetpea and the other two belonged to other people who didn't have stables at their homes and that their owners paid us to care for them.

"Like the people at *Akkerstroom*?" Valdine asked.

"Except our guests don't stay permanently," Anika said which led me to explain what 'permanent' meant.

Harry, Sally, and Woo were waiting for us as we came out of the stable, tails wagging and ears cocked with anticipation. I took a tennis ball from my jacket pocket and demonstrated throwing it in different directions so that each of them got a chance to bring it back. This required throwing it short for Woo and further off for the Rottweilers. Harry and Sally were like galloping horses compared to the dumpy sausage-like Woo. But the Dachsie had developed tricks, like darting under one of the bigger dogs or suddenly swerving in an opposite direction and shooting off with the ball in her mouth.

It took a while, but when Valdine had got the hang of it, I turned to Anika.

"Any news of you-know-who? Did you manage to contact anyone in Bethany?"

"I did." She cast an anxious eye after Valdine. "I was passed from pillar to post, but no one has seen or heard from him in years. Of course, I was often speaking to older folks. Like us, most of our friends have moved away. A number of them are overseas, with careers and jobs and families." She sighed. Then she perked up, especially when she saw how well Valdine was handling the dogs. "We have invitations to come and stay. You remember how hospitable people were? You remember the Maartens sisters? They're still there in the town. They have all the gossip. They remember us. Have the stories about us off pat."

"That should be interesting. The versions of those two old girls." I was going to say old 'maids,' but didn't want to cause offense. I remembered meeting them in the bank. How my father, Roy, rustled up tea for them and how interested they were in our family. "They were always so full of questions, from where had I bought the dress I was wearing, to what were my plans for the future? If anyone would know anything about Strawks and his whereabouts, it would be them."

"Most kids would be afraid of Rottweilers, especially girls," I said, an eye on Valdine.

"I wonder if it isn't ignorance– that she doesn't realize what they're capable of."

"I rather think it's instinct. Plus, none of us are afraid of them. That'll be her guide."

"Maybe... Vally and I are going to Skype my folks. Faye has shown us how, and a nephew is helping Ma and Pa at their end. I'll let you know if something interesting comes out of that."

We strolled back to the house. We left the dogs cooling off on the back steps and I showed Valdine where we kept the balls and doggy toys in the kitchen. Off her bat she began rinsing out and re-filling the dogs' water bowls.

"Do you know whether Faye has changed her mind about having chemo?" I asked, knowing as I did so, that Anika would have told me if Faye had. We were standing at the sink helping ourselves to glasses of water from the tap.

"We did have a little chat. She says she can't face having more done to her. I left it at that."

Anika and Valdine walked through to join the others on the front veranda, while I went to check on Faye. She wasn't in the spare room, formerly occupied by Gunner and now Lyle, but asleep on my bed, clutching a pillow. She didn't stir, even when I pulled a blanket over her. Fergus was curled up near her feet and watched with approval, not minding the share of a woolly corner of the blanket. I stood for a moment assessing how far she had recovered from this most recent inroad on her health. Her cheekbones were sharper, her eyes closed in violet hollows that seemed deeper than I remembered. The smudging beneath picked up the theme of something formidable having been endured. A blue vein throbbed at a temple. Her usually sweetly curved lips were stretched across her teeth, more a grimace than a smile and far too pale for my liking. I shouldn't have been shocked, but I was. Hadn't I expected something like this? Reality, I reminded myself, is ever the leveler.

My throat ached with unshed tears, unsaid words. I thought of Gunner and my disappointment, and it seemed foolish now, a kind of madness. I also realized, watching my friend breathe in and out, that as matters stood, even if I had received a proposal of marriage I wouldn't have been able to engage fully. Until I had solved Faye's problem, which I regarded as my own, I wouldn't be able to give my full attention to something as personal.

I remembered Faye's striving after the unobtainable medication from overseas and my understanding of it: that it was an avoidance tactic on her part. Lusting after unavailable Gunner amounted to the same thing. What a pair we were.

Back on the veranda we chatted about this and that. Henk was being very patient, Anika said, but she didn't know for how long. That Faye hadn't spoken about going back to work was indicative of how she was feeling, I said, and how much her, Anika's, and Valdine's presence was ensuring that she stayed at home. I hoped that she and Valdine could stay a bit longer. Once Faye was on her own, the pressure to go back would get too much. I could be there some of the time, but I was needed on the farm. I had neglected my affairs quite a bit while Gunner was there, but I didn't say that.

Later, Anika and Ellie went off to make tea, and Valdine to wake Faye. I stayed behind to check if the twins' plan to chat with Faye still held. Her nap had interfered with burying Suzi. They thought that we should have tea and then bury Suzi. Her remains were still in the garden shed. After that they would talk to Faye.

Lyle didn't look confident.

"Sweetheart," I said, with an eye on the doorway and an ear cocked for Faye and Valdine's approach. "Why don't you play it by ear? If she seems ill at all, or you have a feeling it isn't the right time, leave it for another day."

Brand said, "Let's do that, *boet*. Have tea and send off Suzi, and see after that."

"That seems a bit airy-fairy, waiting to see how we feel. I sure know how Faye will be feeling. What do you think, Myrn?"

"Your Mom knows your aunt best. It is terribly worrying, not doing anything, but a wrong move, and you're back to square one."

I glanced across at Myrna. It was as though she hadn't spoken.

I said, "Anika told me just now that she spoke to Faye about having the treatment, but with no luck."

"What did Faye say? How did she react?" Brand asked.

"That she'd had enough done to her."

Faye and Valdine must have gone to the kitchen. Voices and the clink of crockery floated back down the passage. Then the sounds grew until Valdine was stepping through with a plate of her *kringla*, and Faye with the raisin tart and jug of cream, followed by Anika and Ellie with the trays of tea things.

Faye was flushed and smiling. "I don't know why I slept so long. It's that bed of yours, Stella. I felt like Goldilocks."

"It's the farm air," Anika said.

In the end, Brand and Lyle didn't bring up the subject of chemotherapy with their godmother. It was a teary group that huddled in the family graveyard. The weather had turned foul. We were battered by wind and then rain as the boys knelt to place the blanketed Suzi into the almost meter-deep hole dug by Isak earlier. Baboons had been known to come down from the mountain and dig up a shallower grave. The fence around the graveyard kept out dogs and the odd jackal (scarcer these days), but not baboons. Each of us took a spade, standing with our backs to the wind as we tipped the red soil onto the lumpy form of the dog. Then we watched as Brand and Lyle shoveled in the remainder, stamped down the mound, and promised to erect a suitable marker.

Sheltering under the trees, I glanced at the other animal graves, each with their wooden plaques, as well as the family grave, a large rectangle bordered with carved stone and filled in with pink and cream gravel. The gravel had to be raked aside and the cement slabs lifted before Arno's coffin could be lowered, but by then he wasn't there, for me, anyway. He was in his favorite sayings ringing in my head: stupid things like 'shove up, kiddo' when he got into bed at night and referring to an early start as 'sparrow fart'. He was in his handwritten check lists in his office, a note beside the home telephone '**RING IVY**'. I've never, to this day, found out who Ivy is or was. He was in his favorite possessions– the small ones, like the fountain pen he used when writing inside a book he was giving someone or filling in a greetings card. He took time thinking up the right words, blowing them dry afterwards with a look of satisfaction. And in his bunch of keys. It was like getting an electric shock the first time I picked them up. He was in the clothes I nosed and breathed in in his cupboard, in the bed linen (until I moved out), in him walking into the kitchen one night as I sat, numb and wrung out. He was so real that I said aloud, "Sweetheart, hi!" I shared this with Willy and she said it was our longing that brought them back. It was usually before they had 'made their home properly on the other side.'

The Gideons weren't a wordy bunch. They preferred to have carved into the different headstones, the name of the deceased, dates of birth and death, topped by a trite *In Loving Memory*. They believed that where love was concerned, words quickly became clanging cymbals. Well, that was what Arno told me on my first visit there, and I saw no reason to break with tradition when my turn came, although I prefer to think of words as failing one, that no word however well-chosen can express how much the loved one is missed.

Faye had elected to stay behind and clear away the tea things, which was loudly protested but in the end accepted. This, more than anything, must have helped Brand and Lyle make up their minds. They knew how much she loved animals and wouldn't normally miss an opportunity to express that love. My understanding was that she had had enough sadness and pain to deal with in the past, and the new pain and worry regarding her health would more than likely result in overload, that is, she would not be able to stop crying once she started. Self-preservation was the least of what we could allow her, could give her.

CHAPTER 33

I gave myself a week to catch up on the office and vineyard and, I guess, my energy. The bank called on the following Monday. They wanted to see me ASAP with a set of accounts and balance sheet.

I spent a morning going over our affairs with our accountant, the retired Mr. Hendon. No one called him by his first name, not even Arno, who had grown up with visits from the portly gent from Leicester, England, a friend of Ada and Frank's, whom they had helped get on his feet businesswise when he emigrated. He charged a nominal amount and didn't expect a bonus of wine (customary in the wine industry for professional services rendered), unless it was to give away to others as he was a staunch Methodist and had made a temperance vow as a young man and saw no reason to break it. Brand was all for replacing Mr. Hendon with one of his mates whom we could get at a good price, he said, because the friend hadn't finished his Articles, but who was at the cutting edge of business models and strategy, tax avoidance and so on. For a young person, the accountant would seem overly conservative, but I felt safe with the white-haired Mr. Hendon who knew the family history and who had steered me through the past three years like I was a piece of egg-shell Spode china.

We had been through my printouts of our finances, which I had already e-mailed to Mr. Hendon so he could decide how and where to arrange everything. He called this putting our best foot forward, but he did admit we were drifting towards the edge. When I told him that I was thinking about making wine he said I should go ahead, which surprised me. He had always had an almost sacrosanct admiration for Arno's wine-making abilities, and I expected him to warn off my ignorance and inexperience– gently, of course. Offer it to the supermarket chains as an Odd Bin line, he advised. But I needed to hurry, as the next harvest and its flush of new wines was around the corner. He said this as he made his final notes and tucked them in with the other papers in our file.

"Arno had an excellent system. Follow that but introduce your own combinations. It might be worth buying in different cultivars. I heard of a new estate that blends something like ten or twelve varieties in one wine. The bank will help if you give them a plan. The wine industry is on the up and up. I don't know if you're aware, but in Elgin they've been uprooting apple trees and planting vines. There's a world-wide shortage of wine. If China comes in as a major buyer, the sky will be the limit."

I did know about the apple orchards. They had some unknown disease without a known cure, which helped the decision. And about the world shortage, both had floated past my head. The habit of leaving everything to do with farming to Arno– even an absent Arno– was hard to break.

"Brand keeps telling me to check Arno's computer. But that is usually for vineyard care. Not for making wine."

"There you are, then."

Mr. Hendon promised to check 'the plan' (it still sounded like fairy tales) and also to accompany me to the bank. He had never come to the bank with me before and for this reason alone, I decided, it was worth a shot.

We had drunk our tea and he was zipping up his briefcase when I said, "I had an offer out of the blue from a friend. You know the man who prunes the cinsaut for us?"

"The Australian?"

I hadn't planned on telling Mr. Hendon about the offer, but now that I was heading that way, it felt right. "Doug Moore, or Gunner, as he prefers to be called."

Mr. Hendon hadn't met Gunner. Why hadn't I thought to introduce them during the latter's visit? I had hoped Gunner and Henk would meet, but that had been on an entirely different level.

"He wants to invest in Gideon's and not only that, he wants to manage us, if I'm willing. I would have to talk it over with the boys. Gunner is in the process of selling his wine farm outside Melbourne. It seems he wants to put down roots here."

Hugh Hendon has soft, pink skin. Like a baby, I sometimes think. (I've heard the boys refer to him as Mr. Porky. 'Mr. Porky's been here again,' they might chirp and collapse with giggles.) Now he seemed to be reddening. I wondered if blushing was catching. I was certainly feeling uncomfortable.

"I would tread warily. I don't mean to alarm you, my dear, but hostile takeovers are happening too frequently to ignore. If you decide to take him seriously, you could have him checked out. But it's a costly business, and I'd prefer to see Gideon's remain independent. You have all the makings of a successful operation. Give it time. Your idea of becoming even more involved than you are will pay off. I'm sure it will."

I was stunned. Mr. Hendon hadn't said as much in all the time I'd known him. Well, not in one go. I watched him drive off in his gleaming Bentley. He bought the car when his wife died. Did it remind him of his wife who had been on the large side with the sort of looks that in a past age were referred to as handsome? I wondered what car I might buy that would remind me of Arno– when my ship came in, of course. Something long (he was tall) and sleek (he was thin) and old-fashioned. A vintage Jag?

Right now, what I needed was Dutch courage. Strong coffee would have to do. I walked back into the winery. It seemed quieter, even though there had only been Mr. Hendon and me there all morning. The men were in the vineyard, in the trellised section of the early chenin blanc topping, that is, hitting off the top growth with a switch to ensure greater leaf growth. The workload was slowly building until we'd be all guns firing in January. The day had started out windless and Brand had seized the opportunity for some sulphur dusting. It was one of those days when the wind was swinging, in this case, from the rain-bearing west to the east, transforming into the soon-to-be chief, dry, cooling and relentless wind of summer, the south-easter. Vine sulphur prevented powdery mildew, a fungus, a wine farmer's nightmare having made its first appearance on Cape vines in the eighteen-hundreds. Before Mr. Hendon arrived, I had been round to check on one of Arno's pet niggles with the men: that they weren't forgetting to go below the ground for shoots on the rootstock. This had to be done while the soil was still moist and soft. With the heat and dryness of summer, the ground would harden making shoot removal difficult, but which were conditions vine root systems thrive on.

"Ag, Miss, we did the *tipping* with Mr. Gunner," Isak reported cheerfully. Tipping was the removal of the first shoots by hand. Topping and tipping. Being out of it for a fortnight had sure messed with my head.

I kept a kettle and tea and coffee things in my office. I made myself a mug of strong coffee and walked the few steps into Arno's office. I was frequently popping in to check on the which, how much of, when, how, and where of insecticides (this morning sulphur), but this felt different.

I walked around Arno's desk. Instead of sadness, I felt a ripple up my spine. Better not examine it too closely. Best keep my mind on the job.

The computer screen looked dusty, and I wiped it with the cuff of my sweater while it booted up. I sat in his chair. *Sweetheart, are you there? Hold thumbs.*

Arno had installed programs for everything to do with wine-farming and winemaking. I clicked on blending. Up came the categorized history of twenty years. I opened a new page, leaving the last one he'd entered open so that I could copy the headings. There were the obvious ones, like blending date, harvest date, time, cultivar, vineyard number, cellar temperature, outdoor temperature, quantity used, and a whole lot of detail that I wouldn't need for this exercise, seeing as it was a one-off and an experiment. But I would put them in anyway. Better to capture more than I needed, or thought I needed. Everything was conjecture at this stage. What I learnt from this run would inform the future– if there is to be a future. I was still not sure if I could bring it off, if what I produced would be palatable, not just for myself, but others.

My first task was to acquire more cultivars. Sometime before this, I couldn't remember exactly when, I'd decided that if I was going to make wine, it wouldn't be from a sole cultivar, and especially not the cinsaut, which meant I needed a greater variety. I already had three. This was for the white wine. Until my confidence levels rose, I was going to deal only with other small concerns. With the third call I found what I needed at a new farm in– you guessed it, Elgin. The young man, Brad Corder, was winemaker for his retired parents who had sunk their savings into the farm. He was fresh out of Elsenburg. We got chatting. Starting the following month, his mother was going to run a restaurant that served lunches. I promised to round up the family and be one of their first guests. For the red, I thought first to ring Perl, caught a flash of Arno's disbelief that I would even consider such a thing. So I called Henk. I knew this would mean a good half hour of chat, but I trusted the man to give me good advice, businesswise, that is.

"How're you, Henk?"

"Grumpy as hell. So make it quick."

"Missing your girl, huh?"

He didn't answer. Then I said, "I need advice. But it's in regard to the wine-making world."

He immediately perked up. "Fire away."

In his present state, Henk wouldn't welcome beating about the bush. "I'm making wine."

"Well, that's good news. And?"

"I'm looking for red wine cultivars three to start, two-fifty liters. Piddling quantities, I know, but I'm using up my remainder of cinsaut."

"A test drive? Let's see. It so happens…"

The evening Henk took me out to dinner, he had that day visited an old friend who had some leftovers, as he put it. This person had had to attend a niece's wedding in the States, which had taken precedence over winemaking, which wasn't much more than a hobby, according to Henk. I wondered if this person would agree. Being late in the season when she returned– she liked to enter the various young wine shows– the tanks had remained unused. To make way for the new wine, she had considered selling them to a co-op. The 'she' part intrigued me. An old flame? Nosiness wouldn't help my cause.

Henk promised to find out if the wine was still unsold and get back to me.

I was tinkering with the headings on my spreadsheet when he called.

"You're in luck. Can you make it tomorrow? Say, twelve. She'll give us lunch. I have appointments this side otherwise I'd offer to pick you up."

I could. He gave me the name and wine estate. Perl Javinski, Perlheim.

I was too stunned to decline. But a gaggle of protestations burst inwardly. I didn't need the complication of this. I didn't need that pro giving me advice. And what about loyalty to Arno? And Strawks, for that matter? I would be supping with the devil. Fortunately, Anika called soon after that.

This was her last week with Faye. Henk had put his foot down. She was *so sorry*.

I understand, I said. You have a responsibility to him. I didn't mention my date with Henk and Perl. It would have meant giving it too much importance and I was already feeling embarrassed and nervy about the blending. Besides, it was up to Henk to square with Anika.

"Now for the good news," she said. "I've tracked down my brother."

I was too stunned to answer.

Strawks had been accepted by a monastery in Durban and was very happy there– The monastery of Jesus the Nazarene. I found this baffling. Was he still trying to be holy, or was he running away from responsibility to his daughter? And this was the man whose help I was counting on?

"Weren't you annoyed that he hadn't contacted you or Valdine?"

"I knew he would eventually."

"But what if something had happened to you or Valdine in the interim– an accident or illness? I mean, with the level of crime in the country…"

"But it didn't, did it?"

It was then that I was reminded how every family has its unique way of functioning. I thought back to how Constance and I had functioned, or not functioned. How weeks would go by without either of us making contact. How that was the norm for me and how it took rubbing shoulders with Ada and Frank to show me that there were other ways. *Except that*

Valdine was just thirteen. My mother hadn't let me out of her sight at that age except for the obvious activities like school and visiting friends. Strawks had tremendous confidence in his sister to leave the care of his daughter so completely in her hands.

Then came the million-dollar question, leading to other questions that would lead to how on earth were we going to get him to talk some sense into Faye?

"Have you spoken to him?"

"Er…no. But-" and here Anika quickly added, "the monastery has in place a routine for the monks keeping in touch with us and we with them. Once a week we can speak to the abbot– he is especially friendly– and get an update and he will pass on any messages from the family that he thinks are important."

That he thinks are important didn't bode well. The mail would more than likely be censored. Here I was thinking of the paper kind. I wondered if the novice monks were allowed access to computers. I would get to that, but first I had to ask, "So you haven't spoken to him?"

"No."

"Nor Valdine?"

"No."

"And she's happy with that?"

"No, of course not. But she knows he is close to Jesus and praying for us."

Hearing this left me feeling rotten. Anika had called me while out shopping. She was respecting my wish to keep my plan to get in touch with Strawks from Faye, for which I was grateful. Besides which she was into the third week caring for Faye– an arrangement that had proved beneficial in so many ways. To wit, I decided against asking if Strawks had an e-mail address.

I had the abbot's telephone number, and I dialed it immediately, although Anika had said to call on a Sunday. I wanted the man to know I wasn't going to take the brush off, if that was what he had in mind.

The telephone was answered by a woman, someone elderly, judging by the tremor in her voice. The monks were on retreat, and she was helping out. After telling me that the abbot would most definitely only be available on Sundays between 2pm and 5pm, she asked if I had any old clothes or bric-a-brac for a white elephant stall. They were having a bazaar on the Saturday. Their main thrust was to bring the poor souls in the area to the Faith. The funds were for a vehicle for the nun who serviced the Valley of a Thousand Hills. There followed a lengthy tale about the sad fate of an ancient Austin Heely. She hadn't seemed to realize that I was calling from Cape Town and that even if I wanted to, I couldn't have gotten anything to her by then. I'd send a check, I said, and took down the details.

I said goodbye with my ear buzzing. I needed someone like that to sell my wine when it was ready. The woman's garrulity was double-edged. Whether the monks realized it or not, it was an excellent deterrent to anyone not of similar belief who might have had plans to hot up the telephone lines.

I left my number with the woman. She only jotted it down, I thought, because of my (feigned) interest in the fundraising.

In the end, I enjoyed lunching with Perl again. It gave me more time to size her up, ask questions about the estate, her family, and inevitably how she went about blending– all without the charge from Gunner's male presence. How he had colored or obscured my view of her and everything. I even found myself wondering if it was indeed Perl who had fired Strawks after a week.

I'd had a massive crush on the man, I realized. How embarrassing, seeing as he was supposed to have had a crush on me. Sitting at her table again helped me gain perspective, reduced Gunner to a businessman with a steely purpose, using whatever was at hand, in my case, friendship, to further his aims. I doubted that I could ever become that single-minded. I could have admired him– businesswoman to businessman– had I not been someone who placed more emphasis on relationships. Granted, I was a fledgling in the area of business, but that didn't mean I wouldn't hold out for the best that I could be in both, always remembering which came first in my life.

The weather was warm enough for us to sit at a table in the garden that led from the main restaurant. Spreading trees shaded the rustic setting. Flowers in waist-high boxes splashed color from a wide circle around the solid wood tables and chairs arranged on stone paving. I found myself noticing details missed on my previous visit. Our meals were served on wooden platters, or in handmade pottery with the farm's logo of a guinea fowl. The birds were underfoot everywhere. I hadn't noticed them when I'd come with Gunner. Had they been elsewhere on that particular day, or had I been too dizzy to notice? Only the glass holding our wine looked refined and befitting the elegance of its contents. I learnt that almost all of the wine was blended by her sons and that, indeed, winemaking was a fun pursuit for their mother. Perhaps that was what drove Arno crazy. There he was, breaking a sweat, and she was dabbling. I'll try a little of this cultivar, more of that one, sip, swill, great. Of all I learnt that day from Perl, and she explained how she went about it and showed me her spreadsheets and her equipment in a special little cottage to one side of the winery, this would be the most important: that I should regard it as play. As soon as I took it too seriously, the magic would go, she said.

Henk and I stood chatting in the parking area before driving off. Spreading trees kept the area cool. Getting into our cars wouldn't be like taking a sauna. You left in a good mood. Whoever had designed the estate has thought of everything.

"You and Perl had a thing once, didn't you?" We stood there looking back at the mountains and the fan of rows of vines, those visible from that corner of the property.

"What makes you say that?"

"I dunno." I grinned. "I'm guessing."

"She's a lesbo. Didn't you know? I think she…" The beard expanded into a rare grin. "Wants to get in your underwear. She doesn't give out her trade secrets to just anyone."

I'd had enough of being told someone had a crush on me, or words to that effect. But Gunner had been right. Perl wasn't into men.

"So what brought the two of you together?"

"We partnered with one another for functions. My wife was sick for years. When she died I still felt loyal. Perl knew she was safe with me."

"Anika must have had something special," I say, "for you to give your heart again."

"You know she worked for me for years? Then one day, I was looking at her and realized. There was this most wonderful woman, under my nose, there for the asking."

"It's about timing. I thought I was ready, but maybe I'm not."

"Oh yeah? Who is this lucky bugger? Do I know him?"

I shook my head.

The next day the tanks of wine arrived. I asked the driver of the truck for the invoice.

"There's no charge," he said.

I rang Perl on my cell phone. "Perl, you haven't given me a price."

"They're to get you started. See you at the next show."

"Are you sure?"

"They're also for the aggro I caused your husband."

"Perl?" The line was dead.

Once Perl's tanks were in and hooked up to the cold sterilizing system, Isak fitted taps. The Corder tanks had arrived from Elgin the previous day and were already cooling.

I was going to make a start on blending the next morning, when it was still dark, *at sparrow fart*. Before I left the winery that evening I made sure I had enough measuring jugs lined up and that the taps on the tanks were all working. A notebook, pen, and the sheaf of printouts of my spreadsheet page were ready on a counter nearby.

My mind reeled with plans for after that. Top of the list was having Isak check that our bottling plant was in working order. I was also going to get him to help me check our stock of bottles. I knew I was going to have to order more. Then there were the labels. Lyle had designed labels for Arno. Now he would be designing for his Mom. At this thought the nerves in my spine shook themselves awake and wriggled upstream. This was real. I was going to make wine.

The strangest thing was that neither of the boys was aware of what I was up to. Lyle had been busy in the salon when both trucks with the tanks arrived and left, and neither of the boys had been into the winery lately. Brand's help had been limited to the vineyard. I was going to have to talk to them that evening if I was going to stick to my plan of action for the next day. Outlining the financial situation, which until then I had kept to myself, would win me support.

But when it came to it, I didn't need help. I think it was the fright in my face and voice as I spoke that did it.

"I'm going to be making wine," I said. To cover my embarrassment, I turned to Ellie, "This Thai curry is to die for. Who would have thought boring ol' pork chops could taste this good. Is this a slice of peach?"

I raised my fork with something orange on it. Sure, we were missing Willy's dependable, comforting fare, but there was no doubt Ellie was up there when it came to imaginative dishes.

"No, Stella, it's mango."

"Mom, did I hear you right?"

Myrna wasn't there, so it was three pairs of eyes that stared at me.

"If I don't try now, I never will. Perl has given us tanks of her leftovers. She didn't get to make wine this year. They are reds." I saw that Brand was going to speak and I quickly added, "And I took it upon myself to buy in some white."

"Perl Javinski? Given us tanks of leftovers." Brand's voice trailed away.

"Henk says she has a crush on me, but *she* says it's to get me started and that she'll see me at the next show. That'll be wine from the *new* harvest. What I'll be making *now* is a test run. Lyle, are you up for some snazzy labels?"

CHAPTER 34

We arranged a tasting for a Saturday evening, a week later. We began by inviting friends– some whom had been at Myrna's housewarming, including her mother, Petra, and her grandmother, and Henk, Anika, and Valdine. These were our emotional support. Then I turned to anyone whose professional opinion Arno had valued, people he had trusted would be honest. For this, I consulted Arno's cell phone, computer, and an ancient rolodex, as well as the files of business letters and documents housed in a formidable steel cabinet.

I was excited by the time I got to 'P' for Perl on my list. I was quite chuffed with myself. I hadn't only blended two decent wines, but I was organizing a tasting.

I sat down with a thump after speaking to her. She had a prior engagement, she said. I had been depending on her opinion. She had been my invisible partner through those dark mornings of tapping off, pouring, swilling, tasting and making notes. Her almost black eyes seemed to gleam at me through the golden liquid held up to the dawning sun at a window. As I turned to the next telephone number on my list it occurred to me. She was staying away deliberately. To be a worthy opponent I had to be left to battle on my own. What did the man in the Bible do when people he knew refused to come to the wedding? He went into the highways and byways. I began calling people randomly after that, among others, the owner of Bella's B+B, the woman at Elsenburg whose son abandoned kiwi farming, and Fr. Rob. I asked him not to refer to our recent phone calls in front of Faye.

Before I went off to shower, I checked the winery. One of the men had brought me armfuls of spring flowers from the garden, which I had arranged in pots at the entrance and in whatever vases I could find to brighten corners as you made your way inside. Two rows of trestle tables covered in white paper ran the length of the room. One row was for the red wine, the other for the white. Trays with jugs of water to swill out glasses, tasting glasses and baskets with score cards and pencils, topped and tailed the tables. There were also plastic waste buckets for tasters to tip their dregs in. Ellie had prepared hot and cold snacks for afterwards. Marie would help bring trays across from the house. We were also offering other wines, soft drinks and bottled mineral water, tea, and coffee. The twins would serve the drinks. Myrna had offered to help with the tasting, of which she had some experience helping at wine shows. We had brought in as many chairs as we could find, and these were arranged at intervals against the walls. Isak and another of the men were going to direct cars into the parking area.

I couldn't resist another look at my bottles. Lyle had rushed through the printing of the labels the afternoon before, and I stuck them on by hand that night. We have a machine that does the job, but I hadn't yet learnt to use it. I picked up a bottle of red. *Quinn's Quest* was printed in an olde worlde script. Below, a loosely sketched knight on horseback brandished a sword. To emphasis the experimental nature of the blending I had handwritten the vintage (last year) and the cultivars and percentages of each used. The white wine, *Quinn's Quaff*, also had the knight on horseback but in this case, he was waving a flag. The diagrams were Lyle's idea. We'd had a think-tank about the names. Myrna said, why don't I use my maiden name? What had resulted, I felt, was fussy, but it was as far away as we could get from *Hart Sag*.

On my way out I cast a look back through the arched doorway leading to the cellar. The rows of tanks glistened under the lights. They were the main players, waiting in the wings for bigger and better things. Cross fingers.

Lyle arrived with Faye just as we were greeting the first guests. Myrna had come on her own steam and was already helping some of them to begin tasting.

"We'll get my bags out later," Faye said. She was staying the weekend. She had on a new blue silk dress with a plunging neckline. "I'm so excited." She gave a little squeal and hugged me. "I can't wait. Lead the way José."

I watched as she took Lyle's arm and sashayed in. I wanted to be happy for her, but I felt uneasy. These days *she* was the Spode china. I was the hand-thrown earthenware.

Soon a buzz was bouncing off the low ceiling. People came in dribs and drabs, which allowed me to greet everyone. When the supply had dried up I ventured inside and Brand clinked a glass so that I could describe briefly what was expected, how the comment explained the score, and the generally accepted scores for varying quality, and that the white wine should be tasted before the red. I had tried to prepare myself, but it was still disconcerting to have people frown over a glass or grimace, even jokingly, as did Fr. Rob. People around him laughed as he cracked a joke. Valdine and Marie followed behind me offering trays of cold snacks. Ellie looked flustered when someone asked for vegetarian, but she quickly returned with another tray and offered it around. The twins poured wine, opened bottles of beer.

I walked over to Henk and Anika, who huddled together over their score sheets.

"I didn't know you could make wine," Anika said.

"That's why you're here."

"I don't know what to write," she said, taking another thoughtful sip of the red.

"Compare the color to something. Same with the nose and taste. Write whatever comes into your head. If you don't like it, say. Or make a suggestion. For instance– could be sweeter or tannin overpowers or lacks aftertaste. Or just fill in the numbers." I pointed to *Taster* at the top of the card. "You can remain anonymous. Get another card and leave off your name."

"It doesn't have to be poetry." Henk had been looking at a cluster of girls. I recognized them from the salon. They were taking it all very seriously, checking on one another's attempts, rubbing out and trying again.

"This is such fun," said Myrna's grandmother looking down her nose through her reading specs and licking the end of her pencil. "Reminds me of a wine gum," she said as she wrote.

Petra said, "I came to one of your husbands' tastings– years ago. But that was for the finished product, wasn't it? Yours is subject to change, I gather."

"Did you?" I blushed. I hadn't recognized her at Myrna's housewarming. I still didn't. "I guess what I am doing is unusual."

"It takes a woman," said Petra. "We don't have the big ol' ego to get out of the way."

When the hot snacks came in, I walked outside for a breather. It had been calm but now leaves gusted against the bottom step. Above the trees, the moon sailed between the clouds. Faye followed me. I thought she was going to ask about Fr. Rob but instead she said, "So Perl didn't come?"

I shared what I thought it meant. "I'm probably making too much of it."

Faye thought for a while. Then she said. "You amaze me. I keep waiting for Arno to walk through the door–"

"–and ask me what the hell I think I'm doing?"

"Something like that." For a moment she looked sad. She seldom dwelt on the past, which I was grateful for. Then she sucked in her breath. I imagined a shudder deep down. "If it was me, I would have sold up and moved to the Isle of Man or some-such by now."

"That's because you don't have kids." I immediately realized what I had said and grabbed Faye's arm. "You don't need that rubbing in." What I had meant to say was that there was no point in running away from loss.

Faye gave me that look of hers that scared me. "They might not want to take over from you. All of this would be for nothing."

"What have they been saying to you?" I tried to imagine what she and Lyle might have discussed on the way over, but my mind kept returning to what might be transpiring inside the winery. So far there had been only compliments, but who knew when my back was turned what might come out.

"Nothing. Just, you seem different. Changed. You don't listen to them like you used to. You're preoccupied."

Of course I've been preoccupied, I wanted to scream. I'm looking out for you in the absence of your looking after yourself.

I looked out across the rows of parked cars. Their presence seemed like a benediction. "I'm doing it for me."

"Are you?"

Brand tapped me on the shoulder. "People want to leave. Shall I say something? Like thank them for coming."

"No, I'll do it. Practice makes perfect. We'll be with you in a minute. Ask Marie to make tea and coffee."

Faye and I exchanged a look. We hadn't fought in ages. The last time– I tried to think– was on the cruise. I wanted to pay for her, and she said I should be keeping my money for my grandchildren. I took the comment as a criticism of my parenting. It was happening again. Who parented perfectly? But somehow we all expected ourselves to.

"We'll talk some more later."

She didn't answer.

"Come and hear me make a fool of myself."

"I think I'll go back to the house. I'm cold." She hugged herself under her breasts.

"I'll get Lyle to get your things out of the car."

I watched her retreating back and then called, "Take one of my sweaters. There's one on a hook behind the kitchen door. Or behind my bedroom door." I was shouting by then. "Or one out of my cupboard..."

She had disappeared around a corner.

I wanted to run after her. The wine tasting and its hype, compared to what I wanted, could do, *hoped* to do for my friend, was so much flim-flam (Ada's word). But I had to finish what I had started, and I went back inside.

There are always stragglers at a function like the one we had just arranged. Henk and Anika were waiting for Valdine, who was helping clear away. I said we had plenty of help, but Anika said the girl was enjoying herself. Fr. Rob stayed to ask me how Faye was, and I told him about her second op and that I had tracked Strawks down to Jesus the Nazarene in Durban and that I planned to call the abbot the next day.

"They're a good bunch. He's in good hands. They have a strong work ethic. Once he's done his novitiate he'll be put to work. Mention you've spoken to me. It might help. Or better still, give the old bloke my number." Old bloke? Ah, the abbot. "I did meet Strawks once. Faye brought him over. She wanted them to go to instruction together. A refresher for him. But he had a lot on his plate at the time."

"Are you surprised he wants to be a monk?"

"Didn't look the type. But you never can tell. I'm constantly surprised."

He left after that with a request to know as soon as the wines, the finished products, were ready.

Henk sauntered over with his tasting glass two-thirds full. He had stayed with my wine for the evening, as had some stalwarts. I couldn't help but be touched.

He took another gulp of the red and said, "I know who your mystery man is. The Aussie you were going to bring for lunch." He leaned in so he could look directly into my eyes. "What happened?"

Just then Lyle told me I should come back to the house. "Faye is throwing up," he whispered in my ear.

I left him speaking to Henk. I didn't know what I would have said to Henk. Lied, probably?

Faye was sitting on the bathroom tiles next to the toilet.

"I told Lyle it was a one-off. I'm going to be fine, now it's out." She grimaced. "It's good stuff, that Quinn's Quirk or whatever it's called."

I helped her up and kept an arm around her shoulders as we made our way to the spare room that Lyle had vacated for the night. I shifted her overnight bag to a chair so she could sit on the bed.

"I'll just lie down a little. Then I'll join you guys."

I pulled back the covers and she sat down again. "Shall I get some Enos? Or water?"

"Just water."

After the water she lay back and I removed her shoes.

"How about I loosen your bra?"

She nodded and I turned her on her side and through the fabric of her dress undid the bra. She sighed with relief, lay straight again and closed her eyes. I pulled the duvet up to her chin.

"Go." Her eyes were closed. "And don't look so worried. You worry too much."

Faye never did get up and join us. Later I took her a cup of tea and helped her into her nightie.

The next morning it was raining. When I got up I saw that Faye was still asleep. An hour or so later I brought her French toast, crisp bacon and maple syrup, orange juice, and coffee.

I thought we might finish our talk of the previous day, but Faye wanted to talk about Valdine, how she was having the girl stay the following weekend so Henk and Anika could get away.

"She doesn't have any friends. I've asked the neighbors' daughters if they'd like to pop over. The three of them had already said hello across the fence. Vally can show them how to make *kringla*, or they can watch a DVD and eat popcorn. I'll see what she wants to do when she's there."

I was about to offer to sleep over to help but she looked so happy and confident– a total change from how she had seemed outside the winery during the tasting.

From there it was talk about work, but the more gossipy stuff, like who was pregnant and having an office romance and how people were still handling her with velvet gloves. Then she dropped her bombshell. Hilliards was up for sale and there was already someone interested.

I did a re-take. "Hilliards is on the market?"

"Almost sold. They're at the point of signing. I've met the new people. They want to keep the staff as is. They're all dripping sweet, full of compliments. But give them three months and they'll be changing everything. Putting in new systems when the old ones are working like spinning tops. Offering people packages, me included. Stel, I don't know if I want to stay on and go through all that. Wait for the axe to fall or the other shoe. I've been with Hilliards since I qualified. I've grown up with them. It's like a divorce. I don't want a stepmother breathing down my back. And a stepmother who is wet behind the ears. I'm going to have to knuckle under the new guys who aren't much older than Brand and Lyle."

Here was why Faye went off the deep end the night before.

"Have you thought of making an offer?" It was a long shot, but I didn't want Faye feeling hopeless. Or helpless.

She leaned back against the pillows. "Buy Hilliards? Me, own the show?"

I got up and removed the tray. She had eaten very little. "Why not? You've run it singlehandedly for years. Think about it. You have your savings, and you could mortgage the house for the balance. Shall I get you more coffee?"

Faye shook her head.

"Jeff might sweeten the pot if it's you." Jeff was the son who had taken over when old man Hilliard retired. He still had his other business. I always wondered how he coped with the two. *Faye* was how he coped. I didn't have to wonder what had changed. He had read the writing on the wall about her. The second op must have done it. I swore under my breath, all the filthiest words I could muster with his name attached.

I stood up again. "*I* need some coffee. I don't know about you." I had to get away before Faye saw how I was feeling. "Also, I must get on with the lunch. I've told Brand to take Ellie out for lunch. She deserves a break after yesterday. Then after that ,Lyle is taking you to check out what he's done to Myrna's house and garden. You'll be blown away. But then you always said he was going to surprise us, didn't you?"

"You're not coming with us?"

"Ends to tie up after last night." Faye's eyes were filling with tears. "Tell you what. Stay the night. I'll drive you home tomorrow morning. At sparrow fart."

Faye smiled crookedly, sniffed. "Arno used to say that."

"I've been saying it a lot lately."

"Star, come here."

I put the tray on the dressing table and lent over her. She pulled me close and kissed me for long moments, while I did my best for her not to look directly into my eyes. Hers were full of tears anyway, so I needn't have worried about her sussing me out.

No sooner was Lyle's car through the main gate than I went to my bedroom. Brand and Ellie were taking a nap. I closed the door carefully. I would have to keep my voice down. As I looked at the number, I felt heat prickle my neck and break out under my arms. I was still steamed up about Faye and her treatment by the Hilliards scion. Now this. I had to contend with speaking to some stranger– not Strawks himself– about a very personal matter.

My friend has breast cancer. The female organ and a man of the cloth were the north and south pole. Being this close, a two-hour flight away, made it all the more frustrating. Damn Strawks. Here were we, all pulling out the stops for his daughter while he wittered away to God in some cell. It must take enormous faith, not to want to be checking on her, that she was OK. What about the works that went along with the faith? What about duty to your own flesh and blood? Didn't charity begin at home? The English crowd must have found out about Valdine and packed the remiss father off to the home front to put things right. How come the second abbot had taken Strawks on? Perhaps he was turning a blind eye due of needing a good pair of hands in the place. The work ethic.

While I sat there trying to sort my thoughts, my cell phone rang. Gunner's number flashed and I diverted it. He had called when he landed in Melbourne, but he had been tired, so we hadn't discussed his proposal. Since then he had called twice. Each time I told him I hadn't spoken to the boys.

For a moment I wished I could have picked Gunner's brains about Strawks, as I had before we visited Perl and Bella's B+B. A man's opinion would have brought balance. A man's opinion of another man. He, Anika, and Henk were the three people who knew what I was dealing with, what I was contemplating. I didn't think Henk would have shifted off his low opinion of Strawks. It would color any advice he might be prepared to give, rendering it unreliable. And Anika would be her usual non-committal self. She was a strong woman in most areas but this one. Her relationship with her young brother bordered on indulgent. No, that wasn't it. The opposite. She seemed to have abandoned him.

But no, I couldn't talk to Gunner about Strawks, or give him a straight answer about what he had proposed. In spite of gaining some perspective at Perlheim, I was still too bruised from what had transpired the night before he left. And I couldn't speak to the boys while vestiges of my infatuation remained. If Gunner only knew what was holding up the decision. I cringed thinking about it, which was no preparation for getting tough with the head monk.

I was tempted to take Izzy out for a run to clear my head, but with Faye at the farm for the weekend, I had organized for Isak and the twins to see to the horses. At this thought I wondered if Faye was right. That I was using the twins. Keeping them on at the farm for a future they didn't want. What she perhaps didn't realize was that they had other plans, tentative in the case of Lyle, and I knew about them and was fully supportive. Brand had enrolled for the MBA. Lyle knew he could pursue interior decorating if that was what he wanted. I wasn't standing in their way. They could leave any time, find alternative accommodation. I hadn't asked them to come home. They had returned home of their own accord. They could leave any time. They knew that, didn't they?

CHAPTER 35

I stared at the phone in my hand. Shock ran through me. Blood pounded in my ears. Strawks wasn't at the monastery. He wasn't in a cell praying to God. I tried to remember what the abbot had said, how I learnt the alarming news. The bottom line was I was wondering if I could have somehow circumvented it, could have got wind of it ahead of time, scooped Strawks up before the thunderclap.

Even before I dialed, I had decided that I wasn't going to pussyfoot about. I'd be polite but firm. Say what I wanted.

After the introductions, I climbed right in. "Can I speak to Strawks Johansen? It's a matter of importance." I could have said a matter of life and death, but I might have been written off as a drama queen.

"You can speak to me. I can convey any messages."

"A mutual friend is ill. I'm sure Strawks would like to know."

"Would you mind giving me the details?"

"It's a delicate matter. I need to speak to him in person."

"That isn't possible."

"It may be embarrassing. It's a feminine matter."

"After hearing confessions in a parish that included the Durban dock area, nothing much can embarrass me."

I snatched a breath and launched in. "My best friend has breast cancer and is refusing to have chemotherapy. Strawks was engaged to her once. If anyone can get through to her, it's he." There, I'd said it. "It's a matter of a phone call. Strawks needn't leave the monastery." An ugly edge had sneaked into my voice.

"I'm sorry about your friend, Stella, is it? But Thorkild is unable to help."

"Do I call you Abbot?"

"Father will do. I'm Father Brian."

"Father Brian, can you allow Strawks come to the phone? Just this once."

"It isn't possible."

"Why? Because he needs to say his prayers?" I imagined Strawks knees glued to a predieux, me tugging one arm, the abbot the other. "Isn't helping a friend a form of prayer?

Prayer in action? Or did I get it wrong. Religion means each man for him or herself. My hands were shaking.

"I can see how difficult this must be for you. Your friend is in great need but refusing help. The frustration must be enormous."

I didn't want sympathy. I wanted Strawks now, his cheeky ol' voice in my ear. *I bet you've done it.*

"I've googled him, visited a former employer, his digs in a country town. That was here in South Africa. Then I began calling people in the UK, another former employer, St Bernard's in Wales."

"Ah."

"So you knew he had been turned away as unsuitable." *And yet you took him in?*

"Ours isn't a contemplative order. That is to say it is less rigorous spiritually."

We were getting off the track. I got up and stood at the window, looking out onto the narrow front garden. That way I'd see Faye and Lyle if I didn't hear them. Beyond the picket fence, the Jeep and Brand and Ellie's cars glinted in the late afternoon sun. I looked down. Harry and Sally were standing in a flowerbed. I flapped a hand, "*Shoo. Shoo.*" Woo trotted over to see what was going on. When they had moved off I looked back into the room at my narrow bed. I was in a cell too.

The man coughed.

"Faye had one breast removed. Recently she lost the other."

He murmured sympathy.

"I know, a total balls up. Considering all of this, could you make an exception?" My voice had risen, and I cleared my throat.

"Thorkild is unable to help, because he himself is not well."

"What –" It's a cliché. But at moments like this you *do* doubt your hearing. "What's wrong with him?"

"At this stage it's unclear."

"Unclear?" I was sure I was being put off. I was angry again, beyond caring. "You'll tell me next he has the stigmata."

"Before we continue I'd like to know more about your relationship with Thorkild."

The man's voice was warm, almost intimate. With that kind of voice, a confession would slip from between a hardened criminal's lips like watermelon pips on a hot day. And yet, for me it felt like a rap over the knuckles. But I couldn't, wouldn't stop now. I dragged breath from some hitherto unused corners of my lungs. Here we go, I thought. This was what I wanted. Get the facts across. But why did it feel like I would be diving into a swimming pool without water.

"Faye, that's my friend, and Strawks and I were very close at one time. We met the year after leaving school in a small town in the north-eastern Cape where Faye and Strawks fell in love. They were to be married the year after they graduated from Varsity, but Faye's father died and she cancelled the wedding to care for her mother. Strawks was heart-broken but did his best to get on with his life without her. She was the one who gave him the name Strawks." I squeezed my eyes shut, swallowed. "I tried to get them back together. I almost lost my friend *then*." There was so much I wasn't saying. Before I knew it would be about me. *Oh hell.*

"Our preparation for the novitiate is thorough, so I know most of what you've told me. Also that he married on the rebound and that he has a daughter."

"You do? Do you know that he hasn't spoken to his daughter in months?" I was back on the offensive.

"That is his choice. We ask that our candidates sort out family relationships to the best of their abilities. She is well cared for by his sister, he tells me. Would you agree?"

"I suppose so. Yes." I was stumped. "So tell me, Father, what's wrong with Strawks? You said he's not well?"

The pause was so long I wondered if I'd lost the connection. I turned back to the window, raising my view to the vines, to the craggy mountains, to the sky where skeins of clouds trailed on the wind.

"He collapsed this morning on the way to chapel."

Phyllis O'Donnell and I had visited Jesus the Nazarene once. She had been looking for a wedding anniversary gift for the teacher I boarded with before I bought the flat. The monks taught crafts to the disadvantaged like basketry, spinning and weaving, ceramics, and jewelry-making all were to be found in the gift shop where we had headed. The artwork of the monks themselves, sculptures and paintings could be viewed in the chapel, which we did, and were suitably impressed.

The living quarters, however, a tall red brick building half hidden by trees, remained a mystery. In addition to the communal rooms, there would be the monks' cells. It was in the doorway of one of these that Strawks was found when he failed to appear in the chapel in the early hours of Sunday morning. All but the bedridden of the community had assembled. The new candidates were going to be blessed for the start of their novitiate. It was the culmination of weeks of interviews, assigned reading, prayer and confession.

At first they thought he'd had a fit. But there was no foaming at the mouth, eyes rolling back or limbs jerking. In fact, he was motionless all but for speech. The abbot had arrived by then, knelt with his ear to Strawks' mouth. He was greeted with a stream of prayer. There was no eye contact.

The abbot ordered Strawks' rather stiff form to be carried to his bed. Leaving him with a senior monk, the abbot went off to call the doctor. After questioning Strawks, a fruitless task, and checking that there was nothing physically wrong, the doctor had booked the patient into a rehab center. The psychiatric wards at the other hospitals in Durban were full. Strawks had climbed into the monastery car 'like a lamb', the abbot said.

He had planned to call the family as soon as he had an evaluation from the psychiatrist at the hospital.

"I didn't want to alarm his sister and particularly not the parents in Norway when there may be a simple explanation. And a solution."

I was on autopilot by then. Questions popped unbidden. "Did the doctor say what he thought was wrong? Had there been any warning? Had he been like this before?"

"No. That is what I liked about the boy. He was down to earth. Cheerful. The first day he was here he washed the monastery cars and helped in the kitchen. One of our elderly brothers wasn't eating. Thorkild persuaded him to take some soup."

The picture he conjured up of my friend was oh-so familiar. What had happened in the interim? "There must have been a lead up. Did something happen, do you think, to upset him?"

"Not that I know of. He came with a clean bill of health. That's one of our requirements, once genuine interest has been established, to have a thorough medical."

"But not a psych evaluation?" It felt like I was channeling *Criminal Minds*. It was all so unreal.

"It hasn't been necessary before. Our interview process is thorough. One of us is a trained psychologist. It was he who consulted with our doctor and came up with the decision to get Thorkild into a hospital."

I heard myself promising the abbot that I wouldn't speak to Strawks' family until he called with the evaluation. To which he said that he would like to be the one that broke the news to Anika, and that it was probably best if she gave their parents the prognosis.

———————————

How I gathered my wits, I don't know. All I could think of was that I had tracked Strawks down, finally. But the tables had turned on me. I had wanted him to help me with Faye. Now he was the one needing help. What that was, I had no idea. He seemed to have suffered some sort of a breakdown. The next few days would bring some clarity, I hoped. All I could do until then was wait. At some stage, I was going to have to come clean with Faye, but I couldn't present her with this worry, not in her condition.

In that moment I felt so terribly alone, so utterly wretched. What had I stumbled into? The can of worms corollary came to mind.

Faye was going to smell a rat if I didn't calm down. I stepped out of my skirt, pulled on jeans, thick socks, and my riding boots. I walked down the passage, shoving my arms through the sleeves of my anorak. All was quiet behind Brand and Ellie's closed door.

"Not now," I told the dogs, slipping my mobile into an inside pocket, breaking one of my rules. A ride was to get away from people and responsibility. Izzy whinnied and tossed her head as I saddled up. She couldn't believe her luck. Sweetpea stamped about in protest as we trotted out.

My phone vibrated against my chest as we cantered towards the neighbors' racetrack.

"We're having a cup of tea." It was Faye. "Myrna's place is amazing. I've booked Lyle for a makeover for mine."

I reined in sharply. I didn't want the rhythmic drag on my voice giving me away.

"Good for you."

At the neighbor's gate, we halted. Then, seeing the gate was unlocked, we walked in. Someone had forgotten to lock up. I hoped to God it hadn't been me on my last visit. Some kids, probably, had partied. Beer bottles, soft drink cans, KFC tubs and paper bags, and chip packets littered the grass. I had a feeling that if I checked the bushes nearby I'd find condoms. I wished I'd thought to bring along a refuse bag. I also wished I'd had someone riding with me. Izzy loved to pit herself against a companion. But soon these thoughts lifted, as did my hair, my backside in the saddle, and it was all I could do to keep holding on, limbs, the length of me focused on eating up the hard earth with hammering hoofs as we followed the curved track round and round and round.

CHAPTER 36

Lyle drove Faye back to town on Monday morning. She wanted him to look around the house and garden to get some ideas, which relieved me from some of the strain of holding back about Strawks. Most of what remained of Sunday we spent with Brand, Ellie, Lyle, and Myrna, and when we were alone Faye returned to her worries about Hilliards. Then the next morning, after the best sleep in ages, she decided she was going to resign, that it was time for a change.

Not for me to knock that. In one sense, I'd be getting my friend back.

"What will you do?" I had asked.

"I've no idea. Probably something to do with Valdine. If she does a course she could stay with me."

"Aren't you jumping the gun?"

"Maybe. But it's nice to dream. There'll be space to dream now."

After Lyle left with Faye, I saw to the animals, checked that Isak and the men had plenty to do, and headed for the winery. The maintenance people for the bottling plant were coming the next day. Mid-week, our order of bottles was arriving. I had to do the final blend. Lyle was seeing to the labels. I still wasn't sure about the names of the wines.

I sat down at Arno's desk with the pile of score cards. I flipped through. Only one had no name. It had to be Anika's. She had scored both wines a conservative *13* each. I found Henk's card. They were word for word. One woman likened the wines to perfume. I had forgotten to ask people not to wear perfume or after-shave. It was good though, as that might have put them off.

I entered the scores under the headings of color, nose, and taste followed by the totals out of 20. The average came out at 11 for the white and 14 for the red. The comments were not so easily sorted. Under the three categories I listed the words and phrases most frequently used and the number of times they were used, followed by other words and phrases used. Of the white, among my favorites were: *you can hear the bees in this one.* Of the red: *brave and unexpected– a triumph*, and *bracing tannin platform to juicy raspberries, figs and honey. This is a keeper.* Fr. Rob squeezed into the column: *I'd have to ask my neighbor to lock this one away or I'll be toyi-toyi-ing in front of the altar.* Myrna's Gran had given full marks to the red, with *bloody* for the color, *my lover's breath* for the nose and *orgasmic* for taste, and a 5 to the white with a no-holes-barred, *use as salad dressing.* The more experienced like Phyllis and the couple of wine writers and sales and marketing people had commented on what they thought were the contributing qualities of the various cultivars. One even suggested cutting or upping the percentages for better effect.

"Definitely a thumbs up," said Brand peering over my shoulder.

"Hey. Why aren't you at work?" He looked good in silver grey. His shirt was charcoal, the tie oyster.

"Mom, could we have a word?"

"Now?" I was like a child on Christmas morning being asked to leave playing with my new toys and go to church.

"When you've finished here."

"I guess I can take a break." I grinned wryly. "This is almost as good as sex."

"*Mother.*"

We sat on a bench outside the winery shaded by a bougainvillea coming into rampant magenta. We had brought bottles of mineral water.

I took a swig and said, "Shoot."

"I've been waiting for you to talk to me about Gunner."

"What about Gunner?" I looked away as heat rose up my neck. "You know about his business proposition?" Brand's eyes told me what I needed to know. "He shouldn't have spoken to you. That was out of order."

I held the cold bottle against one cheek, then the other.

"Mom, what is it? Did something happen between you two?"

I decided I had to be honest. Role reversal has begun early, I thought, miserably.

"Nothing happened. Nothing physical if that's what you're asking. But I did have a crush on him."

"Oh." Thoughts flitted like clouds across Brand's face as he took in this new information.

"He was kind to me when I was sick. I was grateful. It went from there."

"I thought you'd be pleased. That it would take a weight off. I'm going to be out of it next year when I begin the MBA."

"We'll manage." I touched his arm. "Truly. We'll be OK. Mr. Hendon is coming to the bank with me when I have my plan ready for making wine. My business plan."

"Bloody hell, Mom. He's a dinosaur."

"He suits me. He's patient and supportive. Your father and grandfather were quite happy with him."

"Well, if you need a second opinion…"

"Your whiz-kid friends. I know."

"I have a couple of sales coming up. That should cover my fees, plus Ellie will be working."

I was about to protest when he said, "We'll also be OK."

I wanted to tell him then about Strawks. But I would be unburdening. Later, perhaps, when we knew more.

"Funny," he said reaching into his jacket pocket for his car keys. "Ellie said– No, forget it."

"What did Ellie say?"

"Let's just say she didn't trust him."

"Does Lyle know about Gunner's offer?"

"I don't think so. Let's leave it at that." Brand made to get up and I pulled him down. "There's something that's been worrying me. That night after Faye's first op. You had dinner with the boss from Jo'burg–"

"Not *that* again."

"Please." I kept holding his arm.

"Oh, well, it doesn't matter now, as I'm doing the MBA. And looking back, it was just as well I turned it down. I wouldn't have had time to study."

"Turned what down?"

"To run the office in Jo'burg."

"To be manager? A promotion? Why did you turn it down?"

"You know why, Mom."

I knew it. He had been thinking of me and the farm. What could I say? I released him and he was off down the path.

Brand looked good in a suit. Arno had owned one suit, the suit from our wedding, aired for subsequent weddings and funerals. Next year, when Brand was studying, his suits would be replaced with T-shirts and jeans. He was paying for the course without prompting from me. If Arno was with us, we'd be flush and he would have taken care of the fees. Brand was growing up fast. Too fast. But then all of us were growing, being stretched.

I returned to Arno's office and made notes. I called the marketing and sales people, thanked them for their comments, and asked them to send me lists of recent sales of wines of comparable style and quality. All except one said not to pursue the Odd Bin idea but to sell direct to bottle stores, restaurants, and hotels. I should start phoning even before my wines were ready, or simply call around loaded up. They confirmed that at this time of the year shelves were getting empty. For the new harvest I should get a website going, maybe find a distributor?

The way our finances were going, we were going to have to do everything ourselves. I walked outside again and stood in the entrance, straining for the voices of the men above the drone of the tractor as it tipped topsoil out of the trailer onto the root systems of vines in the bottom, irrigated section of the vineyard. The more jobs Isak shouldered, the better he seemed to work. I'd discuss with Brand about promoting Isak to, say, vineyard supervisor, a new job description. He could train one of the men to take over in the stable. We had a few weeks until Brand began his lectures. Our programs needed updating. I had to get more involved so that I could take over when he was on the course. Grafting, pruning, trellising and soil analysis were tasks I had watched being carried out, listened to discussions between Arno, staff, friends in the business, experts he had called in at various times through the years, and Frank in those far off days. Now I had to get hands on. I had to support myself, forget about the boys.

It occurred to me, not for the first time, that I could sell up, save myself the hard work, the worry that went with keeping the balls of staff, vines and the business world in the air. I could live in town, find secretarial work. I would have money left over from the sale of the farm which I could invest to pay for stabling Izzy. The boys could find jobs, alternative accommodation. But did I want that?

I looked back into the winery, breathing in the ripe, stronger odor of fermentation since the arrival of the tanks, remembering how we had worked as a team on the tasting, the twins and I, Ellie and Myrna. I didn't want to lose that. How we gathered to celebrate family events, the braais, meals. I wanted all of that for myself, let alone for them. Memories of departed loved ones and tradition backed us. The work kept me grounded. *The Good Earth*. I couldn't imagine living in a town again. I wanted to wake up to the animal sounds, the birdsong, the fragrance of the garden, the vines– the baked hard soil, or the recently turned and rained-on, loamy soil wafting in through the front door. Even if Brand– and Lyle, for that matter, became hotshots in the city or as far afield as Joburg, they would return for the summer holidays as I had done, to soak in nature, to pace down to the rhythm of the seasons so visually and viscerally apparent on a wine farm. I allowed myself to think on into the future to my grandchildren, tumbling out of cars, leaving the doors swinging wide as they hurried into my arms.

I walked into the cellar and ran a hand along the nearest of the tanks, then another and another. The cool smoothness thrilled me. I was their channel to usefulness, to what the grape had been created for. I didn't know how I was going to wait through to the next morning when the fine-tuning would begin. But wait I must for my senses to be at their best, for when they would be gagging for the creativity that awaited them, for their time to shine. I could tackle my business plan, though. I felt my pulse slacken, reason reassert. Arno prepared something like that for the bank when he bought the new crusher. I sat down again at his desk and opened Strategic Plans and Budgets. With a tweak here and there, I'd make it work for me.

CHAPTER 37

Now every day began and ended in the dark. It took a week to blend the two wines, run them through the filtration plant, bottle, and label. Despite my note taking and modifications, the combination of cultivars ended up very much the same. But I felt satisfied. Well, as satisfied as I was ever going to be. Now I understood what Arno meant when he said, when his wines were ready to bottle, a work of art is never finished. You just have to stop in an interesting place. Not that I regarded my wines as works of art. A craft, maybe? But the process was surely the same.

Then followed a fortnight of Brand, Lyle, and me– mostly me– behind the wheel of the truck or the van loaded up with *Quinn's Red* and *Quinn's White*. I had decided to drop the 'Quest' and 'Quaff'. Definitely corny. The wine estate was still Gideons, which carried clout. When I blended the fresh batch I'd cast around for other names. I hadn't yet been to the bank with Mr. Hendon. I wanted to have the current sales figures under my belt when we did. Having offered a hefty discount, we were delivering COD which kept us flush. With the deliveries in addition to my normal duties I barely had time or energy to speak to my family or the staff– except to bark orders– and least of all, to check on how Strawks was doing. Therefore, it came as a shock on the Sunday, the third Sunday since speaking to Fr. Brian, to receive a call, not from him, but from Anika.

After the usual pleasantries and enquiry after the progress of 'your newfound talent,' she said she had news of her brother.

"The abbot has been in touch. He told me you'd telephoned and that you know my brother has had a collapse."

300 | MERIEL MONGIE

"I'm sorry I didn't get in touch when I heard, but the Abbot wanted to tell you himself. How appalling for you. I am *so* sorry, Anika. None of you deserve this– not Strawks and certainly not you and Valdine."

Only now that we were speaking and I could hear the change in her voice– the thickness, did she have a cold– was I realizing that I should have been the one to break the news. Bad news is always better coming from someone you know.

"I'm sorry for *you*, Stella. You wanted my brother's help with Faye."

I didn't know what to say to that except that I had been too busy to dwell on that aspect of the calamity– for calamity it must seem to Strawks' sister who, in addition to her own needs and that of his daughter, had his health to worry about. Not that big sister Anika would allow a murmur to cross her lips.

"I can't leave Valdine, otherwise I'd go and see for myself. And I can't take her with me because I don't know what I'll find. All the feedback I get is that he has had a breakdown and is semi-conscious. I also don't know what sort of effect seeing her father in a semi-comatose state will have on her."

"I can understand that. Although she'd probably take it in her stride if you explained that he isn't well. That he's in a half sleep. That he needs to remain that way to get well perhaps?"

"You have more faith than I."

"Seeing Valdine might be just what he needs." I was on a roll– a roll brought on by my present hyper state. "Children and animals have a way of getting through to us. Seeing her sweet concern might bring him round."

"You're probably right, but I can't take that chance." Was she humoring me?

"But you must have a plan. Anika, you can't just leave him there– among strangers, among those monks." Icy prickles ran up and down my spine, the equivalent of raised hairs on a dog.

Somewhere during the past few days, I'd developed an aversion to these cloistered individuals. I blamed them, I realized, for not recognizing the fragility in Strawk's makeup, for not grasping what had driven him to seek a monk's cell. Where was their understanding of human nature? Were they so spiritual they weren't any earthly good? Of course, Strawks, in his keenness to get into a cell, might have held back from revealing all, from laying his soul completely bare. But I was done with making allowances. Someone had to take the blame, and these supposed repositories and upholders of virtue had to be first in line.

"He needs a woman's touch, and what could be better than his sister at his bedside, and his daughter– his family. Surely Henk can release you for a week or two to go up and sort this out? You can drop off Valdine with us. She can go to work with Ellie and lick envelopes or file. They adore one another, Ellie and Valdine. Or she could come along in the truck with me."

Had I gone too far?

"You are always so generous, Stella… that I wonder if I dare ask…?"

"Ask me what?"

"Won't you take my place? Go up to Durban for me. See exactly how he is." Before I could reply, she said. "I'll pay the air fare."

We were only halfway with the deliveries. I'd just got myself psyched into my role of wine farmer and I was being asked to pause, to break away. I was a hamster on a whirring wheel. Just thinking about stopping and my shoulders were up near my ears.

But Anika wasn't done. "You could talk to the psychiatrist while you're there. Perhaps they'll agree to transfer him to a neuro-clinic in Cape Town. You can be my spokesperson. No one I can think of knows my brother as well as you do, except Faye and she's in no shape to take on something like this." She paused. "They can fax anything I have to sign. I'll give you a Power of Attorney."

I had to stand my ground for my sake and for the family's. And wasn't this another form of interfering, even though this time it wasn't coming from me?

"Anika, I have to get my bottles out while supplies everywhere are low. In a few weeks, the harvest will have begun, and the new wines released onto the market. There's just Brand, Lyle and me, and the boys have jobs, work." I paused. "Anika? Are you there?"

A muffled, "Yes."

"I have commitments I didn't have a few weeks ago. Things here have changed. I'm no longer a lady of leisure. Anika?"

The ugly sound of sobbing filled my ear. Then the line went dead.

I should have known that Anika would be at her wits end. That the months of waiting for word from Strawks would have become unbearable. The suspicion that all wasn't well and the fear that went with it must have been mounting as he pursued, to no success, the out of character goal of personal holiness via monkhood. And having at her side a companion who had written off her brother as a bad egg would have compounded the feeling of being alone in that fear and worry. By her own admission, she couldn't turn to Faye. Faye would have been ideal, as they were old friends and had spent more time together recently than Anika and me. Then there was me, with my own agenda which must have seemed at times obsessive, archaically romantic, illogical. How could a relationship that had ended a quarter of a century earlier be relied upon to help in the present?

All of this swirled about in my head as I drove into town. That same evening, after Anika's call, I had called a family meeting and came clean about the white rabbit I had been chasing ever since Faye's first op when she refused to have chemo. I waited until we had eaten then summoned everyone to the 'lounge.'

I confessed that I hadn't stood my ground in the hospital when the doctor came to hear what Faye had decided. She might have given in if I had, and we would have been saved all of what I was about to lay at their feet. I had been out of my mind about what to do when I stumbled upon the Bethany album which sparked the idea that Strawks might be the one person that is able to get her to change her mind.

"After all, they were once engaged," I finished.

The boys looked almost disbelieving.

I told them the whole story of how I had been trying to track down Strawks and that he is now in a psychiatric ward in a local hospital.

Myrna was the first to speak. "So the one person who could help change Faye's mind is basically out of the picture?"

"More than that– *He* is now in need."

My audience was silent, chewing over everything I had said.

"Here's the thing. Anika has asked me to go to Durban in her stead. She can't leave Valdine. She also doesn't want to risk the girl seeing her father while he is, to put it bluntly, *non compos mentis.*"

"We could look after Valdine," announced Ellie.

"That's just what I said to Anika. But she insists it is me that should go."

"What about Faye?" Lyle asked. "I mean she knows him the best. I mean, isn't that what all this is about. Getting the two of them together again– Faye and Strawks? Or did it end badly– the break-up? Oh, yeah." He thumped his forehead with the heel of a hand.

I sat back. The children were handling this surprising well. But then, I thought, this was an 'old folks' problem. It was easy to be detached about events involving the older generation. I remembered how I had been able to observe Constance's descent into senility without becoming too embroiled. Her sister, Bev, had been the one to fret at her sister's bedside.

Ellie's next argument confirmed this. "Well, it was a while ago. Seeing her after– how many years is it, Stella? Twenty- odd?" I nodded. "Might have an adverse effect on, er, Strawks." Her usually smooth forehead was creased.

"He might think he has died and gone to heaven. *Really died*, I mean."

Brand shook his head. "Bro, you're something else."

"I'm just trying to be helpful." Lyle was in his little brother mode.

"Getting back to Faye," Brand said. "And I know this sounds– well– tough, but she's the one who needs a shake-up. I think *she* should go. You know, be cruel to be kind…" he ended lamely.

Myrna spoke into the hush. "Brand has a point. Both of you boys have a point."

Lyle cheered up instantly.

"Faye needs to face her mortality. That's what not wanting to have the chemo is all about. If she accepts to have the treatment, she is, in fact, accepting that the disease could kill her. And who better to face this with than a former lover, someone who was prepared to go to the altar with her." She took in our newly stunned expressions– especially mine. "I did a stint for Life Line. Many of our calls were about the 'big C'." She blushed.

Ellie suggested that, considering Faye has had two operations within weeks of one another, I should accompany her. After which she asked for volunteers for the deliveries.

I knew I had to talk to Faye immediately or I would lose courage. Being a Sunday night, the roads would be less busy. It was nearly ten when I stopped at the traffic lights on Belvedere Road. Green flashed and I turned into what I thought of as 'Faye's road,' stopping at her gate. The front of the house was in darkness. I hadn't told her I was coming. If she didn't respond to my buzzing, I could call her on my cell phone. As I leaned out the Jeep window I remembered another time– when having security devices fitted wasn't the norm– when Strawks sat in the driver's seat of Perl Javinski's van just inside the gate, huddled over with misery. And here I was again caught between the two– Faye, to whom I had to present my case, a Faye somewhat worse for wear (that was putting it mildly), and Strawks. God only knew where he was emotionally and mentally, if it was possible to peg those.

I tapped our code into the intercom– one long, two short, three long. These days of heightened crime one couldn't be too careful.

"It's me." I announced.

The gate slid back.

I didn't have to knock. She had the kitchen door open. Fergus barked a welcome and bounded into my waiting arms.

"Hello, young fella." He was shivering with delight.

Faye was in her dressing gown and slippers with her hair extra curly from the damp of bath steam. Her cheeks were pink, her brown eyes round and glistening with the shock of surprise. Whatever was I doing there on a Sunday night and with no warning, she'd be thinking. And yet all I could think of was that if Strawks could see her like this he would sit bolt upright in bed defying the doctor and everyone.

"This looks serious," she said, even though I was smiling. But it was a fixed smile. I was caught between joy, should she agree to what I was about to suggest and panic, driven by what I was about to reveal. "Would you like a drink? Horlicks? Coffee?"

I saw that she had a mug in the microwave and a tin of Horlicks open nearby.

"How about some of that Chivers of yours. No ice. A touch of water."

"This *is* serious."

I followed Faye to the lounge. I put Fergus down and he stood looking from his mistress to me and back. To break the tension, I lifted him up again and sat with him on my lap.

I watched as she took the whisky bottle out of the drink cabinet, mineral water and crystal tumblers so old-fashioned they were probably back in vogue. She poured, handed me my drink and sat opposite.

I sipped, wondering how I should start. Talking to one's children went with the territory. Over the years there had been talks of varying degrees of seriousness from commenting on bad report cards to preparing the boys for the approaching death of Granny Ada, who had wasted away after Grandpa Frank died suddenly from heart failure.

My first thought was to check that Anika hadn't told her about Strawks' breakdown. But looking at Faye, who was unruffled apart from wondering why I was paying her this untimely visit, I thought, not. Just hearing his name again would set the cat among the pigeons, let alone news of the strange malaise that had beset him. Then I thought I would follow the lines of how I had explained everything to the children– with a tweak here and there.

306 | MERIEL MONGIE

"Faye, you must have realized that I wasn't going to take your decision not to have chemo."

At this her lips formed a hard line, and I remembered what Myrna had said and winged a prayer that in time Faye would be able to face the truth.

But I must try. I had to do this. I had to tell Faye about my odyssey and what I had discovered at the end of it. Like Odysseus, I was casting off my disguise. His had been that of a beggar and mine– half truths, silence? And, like him, I would have a struggle ahead of me. But once there were two of us– not just me, but Faye and me, how greater would our chances of success be? I, too, had felt like a beggar, I realized. Begging here, begging there, for information as regards the whereabouts of my quarry.

Having spilt the beans, it would be up to her. I knew what I had to do. I thought of the twins and Ellie and Myrna with the roster they had drawn up for the deliveries, all to be carried out within the next week. If Faye only knew how the five of us were behind her, inwardly cheering her on.

But they weren't here now, just me.

I looked at my hand holding the tumbler of whiskey. Any minute the crystal was going to snap. My glass on the table clinked noisily. Let her see what this was doing to me. All the better to *impel* you, my dear.

"I had to do something, but I didn't know what. Then I found the Bethany album. It was while we were looking at it with the kids, and you came out with how you gave Strawks his name, that I decided I had to get hold of him. That he knew you as well, or even better than me. That–" *That he would be the one to get you to change your mind*, I might have said, but I didn't want to get her back up right there at the onset. "That two heads were better than one. That he would have some good advice for me. He was always so practical. It came from being a farmer's son, I guess."

Her lips had relaxed a little.

"So I went looking for him. Googled him." Her eyes widened slightly. "School, the agricultural college, toastmasters, the wine club. Old stuff. Dated. Then you mentioned Anika."

"You told her I don't want chemo." Her bottom lip was out.

"So?"

"It brought back how you told Mom I cancelled the wedding. I knew you were up to something then, but you didn't say anything more so I left it. It's been a good thing, though, hasn't it, getting in touch with Anika and Valdine? Vally has come on amazingly."

I wasn't going to be side-tracked.

"That day at Akkerstroom," I continued in a monotone, "there was a postcard on the mantelpiece in her cottage. It was from a 'Bro' Thorkild' residing at St Bernard's Abbey. No address but a stamp with Queen Elizabeth on it. *Brother* Thorkild." I looked into Faye's eyes. She stared back woodenly. "So I googled the Abbey. There I found the name of a craft and wine shop and a telephone number in the UK. The shop couldn't help but I did learn that Strawks had been running the orchards at the abbey in Wales. The monks don't like answering the phone, especially when they hear a woman's voice. That's when I contacted Fr. Rob."

"So that's how he came to be at the tasting. Seeing him after so many years was a shock, I must say."

We could have chatted about that, how he remembered me and even more remarkable, the story of how Strawks got his name, but I knew I had to keep going. "Strawks had tried to enter the novitiate but been rejected as unsuitable."

I paused again for Faye to say something or for some sign that she had heard and was absorbing what I had said. Again, nothing.

"He wanted to be a monk. A monk, Faye. He was found unsuitable. He had to leave. Imagine the blow that must have been." I took a swig of whiskey and plonked my glass back down. My hands weren't shaking any more. But I could have been talking about the Queen of Sheba for all the interest she showed.

"After that, he seemed to disappear. Anika didn't know where he was. She was stoic about it. Perhaps it's Norwegian. I would have been jumping up and down with frustration. And fed up, too, wouldn't you think?" I sighed and shook my head. "Strawks had left Valdine with her with no further word. This went on for months. Henk is fed up, of course. If Anika didn't have Valdine, he and Anika could be married by now. Well, you know all that."

Faye said, "No trace?"

"I would have been worried, wouldn't you?" Faye nodded, but like she was agreeing to be shot at dawn. "But he did leave a poste restante address at St Bernard's."

"A poste restante address?" Polite. Non-committal. She and Anika were a pair, I couldn't help thinking. Strawks had this effect on the women that were close to him, I also noted.

"Do you know what it was?"

Faye stared back.

"Akkerstroom farm, Piketberg."

I gulped whiskey. "Then Anika got a call from an abbot. Strawks was having another go at becoming a monk. This time in Durban. Jesus the Nazarene. Heard of it? I had, actually. Phyllis and I went there once, to the gift shop. Great wooden salad bowls and servers, pottery, beadwork. Fab."

I drained my tumbler and held it out. Her drink was untouched. She walked stiffly over to the cabinet and for a moment I felt sorry for her. What must this *really* be doing to her? But I had to press on.

"There was to be no direct contact with Strawks, the abbot told Anika. She could talk to the abbot on Sunday afternoons between two and five. He would be the go-between. Anika seemed to accept all of this, whereas I was going crazy. I tried calling during the week, but some old duck answered with a diversion about needing old clothes and things for a bazaar. All of this was so I could get hold of Strawks to talk to you." I let this sink in, watching Faye, but she seemed to have discovered some superhuman strength because once again her expression had become mask-like.

"Then I got through to the abbot. That was on the Sunday. Three weeks today."

"And?" It was a whisper.

"Bear in mind that Anika hadn't spoken to the abbot again. It was me that made the contact. And guess what he told me?"

Faye said nothing.

"The whole community was gathered in the chapel that morning. The new group of monks were going to be blessed for the start of their novitiate, but Strawks didn't arrive. I suppose they waited and eventually someone was sent to see what had happened to him. Well–" I looked across at Faye. Her big moist eyes blinked.

"They found him lying in the doorway of his cell."

Before I could say more, Faye was up and on her feet. She glanced at me, hand to mouth. Then she was walking faster, then running along the passage to the bathroom, where a sound floated back, a sound muffled through the brick wall.

CHAPTER 38

We went on standby for the crack-of-dawn flight to Durban. An hour before take-off we were booked on. I called Anika afterwards. She seemed happy that Faye was coming with me. Faye left a message for Jeff Hilliard. I also called Fr. Brian who said he would inform Strawks' doctor we would be calling at the rehab center later that afternoon. He warned me that the doctor would want to talk to us beforehand 'to prepare us,' which I didn't like the sound of and which I didn't repeat in quite those words to Faye.

Over the next couple of hours we tried to sleep, but we were too pent up to do more than nap briefly. Drinks were served, and then breakfast. At times we were above the clouds, and then the khaki-colored escarpment would be sliding by. It was too early in the season, for rain and the sun shone relentlessly.

Fresh coffee was served. The pilot warned that soon the descent into Durban would begin. We had to speak about Strawks now. Faye had known that Strawks was working overseas, but only the bare bones. She confessed to closing her mind to knowing more and guessed that perhaps that was why Anika hadn't told her that Strawks had decided to become a monk. We agreed that the failure of Strawks' marriage to Crystal seemed to have been the turning point. That his male ego seemed to have received a shattering blow, aggravated by the fact that Crystal could provide generously for Valdine. Which in turn propelled him into taking employment overseas, thus depriving his daughter of his presence, a rum choice you would think, as Crystal in other ways seemed to have lost interest in the girl. He could have persisted with looking for a job locally, even to taking a low-paid one until something better came along. Which is how the Strawks we knew and loved would have acted. And as to becoming a monk, that was stranger still.

After this, we lapsed into a tense silence once more. Uppermost in our minds was what we might find in that ward and our utter ignorance as regards diseases of the mind.

The steamy air hit us full in the face as we stepped out of the aircraft, and wafted cloyingly around our legs in heavy-weight jeans as we proceeded down the gangway and onto the courtesy bus that dropped us off at the new King Shaka airport building. There hadn't been busses at the old, piddling Louis Botha version. As we walked the short distance to the entrance, I was remembering the last time I had been there. Bidding farewell to a teary Phyllis O'Donnell, I'd had to excuse myself to throw up in the public bathroom. She thought I was pregnant (Arno had spent weekends at my flat, flying unearthly hours to save money) but turned out it was nerves about my new life with him at Gideons. I was surrendering my independence, my hard-won independence. I shared this with Faye as we stood at the car hire counter, realizing from the sad look she gave me that we hadn't been on speaking terms at that stage. I grabbed her hand and squeezed, fervently giving thanks that she was at my side now.

Out on the freeway, we were approaching an overhead signboard. I had switched the GPS off the moment I saw the crowd of new heroes-of-the-struggle street names. I knew where to find the St John Vianney Treatment Center for drug and alcoholic addiction. Anyone who lived in Durban for any length of time knew of someone who had gone to 'SJVs' for a sweat out or dry out. One of the teacher's husbands from the college, a big boozer, had been sent there by his employer.

But for the moment I wanted us to forget where we were headed.

"City?" I said. "It'll take longer, but it's your first time in Durbs."

Faye nodded. Complicit was our postponing of the moment of reckoning. She sighed heavily and returned to watching the lush coastline fly by on our left and the blue of the ocean when we caught glimpses. Soon the outlying suburbs were also behind us and the shoulder-to-shoulder beachfront hotels and holiday apartment blocks sweeping by on our right as we approached the city. With its sub-tropical climate, Durban is a year-round holiday destination. Even in spring, when Capetonians wouldn't dream of dipping a toe in salt water unless they were health or sports nuts, the beaches are sprinkled with umbrellas and the ocean dotted with bathers. The candy-striped roofs of the funfair, slowly turning big wheel and doggem cars bumping against each other as we waited at a set of lights, jolted us to life going on elsewhere, and people enjoying themselves, which only served to heighten the quite opposite nature of our mission.

But we couldn't be gloomy for long. No sooner had we turned towards the city center than I had to stop again. Two rickshaw drivers, resplendent in enormous horned head gear and tossing wild animal skins, were attempting to pass one another in a race that had more to do with impressing their passengers– who innocently or deliberately cheered the men on– than getting to their destination sooner.

The new grid of one-way streets kept me absorbed as we headed through the city and up towards what was formerly Ridge Road, now Peter Mokaba, then through the cross-section of smaller streets with thankfully unchanged names.

We had no trouble at the security gates, as our arrival was expected. We were directed to park around the back of the spreading Victorian mansion. A gentle breeze stirred, but it was too moist to bring complete relief. At the reception, a mumsy person introduced herself as Daphne and asked us to take a seat in the large comfortable lounge.

Four others were waiting for Dr. Nomoka, she told us. One of them, a woman with her hair severely scraped back into a bun pursed her lips in sympathy as we began filling in the two-page questionnaire. After the usual personal details, which included whether we were able to pay the patient's bill and requisite bank details– Faye replied in the affirmative, I the negative. There were questions, probing questions, I decided, flinching more for Faye's sake than my own. We tried our best to explain our relationship and history of dealings with the patient and any previous known psychological traumas and details regarding these.

"What's this Dr Nomoka like?" I asked when I took our completed forms up to the desk.

"He's in great demand— on loan from the government hospital up the road. He gets good results, although some regard him as old-fashioned."

I repeated what Daphne had said to Faye. I'm not sure it helped. She was twitching with nerves by then.

At last, the doctor was ready, and Daphne escorted us to his office, handing the file with our forms to him before closing the door. Dr. Richard Nomoka, a tall, strapping Congolese with the American accent of so many Africans who had studied overseas, invited us to sit across from him. His desk held a leather-framed desk blotter, a desk-tidy bristling with pens and pencils and one of those arrangements of hanging lead balls. One wall was lined with books, the other thick with framed originals of local scenery. If not for the diplomas and certificates announcing the various doctors' professional accreditations, this could have been a study in an ordinary home.

The nurses and staff wore no uniforms, only name tags with profession or job description, I had noticed as we passed in the passage. Everyone else looked normal, friendly. Like a fool, I said something along these lines.

"Except they're all grounded. Everyone but the staff," he replied, chuckling. "Actually, it is only the patients in the cottage ward who are confined to barracks, as they might come to some harm if they wandered off."

The smile with its white teeth and glistening eyeballs against black was almost indecent in its radiance. He's making a joke, part of me realized. The rest of me tensed as I looked at Faye who was staring into her lap.

"D'you mind if I check your homework?" he said opening the file. Another joke falling flat.

A domestic worker entered with a tray with tea and biscuits. I sipped and nibbled while Faye regarded the contents of the tray as if it was poisoned. I looked out of the window. A child's swing hung limply from a jacaranda tree. The purple-blue florets covered the bench and bricked paving below. Again I thought how innocent everything looked, that is, with no hint of the troubled spirits that were harbored within.

The doctor returned the forms to the file and leaned back. "I'll need your assurance that you will cooperate with me and the staff in helping Thorkild to regain his equilibrium."

Again the fulsome smile.

We nodded. At least, I did. I looked at Faye once more, but she wouldn't look at me.

"It's all my fault," she began. Tears dripped into her lap.

"No, no, no," said the doctor. "The patient is an adult. He is aware of where he is and what he is doing. He would have had warnings of the approaching crisis. Lack of concentration, for example, anxiety attacks, thoughts of suicide, hallucinations and so on."

He stopped and addressed me. "*Madame,* why don't you scoot up to your friend. Here, let me help you."

As he spoke, traces of the French that he had begun life with emerged. He came around the desk and I stood up while he pushed my chair up against Faye's. Seated once more, I stretched an arm across her shoulders.

"He took no notice of the warnings. Is that it?" Faye asked in a shaky voice.

"It's my guess. What began as reactive depression, that is, depression as a reaction to an event. The death of someone close, for example, or a relationship ending, being fired from a job, financial ruin, these are some of the common triggers. But the catatonic development– that is, the collapse– would be due to some choice having to be made, something looming, and being unable to decide against it or change the circumstances until breaking point was reached. It's a shutting down where action or volition or choice of action of any new and fresh kind is made impossible."

"Is it like dying while you're still alive?"

The doctor looked at Faye, surprised. For a moment a brief heaviness collapsed the good cheer. "Suicide would be a decision you see, and with catatonic depression the decision is *not* to decide. In fact, to do nothing. To bring life to a complete halt without actually dying."

"Then the patient really wants to continue living."

"Quite." I could feel Faye relax. She turned to me. "When you told me about Strawks, the lead up, how someone went to see what had happened to him, I thought you were going to say that he was…dead. From a heart attack or something." Much later, she was able to confess that she thought he might have taken his own life.

I squeezed her arm.

"At this stage Thorkild is unable to move or speak voluntarily. He seems also to be repeating certain prayers. That is, he is unable to stop."

Faye and I murmured dismay.

"Once the stressor or stressing factor is removed and the patient feels safe again, volition will return. It may take time– weeks, months, depending on severity. Remember, it takes time to reach this state and time to recover from it."

"Do you think he will recover?" Faye asked.

"There's no doubt in my mind. Especially with friends like you to cheer him on." The doctor leaned forward. "But we have to be patient."

"The abbot told me that treatment has begun," I said.

"A course of benzodiazepines have been prescribed to alleviate anxiety, sleeplessness, agitation, muscle spasms. That's Valium, to you. We may have to use other methods, if Thorkild doesn't look like waking up on his own. But we'll talk about that another day."

"So he's not in pain?"

The doctor nodded.

"Will he be able to talk to us?" Faye asked.

"I'd be very surprised if he did. But he'll hear you. You'll need to keep it simple. Responding may take a while."

The doctor stood up. "I need to take the other visitors through. I give them a weekly update. Unfortunately for you," he looked at each of us in turn, "this is that day of the week. If you don't mind waiting, a nurse will call you when I'm done. Then we can say hello to your friend and see how he's feeling today."

Everything was uttered cheerfully as though there was nothing out of the ordinary about anything that had happened so far.

We returned to the waiting area, a tortuous hour. At last, the nurse appeared.

The cottage had a latticed metal security gate in front of the door. While the nurse was entering the code, Faye and I conferred. Who should go first? We were allowed no more than fifteen minutes each. The doctor would be nearby at all times. "

You take the half hour," I whispered.

I was going to wait and see how Faye managed before I ventured beside that bed.

At the ward, Nomoka beckoned for us to enter.

"You go," I said, stopping just inside. I had been going to stand beside her– to offer her support– but a glance around the ward had swallowed up my good intentions. All the patients were lying down, all except one man who couldn't seem to lie with his head on the pillow and every so often shouted something unintelligible.

The first thing I saw was the hair. The bright sun of it.

The nurse rolled him onto his side so that he was facing Faye. His eyes were closed, but his lips moved. I wasn't close enough to see his expression, or lack of it. He could be acting, I thought, remembering how Strawks loved to dress up and play parts. Maybe that was what this was, a game, by anyone's standards a diabolical one, but utterly convincing, the means of bringing his beloved to his bedside.

The doctors would have seen through the charade in no time, I told myself. The reality of where I was and what I was seeing was beginning to strike home with force. I was trembling all over. Marshalling will power, I stepped further back so that I was just behind the door. I wasn't the fainting type, but my legs felt like they might collapse under me.

I breathed in and out, trying to stay calm. How must Faye be feeling? Was she touching Strawks? Was it allowed? Thoughts like these were hardly a match for the weight of guilt I was feeling at having deserted her in her most acute moment of need.

"Strawks, honey, it's me, Faye." I had to strain to hear. She said something else which I couldn't make out. Then, "I've come to visit you. I've come to help you get well."

The doctor murmured something then Faye tried again, "Strawks, it's me, Faye." And she repeated about coming to help him get well. Her voice dropped to a whisper. I didn't mind. The less I heard the better, I thought, in true coward fashion.

Moments passed with more of the same. I was about to slip away, having convinced myself that I was of no use there anyway, when Faye began to sing. She kept her voice soft and low, like she was singing a lullaby to a baby.

"You are my special angel, sent from God above…"

I listened through the whole of it, mesmerized, my throat aching with unshed tears. When Faye began her supplications once more, I decided I really couldn't take any more. I turned tail and headed for the cottage's waiting room.

Once there, I found myself desperate for something to stop me from thinking about what was going on back in the ward. We hadn't yet booked somewhere for the night. I delved in my bag for my cell phone and was about to call a B+B when I thought of Phyllis.

"Stella. You're in Durban? *Oh how marvelous.*"

Those crisp English consonants spoke of a Boadicean capability that had seen me through many a crisis, the most noteworthy being the day Arno followed me to Durban. I had to explain to her why I hadn't turned up for work and that Ensign didn't have horse flu or strangles. She organized for a student to man the reception so I was free to spend time with Arno. She would have done more if he had been able to stay longer. But we did avail ourselves of theater tickets and a late-night supper at a favorite restaurant, paid for by her and 'no back-chat.'

We didn't have a honeymoon because the twins were due to arrive any day after the wedding (they could have made their entry with mine down the aisle) and although we never said as much to one another, that night more than made up for it. All of which gave me courage some weeks later when I had to announce that I would be leaving her employ and moving to Cape Town due to being pregnant. She wanted to have me checked out again by another gyno, which I assured her was unnecessary. (I hadn't been to a gyno or doctor. But I had skipped a period due to fretting about a possible move to the Cape.) She wanted to drive me down. Flying was dangerous when you were pregnant, wasn't it? Within twenty-four hours, she had bought a full layette at Stuttafords and would have bought and had delivered from the same expensive source, an entire suite of baby furniture and paraphernalia half across the country if I had allowed it. (The layette came in handy a couple years later, doubled up, of course).

I wasn't pregnant, I'd had to confess. It had all been in my mind. She had even forgiven that and allowed me to stay on for longer in her employ until I had finally gathered the courage to end my single existence and begin the shaky steps towards marriage with a very patient Arno.

This gave me the courage now to tell her briefly where Faye and I were and why. She knew Faye and Strawks' history, the broad strokes of it, gleaned during her holidays at the farm, her last being the previous summer. I promised to fill in the details later. She shrugged this off as unimportant. What was important was that we had a comfortable place to stay during our time in Durban, however long that was, starting with that evening. We were to come around immediately our visit at the center ended. After speaking with her, I headed for the toilet where I sobbed like a baby.

CHAPTER 39

Faye giggled as Phyllis directed them runway-style into the visitors parking at her apartment block in Musgrave Road. It was good to feel, even briefly, something other than dread, good to feel her once happier self was still there, that life as she had known it was waiting for her to resume it, when she was able, when the nightmare was over.

Phyllis had taken to wearing caftans, a not always successful attempt to hide the weight gained since she retired. This number was in jewel colors evocative of a peacock spreading feathers for these womenfolk. Someone else might have given them instructions at the car window or indoors from a cell phone, not to mention that Stella had been there before, but to give Phyllis her due, that was ages ago. Everything about Phyllis was big and bold. There had been a time, at Stella's wedding to be precise, when Faye had been jealous of her friend's friendship with her one-time boss, since replaced with a growing appreciation because the woman had been nothing but kind. Besides, the vacuum left by Glad and Constance and then Ada, begged to be filled. Or was it the other way round?

No sooner were they inside and freshened up than the G+Ts were out, which Faye and Stella downed like they were a splash of water hitting a sunbaked rock. Phyllis was on her feet again offering a top up. Behind her in the dining room, a table was laid for a meal of Woolies meat cuts and salads, and the crunchiest looking bread rolls. Faye had picked at the airplane food, and lest she forget, had the night before been relieved of her supper which was enough to make her feel starved now.

She sat there thinking, *Mom would have loved this*. Ornaments were everywhere, a whole cabinet full of them. A RAF Spitfire prop clock took center place on the mantelpiece and pouffes and side tables interspersed the heavier furniture. It reminded Faye of the home of an aunt visited on a rare holiday in England. The flat was prewar and would have seemed cluttered, had not the tall windows been tastefully draped in velvet, and silk carpeting in matching cool eau-de-nil flowed in and out of the colonially indulgent rooms.

"So. What's been going on?"

On the way over, Stella had asked if Faye wanted to skirt the chemo issue when they described the lead-up to coming to Durban and Faye said, *nonsense*. That it was essential to the story and that Stella should go ahead and speak about it. But that was a far as it went. All she could think of now was Strawks and helping him get better.

Stella did her best to recount the events, ending with Strawks collapsing in the doorway of his cell and being diagnosed as needing some kind of psychiatric treatment. Phyllis wanted to know if they knew what had caused the breakdown.

"More than likely he's going to want to forget it once he's recovered. I know I would," said Stella. Faye knew that shudder. "But it does seem like he couldn't go through with becoming a monk. Being rejected by the monastery in England probably knocked his confidence in that regard. A failed marriage didn't help, either."

"Doesn't something like this have its roots in childhood?" Phyllis cocked an eyebrow at Faye as she offered a dish of cashews.

"He never said much. He was terribly loyal. His parents were in their forties when they had Strawks and his sister. They were old-fashioned and a tad rigid. But he gave no hint that he had suffered in any way or came away with hang-ups. He was one of the most balanced people I know."

Why try to explain which only showed how little she really knew. Irritation rose like prickly heat, which Faye was sure she would have been breaking out in had it not been for the air-conditioning. She wriggled in her chair and some of her drink slopped onto her lap.

"*Sorry.*"

Phyllis was on her feet again, handing Faye a napkin. "I'm the one that should be apologizing. I get so greedy for news of you Capies. You must be exhausted. Both of you. I'll fetch that wine of Stella's. If you don't mind, Stella, we can pop ice in it as it hasn't had long enough to chill. I can't wait to try your Quinn's. We'll open the white this go-off, shall we?"

During the meal, Faye found herself longing for bed, but once there, sleep evaded her. Or if she did fall asleep, it was to flail about in a pit of nightmares. Her head was an open wound and birds pecked at her brains. She woke up trying to hit them off. Or when she tried to speak, a snake crawled out of her mouth, and she tugged and tugged trying to get it out with no success. All through, Dr. Nomoka was saying, *"Here, let me help you."*

She didn't dream once about Strawks as she would have expected. It got so bad, she didn't dare fall asleep again. Once, she stood at the window which had a view of the spot-lit, park-like garden and hugged her chest, forgetting until the scars hurt and rubbed her arms instead against the suddenly too-cold artificially cooled air. The garden seemed like a dream as well, which was hardly any help. In the sauna-like climate, plants reached grotesque proportions. Feathery pampas grass stood six feet high, strelitzia like prehistoric birds stood poised to attack while cannas bared petal tongues in colors from blood through bile to jaundiced white. She heard a floorboard squeak, thought it might be over-solicitous Phyllis come to check on her, and she tiptoed back to bed.

———————

Stella could only stay a week. Faye was dreading being without her. She didn't know how she was going to handle Phyllis. The woman was a bull in her china shop, but she wasn't going to think about that now. It was Friday, and Strawks was having shock treatment. They had the weekend to recover. Stella was flying out Monday morning.

"Thorkild has been booked to have electroconvulsive treatment," the doctor told them the day before. "He'll be given a pre-med and a mild anesthetic will be administered prior to the treatment. He'll be closely monitored. There's no need for worry."

They had been in the waiting room at the cottage since six. Now it was eight. While Stella made calls to the farm, Faye sat with Strawks. She searched his face, hoping he was awake, that by some miracle he didn't need the treatment. She had never given up hoping that *this* day, *this* moment would bring her friend back to her. One of the worst things for Faye was the change to his face, the blankness, those dead eyes she found staring at her whenever he was handled, like dressing him that morning in the clean gown and long white socks she remembered from journeys into her medical minefields.

Luckily, Strawks didn't know what he was headed for. Since the drops of pre-med on his tongue, the gabble was less intense, which was disconcerting. She had come to rely on it. Over the few days of her being there– to relieve boredom, God forgive her– she had begun listening for content. From her brief encounter with Catholicism she recognized parts of the mass, and what she supposed was a morning and night prayer, and the Litany of the Saints. The woman with the bun, a Catholic, had given her this last clue. There was this astounding side to it. It reminded her of the movie, *Rainman*, and the ramblings of the savant brother who was a genius with numbers. Who knew what was stored in any of their heads, what might come pouring out given the backing down of the conscious mind?

At last, the ambulance was there. The small band of 'cat' ward visitors gathered to wish them good luck and waved them off, which brought Faye close to tears as she and Stella followed the nurse with Strawks in the wheelchair.

The attendant, a hefty Zulu called Mano, rolled Strawks onto a gurney that had wheels that folded underneath before it locked into place in the back of the vehicle. Both Faye and Stella were given a hand in. She sat up front with her hand on Strawks' nearest hand, the attendant and Stella opposite.

Thankfully, the siren wasn't going to be activated. She asked for Strawks' head to be turned so that he was facing her. He was dribbling and his nose running, which she took care of with a tissue, careful not to remove the lip balm she applied whenever she was with him, which had no real salubrious value but in her troubled state these small acts took on heightened importance like a hand placed against a pane of glass you sometimes saw in movies.

"Surely an ordinary car or van would have been better? I mean, Strawks isn't actually sick," Stella remarked as they travelled uphill along roads that took them to the highest point, Durban's Ridge.

He *is* sick, thought Faye, so there was no point arguing. Through a small window, buildings, trees and hedges and walls passed by. Everywhere was densely green, as stultifying as cotton wool in your ears (the interior of the ambulance shut out most sounds). With a pang, Faye realized she was missing openness and mountains. You only realized when you were away how a familiar landscape contributed to your sense of wellbeing.

"We never know how the patient will react," the attendant replied. To underscore this, he checked the blood pressure apparatus for a reading and that the clamp on Strawks right index finger was secure. He was confident to the point of arrogance, quite different in approach to the staff at the cottage.

"I bet you have some horror stories to tell?" Stella said. The man perked up. "But do you mind keeping them for Halloween?"

Stella placed her hand over Faye's and winked. The attendant sat back, deflated. In other circumstances Faye would have felt sorry for the man, but the reek of his deodorant, or was it the sway of the vehicle? was making her nauseous– that and concentrating on being calm by placing her hand over Strawks' was enough to think about.

They should have coffee in the cafeteria while they waited, Nomoka said, ushering them towards the lift. Faye had stolen a look back over her shoulder into the treatment room before the nurse, having wheeled Strawks in, shut the door. Various restraints lay on or dangled from the

324 | MERIEL MONGIE

padded treatment table. A bank of machines lined the wall. Anything else that might have been there was a blur.

Forgive me, honey, she murmured under her breath as the lift door slid closed. Anika had given her power of attorney to sign for whatever treatment was necessary for her brother. Now Faye quaked inwardly at the enormity of what was to take place, what she had signed this innocent creature up for, this good man, this dearest of friends. If she could have cried, it might have helped. Instead, she was frozen with terror.

The instant they were in the cafeteria, the nausea returned, and she had to go outside and wait while Stella ordered the coffee which they took out into the grounds. While seated on a bench under palm trees, Stella's mobile rang. It was Anika. Stella, as she always did, offered for Faye to talk, but she shook her head. She would talk to Anika when there was something positive to report. "But give her my love. Oh, and how is Vally?"

While they drank their coffee Stella relayed news of Valdine. She had started on the next grade of her home studies. Any other news, Faye seemed unable to absorb, and Stella began instead to describe local places of interest she hoped Faye might visit while in Durban, nothing that required deep thought or an immediate decision.

They were still there when Nomoka came out. Refusing their offer for him to join them on the bench, he began, "As I told you, we won't know the full effect until tomorrow. He is sleeping now. But it went well. There was a healthy reaction."

"Excuse me, but what does that mean?" Faye asked, sitting on her hands to stop them shaking.

"Put it this way, the words he used were very un-monk-like. We had to put the mouthpiece back in a couple of times."

Stella dug Faye in the ribs. "See? Our boy is his old self."

Mouthpiece? The coffee rose bitter as bile in her throat.

"*Madame,* I wouldn't put it quite like that." He always called Stella *madame.* "We've scheduled half a dozen treatments. He may not need them all. After which we begin counseling."

Stella looked at Faye. "How long will you stay, d'you think?"

Faye shrugged. "I might have to find digs. A B+B?"

"Phyllis will never allow that."

"That's what worries me," said Faye.

"Right," said the doctor. "I see I've set a cat among the pigeons."

And he walked away.

The first treatment put an end to the gabble. Strawks was still semi-conscious, however.

"Great strides," Nomoka remarked, beaming.

On Monday of the fourth week Faye was allowed to take Strawks into the front garden of the center. It was going to be a celebration of sorts. There were to be no more trips to that destination of horror, the ECT room. The previous night she had tossed about, this time in a whirl of delicious anticipation.

Phyllis, in her ancient Volvo, wished Faye luck before dropping her off at the center. Faye hadn't booked into a B+B, more for Stella's sake and the sake of their friendship than anything. Soon, however, exhaustion set in. After a day at the center, she was only too grateful, not so much for the lift and a drink and a delicious meal waiting for her, although these were tip-top, but for having someone to speak to, to share the events of the day with, someone who wasn't a complete stranger, someone who seemed free of worries of her own, a fresh face and voice after the demands of the ward. Phyllis had a way of getting Faye to speak, to unburden. She knew, for instance, that Faye, apart from the many longed for and welcome changes in Strawks since the introduction of the treatments, had yet to hear him utter her name.

He was looking more handsome by the day. The unbearable slackness was gone, only to be replaced by gauntness. But even this was an improvement. Today he looked scrubbed and groomed. She had been allowed to give him a bed bath, but now that he was 'awake' a male nurse came over from the main building and helped Strawks shower. He also helped Strawks shave. A couple of days earlier, a barber had called offering to cut the patients' hair and Faye had asked that Strawks might avail himself. The man wouldn't take payment. He was a Christian and said he tithed his time. There were a number of these generous souls who had to be vetted, of course. This individual, for instance, wasn't allowed to talk about Christ or pray with patients. But what better sermon than his selfless service, Faye found herself thinking.

Strawks was wearing one of the shirts and Bermudas she had bought for him. He had given away all of his civvies when they kitted him out for the novitiate, the abbot told her when she asked for Strawks' clothes to be brought to the center. He hadn't known Strawks had done this, he said, which Faye thought was quite lame, although the finality of the action was a clue to how serious Strawks had been considering the calling. Stella said Faye should have it out with the cleric about not twigging onto the fragility of Strawks' mental state. But blame wasn't the way. Faye had learnt that lesson dealing with the loss of first her Dad and then her Mom. You could blame the other spouse, other people, yourself, anything and everything, but at the end of it all, what was needed for peace to flow into one's heart, was acceptance. On the issue of his clothes, however, she was amazed to discover she remembered his measurements. He had been happy to leave ordering his suit for the wedding to her. Typical farmer, she thought at the time. When she handed his measurements to the assistant at Hamilton's Men's Outfitters, he had told her flatly that she had the numbers wrong. The chest measurement was too wide for the length of leg. She had checked with Strawks. The numbers were correct. That's my man, she remembered thinking, big chest, big heart.

And he was still her man. Smoothing his collar, she noticed that the shirt, blue to match his eyes, open-necked and short-sleeved, was a tad loose, as was the waist of the Bermudas. But he would gain weight in no time, Nomoka said. When you are able to register the sight, smell, and taste of the meal before you, your appetite is bound to improve. And boy, was he eating. She burrowed in the box of Romany Creams for the last one and handed it to him. It disappeared in two bites. She wished he was as keen on talking. But she had to be content. He was taking an interest in his surroundings. He was listening to her. But it was hard work, as his replies were monosyllabic. And then there was the matter of her name. She was being finicky and childish but try as she might, she couldn't shake the need for him to say– not the two-syllable, "honey" or "darling," which would be too much to expect anyway– but the one magic, Faye.

He was only able to focus on one thing at a time. Eating done, she began commenting on their surroundings. One of the florets of the jacaranda tree had landed on his knee and, hoping for a reaction, she lifted it up to his line of vision. He merely looked. He had always been a smiley person, so the smile didn't mean much. It was words she wanted. She remembered an incident with the twins in the 'double cab' at Kirstenbosch gardens. How she had bent the long stem of an agapanthus to within inches of each face in turn. It was always with a sense of wonder she observed the differences: blue and brown eyes, smile and solemnity.

"Fly," said Brand and then Lyle.

'Fly', instead of, 'flower'. OK… she thought, until she spotted a bee landing on the massed head of blue corollas like it was a helipad. She released the stem as though it was red hot, her heart thundering in her ears.

She told Strawks the story, wondering if he remembered the twins.

"It was a bee, not a fly," she prompted.

"Bee, not fly," he said.

Suddenly she didn't have the energy to go into who Lyle and Brand were.

They watched as *Pure Earth*, the van from the recycling company, entered at the gate and how, with the engine still running, the driver took the clipboard from the guard and scribbled an entry. Through the van's open window, they watched as the man lifted a can of Coke and sucked through a straw before taking hold of the steering wheel once more and driving in.

Faye was thinking that perhaps they could talk about that when Strawks said, "Thirsty."

"Yes, it's thirsty work," she replied. Progress at last.

Strawks looked at her.

"Oh, *you're* thirsty. Sorry." She got up. "Wait there. I'll get us something to drink."

At the desk she asked Daphne for change for the dispensing machine. The receptionist looked harassed.

"I'm on a call with a parent. *Again*," she said, a hand over the mouthpiece, taking the bank note but handing over the couple of coins needed instead of all the change.

Mothers of the younger patients often rang wanting to speak to one of the doctors, not taking no for an answer, they harass the receptionist with questions about their offspring's progress.

Returning with her purchases, Faye leaned over the desk. The receptionist was still on the call.

"I'll bring the money out to you," she said. "But hang on."

She saw that Faye was struggling with the cans, packets of crisps and *Lunch bars*.

"Do you mind holding?" she asked the caller and walked with Faye to the front door. "Hopefully the line will be dead when I get back." Daphne grinned wickedly.

"Where's your man?" she said, holding the door open and peering into the garden. Faye liked the sound of 'your man,' but not the fact that he wasn't on the bench or anywhere on the small stretch of lawn.

Over at the gates, the *Pure Earth* van was back, and the guard was once again handing over the clipboard. Behind him Strawks was edging through the space opening up.

"*Strawks*." Shoving the cans and chip packets at Daphne and kicking off her flip-slops for greater speed, Faye ran down the small slope that led to the gate.

He was out on the grassed verge when she got to him. He was a little unsteady but looking from side to side as though he was not just regaining his balance but getting his bearings.

"Strawks. Thorkild Johansen. What the hell d'you think you're doing?" She was shouting and holding his arm while propelling him back to the gate that had to be opened once more by the shell-shocked guard.

Daphne tut-tutted and went back inside.

Back on the bench, Faye tried again. "Strawks, where did you think you were going?"

He looked back, as puzzled as she.

"You will be able to go out one of these days. You're just not ready." She shook her head. "As soon as Dr Nomoka gives the word, we'll go out, anywhere and everywhere. But you're still on medication. If anything happened to you, I wouldn't have been able to forgive myself."

Those traitorous tears were on their way and Faye shut her eyes. She hung her head and, too late, they dripped.

"Faye... sorry."

———————

She didn't have to explain what happened when Phyllis collected her later. But Faye wanted to, all the cute details right up to Strawks saying her name. Later at the Curry Bar in the Royal Hotel, where Phyllis had taken her to celebrate, Stella called. Faye told her what had happened, up to Strawks slipping through the gate. She kept it brief, knowing how busy Stella was.

"He's getting crafty," Stella said, laughing.

Faye was affronted. "What do you mean?"

"Didn't you say he was looking around like he was planning to go somewhere?"

Faye felt herself bristle. "Did I? I gave you the wrong impression. He isn't able to string words into a sentence, let alone plan anything. Plan an escape."

She had shocked herself with that last word. Escape? Is that what he was trying to do? She squashed the thought.

"Remember how Nomoka said getting fried was like being born again. Today he said Strawks is quarter way through recovery, which means Strawks is in the child phase. Like a child, he saw the gap and went for it. A childish impulse." Why was she making a big deal of it?

"OK. Heck. I was just trying to point out how well our boy is doing."

There she was again, refusing to acknowledge that recovery took time. She pictured Stella, exhausted after a day in the vineyard, up early to blend wine, supervising staff, seeing to the animals. She was a world away from where Faye was. It occurred to Faye then that telling Stella that Strawks had said her name, how important it had been to her, would be a waste of time. And she'd end up getting offended– if she wasn't already. She smiled wryly at Phyllis, who offered a little moue of sympathy.

"It'll be better once you're back and can talk everything through," Phyllis said, nodding for emphasis. "I'm going to be envious then, I'll tell you. In the meantime let's enjoy the time we have. Shall we order?"

CHAPTER 40

FOUR MONTHS LATER

They would be home for Christmas. Their seats had been booked. The last fortnight had been a countdown of the sights, from nearby Mitchell Park and the Botanic Gardens to day trips to Umhlanga Rocks on the north coast and the Valley of a Thousand Hills. Phyllis had been with them most times but in Cape Town, it would be just the two of them. Faye couldn't wait. Phyllis' flat had been home from home but now they would be *really* home.

They were in Phyllis' car the day before leaving. Strawks had asked if it could be 'just the two of them' that day for lunch, which, of course, Faye didn't mind, but as they were going to be together indefinitely from the next day it seemed overkill.

Strawks had been thoughtful during lunch. She had quizzed him, but he wouldn't say much. She imagined it was having to say goodbye to everyone at the cottage but mainly, Nomoka, or 'Doc,' as they were calling him these days. The previous night, Faye and Phyllis brought snacks and soft drinks to the cottage (no alcohol was allowed on the premises). Daphne and Mano, the ambulance driver, now a firm friend, had joined them for some heartfelt thanks expressed by both Strawks and Faye. Faye felt nervous when Strawks stood up until she remembered Stella mentioning Toastmasters, when fear gave way to pride. Everyone exchanged phone numbers and promised to keep in touch. Not all the patients had rallied, but Faye tried not to dwell on those poor souls. Promises of prayers were all one could offer while trying not to feel a heel for her and Strawks' good fortune.

Now he laid his hand on Faye's in her lap at the wheel. She drove everywhere in Durban but once they were in Cape Town, Strawks was going to drive. Stella had already promised he could use her Jeep to enable him to commute between Faye's and Gideon's, where he would be working on a two-way trial basis.

"This time tomorrow we'll be home."

She couldn't keep the excitement out of her voice. And why should she? It was the reward of the months of waiting. They would be free of the restrictions connected with the center. They could begin normal life. She wasn't expecting romance. Recent events had been too off the wall for that. Just everyday things, routine, was what she was hoping for. She pictured them listening to music, reading aloud from books they were reading (then she remembered Strawks didn't read much). They could try cooking, making bread, something she had always wanted to do. Kneading bread flashed a scene from classic, *Ghost,* with Demi Moore at the potter's wheel and Patrick Swayze saying, in her head, "Ditto" to her "I love you". Over by the gate, two nurses stood smoking, and she waved.

"About that," he said, removing his hand. What had she said? Prattling on about making bread, maybe? "I don't want us to rush into anything." He took a deep breath. "So I've booked to stay at the neuro-clinic for the first month."

"What d'you mean *stay*?" Her heart was hammering dismally. She felt out of control. Then she got it. Not so long ago, he had been contemplating a life of celibacy.

"You can sleep in the spare room." Why hadn't she thought of that? Doc was always saying, take it slow. "The neuro-clinic is ten minutes away. You can go back and forth." He was booked at the clinic for weekly group work. He didn't need to stay there for that.

"I don't want to discuss it," he said, climbing out of the car. He stood at the window, motioning for her to open it. "And I want to go straight there from the airport."

What? She watched as he walked towards the gate. He refused to talk about being a monk. And she understood, or rather, she also wasn't talking about something important, so it was quid pro quo.

There in the car she called Nomoka. "Strawks is refusing to stay with me. He's booked into the neuro-clinic. Did you know?"

Of course, he knew. After which she got a lecture, the Humpty-Dumpty one. When you had a breakdown, the ego collapsed, like Humpty falling off the wall, all the horses and men couldn't put him back together again. Same with the ego. No one could do it for Strawks. Only he could do it. It was a re-think on a gigantic scale, frightening, exhausting.

"He'll need the quiet of the single ward we've arranged for him. And there's something else to consider. Rushing the process could set him back, though it is highly unlikely. He is strong, make no mistake. But it is possible he could regress."

She wanted to scream at him, I'm not a saint.

And neither was the doctor. You tended to forget that. Everyone was hailing him as some kind of wonder worker, but Faye wondered if his judgment wasn't off. Instead of a much-needed nudge, he was babying the patient. She remembered Stella allowing the twins to cry. And look how they had turned out. Perfect.

She had to try again. During dinner at Phyllis', she itched to get started but on the drive over, couldn't get up the courage. In the dimness of the cab, he looked sad.

Stopped outside the center, she rambled a little, saying how she had ordered the gardening service to get everywhere ship-shape, Madam and Monsieur to spring-clean. "I've almost forgotten what Cape Town looks like."

Get on with it, she told herself. "We can live any way we choose. You can live monklike… forever, if you want. Just let's be under one roof. This is so unfriendly, what you're doing, what you've arranged." And without consulting her. They were in this together, she had assumed, together in this thing called Life.

The plastered-on smile was slipping. A tide of pink crept up his neck as he hunted for words, swore under his breath, until out it came, bitter, hot as larva, like the words had to be gone, released instantly they were spoken.

"I've told you. I want to be alone. I need to be alone."

Go stuff yourself.

All the way back to Phyllis' she fumed. She had to sit in the car until she was calmer. After which a difficult hour followed, with Phyllis, eyes at times bright with tears, chatting on about Christmas in the Cape when she would be with them all– Faye and Strawks and the Gideons. She had yet to meet Myrna, Henk, Anika, and Vally.

She hadn't wanted to count the cost, to think back to the early weeks, holding everything in, half the time bored, the other full of fear, waiting for minuscule changes for the better while attentive to every drink of water needed, special dishes requested from the moody cook, crumbs brushed off his shirt front, blinds opened and closed (he had become ultra-sensitive to light), needs and favors begged of the rest of the staff, the doctor, the maintenance person. The air-conditioner was noisy, could they find another one? Could the sleeping pills be changed, the anti-depressant, so he could feel energetic again? She almost longed for the first days when she could think of him as a child, wipe his mouth, his bum, give him a hug when he got something right, like remembering the names of the twins, only to be shoved away (even then). Then the teenager who believed the world revolved around him. He had to win in games of Ludo and Scrabble. Some days he spoke to everyone but her, complained to the nurses and Doc that she was suffocating him with her attentions. But thank God that stage, too, came to an end, and the adult finally emerged. They had been getting along like in the old days, famously. Until this.

She called Stella who said Faye should speak to Anika about this latest development.

"It's more her territory," Stella said. "I mean, she's known him forever."

Anika had been silent at first, then said, "I must apologize for my brother. He doesn't mean anything by it."

What could you answer to something like that? She had sounded almost happy at the news, although happy, sad, or any other emotion were hard to imagine, even a ripple disturbing the flat, glass-like surface of the woman's personality. Was she jealous, Faye wondered? She banished the thought, remembering that it was Anika who asked Stella and herself to go in her stead. Correction. Anika had asked Stella to go in her stead. Prompted by the twins, Stella had asked Faye to come along. But surely, everything taken into consideration, Anika would be nothing but happy that her brother was well again.

There had to be something, a clue, like a key to a locked door.

Remembering Phyllis' query about their childhoods, Faye said, "Did anything happen to Strawks when he was a boy that might have led to him closing himself off like this? I know I hurt him once but surely, what the two of us have been through together lately would have shown him I've changed. That I'm a hundred percent on his side. That I will really do anything for him."

"He knows all that. We're very grateful." After which she began a list of Valdine's latest achievements in schoolwork and new recipes successfully tried. Another door effectively shut.

She rang Stella on speed dial.

"I wanted to shake her," Faye said. "How you got her to tell you where Strawks was beats me. I'm wondering if I know the woman at all."

Faye imagined Stella settling down at the kitchen table with a hundred-and-one things buzzing in her head and trying not to sigh.

Then she remembered the welcome back lunch for Strawks.

"Stel, he wants to go straight from the airport to the clinic. I'm *so* sorry. I should have told you sooner. But all the time I've been thinking he'll change his mind." All that time talking to Phyllis when Stella could have been calling everyone. "Could you call everyone tonight? All the food…"

"Forget the food."

Stella was quiet, then she said, "Anika's picking up labels Lyle printed for her so I won't put them off. They don't know about the lunch. Brand can give her the labels if I'm not back from dropping you and Strawks off. Or Lyle. Ellie can decide if she wants to go to work. Myrna is the only one I need call."

"Stel..."

"Don't you worry about a thing. See you at the airport, OK? But I can't promise I won't smack that man of yours on the head."

CHAPTER 41

I should have known that Faye and Strawks wouldn't just fall into one another's arms. But it had looked so good. He had responded so quickly to the treatment. I had been there to see that first smile, admittedly at some dream he was having. But that gibbering, shut-off zombie that had shocked us rigid when we arrived from Durban was gone, vanquished, cast out into the ether.

Then there was the amazing Dr. Nomoka. He had put his annual leave on hold until Strawks was discharged, Daphne told Faye recently. He had a way of filling us with hope and faith, faith in him and faith in our love for the patient that it would deliver him onto the sparkling shore of recovery. Our roguish, fun-loving friend would be restored to Faye, to us, to his family. Not this contrary person, this mean-spirited person, this person that I had hoped would be the answer to my problem.

It was a while since I'd thought about it, my/Faye's problem. I suppose I hadn't dared while Strawks was out of it. But now, I have to do something, or he would be lost to us again. (Was he still intent on becoming a monk? Was that it?) And Faye, having found him only to lose him again, would be in a worse state than before.

It is midnight. I decide to call the doctor. He should be used to having his sleep disturbed. I walk out to the front steps and plonk myself down. I stare into the purple shadows with cell phone to ear.

"*Madame.*"

A whole minute passes, and then he is effusive. How was I? How was Cape Town, the farm, the family? Since when was he interested in me and my concerns? He sounds wrong-footed, guilty. The fine doctor at a loss?

"You know why I'm calling. It's Faye. She's not pleased with Strawks, he has decided not to stay with her in Cape Town."

"Eez choice." I feel irritated by the accent. Since when was he *that* French? "It is how he is choosing to proceed."

"Why, for heaven's sake? I don't have to remind you they were once engaged."

"The young man has registered for a course. It involves group work. He has to create a whole new modus operandi for handling people." He waits for me to say something and when I don't, he says, "The couple will benefit from time apart."

I see that I'm not getting anywhere and am about to end the call when he says, "I want you to remember this when he is back with you. It is the family you should be focusing on. It is a *family* in crisis." And then he is gone.

Family? He and Faye aren't a family yet. The Johansens? Of course they are in crisis. The main breadwinner of the family has just spent four and a half months in a mental hospital. At enormous cost to my friend, I might add, although she considers it so much tosh compared to having him, her dearly beloved sound of mind, ready to take on the world again.

I feel cheated. What had I expected? That he would talk Strawks into giving up this isolation lark of his? Which turns out, is a positive move and therefore acceptable? Acceptable to whom? Faye would argue that he doesn't have to live in in order to do the course. I could try talking to Anika, but if Faye's attempt registered nil then chances are I would do no better. Better to expend energy on this lunch for Strawks.

Just before floating off, I have an idea. I'll send Lyle to collect Faye and Strawks from the airport. Strawks won't be able to resist Lyle's brand of enthusiasm.

CHAPTER 42

The next day is full summer. It is only nine o'clock, but already Harry and Sally pant in the shade. Woo, languishing on the kitchen doorstep, can probably hear the stream bubbling high up the rocky slope before it begins its hidden descent. Reappearing at the bottom of the garden, it will be shouted down by the cicadas. I stoop to pat Fergus, who seldom leaves my side. Faye speaks to him daily on the telephone. Being without the little dog has been one of the hardest things for her. His ears are super erect. He knows something is up, but whether it is because I told him this morning that she is coming today or by means of the subliminal messaging system that dogs reputedly possess, I'm not sure. I am grateful for the breeze that rifles the skirt of my cotton dress and dries my underarms as I twist my ponytail into a bun and secure with a rubber band. And, yes, it will make our guests more comfortable. But more and more these days I am thinking of the vines.

We've had rain the last few days, which is great for the young plants with their shallow roots but unwelcome for the mature ones with their growing weight of fruit and susceptibility to botrytis. On this cautionary note, first thing this morning, I dispatched a couple of the men to dig out weeds missed last month, especially the taller ones that could keep the air around the lower bunches warm and moist with more disastrous results. The first harvest, that is of the chenin blanc, should begin after Christmas. With this in mind, I've dispatched Isak and the rest of the staff to clean the wine-making equipment. Some of the bins may need a good scouring with steel brushes, followed by a coat of paint. I make a mental note to check quantities of the acid-resistant variety. While doing so, I know I won't be able to resist double-checking our stock of chemicals and yeast.

Willy is in her element. She has gone all out for the cold lunch with all the trimmings. She doesn't need me, she says, as I hover after I have done the flowers and checked that everywhere is neat and clean, towels, soap, and toilet rolls are in the bathrooms, have counted chairs on the veranda as well as ensured that plates, champers flutes and other glasses, cutlery, and so on are in abundant supply on the extended table draped in one of Ada's best Madeira tablecloths. She has Marie to help her, which is code for having someone more malleable to her bossiness.

The day I flew back from Durban, I discovered Willy amid the pots and pans for a special lunch for my return, and Marie giving the front steps a vigorous buffing. Later, when we talked, she asked if Marie could stay on without pay as it was easier to get a job when you were employed than if you were home, especially when home was the small town of Uppington, way up the west coast. There were always more opportunities closer to the city. Subsequently, however, I nabbed Marie, much to Willy's pique, to work in the cellar at a salary to be increased as her competence grows. She has a moderate amount of schooling, is a quick learner, but best of all, has taken to winemaking. She told me the other day that just the smell of the cellar made her happy which, of anything, is a recommendation.

I had no word from Willy during the weeks that she was away. I hadn't even been sure that her mother had survived her illness. Willy is close on seventy, the mother around ninety. Willy explained it this way: "The butterfly dream was for me, Miss. My Mommy wanted me home. The minute I got home, she was better. My brothers are giving her money now, so she doesn't need my salary. But, Miss, I like working. And I'll go *mal* being stuck in Uppington. A butterfly is happy, isn't it? The butterfly was saying I must be happy. So, I decided to come back to Miss. I just hope my Mommy doesn't make herself sick again to get me to come home."

"We'll cross that bridge when we get to it," I advised, shamelessly aware that I had Marie as back-up.

As soon as I calculate they are airborn, I call the airport. The plane left on time, estimated time of arrival approximately two hours after take-off. After an hour and a half's office work, I dispatch Lyle.

"If they wonder where I am, say I'm expecting tanks of wine." He leaves in Gunner's Lexus while I try not to dwell on his fondness for speed even as I imagine him tearing along the freeway in that stallion of cars.

I don't want to think about Gunner, especially today, although I am ever aware of the unfinished business where he is concerned. He pays whatever the car needs by EFT into Brand's bank account. It would come across as nitpicking, if not downright churlish, if I argued for the car's sale, or in blunt terms, for it to be removed from my property into a lock-up garage or some-such. The bottom line, though, is that it would reflect back to Gunner the true state of my feelings. When he calls I am friendly but restrained. I still find a way to put off the decision about his business proposal. What is behind it, I have to admit, is that I want to stay in touch so that ultimately I can show him that I and the business are doing fine, thank you very much. Faye doesn't know about Gunner's proposal or my lingering schoolgirl fantasy. I suspect that if she did know, she'd waste no time calling me a heartless bitch and to let him out of his misery.

The intercom bleeps and Henk's bark tells me that he, Anika and Valdine are at the gate. *They are early*.

This is exactly what I didn't want to happen. I had expressly asked them to come around two so that they wouldn't be on hand when Faye and Strawks arrived, allowing time to settle in. One glance at the ice buckets, silverware and the number of chairs and Henk will guess. I need a plan, a plan B.

I sound quite normal as I greet them over the intercom. The labels are at the winery, I say, and wouldn't they like to drive up and have a look around– not possible on the evening of the tasting. Henk growls interest.

I pop my head into the dining room where Brand looks up from his computer screen. Henk and company have arrived early, I say. We're going up to the winery where we'll stay until everyone else has arrived, I shout above the din of the vacuum cleaner that Willy has on to annoy me.

"No probs," he says.

Fine for you, I think. Myrna and Ellie are ad-libbing ingredients for an enormous bowl of punch.

Farmers are continually learning from one another. They can spend hours discussing the weather, the effect of a late or early season and our efforts to make good all the small and big failures and successes. Henk, Anika and I are no different. I am hard-pressed answering their questions about sales, advertising, and the over-all success of the Quinn's wines which is modest as far as the industry as a whole is concerned, but far exceeded my expectations given my inexperience and spur-of-the-moment decision to produce any wine at all.

We are examining the state of the bottling plant when, in the distance, I hear car doors bang. I sidle up to an open window while Henk is asking Isak what is in the cardboard boxes against the opposite wall. My main man, as I refer to Isak privately, answers correctly– sulphur dioxide and bentonite.

"Sulphur dioxide sterilises *alles*," I hear him say, and note the wide sweep of his arms, "and we filter the wine through the bentonite. Ag, it's a *spesiaal* mud. Clay. It comes from *oorsee*. America."

My every nerve is strained for voices. Is that Ellie's girlish laugh, Brand's manly retort? I sneak a look at Henk and Anika. They seem unaware. In my heightened state, I have imagined the sounds.

Valdine, who has been commendably patient, asks, "Can I take Wolraad to meet your dogs, Stella?"

The smelly old German shepherd has been following our progress through the production area of the winery, obedient to commands, especially where the workers are concerned. He hasn't barked or growled once. This seems as good a test as any. When Valdine asked if she could bring Henk's dog today, I thought it couldn't do any harm, but I imagined being present should Harry and Sally, and especially Harry, take umbrage. Then I have another thought. If her father arrives while we are in the winery, so much the better. I imagine the reunion between father and daughter, the longest and most enormous hug ever and a resounding kiss, a meeting without the Supreme Court Judge, the Chief Executioner, Henk, present. Maybe the early appearance of the party from Akkerstroom isn't such a disaster after all.

"Sure," I say. "But Vally, the minute Harry looks aggro, stop in your tracks and wait for Brand. He'll need to be on hand when you go into the house, in any case."

"Brand is here?" asks Henk as Valdine leaves with Wolraad on a leash.

"He's at home most days, studying. Unless he has a lecture or group work in Cape Town. He's doing an MBA and paying for his studies. So he still has to sell houses and take a turn with a show house on weekends."

"Most enterprising," says Anika. She turns to me. "I only met Arno once, in Bethany, when your father had just died. But I could see what kind of a person he was. He would be very proud of your boys."

"Thank you," I say, feeling tears spring to my eyes at the unexpected compliment. "I didn't know you met Arno."

"It was after you had left for Cape Town. We applied again for a loan. It was refused."

"Oh, I'm sorry." Suddenly, in the midst of the excitement about the party, I am back with young Arno and Anika and her parents.

Henk is restless. Plus Isak is finding it difficult to get the attention of the workers who are curious about our visitors. We need something else to keep us busy. I head for the office. Henk plays into my hands when he asks to see the program I use for stock control. Anika is happy with her handwritten records, although Henk is pushing for her to convert. I sit at the computer with them each looking over a shoulder. I begin by apologizing for the outdated version inherited from Arno, but from their silence, I conclude they are interested. Henk brings a chair across, and I another, and they sit either side me. I explain how it works, while they stop me every so often with a question.

We are startled with a cheery, "Hi all." Faye is in the doorway, Fergus under her arm. Before I know it, I am out of my seat.

This is also something I didn't want to happen. Henk is bound to guess that if Faye is here, Strawks can't be far behind. And sure enough, in he swaggers.

I rush forward, hug each in turn. Our arms crisscross and we are in a circle. A sandwiched Fergus doesn't complain.

Anika is the first to recover and greets Faye. There is no kiss or hug. My disappointment on Faye's behalf flares hotly. I try to tell myself that she is behaving this way out of deference for Henk. I only just stop myself from blurting something. Then Henk steps forward and takes Faye's hand. He holds it between his two spade-size ones. Throughout this, Faye smiles while Anika and Henk remain solemn. Strawks is ignored.

The tension is palpable. I am almost sorry for Anika and Henk, except that Faye and Strawks by their very presence are good news, for me at least, and I feel the joy at seeing them together pump through me. My friends look well and healthy. In fact, they look shockingly normal.

Strawks steps forward and pecks Anika on the cheek and says, "Hi, sis."

This can't be all, surely? My heart aches on their behalf. Perhaps when they are alone their true feelings will emerge? I remind myself that she plans to visit him when he is at the clinic. They are private people, more private than I have allowed for. I try to remember how brother and sister were with each other previously. At Faye and Strawks' engagement, for example. And come up blank. My focus at the time was on the engaged couple. Then shame has me blushing. How self-obsessed I had been in those days.

Well, I can feel happy now. I can make up for those days.

But it is not going to be easy. Once again I am back with the unfolding of the present.

Strawks and Henk remain with as yet no word or action between them. My heart lurches. What did I think I was doing, bringing these two opposing forces together? I wing a prayer, *do something*. Then Strawks is stepping forward and offering his hand to Henk.

It should be the other way around, but no matter. Henk looks thunderous but Strawks keeps smiling. I look at Faye. Her eyes magnify what I am feeling. Then they shake hands. They've called a truce, I decide.

Even so, a silence settles. Again the five of us are immobile. I'm the hostess; I'm the instigator of this meeting. I need to say and do something, but what?

Then Anika says in her flat voice, looking at Faye. "We weren't expecting you."

It comes out in a tumble. "We weren't meant to be here, but then Stella had some tanks of wine arriving and couldn't get to the airport. And we would have continued to Cape Town." For a second Faye looks worried, then her eyes clear. "And Strawks wanted to see the farm. So here we are."

"That's nice." Anika is woodenly courteous.

"What tanks of wine?" Henk barks into another silence.

Just then a sound erupts at the entrance. Valdine is calling, "Wolraad, Wolraad," which grows louder until first dog, and then girl, burst into the office. Wolraad is straining against the leash, whining, his long red tongue dripping saliva. He is a puppy again, jumping up against whoever's legs cross his path. Fergus, from Faye's arm, yaps, puppy-like himself. Henk, swearing under his breath, grabs the leash, which results in immediate order.

The girl is close to tears with words tripping up on one another. "He– was– so– good– at– the– house."

Strawks slips an arm around her shoulders and pulls her close.

"Now you've all met, let's go down to the house. I'm sure you're all famished– and thirsty."

Henk and Anika exchange a look.

The others walk out towards the entrance while I check a few things with Isak. I instruct one of the cleaning team to follow Henk to his truck with the box of labels.

While we begin down the path, Henk remains beside his truck, his hand on the door handle. Is he thinking of leaving? I decide the best I can do is continue down the path. Anika looks stricken, but hurries after us.

346 | MERIEL MONGIE

Just then, Faye calls back, "Come on Henk. That appointment with the bank can wait."

He walks towards us with big strides until he is flush with Faye. "I don't have an appointment with the bank."

"Oh, Henk," she says, and on tiptoe, kisses his cheek. "It'll be no party without you. All of you," she says including Anika and Vally. The girl has taken hold of Wolraad's leash once more and is out front with the dog again tugging.

"What party?" Henk says.

"Just come."

"It's like you knew," Anika says to me. For the first time I notice the antique diamond ring.

We all stop. At last Anika is smiling. She has been waiting for this moment, I realize. Faye and I examine the ring, offer our congratulations. Valdine hears the commotion and runs back to us with Wolraad, who thinks this is another game and jumps around, entangling the leash around various ankles.

Ellie, Myrna, Lyle, and Brand are in the kitchen to greet us. Willy and Marie stand by. I introduce Henk and then tell them about the engagement. More congratulations follow, and inspection of the ring by Ellie and Myrna. I lead our guests through to the veranda where the cold lunch is laid out on the table.

A champers cork pops. Lyle fills flutes, while Brand takes alternative drink orders. When everyone has a glass in hand I say that it seems like fate that we have more than one reason to celebrate.

"To Anika and Henk and their forthcoming marriage."

"To Strawks, welcome home."

Chatter gives way to perusal of the food and filling of plates. Conversation becomes more general.

My attention quickly turns to Faye and Strawks, who describe that morning's flight for anyone who will listen. The flight was on time, Faye remarks. Due to there being no head or tail wind which was unusual, Strawks adds. Discussion about aerodynamics ensues among the men, and

Faye and I grin, remembering instances in the past when male company honed in on a topic.

Valdine is grappling with a description of Wolraad's peaceful introduction into the Gideon menagerie. Anika is distracted, and I step in with prompts. Valdine had waited for someone to come to her aid, and it is Ellie who finally appears and holds Harry's collar and speaks to the two animals until friendly relations are secured. What occurred between Henk and Strawks in the winery earlier seems suddenly similar, although sans help from a third party, and I want to giggle.

Instead, I sit back and release a surreptitious sigh. Conversation settles into pockets. Ellie disappeared, I presume to the toilet, and returns looking pale. A number of patients at the med-clinic have come in with a tummy bug and I wonder if she is another casualty. Faye is absorbed in Valdine's chattering about a mail order for her bridesmaid dress. High spots of color in Faye's cheeks contrast sharply with her pallor. I will encourage her and Strawks to leave early. Before she can flop on her bed, there is the drive to town and the clinic. Most taxing of all will be saying goodbye to Strawks. Fergus, in her lap, throws me a look that says, isn't there something you can do, before resting his head once again on his paws.

Strawks tells Brand that he would have liked to check out the vineyard, but it will have to wait. Brand replies that he will be only too glad to give his 'uncle' a tour, anytime. Addressing Strawks in the same way, Lyle asks the older man if he and his brother met him.

"You were *lighties* that time. We were kicking a ball out there on the front lawn, but your Mom," he grins across at me and I wonder what is coming, "whisked you smartly off to bed. She was a real killjoy, your Mom. Is she still like that…?"

He winks at Lyle, who nods with a corresponding twinkle.

A discussion follows of how far back people can remember. I am captivated as Lyle describes being lifted onto Arno's back so he could pick pods off the kaffir boom, the seeds which provided ammo for his catapult.

"Dad seemed huge. As big as the tree. Always when I read stories about giants I thought of Dad."

And then Ellie tells us how on an outing in the country with her father, their car broke down, and while waiting for the pick-up truck, she took off her panties, washed them in a nearby stream and left them on a rock to dry. At home later her mother asked where her panties were. Her mother was very proud of the dress and matching panties that she had made. Little Ellie had forgotten but her father supplied the answer.

Ellie chuckles, "Dad got a real telling off."

Anika has been listening. She turns to Strawks. "I haven't seen that shirt before. Or those pants."

"Faye bought them. I gave away all my civvies at Jesus the Nazarene."

"I see." Anika leans over and tucks in the label at the back of Strawk's neck.

People talk of heightened awareness. Perhaps it was Lyle's vivid picturing of Arno, propelling me back in time to the bigness of him across me, under another tree with Ensign cropping grass nearby the day he followed me to Durban. Or Ellie's tale of the forgotten panties, so childishly innocent but which set me wondering if there had been something sexual that had happened and which she was unaware of or had suppressed (which I immediately discounted as none of my business). In this age of media scrutiny we are continually being bombarded by such things. Every other article or news item dredges up a horrific account of some father or mother, some uncle or aunt, brother, sister, neighbor, or trusted friend interfering with a child. All of which resounds through me, holding me spellbound to the scene playing out before me.

So that even when I had finally closed my eyes I kept seeing *those* fingers on the skin of *that* neck.

I felt my heart thud down, down to my crotch. A tingling followed by a sticky warmth warned of an arousal. And there, in the presence of my friends and family, I felt the telltale throb that wouldn't be stopped until it was spent, every unwanted yet exquisite pleasure fanning up and outwards, all the while I scold myself for this poor choice of a moment. And as if this wasn't enough, I feel heat travel up my neck, flood my cheeks and bring tears of shame to my eyes.

I stand up, wondering if anyone has noticed. I glance around, forcing a smile, hoping I look like the hostess I am meant to be. But, no, I am alone in this indignity. I immediately wonder what had brought this on. I am sex-deprived for sure, but usually the need is attended to in bed at night. Never before in plain sight and elbow to elbow with others. Riding horses as a young woman had at times triggered an orgasm, even as an older woman. In horsey circles such an occurrence is common and joked about. But what had just taken place was prompted visually.

During the brief moments of loss of control, I had looked everywhere but at the two that seemed to cause it. Now my gaze returns to them. Had they noticed? On some level, were they aware?

Strawks is trying to catch Faye's eye, and having succeeded, is pointing rather rudely, I decide, at his wristwatch. Anika and Henk are also exchanging a look, a more discrete look that suggests they make a move. Before I know it, my party will be breaking up. And we haven't had dessert, an oversight Ellie will never forgive me for.

"Who's for berries and pavlova?"

Willy had been waiting in the doorway and instantly prods Marie who collects the used plates and cutlery while she wheels in the loaded trolley.

CHAPTER 43

Shock was still pulsing through me as I watched the small procession to the table.

At that point, I decided that I had exaggerated the incident between Anika and Strawks. That my suspicions were the result of an over-active imagination, driven by my own base needs. It wasn't surprising that I had gotten myself worked up, given the events of the day. It wasn't every day an engagement was thrust on one, or archenemies reconciled, if one could go so far as to describe the handshake between Strawks and Henk in those terms. Or a friend returned from mental hell. Those of us close to him were bound to be affected. Made a little mad ourselves, I thought, as I saw my guests off. There were bound to be glitches until our lives were more settled, until we had lived with the newly born Strawks for a while, had more of the facts enabling us to understand better what had happened to him, until, finally, we saw the benefits in his re-entry into life.

But that night in bed, the validity of the incident struck me. As I probed various events of the recent past, impressions, things not said and things left hanging, it began to make sense. Pieces of a puzzle began to zoom into place until the enormity of what it meant– or could mean– had me throw back the one sheet covering me and stand there trembling with the appalling nature of my thoughts, my revulsion of Anika and Strawks and the shock and horror, the anger, pain and disappointment of what this was going to mean for Faye.

I slipped on a thin gown although I was in a cold sort of sweat. I peed but didn't flush so as not to wake the hopefully sleeping Ellie and Brand, and Lyle. I heard the clock in the lounge strike two as I stepped barefoot into the passage.

I refrained from switching on another light. Courtesy lights glowed at floor level along the passage but otherwise I would be in darkness as I proceeded through the house. I would have dearly loved to be able to wander through the garden. Being close to nature would have calmed me, helped me gain some sort of perspective. But security lights would be activated immediately if I stepped outside. Someone was bound to wake up, raise an alarm, putting paid to my need for some intense reflection. As a result, I had to be content with sitting on the veranda.

Harry, Sally, and Woo joined me at the French doors, which I unlocked with concentrated care. They sensed that silence was required, and I patted each to show my gratitude. We padded down the steps and out into the cool shadows. The moon was off elsewhere. It would be, I thought grumpily. This reassured me instantly. My old self hadn't completely gone aground. And yet, sitting there on the bench in the dark felt unreal. Willie and Marie had removed all traces of the party the day before, adding weight to the idea that my imagination was responsible for the dilemma I was facing. Had I concocted all of yesterday or just that one excruciating moment? I pulled the dogs closer for warmth as much as comfort– the Rottweilers against my legs, Woo, against my middle. Inland, the temperature drops considerably compared to living closer to the ocean. I thought of Faye then, hoping she was sleeping comfortably and soundly. If I was on the right track, if what I suspected was indeed true and she had already suspected, then that peaceful sleep would be the last of its kind for some time.

Through the next few hours I picked through my recent experiences with Anika, her non-interest in Strawks' welfare and her fearful handling of Valdine. Henk. Did he know? Had he guessed? Worst of all, had he discovered them together and sent Strawks packing? Typically male, he would blame Strawks and think that he had forced himself on his sister. Then Strawks himself– not able to get as far away from his sister, who represented temptation, even to forsaking his precious daughter. His guilt had driven him to madness, not the prospect of a monk's existence, as I had thought. Or maybe the craziness of that, the lengths to which he was prepared to go to escape that guilt or deal with it, had tipped him over the edge. Then there was the out-of-sight wife, Crystal. Did she even exist? One never heard her mentioned in the present. Not a squeak.

Which brought me to Strawks' recent behavior as regards Faye. His boorish insisting on winning board games. Refusing to stay with her in Cape Town. He had been trying to push her away so she wouldn't learn his filthy secret. Don't come too close, he'd have been thinking, I'm grossly unworthy. That clumsy, bumbling idiot might also be trying to spare her the pain.

I knew that I had to have a plan before the day began. I still had a farm to run. The first harvest was around the corner. In order for me to appear as normal as possible I had to have decided what to do about my suspicions. For suspicions they still were. Part of me longed desperately to be proved wrong, but even as I contemplated being put wise by a horrified Strawks, I knew that I was right. He might bluster and fume, act dumb, but in the very deepest, darkest part of myself I was convinced, a part that is within every person whether they admit to it or not, a part that knows that being faced with a similar situation, that being brought low enough, desperate enough by circumstance and need, he or she could and would do the same.

I had to speak to Strawks. In the meantime, if I had any contact with Faye, I had to behave in exactly the same way I had behaved before witnessing what could mean the end of every plan and dream she ever had concerning Strawks. That was enough to think about for now.

I was finally able to fall sleep, there on the bench. I was tapped awake on the shoulder by Ellie.

"What are you doing out here, Stella? This hard bench. It can't be too comfortable."

"Excitement," I said, casting around for a reason and coming up with Anika and Henk's wedding. At some point in the previous afternoon, I had offered to have their nuptials at Gideons. I could tout that out if Ellie probed.

"I'll get us coffee," she said.

I was still sitting there, arranging my face in what I hoped was my usual morning doziness, when Ellie returned.

"You're not having coffee?"

Ellie nibbled on a dry biscuit in reply, a huge grin splitting her rather pale face.

I stared back, blank.

"I'm pregnant."

Brand was standing in the doorway.

"Come here," I said.

Ellie and Brand's news carried me through making the call to the neuro-clinic and to insisting Strawks see me that very day, all achieved well out of hearing of everyone, including Willy, who, after Ellie, would be sensitive to changes in my demeanor. I walked back inside saying that I had to check on another label order for Anika and would be out for the afternoon. The course was in the morning, the manager of the clinic informed me. I could visit Thorkild after lunch. She would make sure he knew and was ready for me. I was grateful that I hadn't had to speak to him. What in heaven's name would I have given as my reason for visiting him so soon after his visit to the farm and that couldn't be dealt with on the phone?

The children's news completely overshadowed any hint I might have given that I'd had an enormous shock and was having to face dealing with it. Ellie was already twelve weeks with an absence of morning sickness until the party, strangely enough. Hence my failure to detect.

"Stella, you're going to be a grandmother," Myrna said. She had popped in to see if she could help with any clearing up from the party, but I suspected that she didn't want to miss out on any of the family excitement.

"I'm not ready for this," I confided, keeping my voice low. But the positive nature of the news helped steady my nerves. Already I could feel the emptiness associated with Arno, that had loosened its hold a tad for Gunner, begin to soften with receptivity for the little treasure's arrival in our midst, a pale but not impossible facsimile of what was happening in Ellie's uterus.

It occurred to me that what I should have been doing was popping in on Faye with some supplies; help her sort out the house, clean out the fridge, for starters. Ellie was at work by then. Brand had a conference meeting via the internet with his course companions, Lyle working through appointments. Myrna, on hearing my dismay about Faye, offered to go in my stead.

The landscape is bleached of green except for evergreen trees and private gardens that surely defy water restrictions. I take the Mowbray off-ramp, but instead of turning left as I would have to visit Faye, I continue up past the supermarket, restaurants, filling station to link with the Liesbeeck Parkway which skirts the lower part of the suburb of Observatory. The mountains offer a comforting solidity in the background as I cross the Liesbeeck River and double back along its length almost stagnant in summer's aridity. The crenelated towers of the hospital proper beckon from among a guard-like cluster of trees. It resembles a small castle, more Count Dracula than Walt Disney, such is my dread of what lies ahead.

I park the Jeep and head for reception where I am directed out of the main building towards the side of the property closest to Observatory. A covered path leads to rows of prefab wards that form sides around a grassed quadrangle complete with a central and, not surprising, dried-up fountain. This is the volunteer phase of occupancy I was told at reception. Strawks is in ward number twenty, the last of the wards in this section.

I knock on the door and the familiar voice invites me in. The door opens. After the brightness I am almost blind. Strawks stands there, smiling. Even so, my heart is thumping at the prospect of what I am contemplating. This awareness short-circuits a greeting. He seems to understand and steps forward and hugs me until I find my voice.

"Strawks, hi," I say, pulling away. I feel a blush begin and turn away quickly. I am thoroughly mortified. This is a nine to the ten of finding Arno on his office floor.

"Welcome to my humble abode." He points to an easy chair. "Sit."

I envy his apparent calm.

"Tea or coffee?" he asks.

I say tea, it is more refreshing, and he walks the couple of paces to fill the kettle from a tap over a sink. A small mirror perches on the window ledge where I imagine he washes and shaves as well as attends to used crockery and cutlery. While the water boils he takes a plastic bottle of milk out of a bar fridge. A hotplate with griller replaces a stove. From the cupboard beneath the sink, he takes two cups and saucers and a plate onto which he shakes several biscuits from a tin which sits beside a glass bottle of sugar.

"Can I put in sugar for you?" he asks, "Then I must close this. Ants," he says by way of an explanation. "We also have fleas. The woman before me kept a dog. Which is against the rules."

"You're not tempted? I mean, to keep an animal?" I remember that he once had a tame rat.

"I'm not good at secrets," he says. He is blushing.

We stare at one another. The word 'secret' buzzes between us like a bee about to sting. His high color tells me he has some idea of why I have come. It's going to be OK, I tell myself. This is my old friend, Strawks. A picture flashes of us riding on a farm. We're racing. Who won? I can't remember. We are going to sort this out together. He hasn't refused to see me, which he could have done. Instead he has welcomed me.

I look around while he attends to the tea. A door leads to what I imagine is a toilet. The room is sparsely furnished with a small octagonal wooden table, a single bed covered in an ancient honeycomb cotton counterpane, a small bookcase, another upright chair against the outer wall and a couple of framed prints of Cape scenery on the hardwood walls. A small rug made from knotted fabric scraps is the one softening detail on the lino-covered boards.

Strawks sees me looking around.

"All donated," he says.

I glance out of the window, which has a thin cotton curtain pulled to one side along a length of expansion wire. A bird lands on the rim of the fountain and almost disappears as it hops down into the bowl, pecking away happily. It has probably found seeds blown in by the wind. Or it is drinking water provided by someone like Strawks.

This thought encourages me as I accept the cup of tea. He fetches the other chair and places it so that he is sitting across from me.

"You've come about me and Anika?" He takes a sip of tea and then places it on the table between us. It will have gone cold by the time he takes another sip.

I, on the other hand, am frozen into continually sipping until the cup is empty.

CHAPTER 44

The day he tried to leave through the gates of the St. John Vianney Centre was the start of realizing that there was something worrying him. He hadn't known what it was, just that he had to get away from Faye. Of course, part of him was only too pleased to be back sitting next to her, to be looking into those warm brown eyes that said so much but which he couldn't comprehend, not at that stage. And to watch the tears form. To hear her reassuring him. He had always been partial to feminine comfort and sympathy.

Nomoka hadn't yet begun their sessions. Strawks was allowed recovery time from the last of the ECT, but already he was aware of some inner conflict that was at the root of what ailed him, that had sent him looking for a way out. That had him ready to flee. It would be some weeks with some extensive digging about in his psyche with the help of a number of the tricks of the trade by the medic before they were able to piece together what had led to his collapse in the doorway of his cell at the monastery. Regarding which one might have expected some shock and self-disgust when the facts were revealed, if one didn't know that he had been living with the weight of it for some time, had attempted to come clean via the confessional, and in true Catholic tradition embarked on a course of penance. But somehow that hadn't been enough. This psyche of his, this psyche that he was to become more and more startlingly aware of, that had a built-in set of rights and wrongs, that hadn't been content, couldn't leave it there but had to pull the rug out completely, leaving him stranded until help came in the form of this Amazon of a man with a matching heart, who was beyond shocks, he once said.

The trouble started way back in Norway. His parents weren't only not suited to pig farming, his mother had been a high school teacher while his father worked in a men's outfitters, but they were already well into their forties with a little girl and another child on the way when his mother's parents died, leaving a sizable inheritance.

His father had been a dapper man-about-town and might have remained the carefree bachelor if not for an incident with a customer irate at being overcharged. His father had been at his wit's end with sales discounts and alterations fees muddling his head by the minute while the customer demanded to speak to the owner of the shop. These demands rose to yelling level, overheard by a woman passing by, who stepped into the shop and inquired if she could help. She did, quietly and efficiently. She had been married to her pupils until he came along, his father quipped. He had persuaded her to divorce them and marry him instead. To the children, he was never funny because all too soon the jokes would sour.

Deciding how to best utilize the windfall was heavily influenced by responsibility for their growing family. A life lived close to nature with all the space in the world and unlimited amounts of fresh air seemed infinitely more desirable than buying a bigger house in the already over-populated Norvik, where you often had to stand on the bus on the way home and wait in crowded doctor's rooms and shops. So they bought a pig-farm, a running concern with the latest in machinery, giving them a good return on their investment.

However, they hadn't counted on the ravages of winter and the unrelenting physical aspect of pig-husbandry itself.

By the age of five, young Thorkild could swill out one of the pig's enclosures as quickly and cleanly as one of the adults his father employed from time to time. He didn't mind the work. In fact, he loved it. He loved how strong and capable he felt wielding a broom or a spade. He grew to respect the animals themselves, who instinctively kept their sleeping, eating, and defecating areas separate, who seemed to sense when he was unhappy and would shove up against him with their soft, pink sides, grunting sympathy. The thing is, he wanted to make Pappa happy, but there was no pleasing him. Often, the boy was told he was useless and lazy when Pappa found him playing with the dogs or riding one of the goats. Later, it would be a pony and then a horse, all as a result of Mamma's intervention. She kept a hold on the purse-strings and perhaps this contributed to Pappa's bad temper, Thorks would wonder as he got older.

At first, school seemed like an escape. All too soon this was just another means of making his son's life a misery. Thorks would get the belt if he came home with a bad report, so he devised every trick for hiding such evidence, mostly with dire results. Pappa himself had very little schooling and depended on his wife to keep the farm records and handle the income tax man and their many creditors, so he wanted Thorkild to do well at school.

Thorkild, as he grew up, wondered if his father had married his mother solely for her education, because there were little or no signs of affection between the two and even less for Anika and himself. So, in a way, he was thrust on the animals, and then when they couldn't supply the reassurance he needed, he turned to his sister. When he was little he'd be jolted awake from a nightmare and staggered to her room and not his parents,' who would have sent him right back to his room. In sweeter dreams it would be soft, pink flesh comforting him, the pigs or his sister, he wasn't always sure.

In their family, it seemed it was the women who liked books and learning. Anika excelled at school, but Pappa had already warned that it was he, Thorkild, who must carry the can in this respect, he who would go on to college or university, so he had to keep at his studies. She felt angry about this, he knew, but it didn't stop her from helping him with his math and his languages. Science could be linked to farming, his chosen career, so he did work at that.

In some ways it was a love-hate relationship between Anika and him. They were bound together by necessity. She suffered under their parents in a different way. Hers was neglect. She was ignored. She was desperate to please, to hear for once that she had done well, but it never came. Their mother was of the mindset that to praise was to spoil. When they emigrated and he was sent to boarding school, it was Anika who took his place at the farm, doing his outdoor jobs as well as her domestic ones of running the milking of the goats and cows, making butter and cheese, curing bacon and ham. When enrollment at Elsenberg came up and their parents were deciding to return to Norvik, he and Anika made a pact. He was to be her get out of jail card. She would help him with his studies. In return, he would help her find employment, a place to stay, support her when he was earning.

That was why she didn't mind when Faye broke off the engagement. She was only too happy to take him in, brokenhearted him. She had suffered Faye's help with his studies only because she was unable to get away from the farm where she worked. Oh, he tried to be independent. He had a new job every few months, but he seemed destined to make a hash of each. It was like there was a jinx on his success. Each time he was asked to leave, he'd head back to his sister. She was working at Akkerstroom by then. She made herself indispensable helping to care for Henk's ailing wife. Anika was good at that, making herself indispensable.

But Anika was burning up with hate. First towards their parents. Then when they were out of the way she transferred it to Faye. But he couldn't see it while it was happening, didn't understand how she could abase herself, how she could give herself to him, how she could bind him to her in such a way that he had to get himself out of there to another country. Not Norway, for heaven's sake, which was too full of the old misery, the rooted ties, but somewhere he could make a new start, could sort himself out, could get free. Above all, where he could get free. Which was a fallacy. He had a daughter. *They* had a daughter by then and it almost killed him, leaving her.

CHAPTER 45

"I would never have guessed how Anika felt about Faye. When we met up again recently she welcomed Faye like they were long lost friends." The ill-chosen words made me shudder. It also wasn't strictly true because Anika seldom, if ever, gave away her true feelings.

"Believe it."

I sat for a moment. Strawks had been breathtakingly honest. But most of his story was about the past, about a Strawks I hadn't known. I wanted to understand how the Strawks of Bethany, and later Cape Town, the Strawks who had been going to marry Faye, the Strawks who had visited Arno and I and had played with the twins, had been able to pursue such a demeaning personal route.

I took a deep breath. "When did the intimacy start?" *Intimacy*. I'd found an acceptable word. "As adults. I mean, how recent had you pursued it? Was there really a girl called Crystal, and did you marry her?"

He stared at me. "You think we made that up?"

"You'd already gone to enormous lengths as far as I was concerned… leaving the country, hiding Vally away on the farm. Anika added her bit."

"What did she tell you?"

"That Valdine is you and Crystal's daughter. That she, your ex, gave you full custody." I decided to leave the bit about the allowance out. It didn't matter now. Going overseas to make money was the least of it.

"Holy cow." He sat there for a moment allowing this new piece of information to sink in.

"Crystal is very real. She is living in Joburg. We moved there soon after we married. I met Faye once on a flight to see my sister. Faye didn't tell you?"

I shook my head.

"I told her I had gone up to Joburg for a job interview. It was easier than admitting my marriage was crumbling."

"And?"

"I suggested getting together."

"And what did she say?"

"She didn't want to have an affair with a married man. Or words to that effect. I put on this act of the big businessman." He paused. "That was a pivotal moment. We could have been together."

He squeezed his eyes shut. Lines appeared either side his mouth and on his forehead. I had a flash of how he might look as an old man.

"The marriage was a disaster. To begin with, Crystal and I hit it off. We had this banter. She is a pretty little thing. She thought I was fun. Crystal's father was going to help me– us– buy a farm. That was the attraction for me. My dream would have come true. But Crystal had to be with people all the time. We weren't married a month, and she was seeing other men, men she met at clubs, parties, and who knows where else. I was no longer fun, she said. I had conned her. She'd be off and out while I went looking for farms for sale with her father or worked on a business plan for running one. Then she wanted to move to Joburg where the farming is cattle and sheep, an unknown quantity to me. Even then, I might have made it. But she was never going to be a farmer's wife. Our fights were hellish. Funny, once we decided to split up, peace reigned. We divorced after one year."

Strawks picked up his cup, put it back on the saucer without drinking. "It was the divorce that got to me. I realized that I wasn't going to be able to love another woman. I still loved Faye. It was a life sentence. I was going to be alone forever.

"After Crystal and I signed the papers I headed straight for Akkerstroom. Henk's wife had just died. He had become more and more dependent on Anika, and I was jealous. I wanted my sister to myself, and there he was, demanding she stay with him at his house, serve him his meals, stroke his brow. He was going to marry Anika as soon as he could. And my sister,

God bless her, saw her financial salvation. She was going to be mistress of Akkerstroom, and why couldn't I see that?

"I was raw from the divorce. Once again, I had been rejected. My dream of the farm was in ruins. I never seemed to be able to stay in a job. The future looked grim. And there was Henk, cock of the roost.

"I don't know. I went a little crazy. We were in the cottage and Anika was defending Henk and saying he was crazy with grief at the loss of his wife and that he needed her. But *I* needed her. I was shouting by this time. She shouted back, my soft-spoken sister. We had had minor arguments before, but nothing like this. She was threatening to marry Henk, who never liked me and me him. I was going to lose her. I had already lost the woman I loved. I had even lost Crystal. I could have worked at it. Changed. I was in denial. I'm told it's quite normal.

"Now I was going to lose yet another woman. Anika hated that I loved Faye. She had always been jealous of Faye. Crystal hadn't bothered her. She had known it wouldn't work, she said, gloating. Why hadn't she warned me, I yelled. I was in a fury. I grabbed her, trying to make her see how I was feeling, the extent of it. We tussled. Began slapping one another. On the face, the chest. I tried to kiss her to say sorry. The next thing we were tearing each other's clothes off and rolling on the floor.

"I left soon afterwards. I couldn't believe what had just happened. What we had done. I was going to try and forget it. Keep away from her. I went and found myself a job. Didn't see Anika for weeks. Then she phones me to tell me she is pregnant."

I stared at him, him at me. He was expecting outright rejection, I could tell.

But even as I met those impossibly clear blue eyes a question was forming. I hesitated. How could I put him through more of this, this inquisition? Then something like courage surged. Or obstinacy. I remembered feeling the power of this when I told Constance that I was staying in Durban, that I was not coming back to Cape Town to live and work. I reminded myself that for all our sakes and especially for Faye, I had to have it all, the whole ghastly mess spilled out at my feet. I was like some surgeon preparing to wield a knife without a drop of anesthetic in sight.

"I know I have no right to ask, but was there just that one time?"

Strawks nodded. "One weak moment that ruined two lives. Coming to South Africa had been a fresh start for Anika and me. As teenagers and as young adults we had gone our separate ways. But here we were, linked ineluctably. We were going to be parents. People would find out. We would be ostracized. I wanted her to have an abortion, but she refused. Something I'm not proud of, the knowledge of which I'll have to live with for the rest of my life, besides everything else.

"She told Henk what had happened, how she came to be pregnant. I told her to make up a story. But she said that if she was to have a relationship with him that was worth anything she had to tell him the truth. I thought that that would be the end of him. But he still wanted to marry her. I think that he believes that I forced myself on my sister. Believing that helped him to accept what had happened. Or maybe it was simply need. For her part, though, she felt that she couldn't saddle him with our little daughter. We were both very afraid that Valdine would be handicapped in some way. At her birth we were expecting blood transfusions, fits, heart disease. We never told the doctor we were the parents. If there were complications we agreed that we would. We went through hell when she was born, looking for signs that she was retarded. We convinced ourselves that she was, I see that now. And keeping her away from other people, children, didn't help. Meeting you and Faye broke the grip of that fear. Faye told me how you engineered the meeting. Now that I've seen Vally again– it's been almost a year– I've realized how very normal she is. She'll never be a brain box, but she is certainly more capable than both Anika and I had given her credit for."

I stood up, swaying a little. Hearing the girl's name, that she might never have been, shocked me. She was the one bright spot in all this darkness, the ugliness. That beautiful creature, that sweet child, that budding woman. This was a different sort of shock. And yet I wouldn't have blamed either Strawks or, indeed, Anika, for going ahead.

Finally, it came to me. Anika had been brave. *Was* brave.

He was ashen beneath the freckles. Only his eyes were undimmed.

"Don't go yet," he said. He reached out a hand. Let it drop. "More tea?"

"Sit. I'll get it."

We were quiet as I waited for the kettle to heat up again. The window overlooked the boundary fence, some wattle trees that had escaped the pogrom against alien growth. Above, the sky stretched cloudlessly, and the blue faded like everything else by the sun.

Over my shoulder I added, as the means of defusing some of the shock, "That job... after, you know, what happened... was it at Perlheim?"

Strawks looked surprised.

I thought of Gunner and me, clueless about where our search had been heading.

"I guessed. A friend and I did a little digging. I was still trying to find you. I remembered you worked for her the time you popped in on Arno and me. I thought you might have returned there." I handed him a cup of tea.

"Ol' Perl got one of her sons to fire me." He had spotted my flush of anger. "*No*, I don't blame her. I was a mess. No use to man or beast. *I* would have fired me."

I wanted to go over and at the very least put an arm around him, but I could see he needed time to adjust to having revealed so much, so quickly. It was another kind of abortion, I thought, this very personal tale wrenched out of him by my questions, my presence. I was also beginning to realize that he needed this time away from Faye and all of us to adjust. Nomoka wasn't the soft touch, the manipulative soft touch, I thought he was. He was wise.

"Tell me about the course."

He filled me in and also about the list of repair jobs he had been given to pay for the course and his keep. He began to regain some of his color, but I imagined him collapsing on his bed once I was gone and sleep the sleep of the utterly spent. Coming clean with a professional was one thing–

a professional who had purportedly heard it all– but to a close friend, someone whose respect you valued, was another thing entirely.

There was still so much to talk about– his time in England and attempts to become a monk, but I was afraid that if I pushed too hard he might have some sort of a relapse. But I had to mention our mutual friend. I winged a prayer to find the right words.

"Faye doesn't know?" It was more a statement than a question. I could have told him of my fears with regard to her health. I could have shared why I went looking for him in the first place, but I knew that it would make his task more difficult than it already was. And although in my mind it was like throwing a bus that was hurtling down a hill into reverse, I knew that all that would have to wait.

"I'm working up the courage."

"Don't leave it too long."

We finished our tea, and he walked me to the Jeep.

"Thank you, Stella," he said as I was about to climb into the Jeep. I turned around. He took a step towards me, and we hugged.

"It's going to be easier from here on," he said at the open window of the Jeep. But his smile trembled around the edges.

CHAPTER 46

I didn't hear from Strawks until the Sunday when Faye said they were coming over to talk. "No need to feed us."

"No one leaves here hungry." Pure Ada.

Faye was radiant. Perhaps with an edge? But it could have been worrywart me, looking for snakes in paradise. And Strawks looked a whole lot more relaxed since I visited him at the hospital. I had to wait for lunch to be over and Strawks to be taken off to inspect the vineyard with Brand *and* Lyle, who were curious about Strawks and, I suspected, didn't want to miss anything. He hadn't forgiven me for withholding on Faye not wanting chemo. Ellie was resting on her bed. Myrna was visiting her grandmother. Faye and I took our coffee onto the veranda trailed by Fergus and Woo. Harry and Sally were with the men, galloping up and down between the rows of vines as they did when they got a chance.

Faye looked like she might burst with her news. I was feeling relief loosen muscles even before she spoke.

"Strawks has told me everything. What a relief. I knew there was something bothering him. Why he was behaving like a jerk."

"You're not disgusted?"

"The way he told it, I understood. They were desperate, he and Anika. Two very lonely people. And that strange childhood in Norway. I'll never be able to look a pig without feeling, I dunno, weird." She laughed drily. Don't blame the pigs, I wanted to say, but animal lover must give way to human friend in certain situations, and this was one.

"It's karma. After the way I treated Strawks. Now I get to do something. He's been punished, if you want to look at it like that with the breakdown. The two of them. What they've been through. Their worries over Valdine."

I sat back. I was flabbergasted. And yet I should have expected nothing less. Hadn't I banked all on the strength of her– of their love?

"You know, he came around that afternoon after you left." And when I frowned, she added, "When you left him at the hospital. He got a lift with one of the nurses. Hid his suitcase in a flower bed. He didn't know whether he'd be thrown out after he'd spilled the beans. We've been together since." She came over and hugged me. Her eyes were dry. "I just want us to get on with our lives."

I knew that there was more, but for now I had to be satisfied. Of course, it was over to them, but I wasn't ready for that, not yet.

———————

A blessing out of Faye and Strawks' visit that Sunday was that he offered to stay over and work in the vineyard. Faye didn't mind. In fact, she looked pleased. Someone else would have been pleased. *Arno.* It's not often you get the chance to right wrongs. Brand looked relieved. I wanted to discuss a salary, but Strawks wouldn't hear of it.

"When the wine is in the bottles we can discuss a possible future. A pow-wow with the boys and Mr. Hendon. You still have him?"

I nodded.

"But for now, this is therapy. I should be paying you." He would inquire if there was an opening in the Saturday group of the course.

While Strawks is with us, Lyle is staying at Myrna's, sleeping in one of her spare rooms as they were no longer an item, I was informed by my son in no uncertain terms. I had suspected this was the case, but even so, I was relieved. He also told me that she has a spastic colon, fallout from the divorce, which explains why she isn't able to blithely down even the most delicious-looking food. I find that I like having her around. She has a calming effect. And I'll always be grateful for her word of wisdom about Faye.

Faye returned to town that Sunday evening, alone. She was helping out temporarily at Hilliards. They were having problems. She was being hailed as a savior. If Strawks continued with me she might go back on contract basis, she said. Once Strawks' work routine was established, he was going to spend weekends with her. She had promised Valdine a weekend visit as soon as a routine was established. Valdine still thinks she's adopted, Faye told me when I asked what the girl knew of her parentage. Anika and Strawks may tell her the truth when she is older and more able to understand.

"May? I think they must," I said. "They shouldn't wait until a crisis forces out the knowledge, some health issue where blood groups of the parents is required, or DNA. Children hate to be lied to, whatever the reason. You, Anika, and Strawks need to talk."

Here I was, going on about Valdine, and the matter of Faye's advised chemo hadn't been addressed. I was waiting for Strawks to find out, and all too soon, he did.

I had an idea what was coming, when on the Monday morning, Strawks asked if he could talk to me, privately. We met on the veranda at the end of that first day. Ellie was at work and Brand was writing a test on his computer in Arno's office. Lyle was decorating a house. Like most salon owners, he considered the working girl and closed on Mondays, opening instead all day on Saturday.

Strawks looked perplexed when he asked to speak to me. I might have worried that he was regressing, but there was a spring in his step as he took the front steps two at a time. I thought he might have come over during lunch, forgetting he ate with staff. He liked to stay on friendly terms with them. He had always been strong on solidarity and an open forum among workers. They felt they could talk to him about their problems. As a result, they would go the extra mile for him.

I had asked Willy to bring us coffee and he waited until she had gone before opening on the matter so obviously worrying him.

"What's going on with Faye?"

"What d'you mean? She's OK, isn't she?" My heart thumped so hard I felt sure he could hear it.

"She's fine. But there's something not kosher."

"Not kosher?"

"Something doesn't add up. She's had breast thingies. Enhancements. Faye had the most perfect pair of hooters. 'Scuse my French."

"She hasn't told you?"

"It's true, then? Bugger." He stood, wiping spit off his chin. Bright spots flared in his cheeks. "She has a boyfriend? When was she going to tell me? When the bloke came knocking on the door?" He was pacing up and down but stopped. "Is she afraid I'll go off my head again?"

I laid a hand on his shoulder and pressed him into a chair. I waited until his breathing slowed, until he was looking me in the eye. Faye has only ever loved you, I could have said. But what did one really know about another person? There were the years when she and I hadn't been in touch. And what did it matter if there had been someone. Strawks was all she had now, all she wanted.

"Faye has breast cancer. What you're seeing is reconstructive surgery."

"*Christ.*" He had gone pale, and I thought he might faint or worse, collapse.

At last he spoke. "She never said. All these months, and she never said."

All these months, I was thinking, *and here we are at last.*

"Did she say anything else?"

"What now?"

"She hasn't told you, I suppose? No, why would she? The one follows the other." I took a big breath. "She won't have chemotherapy."

"Good God."

"It's recommended, even though the doctor says he's got it all."

"Of course it is. And she doesn't want it. Why?"

"She won't say. Won't talk about it. Myrna, who has counselled people with cancer, says it's because Faye doesn't want to face that she has a disease she could die from."

"And there's nothing you could do short of tying her up and dragging her there?"

Despite the weight of our thoughts, we looked at each other and grinned.

"That's why I was trying to get hold of you, stupid. If anyone in the world was going to be able to convince her, it would be you."

CHAPTER 47

After Stella told Strawks about the cancer and that Faye didn't want chemo, he held it together until he was in the Jeep. He could scarcely turn the wheel onto the road leading to the N2, his hands shook so much.

How dare they keep it from him? Stella, his sister, everyone. With his foot down hard, his thoughts grabbed at the times he might have been enlightened, beginning with Stella's visit at the hospital in Cape Town and working back, all of it crashing into his head shooting splinters of shock through every nerve. That moment when he had stood at the Jeep window. Why couldn't she have told him then? The day they arrived from Durban. She could have found a moment at the lunch, taken him aside, not let them waltz off to Cape Town and the hospital. His sister. There was an unspoken pact to avoid one another, so no help from that quarter. Although there was that moment when she remarked on his new clothes… Had she been thinking about Faye then? And Faye herself. All those weeks, especially the last couple when he was to all accounts normal again. Faye. *Faye.* He had to pull over.

She was going to die. His beautiful darling was going to die. His forever love. *Forever?* How much time *did* they have left? He switched off the engine and sat with his head on the wheel. He banged his head, once, twice, again and again. The minute he stopped the flood began. He hadn't sobbed like that since he was a kid. Or maybe when she cancelled the wedding. But he didn't want to think of that time, because it would end up being all about him.

That sobered him. He tried to think. Think about her. How this was for her. How to let her know he knew. He swallowed fresh tears. Nomoka would be pleased. He had wanted his patient to cry. But Strawks hadn't, ever. He tried to remember if, perhaps, Faye had let on, had tried to tell him, but he came up blank. She had always been a crier, and yet recently she had been dry-eyed. Never a tear. Not since his recovery. *That* should have alerted him. Privately, however, she must be in a panic, must have moments of sheer terror or blackness. Again he considered, how on earth was he going to broach the subject? The memory of her shutting down on him all those years ago gonged a warning. But he had to forget that. Push through.

It was so unfair. They had only just found one another. He could lose her all over again, this time for good. He hammered the steering wheel, this time with his fists. How much worse must her pain be, the fear of death, dread of further physical suffering, all locked away, endured without a murmur.

Of all the luck. Of all the damnable things that could happen to them. Whatever happened to Faye happened to him. And conversely, whatever happened to him, she took on with every fiber of her being. At the end of his tale of woe about himself and Anika she had exclaimed, "Thank God." And between sobs and hiccups croaked, "And– all the while– I thought– you didn't love me anymore." What seemed to disturb her more than his and Anika's mindless coupling was his offish behavior those last weeks in Durban, crowned with his cowardly plan to keep her at arm's length by holing up at the hospital.

He thought back to the past weekend. They had been very careful with one another that first night. Oh, they were thrilled to be together again, had cuddled, kissed, the old endearments rolling freshly off their tongues, skin electric with desire. Had breathed in the familiar smells, touched, tasted, but stopped before a tidal wave of passion could carry them away. That had been a shock. Faye holding off. After the months of the novitiate, he expected to be the one that would find it difficult to let go, not to mention wondering if that part of him still worked. He told himself he must accept her reluctance, be patient. They were no longer uncomplicated young things with no water under the bridge.

The second night, Saturday, it happened again. And again he bit the bullet, the flood of lust hammering away for release as they lay there in the dark until it had subsided enough for him to be able to reach a hand across and whisper that he loved her, that sex wasn't love, and not to worry about it. That love and affection were what counted.

On Sunday, he was awake before she was. He wanted to linger over every inch of her. He found himself longing for the light, wanted to open the curtains, but he also didn't want to wake her out of what must be the deepest, most satisfying of sleeps. He felt her stirring, called her his wicked, wanton woman, his breath in her ear. He'd always loved her giggle, that naughty laugh.

She seemed to remember something and sat up. Before he could stop her, she was throwing her legs over the side of the bed and wrapping herself in her gown. He thought she might want to use the toilet, but she was already at the passage door.

"Forget about breakfast," he called after her. He felt stupid saying it.

Since when was she domesticated? Fergus, hesitating in the doorway, looked back at him equally puzzled before padding after her.

She returned with mugs of coffee, saying, bright as a button, "What shall we do today?"

He sat up and took the mug. "Thanks, honey. You shouldn't have."

But it was like she'd poured a bucket of cold water on him. Soon, however, she was listing possible things to do, fun things, and he was filled with love all over again. How lucky was he?

But she did rustle up scrambled eggs and toast, left him with a second cup of coffee and the weekend Argus.

"I think I may have my friend," she said, demurely. Ah, he thought, her period. He shook his head. That's what must be behind the reluctance to climax.

She was gone a while, so he went looking for her. With their physical status reinstated, even frustratingly reinstated, he didn't want to miss a moment. They could kiss and cuddle– unless she wasn't feeling well?

He heard the slap of water and walked into the bathroom. Eyes, nose and toes peeped out from the bubbles. How cute was that?

"Mind if I join you?"

"The water isn't clean…"

"I'm a farmer's son, remember?"

She's playing hard to get, he thought, and stepped in. He wondered if, in fact, she did have her period. There was something premeditated about her bathing ahead of him. They splashed one another, touched balls of feet together and explored with toes the secretly delicious places. She added more hot water. He kissed her on the lips, her neck, stroked her breasts, rolled her gently onto one side and lay with his length against her, his front against her back. But her heart didn't seem in it. There was something puzzling in her manner. It must be the bath. It didn't spell romance for her. That was it.

There was only one thing for it. He was going to carry her to the bed. He threw her a saucy look. He was sitting at the tap end and reached under and pulled out the plug. She took her time standing up, suds sliding off in bunches, off her breasts. Could it be the cool air making them so pert? The final slew of water gurgled noisily. He stepped out of the bath, reached for a towel, and enveloped her in it. He lifted the parcel of her in his arms and carried her to the bed. He didn't want to wet the bed, so he drew a towel around himself before joining her. He sat, watching her dry herself. Everything about her thrilled him, which deepened into an aching tenderness. God, he loved her.

He took a second look at her chest. There was something very different about those boobs.

"I had a lift," she said.

Faye hadn't struck him as being vain. And it wasn't as though she'd had children. She hadn't, had she? She wouldn't have been able to keep something as enormous as that from him, he didn't think.

"Do they have to be so firm?" He tried making a joke of it, "I'm going to get poked in the eye if I'm not careful."

Her eyes widened.

"I preferred the old ones," he said, pretending to sulk.

"They have to be firm to begin with," she said huffily. "Like new shoes that have to be worn in. Get it?" *She* was the jokster now.

He tried to respond but failed. He was being made a fool of. For all he knew, she'd had a lover and wanted to impress the git, the lucky bastard. She felt guilty about going back to the guy because he, Strawks, had been in the looney bin.

"You messed with perfection," he said, trying to sound normal.

She feels too sorry for me to come clean, he thought, but didn't dare say. He left her to get dressed, all the while struggling with the new, slamming thought that there was someone else.

"Let's go see Stella," he said, on impulse. He could corner their friend. Get to the bottom of this.

"But we've just been there. Stella needs to recover from Friday…the lunch."

"Call her. See what she says. If you're worried about food, we can bring something."

He'd forgotten how much he missed farming. Once there, he was immediately drawn in. There were a hundred and one things that needed immediate attention– things Stella and Brand and the staff hadn't thought of– and he found himself offering to stay over. Faye, unbeknownst to him, had had an SOS from her old firm the previous week and offered to go in and help them. She had looked relieved when he offered to stay, and he had a moment of wondering if she was glad to be rid of him. But she loved him, the past four months proved it. The question was, was it purely altruistic? And yet, she had responded to his advances. She hadn't said no. She had just not been able to let go completely. Something seemed to hold her back, but what?

Lying awake in Lyle's bed on Sunday night, he wondered if he'd got it wrong. His suspicions about another lover might be brought on by frustration. If they could just make love fully, once, he was sure all would be well again. And the boobs… She might simply have wanted to look her best. Women worried about age. He'd heard her and Stella joke about the effect of gravity. She had said goodbye with such feeling.

"I don't know how I'm going to last the week without you," she said. "We've been together every day for four months. We're almost like an old married couple."

After a night's sleep, albeit restless, he expected he would feel better, but he woke up just as worried and confused. He needed to have that chat with Stella, the one he had allowed himself to be side-tracked from the previous day.

And here he was, on the way back to town after saying he would stay over at the farm for the week. Faye hadn't sounded surprised when he said he was coming home. He hadn't said why he'd changed his mind, just some lame blurt about not being able to stay away from her. He looked at his watch. He said he'd be there around seven. It was close to eight. She would be wondering what had happened to him. Before he spoke to her, though, he had to get himself under control. He had to find the right words. He didn't want what he said to come across as blame, criticism, or accusation about her holding out on him for so long. He didn't want to hurt her any more than she already was, his poor, sick, injured love.

He nosed Stella's Jeep back onto the freeway – now less busy. He took deep breaths thinking about everything and what laid ahead. A few blocks from the house, he stopped outside a superette and called to see if she needed anything for supper. He would have liked to wine and dine her, but he was skinned. Then again, what Faye and he had to discuss was probably best handled at home. He expected a watershed, however he put it across.

Everything was under control, she said. Funny that. She had bought a cooked chicken and salads, crusty bread, cheeses. She still had some of Stella's wine.

Sun streamed in through the entrance of the shop. He had a hundred rand note his sister had slipped him at the lunch, and he bought some exhausted looking pink roses and chocolates that he hoped hadn't melted into scummy globs inside the box.

He let himself into the kitchen, called her name. Fergus appeared and led the way to the lounge. She had an old photo album out.

"That's us. In Bethany?"

She had it open on a scene in a bore hole pool. He could feel tears pushing behind his eyes, hot tears, a mixture of anger and love. What had happened to the kids that they were back in Bethany, those carefree, innocent babes in arms? How had they arrived at this appalling juncture?

She was smiling, but he wasn't going to be side-tracked.

"I had a talk with Stella." He sat on the couch beside her, swallowing hard. His heart beat like a tractor engine.

"What about? You're quite in your rights to talk about a salary."

"I had some questions. Not about money."

"Oh."

She closed the album and laid it on the coffee table. She turned to him. Damn. A tear had sneaked out. She was bound to have noticed. Faye was like that, spotted an ingrown beard hair on his chin, crumbs on his shirt front. But she wasn't checking him, doing the caring thing. She was looking deep into his eyes.

"I'll have it. The treatment. The bloomin' chemo. No need to get your knickers in a knot. Er, your underpants." She took the flowers and chocolates from him and put them on the table beside the album.

"How…"

She reached over and wiped the tears away with her thumbs. "Never mind how. Give me a kiss."

CHAPTER 48

After warning Faye that Strawks was on his way over and why, I waited to hear from them, especially from Faye. But there was nothing. Not for the rest of the weekend. There was always plenty to do, office work, the animals. Ellie and Brand were off to Worcester and Cape Town to spend time with her folks, filling them in about the baby. Myrna was helping Lyle with another decorating job.

Early Monday, Strawks called to say they were with Faye's doctor. She had jumped the queue for a scan that afternoon.

"Say no more," I said.

I wanted to feel happy for them, but what I felt was stunned. In the past, Faye had to wait a week for an appointment. I worried a little then. The doctor must feel he had to act speedily, that Faye's condition warranted it. Somehow I had imagined being with them when they visited the oncologist. There was still the treatment. A picture flashed of Strawks and me on either side of Faye. Would she be in a chair or a bed, I wasn't sure– but definitely, each of us holding a hand, a picture that had formed somewhere in the weeks since I had the idea to find Strawks and enlist his help, a picture I had been only dimly aware of until now.

Mr. Hendon and I had delivered the business plan to the bank, had been in to discuss and make alterations twice. A fortnight ago, the manager called with news of a hefty extension to the overdraft. As I sat at my desk to pay the first batch of accounts, I expected to feel joy and relief at having the means to meet our commitments. Instead, images of Faye cut in. Was she sliding through the cavern of the scanning apparatus or maybe in a waiting area receiving sympathetic glances from other patients– something she hated. To distract myself, I got up and walked through to the winery to check that the list of tasks left by Strawks was being carried out. The rest of that day passed in an equally frustrating way. Even a gallop on Izzy proved futile against wondering how my friends were faring.

Strawks called around nine that evening. Brand and Ellie had stayed over with her mother in Worcester. Lyle was with Myrna. I was alone for the first time in— I couldn't remember.

"Faye is crashed on the bed. I've covered her with a blanket." He added as an afterthought, "She sends her apologies." He was calling on the landline, to save money, he said. "We start the treatment tomorrow. I *know*," he said when I didn't reply, "we're as surprised as you."

"The scan?"

"Clear for now, but the doc's not taking any chances."

"Where are they doing it? And what time?"

"There's no need for you to be there," he said, thinking he would be saving me the bother. "This is my go, my call. Stella, you've done enough."

It wasn't a bother, heaven's no. I was feeling… I couldn't say. Empty? Beached? I had to force myself to take in what followed. Strawks asked if he could be there for each first day of the twelve weeks of treatment, and take further time off if there were complications, although the doctor had assured them there would probably be just the usual minor skin, nail, hair and stomach aggravations, headaches and so on. But probably not much to begin with. When the treatment started, the chemicals were busy fighting the cancer, but later, when the disease had been overcome, it would the patient's body they would assault. Anika and Valdine were ready in the wings should Faye feel she needed help while Strawks was on the farm. Faye was going to work the next day.

I had murmured agreement to most of the plans but this last had me muttering, "Faye's the giddy limit."

Strawks chuckled.

It was so typical of Faye, wanting to go to work as though nothing untoward was happening, as though no poison would be making its way along veins and arteries, infiltrating organs, waging its scorched earth policy of cell destruction, exposing the body to bacterial infection. After the months of worry and heartache, of being stretched beyond imagining, my friend seemed unchanged. This, too, left me floundering. What was the point of everything, what we had been through together? Had she learnt nothing?

"Nothing stops my girl, does it?" He said, trailing away to a rather subdued goodbye.

The man must be exhausted. I felt that way just listening, and something else. Irritated? The 'we' had grated. And fed up, if I was honest. I never thought the longed for, largely good news, would leave me with a feeling of being cast aside like an old sock.

Faye had *crashed* on the bed. It reminded me of how soundly she had slept the night she found the lump. And as I thought about wending my way to my miserable little bed I feared a repeat for me, of the opposite. Until I had sorted my feelings, I had as much hope of a good night's sleep as turning back the clock and wishing Faye hadn't found the lump and cancer reared its ugly head. I couldn't seem to get around this new development. What I had wanted and worked for was at last going to happen, but I wasn't rejoicing, not even a muted hurray, considering the discomfort Faye was likely to endure while undergoing the treatment. Instead, it was like a carpet that had been carrying me onwards and upwards for months now had been yanked out from under me.

This must be how a runner feels in a relay race when the baton is wrested from her grasp. Only she would be heart-thumpingly caught up in the remainder of the race, and then the win. Oh, the win, the joint win when the team met minutes later, the joy, the triumph. Heady stuff, tear-inducing. I had so often seen winners jump around, shout, throw up their arms, group-hug, the team leader running alongside the cheering crowd holding high-as-the-sky their country's flag. Not irritated like I was, not morose and dangerously close to staggering under a load of self-pity. Had my quest been selfish, all about *me* getting what *I* wanted?

As I padded out onto the front steps with Harry and Sally and Woo, old hands now at holding in barks, I thought back to other times recently when I had sought the night air as the means to solving a problem, most recently when I suspected the intimacy between Strawks and Anika. And look how great that had turned out, I told myself, trying desperately to chivvy myself into feeling upbeat, joy, triumph, the race won– something other than this emptiness. This time the problem seemed personal. I knew it wasn't about missing Arno. I would always miss him, terribly, but I had made peace with his death, proof of the pudding being my readiness to love again should the right person come along.

But I couldn't sit. Whatever was bugging me needed movement to dislodge it. For once, I ignored lights coming on. There was no one in the house to raise the alarm. In any event, the lights would go off again once we were out of reach, because I knew where I was headed, what or who was calling me to a conference of sorts.

A crescent moon and adjustment to the dark outlined Suzi's mound of earth and rough wooden cross, the headstones and wide gravel rectangle of the family grave. I sat on the bench while the dogs sniffed around and finally came to sit, Harry and Sally, at my feet and, Woo, to beg and receive a hand up.

Everyone was here that mattered, I found myself thinking. (I would remember thinking this later, cringingly). From their position, beyond physical life and its concerns and demands, my puzzlement would seem minor. Arno would tell me to give it time and that I always came up with a solution, didn't I? Ada would say there was bound to be an anticlimax, even depression at the end of a journey like the one I had just completed, how when they handed over running the farm to Arno they were miserable at first, until they found other things to do. She had begun reading the classics until her eyes failed, Frank carving pipes. He smoked one to the end. He would tell me to open the riding school again, that I was happiest when I was with horses, mine and other people's. Leave Strawks to run the farm. Dabble with blending wine, yes, but leave the bulk of the winemaking to him.

I sat back after that. It all seemed so simple. But I wasn't feeling any better. No "aha" moment had broken through. I returned to the house to a sleep full of dreams which, when I woke, had disappeared like morning mist.

———————

Strawks appeared at breakfast.

"Nothing to write home about," he said.

Faye was off to work none the worse, it seemed. This only added to my feeling of ennui, not shifted by the night's musings.

He helped himself to coffee and toast. This was his time for checking with Brand and I for a plan of attack for the day. Ellie was taking a personal day. Brand was already at his computer in the dining room. It was too early for Lyle and his clients.

Ellie said, biting gingerly into dry toast, "We've been thinking of names. For a girl, although we don't know yet what we're having. I like the old-fashioned ones like Victoria and Elizabeth. In my mother's family– they're Afrikaans– it's common to combine your mother and grandmother's names. They are Anna and Sarie, so you'd get something like Ansar or Saran. I don't know if I want to go that route, though. Brand likes cute modern names like Demi and Torey. If you had a girl, Stella, what would you have called her? What were your mother and grandmother's names?"

"My mother was Constance. My grandmother... she was from the Transvaal... I'm not sure." I blushed. "She died before I was born."

"Would you be able to look it up? Do you have a family Bible?"

"We're a lot of heathens, so no family Bible. I'm not like Faye keeping albums, photos of her parents on her dressing table."

But Ellie kept looking at me. Strawks grinned at my embarrassment but added, trying to be helpful, "I'm like Stella, unsentimental. Anika has framed ones of our folks and grandparents on her walls. That sort of thing matters to some people."

"What if you have a boy? Have you thought of boy's names?" I asked, eager to shift the source of what was proving to be of considerable discomfort for me.

After lunch, when Ellie was resting, I took the key to the rondavel off its hook in the kitchen and made my way there. I thought, how opportune, as I shoved aside the old cots and highchairs and the 'double cab'. But then again, Ellie would probably want to buy a new one for her baby. A pram at least, some multi-tasking spaceship on wheels. At the top of an old wardrobe, its usefulness usurped years ago by built-in cupboards, was what I was looking for– Constance's wedding trousseau hamper. I wrestled into a place beneath the wardrobe, placed an old wooden chair on top of one of the twins' desks, climbed up, and brought it down.

With it on the cleared desktop, I lifted the wicker lid, releasing a cloud of dust and a sticky mess of spiderwebs. I remember remonstrating with Aunt Bev, as I knew it would mean more to her, but she insisted that as 'the daughter' I should have the hamper. The creamy white satin lining reeked of moth balls, but was surprisingly well preserved. I remember giving the contents a disgusted grunt. Then made sure it was stowed well out of reach, and sight. I flipped through an embroidered sampler from girlhood, long white satin gloves with faintly soiled fingertips, short pink lace gloves, an album of pressed flowers abandoned midway, a Chinese fan, saved programs from concerts at my various schools, a brown A4 envelope with my report cards, a menu off the Blue Train, the celebration of a special wedding anniversary when I was left with Aunt Bev and Uncle Clive. I had no interest in the contents of the jewelry box but Ellie might, I thought, and put it to one side. Aunt Bev said my mother's pearls had gone missing in those last months at the home. I said she should have my mother's rings, and she had taken them without argument. Photos were in another box. The wedding photo of Constance and Roy was oddly touching, bringing Ellie and Brand to mind (there were the long white gloves). How unprepared Arno and I— all of us-- were starting out. The two of them posing beside an old Chev, picnicking at the Vaal Dam, one at a dance, my mother in a dress with a puffy skirt and teased hair. Me in a christening robe, first day at school in a gymslip, satchel on my back, and on through the years, running races, hauling myself out of a school swimming pool, with the 'first' hockey team, me on a horse on a holiday camp near Knysna. I hadn't known she had that one. I turned it over. *Stella Viviene on her dream horse.* The photos slid through my fingers while I swallowed and swallowed. Viviene was Granny Turner's name. I signed S.*V.* Gideon almost on a daily basis. Who forgets something like that?

Aunt Bev organized the simple service at the crematorium chapel. She and Uncle Clive were with me when I shook my mother's ashes over the wall at Cape Point. If not for Aunt Bev I wouldn't have known my mother's last wish, which I thought at the time was typical— my mother not sharing with me, especially when the shower of ash disappeared over the glittering ocean, leaving me with the empty garishly brass-colored urn. I remember a gasp from my aunt as I chucked it over as well. After the nothingness that was my mother. Oh, there was a plaque at the Garden of Remembrance, but no remains. No Constance lying there for me to visit like I visited Arno and Ada and Frank, Suzi. Even our dogs were there for us to visit and remember.

I thought back to how she didn't remember my name when I visited her and how I couldn't wait to get away from the growing awareness that she was ill, from the burden of it and to put those umpteen miles between her and me, hightailing it to Durban and Ensign. How when she died, Aunt Bev had cried, even Uncle Clive. But not me. How I told Faye that when I was crying for Bathsheba I was really crying for my mother. Tosh. Junk. Lies. I hadn't cried for my mother because in my heart I had given up on her. My visits to the guest house and later the home were me doing my duty. Sparing visits. Visits doled out when it suited me. I hadn't tried to understand what she was going through. Hadn't spoken to the doctors, asked whether there were other medications that might have been used, other treatments. I hadn't allowed her suffering to touch me. I hadn't allowed myself to *feel*. Above all, I hadn't loved her. Faye was right to call me the Ice Maiden. In Bethany, I had cared. Her taking Valiums and drinking had bothered me, and that she didn't have friends and didn't seem to be enjoying life. But Roy had been there, and I expected him to do the caring. Then he was gone, and I turned to wanting a horse to fill the emptiness of his loss and went off to Durban, and all my caring was lavished on Ensign and every horse and dog and animal that came within my orbit. But not my mother.

A terrible anger flared up in me, and with it tears and sobs that tore at my throat. I was angry with my mother, for the illness that sucked the life out of her, with my father for leaving us, and at last, with myself, with my gross neglect, my cold as ice heart.

CHAPTER 49

I stand back to admire my handiwork. Arno would have approved. Besides the woody mustiness of the proteas and ericas, there is the smell of freshly turned earth that has me breathing in long and deep. The shrubs are hardy locals, able to stand up to whatever the weather throws at them. In fact, they should flourish, unlike the stunted aloes in the black bag I unceremoniously toss into the back of the Jeep. The long overdue task is just what I need. With Woo on the seat beside me, and Harry and Sally loping alongside, I drive back to the house.

I am a little edgy this Christmas morning. They should have been here by now. It is a good hour since Brand, Lyle, and Valdine left to collect Phyllis from the airport. Has the Lexus broken down? Highly unlikely. Or is a strike of airport staff something we have missed in our eagerness to get the farm and animal chores done so that we can enjoy a leisurely lunch? Keeping to tradition, the staff, including Willy and Marie, have the week between Christmas and New Year to spend with their families.

Edgy but happy, I think as I stop to admire– make that commiserate– with the rows of chenin blanc which, if they were milk cows, would be mooing miserably so considerable is their load. *Not long now, my lovelies.* Our pickers, consisting mainly of the families of staff from grandparents to youngsters and a stalwart bunch of old faithfuls, are on standby for what promises to be a bumper crop. As usual, word will go out a couple of days beforehand and a small army of first timers and even some who proved unequal to the job previously will be waiting at the front gate.

But first, Christmas. Ellie, over the worst of the morning sickness, and Myrna, are busy with lunch so I am able to sit a moment. I'm still amazed at how different I feel. I am the total opposite of those vines. After my catharsis in the rondavel, I left light of foot, ready to sing and dance my relief, and yes, my joy. I had been carrying the load of guilt so long it seemed part of me until Faye came along with her lump. Trying to get help for her had been me trying to right the past. Often I find myself wanting to pop in and take a peek at my parents' wedding photo, framed and on the table next to my bed. There have been times, I, hardcase Stella, have to admit, that I've gone to sleep with it and hugged to my chest. Now I want the world, starting with my family and friends, to know how precious these two people from the past are to me and so I've commissioned a painting to be made from a copy (with other photos to ensure likeness), which will take pride of place in the lounge.

Back at the house, Ellie and Myrna tell me to, "Shoo," not before I make tea, slice Anika and Aletta's Christmas cake, and take the tray out to the veranda. The braai is laid with apple wood from another stripped orchard, ready to light when the boys are back (we'll use the Weber when the weather demands it).

"Isn't this nice, just us," I say as I join on the veranda Faye in her blonde wig and Strawks, deeply tanned with a pale strip on his forehead from his work-a-day hat. These days such moments are rare.

"Anika and Henk– especially Henk, might be saying the same." Faye is referring to the tension that sparks off Henk whenever he encounters Strawks. "So good of Aletta and Dop Myburgh to invite them over."

"And we have first prize, Vally," Strawks says, chest big with pride. "I can leave Faye with her when I come to work."

I feel sad as I say, "She seems so grown up."

"It has a lot to do with how we treat her. How Anika and I treat her. Like a grown up. She took it so well, finding out she isn't adopted and that we are her real mom and dad. It was like she knew. Thank you, Stella, for the nudge." Strawks pours and hands me a cup of tea.

"We did tell her not to go blabbing to Jan Publiek," Faye adds.

Strawks grins.

"She is so beautifully open. Has such a warm heart. You wouldn't want her any other way."

Faye is on medication for nausea, thrush in uncomfortable places, and diarrhea, but doesn't want to miss out. But she does nibble the cake gingerly. She goes to work most mornings. Valdine has added nursing to possible career choices.

"But mostly, she is caught up with the wedding. She had me turning out my cupboards the other day. She says I have to get a dressmaker to take my clothes in."

"Faye has lost weight." Strawks frowns.

"One good thing out of this."

We all know there is so much more, but we allow her the little joke.

The quiet is suddenly shattered as Harry and Sally charge back through the house, barking, while Woo follows at an elegant trot and Fergus checks with Faye before padding after his friends. Car doors bang. Soon there's another kind of commotion in the direction of the kitchen.

Phyllis, red-cheeked and beaming, appears at the French doors and totters into my arms.

"I had a drop too much vino on the plane," she confesses, giggling. "Not as good as yours, though, Stella."

Faye and Strawks had kissed fiercely and hugged.

As she flops into a chair, a dark-bearded head on broad shoulders appears in the doorway. Navy blue eyes glint.

I cast accusing glances at Faye, Strawks, and then Phyllis because, simply, I don't know what else to do. Faye shakes her head. *No idea,* her eyes blink across. Strawks also feigns innocence and Phyllis has her Miss O'Donnell look, prim, unrelenting.

"Two little birdies are responsible." Gunner looks back over his shoulder.

"Several little birdies, more like it," says Brand while our visitor moves closer and kisses me.

"Hi, Stella," he says.

I must have been gawping because Faye is left to do the introductions.

"So this is Gunner." Strawks looks the man over like he is a bull at a livestock market, a prize bull.

Faye looks from Gunner to me, radiant.

"So you knew?" I shake my head at her.

"We all did," says Strawks.

"Even me," says Valdine appearing in the doorway with Ellie and Myrna. "Lyle told me in the car on the way to the airport. Ellie told me to hang back until Gunner said hello to you, Stella. And I did."

"Except me," says Phyllis. "But I'm no dope. This is your pruner man, isn't he, Stella?"

"How can you tell?" says Gunner.

Everyone laughs except Valdine and me. Valdine, because she is unaware of Gunner and my history, and me, because already I am giving too much away.

Soon everyone is occupied. Ellie and Myrna, Lyle and Brand return to the kitchen. Valdine is on her father's lap. He whispers something in her ear, and she smiles. You did good, he is probably saying and/or explaining about the 'pruner man.' Phyllis and Gunner reply to queries about their flights by Faye which releases me to slip away to the kitchen, mumbling something about seeing to the lunch, where I lean on the table, strangely out of breath.

"Are you OK, Mom?" enquires Ellie. "I told Brand he was playing with fire."

Being called 'Mom'. A day of surprises.

"I'll get us rolling with these canapés," says Myrna exiting, loaded tray aloft.

Lyle hands me a glass of champers and I look at him inquiringly.

"I'll go get the fire started," he says, not making a move.

"Mom," my eldest begins. "Faye asked what happened to Gunner. We went from there."

I know I won't be able to drink, or eat, for that matter, so I put my glass down and head for the stable. I am stroking Izzy's nose when I feel a hand on my shoulder. There's weight in that hand like it is ensuring I don't bolt.

I'm going to nip this in the bud, I think, and turn and face him. "I'm sorry about keeping you hanging. I was getting around to telling you I didn't want your business proposal."

"I didn't want it either."

"What?"

He stares back steadily. "It was a cover up. I had to secure you somehow. I didn't want to rush you. I didn't think you were ready for... the other."

"The other?"

"Marriage."

A hand is under my chin, the beard close. If he only knew, I was *so* ready.

MERIEL MONGIE was born in Chester, England and grew up in the rural Eastern Cape of South Africa. A retired high school teacher and a proud great-grandmother, Mongie draws upon her rich life experiences to craft narratives that speak profoundly to mature readers. Her background provides her with unique insights into the emotional landscapes she explores in her writing. She lives in Cape Town, South Africa.